CRIMINAL BEHAVIOUR

AMANDA STEVENS

A COLTON TARGET

BEVERLY LONG

MILLS & BOON

First Published in Great Britain 2019
by Mills & Boon, an imprint of HarperCollins*Publishers*
1 London Bridge Street, London, SE1 9GF

Criminal Behaviour © 2019 Marilyn Medlock Amann
A Colton Target © 2019 Harlequin Books S.A.

Special thanks and acknowledgement are given to Beverly Long for her contribution to *The Coltons of Roaring Springs* series.

ISBN: 978-0-263-27417-2

0519

MIX
Paper from responsible sources
FSC™ C007454

CRIMINAL BEHAVIOUR

AMANDA STEVENS

Chapter One

Located at the end of a dead-end street, the derelict
Victorian seemed to wither in the heat, the turrets and
dormers sagging from time, neglect and decades of in-
clement weather. The gardens were lost, the maze of
brick pathways broken and forgotten. The whole place
wore an air of despair and long-buried secrets.

Those secrets and the steamy humidity stole Detective Adaline Kinsella's breath as she ducked under
the crime-scene tape and pushed open the front door.
It swung inward with the inevitable squeak, drawing
a shiver.

She had the strangest sensation of déjà vu as she entered the house, and the experience both puzzled and
unsettled her. She'd never been here before. Couldn't
remember ever having driven down this street. But a
nerve had been touched. Old memories had been trig-
gered. If she listened closely enough, she could hear the
echo of long-dead screams, but she knew that sound
came straight from her nightmares.

She was just tired, Addie told herself. Five days
of hiking, swimming and kayaking in ninety-degree
weather had taken a toll, and now she needed a vacation from her vacation.

For nearly a week, she'd remained sequestered in her

aunt's lake house without access to cable or the internet. One day had spun into another, and for the better part of the week, Addie had thought she'd found heaven on earth in the Blue Ridge Mountains. But by Thursday she'd become restless to the point of pacing on the front porch. On Friday she'd awakened early, packed up her car and headed back to Charleston, arriving just after lunch to explosive headlines and the police department abuzz with a gruesome discovery.

The details of that find swirled in her head as she hovered in the foyer. The previous owner of the house, a recluse named Delmar Gainey, had died five years earlier in a nursing home, and the property had remained vacant until an enterprising house flipper had bought it at auction. The demo crew had noticed a fusty odor, but no one had sounded an alarm. It was the smell of old death, after all. The lingering aroma of disintegrating vermin and rotting vegetation. The house had flooded at least once, allowing in the deadly invasion of mold and mildew. The structure was a public health hazard that needed to be razed, but the flipper had been adamant about renovation—until his workers had uncovered human remains behind the living room walls.

Skeletal remains had also been found behind the dining room walls and beneath the rotting floorboards in the hallway. Seven bodies hidden away inside the abandoned house and seven more buried in the backyard. Fourteen victims so far, and the search had now been extended onto the adjacent property.

"Hello?" Addie called as she moved across the foyer to the rickety staircase. The house was oppressive and sweltering. No power meant no lights and no AC. Sweat trickled down her backbone and moistened her armpits. Furtive claws scratched overhead, and the sound deepened Addie's dread. Ever since she'd heard about the Gainey house, images had bombarded her. Now she pictured the ceiling collapsing and rat bodies dropping down on her. She had a thing about rats. Spiders and snakes she could handle, but rats...

Grimacing in disgust, she moved toward the archway on her right, peeking into the shadowy space she thought might once have been the dining room. The long windows were boarded up, allowing only thin slivers of light to creep in. She could smell dust from the demolished plaster and a whiff of putrefaction. Or was that, too, her imagination? Delmar Gainey's victims had been entombed in the walls for over two decades. Surely the scent would have disintegrated by now.

A memory flitted and was gone. The nightmares still tugged...

Addie suppressed another shiver and wondered why she had come. As of Monday, she had a new assignment. Handpicked by her captain to train with the FBI's famous Behavioral Analysis Unit, she'd been temporarily reassigned from the Charleston PD Investigations Bureau. Soon she would join select law enforcement personnel from all over the Southeast for six weeks of specialized training conducted by one of the brightest minds to ever work in the BAU. But for today, right this moment, she needed to focus on her perilous surroundings. She needed to find out why so many alarms were tripping inside her head.

"Boo!" a voice boomed from the shadows.

Addie jumped in spite of herself, and her hand went automatically to her weapon. Then she let loose a string of expletives that seemed to echo back to her from the hollowed-out walls. "Are you crazy?" she scolded her partner. "I might have shot you."

Detective Matt Lepear laughed as he emerged from the depths of the gloom. "Oh, come on," he drawled. "I've never known anyone less trigger-happy than you." He somehow made it sound like a shortcoming.

"Maybe I've changed."

"Not you, Addie Kinsella. You're as predictable as the day is long. I knew you wouldn't make it a week in the mountains all by your lonesome. What happened? Couldn't stand your own company?"

"Figured I'd better head on back and see how badly you've screwed things up in my absence."

"Can't say as I've missed that mouth." He shoved his dust mask to the top of his head, allowing a lock of brown hair to fall across his brow. "Seriously, girl, you couldn't find anything better to do with the last few days of your vacation? Go to the movies or something. Go shopping, get your hair done. Just go. Get out of here. We've got this covered."

"I know you do, but I wanted to see this place for myself."

"You're a strange bird, Addie. Anyone ever tell you that?"

"Yes, you. All the time."

He leaned a shoulder against the door frame and unwrapped a stick of gum. Like Addie, Matt Lepear was a ten-year veteran of the Charleston PD. They'd gone through the academy together, patrolled the streets together, and their partnership in the Investigations Bureau had seemed a natural progression of their bond. They were as thick as thieves and as different as night and day. Addie had a tendency to overthink and second-guess, but nothing much fazed Matt Lepear. He took it all in stride. Serial killers, hurricanes, even his two ex-wives.

He was a good detective, one might even say gifted, but his career would always be held back by his disdain for rules and neckties. He preferred to follow his gut rather than the book, and he insisted on dressing in his own uniform of jeans, sneakers and T-shirts. His insubordination had become legendary, but he and Addie led the department in percentage of closed cases, so the powers that be tended to give him leeway. Addie was under no illusion that she would be afforded the same consideration with a different partner, no matter that the deputy chief was a man she once called uncle. Addie was smart, meticulous and persistent to a fault, but she would never have Matt's instincts.

His irreverence had rubbed off on her over the years and now she was in no position to criticize anyone's style, she acknowledged, wiping clammy hands down the sides of her faded jeans. She hadn't bothered going home to change before stopping by headquarters. When she heard about the Gainey house, she'd driven straight over. Come Monday, she'd make more of an effort to look presentable. It was in her best interests to get off on the right foot with the retired supervisory special agent-turned-consultant who would be in charge of her training. If there was anything Gwen Holloway had been known for at Quantico, besides her uncanny profiles, it was her rigid standards on dress and conduct.

"You want the twenty-five-cent tour?" Matt asked her.

"Of the house? No, thanks. I'll just poke around on my own." She turned back to the foyer. "How do you think he got away with it for so long? The stench must have been unbearable, especially in the summer months. Yet none of the neighbors ever filed a complaint? Even now I can smell the decay."

"You're smelling the rats," Matt said. "This place is lousy with them, dead and alive."

Addie lifted her gaze to the water-stained ceiling. "I can hear them."

"Wait until they start nipping at your feet. As to why the neighbors never complained, you have to remember that back in Delmar Gainey's time, this area was a lot less populated. The houses damaged by the hurricane were either torn down or abandoned. Gainey's mother died the same year the big one hit. He moved in after she passed, and that's likely when he began his spree. Her death may even have been the stressor. Being isolated as he was, he could come and go as he pleased—bury bodies in the backyard at all hours—and no one would have noticed."

"And then he just stopped?"

Matt nodded toward the murky sidelights that flanked the front door. "Didn't you notice the ramp by the porch steps? Three years after Gainey moved in here, he had a car accident that confined him to a wheelchair. His mobility became limited. He couldn't go around unnoticed like he did before the accident, so for the next quarter of a century, he had to content himself with reliving the kills in his head. Probably why he stayed in this squalor for as long as did. Couldn't bear leaving his conquests behind."

Addie glanced around the gutted room. The remains had already been removed and the scene processed, but the exposed wall studs were a reminder of a madman's gruesome pastime. "That explains how the smell went unnoticed, but how do fourteen people in a city this size just disappear?"

"Fringe dwellers, most likely. Street people have always been easy prey. We'll have to check the files to see if any of the disappearances were reported. That far back, nothing is computerized. Someone will have to do some digging."

Addie nodded absently, her gaze still raking over the walls.

"There's also the time frame to consider." Matt's voice sounded hushed, as if he had intuited her unease. "Could be the reason the disappearances never made the news is because Gainey's spree overlapped with a more famous predator."

Addie nodded again, but she found herself oddly short of breath. Why Matt's observation should hit her so hard, she couldn't explain. She'd already considered the timeline, but the spoken word had power. In one sentence, her partner had illuminated a connection, no matter how tenuous and indirect, to Addie's personal nightmare. The déjà vu she'd experienced upon arrival hadn't been conjured by this house, but by the icy touch of another monster.

"Think about everything going on in Charleston during that time," Matt said. "The city knee-deep in hurricane recovery and every headline and news broadcast obsessed with the Twilight Killer."

The Twilight Killer. The very real bogeyman of Addie's childhood.

"Little wonder someone like Gainey was able to fly under the radar."

"I guess." Addie turned to avoid her partner's penetrating gaze.

His voice softened. "You still don't like to talk about it, do you?"

"I don't mind talking about it. I just have nothing new to offer. And it happened so long ago. I barely even remember it." Not true, of course. She recalled only too well the woman she called aunt standing in the bedroom doorway as Addie had pretended to sleep.

How do we do this, David? That child is barely seven years old. How do we explain to someone so young that her mother has been brutally murdered by a serial killer? Only, it couldn't have been Orson Lee Finch, could it? You arrested him. Which means there's another one out there. A copycat...

We're not going to explain anything tonight. The news can wait until morning. Come away from the door, Helen. Let the girl sleep.

In a minute. I just can't bear to take my eyes off her. My poor angel...

Orson Lee Finch's spree had lasted five months. Nine young women had been brutally murdered, all single mothers from affluent families. All slain in the twilight hour by a demented gardener who had left as his calling card a crimson magnolia petal placed on the lips of his victims, as if to seal their deaths with a kiss.

Unlike Delmar Gainey, who had sequestered his victims in his home, Orson Lee Finch had flaunted his kills, leaving the bodies broken and exposed.

Addie's mother had been the ninth victim—or the first, depending on one's perspective. She hadn't been killed by Orson Lee Finch, but her death was a result of his spree. She'd been murdered in cold blood by the FBI profiler who had mind-hunted Finch. For months, SSA James Merrick had tireless tracked the Twilight Killer, only to become the monster he had so obsessively stalked.

"I watched a documentary the other night about the Twilight Killer," Matt said. "They interviewed people who still think Orson Lee Finch is innocent."

"Death-row groupies. I've run into a few of those over the years," Addie said.

"No, these people were different. Articulate and respectful, and they made some good points. Got me to thinking."

"Had to happen sooner or later."

Matt grinned and folded his arms, which meant he had no intention of letting the subject drop until he'd said his piece. "The case had inconsistencies that I was unaware of until I saw that film. They also ran a segment on Twilight's Children." He paused. "They showed your picture, but it didn't look much like you."

"Probably an old shot," Addie said, still avoiding his gaze.

"They said you declined to be interviewed."

"Because I'm not technically one of Twilight's Children. Orson Lee Finch didn't kill my mother."

"Yeah, but they lump you in just the same, and they still consider your mother the ninth victim. You have to admit, it was one strange, messed-up case."

"*Messed up* is an understatement," Addie muttered.

Matt continued, undaunted, "An FBI profiler with an almost godlike reputation helps capture the psycho and then ends up stalking and murdering a victim with the same MO in order to continue Finch's mission. Talk about crazy."

"Merrick obviously had a psychotic breakdown," Addie said. "Which is why he remains to this day in the state psychiatric hospital in Columbia. He's where he belongs. End of story. Let's get back to Delmar Gainey. We're standing in his house of horrors, after all."

"Yeah, sure. We can get back to Gainey. But there's a lesson to be learned from James Merrick. Especially for you."

She frowned. "What are you talking about?"

"Your new assignment." He let his head fall back against the door frame as he observed her. "It's a game changer. I'd be the last one to ever stand in your way."

"I know that. I also know you deserve this assignment more than I do."

"That's not true. You're a good detective, and you're smart. You need to stop selling yourself short because of a stupid rookie mistake."

Addie winced.

"Just stay smart, okay? The people who'll be training you are a different breed. Next-level intense. What we found here is nothing compared to what they deal with on a daily basis."

"What's your point?"

"Sooner or later, what they do takes a toll. It has to if you're human."

"You don't think I can handle it?"

"Oh, I know you can handle it. Just be aware. Profiling is a powerful tool, but it's not without a dark side. It can mess with your head if you're not careful."

"You mean like James Merrick."

"He entered the mind of a monster and created an opening, allowing the monster to slither back into his." Matt's gaze deepened, and he seemed uncharacteristically sober. "You go into that training with an open mind, Addie. Learn everything you can from this Gwen Holloway. Be a sponge. Soak it all up. Then you come back to the Charleston PD and put that knowledge to good use. But always keep your guard up. Always protect yourself. The moment you let that monster crawl inside your head and make a nest is the moment you become the next James Merrick."

SPECIAL AGENT ETHAN BARROW stood at rigid attention beside his rented SUV as he eyed the abandoned house through his Ray-Bans. His gaze traveled over the crumbling roofline and then dropped once more to the sagging porch. The place was as dark and creepy as one might imagine the lair of a ruthless predator would be. Even the sun shining down through thick curtains of Spanish moss seemed muted, casting the house in perpetual gloom.

Ever since Ethan's return to Charleston, the news had been dominated by the gruesome discovery inside that house, managing to overshadow the upcoming anniversary of Orson Lee Finch's incarceration and James Merrick's subsequent confinement to the state psychiatric hospital. Twenty-five years after the fact, Orson Lee Finch remained at Kirkland Correctional Institution, housed in a specialized unit for the state's most violent inmates. Most people thought he deserved worse. James Merrick remained a patient on the infamous fourth floor, a ward for the criminally insane. Most people thought he deserved worse.

Ethan wasn't one of those people.

He shifted his position so that he could glimpse around the corner of the house. He heard voices over the fence, but no one approached him. That was good. He needed a few minutes to plot his strategy. Or to work up his courage. No reason in the world Adaline Kinsella should agree to hear him out after what he'd once put her through, but she was the only person he could turn to right now. The only person he trusted with the potential bombshell that had fallen into his lap.

He moved back to the other end of the SUV, killing more time. It had now been twenty-four hours since his arrival in Charleston, and he had yet to make contact with Addie. He hadn't slept much. He'd eaten poorly, consumed too much coffee, and now he was starting to feel the strain. He'd forgotten just how hot and humid the city could be in the middle of summer. Virginia was bad enough, but coastal South Carolina was a whole new level of misery. He wasn't dressed for the weather. He loosened his tie and tugged at the collar of his starched shirt, but he didn't remove his jacket. The dark suit was his uniform now. Both his identity and his camouflage.

His first order of business upon landing at Charleston International Airport the day before had been to rent a vehicle and drive to Columbia to interview Orson Lee Finch. Over the years, Ethan had studied dozens, perhaps hundreds, of photos and videos of Finch, but he'd never met him in person. Face-to-face, Finch's appearance had taken him by surprise. The Twilight Killer was a small man, pale and wiry with bright blue eyes magnified behind the thick lenses of silver-framed glasses. His grooming was fastidious—crisp khaki uniform, combed hair, clean and clipped nails. He resembled a scholar or historian. He did not look like a serial killer. Ethan couldn't help but wonder how Finch had managed to survive for as long as he had behind bars. Maybe he was small enough and his appearance so nondescript that he'd managed to go unnoticed. Or maybe his looks were deceiving.

They'd sat on plastic chairs, eyeing each other warily through the partition until Finch had picked up the phone. A few minutes of awkward conversation had ensued while Ethan tried to get a feel for his subject. Finch had struck him as quiet and reflective, a man who'd long ago made peace with his deeds and circumstances. His placid demeanor never altered until Ethan had broached the topic of Finch's mother. Then the blue eyes seemed to intensify behind the glasses and the corner of Finch's mouth twitched, as if he were suppressing a painful memory.

"Your mother never married, did she?" Ethan had spoken in a conversational tone, trying to draw the man out. "That must have been tough. Children born out of wedlock were stigmatized back in your day. You were probably teased in school, maybe even bullied."

Finch said nothing.

"Your mother worked as a housekeeper, so I imagine money was tight. Barely enough for necessities, let alone extras. You wore hand-me-down clothing from the people whose houses she cleaned, and as much as you enjoyed having those nice things, you resented where they came from, didn't you? You were hostile to the hand that fed you."

Finch watched him avidly through the partition.

Ethan glanced down at his notes even though he had everything memorized. "Despite your disadvantages, you were a good student. Always the brightest in your class, but your financial situation limited your prospects. A full-ride scholarship must have been the answer to all your prayers. A dream come true. You studied horticulture at a state school, right? You wanted to be a landscape architect. Then your mother became ill during your junior year, and you were forced to drop out of college to take care of her. That's when you got your first job as a gardener. You had to go back, hat in hand, to the people who had given you their throwaway clothing."

Finch had stared at him for the longest moment before answering. "Is this your way of establishing rapport, Special Agent Barrow? Or do you wish to impress me with the amount of homework you've done?"

"How's this for homework? You have a daughter out there somewhere. No one knows her name or where she's been since your incarceration. Some believe her mother was your first victim. Did she fit your criteria? A single mother without morals. A loose woman who valued her freedom more than her child. What happened? Did she refuse to marry you? Is that what set you off?"

Finch's expression never changed, but something dark glinted at the back of his eyes. "After all these years and all the files you people have amassed—mountains, I'm told—no one has ever gotten it right. Not even the esteemed James Merrick."

"Is that a denial?"

Finch studied his hand for a moment. "Merrick's profile was flawed from the start. It was written from the cynical presumption that I harbored ill will toward my own mother. Nothing could be further from the truth. I was a happy child. We didn't have money, but I never wanted for affection. I wasn't starved for attention. Your psychological evaluations to the contrary, I wasn't bitter then about my lot in life and I'm not bitter now. That must surprise you. You're thinking, if he's really innocent, how can he be so accepting of such a cruel injustice?"

"How do you accept it? If you really are innocent, that is."

A smile flickered for the first time. "I could never give an explanation that would satisfy someone like you. Acceptance isn't in your nature. A man like you will always be at war with his emotions. Tormented by what he can't know. Unable to make peace with his past."

Damn if the observation hadn't been insightful and perhaps even prophetic.

After Ethan had left Orson Lee Finch, he'd driven to the state psychiatric hospital. He was no stranger to the layout of the parking area or the maze of hallways and wards. He'd visited regularly for years and was afforded certain privileges because of his position and background. He had signed in and then been escorted up to the fourth floor, where an orderly had unlocked a small room and waved Ethan inside.

James Merrick had been at the window, gazing out over the shady grounds. He hadn't turned when Ethan entered, nor had he acknowledged Ethan's presence in any way. That wasn't unusual. He never gave any indication of recognizing Ethan from one visit to the next. Ethan had learned to ignore the long silences and unblinking stares, as well as the disturbing sounds that came from deep within the facility. He focused his attention instead on the patient's journals, poring over pages and pages of painstakingly scribbled gibberish in the hope of finding the one clue that would break everything open.

He had that clue now. The last piece of the puzzle was finally within his grasp.

"I came here to tell you that new evidence has turned up in your case," he'd said to Merrick.

The man had given no indication of comprehension, but Ethan hadn't let the prolonged silence discourage him.

"I won't go into the details yet. It's early stages of the investigation. But I wanted you to know that I'm still out there looking for the truth. I never believed you were guilty. Not once in all these years." Ethan walked over to the window and placed his hand briefly on the man's frail arm. "Do you remember me?" he murmured. "I'm Ethan."

Nothing so much as a blink.

"I work for the FBI just as you did. I even do support investigations for the BAU. Back in your day, it was called the Behavioral Science Unit."

Still no response.

"My stepfather is Richard Barrow. You knew him once. I took his name when he married my mother, but he's not my dad. My real name is Merrick. Ethan Merrick. I'm your son."

Chapter Two

The muted thrum of a car engine drew Ethan's attention, pulling him out of that twelve-by-twelve room, away from the power of his father's vacant stare and back to his roadside vigil in front of the Gainey house.

He turned his head toward the sound, noting the presence of a black Dodge Charger—the preferred FBI pursuit vehicle—at the end of the street. The car did not approach, nor did the driver pull to the curb to accommodate oncoming traffic. The Charger sat idling in the middle of the road as if daring Ethan to notice.

Any hope he'd had of flying under the radar vanished. He'd seen that same vehicle or one like it parked outside his hotel that morning. Ethan had gone about his business, taking tortuous routes as he ran aimless errands, and eventually he'd lost the tail in downtown traffic. He had no doubt, though, that whoever was keeping tabs on him had already heard about his trip to Columbia and his visit that morning to the Charleston Police Department. He supposed he shouldn't be surprised that they'd found him again so quickly—they were pros, after all—but it had only been by sheer luck that he'd overheard mention of Adaline Kinsella's name and her whereabouts. He had no idea why the agents had thought to look for him here unless they'd known all along he would come to Addie.

He glanced around, once again scoping out his surroundings. He needed an exit strategy in case the occupants of the Charger got too curious. The house sat at the end of a dead-end street, nearly hidden by a canopy of live oaks and palm trees. The nearest neighbor was a block away, but Ethan was hardly alone. While he stood contemplating his options, the voices behind the fence grew louder, and through one of the grimy sidelights, he caught the silhouette of a woman.

Was it Addie?

Had she spotted him?

Probably not, he decided. If she had an inkling of his presence, she would have already come outside to give him a piece of her mind. Not that he could blame her. He deserved every insult and condemnation she could heap upon him. Still, he'd come here with *his* hat in hand, offering her the chance to help solve the case of a lifetime.

He squinted down the end of the road, trying to determine if the car had crept a little closer. Even from a distance, he could tell the windows were tinted and the license plate obscured. He wondered briefly if a tracker had been planted on his vehicle. Maybe that was how they'd found him again so quickly. More likely they'd used his phone's GPS. Electronic surveillance usually meant clout and someone with serious intent.

The surveillance had annoyed him earlier, but now he was just plain pissed. He resented having his every move scrutinized and disseminated. He'd used personal days to come to Charleston on his own dime, relying on his own resources. As far as he was concerned, this was not the FBI's business, but of course, his section chief would likely see things differently.

So be it. Might as well give them enough rope.

He climbed into his rental and made a U-turn in the street, picking up speed as he headed toward the Charger. The acceleration thrilled him. He pushed the pedal to the floor, and the powerful V-8 roared. The scenery blurred in the side windows as the vehicle shot forward.

For a moment, he wondered if the driver meant to call his bluff. The vehicle remained immobile for so long that a crash seemed imminent. Ethan braced himself and was just about to swerve when the car reversed down the street and backed around the corner in one smooth move. Then the driver shifted and the Charger catapulted through the intersection.

Ethan made the turn without slowing. He gripped the wheel as the SUV fishtailed and the tires spun on the graveled shoulder. Up ahead, the Charger careened around another corner and blasted through a stop sign, narrowly missing a woman and two small boys as they stepped off the curb. The mother had plenty of time to pull the children to safety on the sidewalk, but she froze. Ethan could have sworn he saw her lips move in prayer a split second before he hit the brakes.

The tires squealed in protest as the rubber gripped the pavement and the powerful vehicle skidded to a stop.

He hopped out of the SUV and called to the woman, "Are you okay?"

She spoke in a heavy accent. "Are you crazy? You could have killed us!"

She kept screaming at him, gesturing wildly with her arms as the boys clung to her legs. Ethan stood silently by and took it. She had every right to call him out. What had he been thinking, engaging in a high-speed chase?

He scanned the neighborhood from his periphery. Many of the houses along the street were in various stages of disrepair, but he could see signs of gentrification creeping in. He wondered what the upwardly mobile millennials would think of their fixer-upper investments when they learned about the house at the end of the dead-end street.

Apologizing profusely, he got back in his vehicle. He waited until the woman was safely across the street with the children and then he circled the block and headed back to the abandoned house, parking in the very spot he had vacated only a few minutes earlier. The incident left him shaken. He'd been able to stop in plenty of time, but that was beside the point. What if his brakes had failed? What if he'd lost control of the wheel? He'd behaved recklessly, and that wasn't like him. Not anymore. Maybe he'd played the game for too long, kept his head down and his nose clean for so long that his dangerous impulses were rebelling. Ever since he'd received the first email from a woman named Naomi Quinlan, his life had been one risky decision after another.

He locked the vehicle and walked through the tall weeds in the front yard, pausing at the bottom of the steps to scan the ramshackle facade. He could no longer see anyone inside. Whoever he'd glimpsed earlier had moved into another part of the house or perhaps had left the premises altogether. He hoped that wasn't the case. Far better that he approach Addie on neutral ground than to show up unexpectedly at her house.

He lifted the crime-scene tape over his head and opened the front door. Before he could step into the foyer, a male voice halted him. "Stop right there. In case you can't read that yellow tape, this is a crime scene. You need to get back behind the barricade and stay there."

Ethan took out his wallet and showed the man his credentials. "My name is Ethan Barrow. I'm with the FBI."

The man glanced at the badge and scowled. "No one said anything about federal involvement."

Ethan returned the wallet to his pocket and removed his sunglasses. "I didn't catch your name."

"Detective Matthew Lepear, Charleston PD." He glanced behind him into the gutted room. "Delmar Gainey's victims have been dead for over two decades, Agent Barrow. The man himself died five years ago. Why would the feds be interested in this case?"

"I'm not interested in your case, Detective. I'm looking for Adaline Kinsella."

"What's your interest in *Detective* Kinsella, if you don't mind my asking?"

The slight proprietorial edge in the man's voice caught Ethan's attention. He gave him a sharper scrutiny. "I'd rather discuss my business with her."

"Detective Kinsella is on vacation this week."

Ethan turned to glance out one of the sidelights before resettling his gaze on the detective. "Isn't that her silver SUV at the curb?"

The man shrugged. "New cars all look alike."

Ethan folded his sunglasses carefully and tucked them into his inner jacket pocket. "Detective Kinsella is your partner, isn't she?"

"Why do you ask?"

"You seem overly protective. I can appreciate your concern, but I'm not sure she would."

Something flashed in Lepear's eyes, a fleeting acknowledgment that Ethan had hit a little too close to the truth. "You could be right. Addie's got a mind of her own, that's for damn sure. The one thing I do know about her is this—she won't be happy to see you."

Ethan tamped down his annoyance. "You know her well enough to make that assessment?"

"We go back a long way. Ten years, to be precise. She's not just my partner. She's also a friend. And you're the SOB who almost ended her career."

Ethan was jolted by an uncomfortable truth. Lepear knew who he was.

Anger mingled with remorse. "I never meant to cause her trouble."

"People like you never do. You just tell yourself the end justifies the means."

Ethan waited a beat before he continued. He didn't want to lose his temper. Lepear was defending his partner and friend. Ethan would do the same if the positions were reversed, but it wasn't like he'd walked away from the relationship unscathed. It wasn't like he'd gone back to Virginia and forgotten all about Adaline Kinsella. He'd spent many a sleepless night staring up at the ceiling, wanting to call just to hear her voice but knowing she would never pick up.

"I'm not looking for trouble now," he said. "I just want to talk to her."

Lepear gave him a derisive look before he finally acquiesced. "She's out back. You can go through that door." He nodded toward the crumbling archway. "But if I were you, I'd watch my step. I mean, I'd *really* watch my step, Agent Barrow."

Their gazes held for a moment longer before Ethan nodded. "Thanks for the heads-up."

ADDIE STOOD ON the back porch, staring at the mounds of dirt and empty graves where the remains had been excavated and removed. A broken wheelchair had been pushed up under the porch railing, and she couldn't help but imagine Delmar Gainey sitting there alone in the dark, admiring his gruesome garden by moonlight. Another ramp had been built beside the back steps, and if Addie closed her eyes, she could see him out there among the graves, enjoying the mingled scents of jasmine and death wafting on the afternoon breeze.

She felt light-headed from the heat and from old memories, and she curled her fingers around the wood rail, clinging for a moment while she tried to beat back her emotions. She was no stranger to death. She'd lost her mother to a brutal killer and her grandmother to the gentler reaper of natural causes. As a cop, Addie had seen all manner of death and violence, but those empty graves reminded her of the thin veneer of humanity that could too easily be peeled away.

A sound brought her around with a start, and she felt a shudder go through her as her gaze connected with the man in the doorway. Tall and fit, he stood ramrod straight in his dark suit and tie, hardly more than a silhouette against the dim backdrop of the house.

"Ethan?" Even as she spoke his name, her chin came up in defiance. Before she could demand to know the purpose of his presence, she heard a crack, followed by a splintering sound as the rotting floorboards gave way beneath her feet. Her arms flailed wildly as she tried to catch her balance, but the wood disintegrated and she crashed through the porch.

She saw Ethan lunge for her, and then she saw nothing but blackness as she found herself in a free fall.

Chapter Three

Addie reached out instinctively, grasping, grasping until she made contact with a rope. She grabbed on with both hands, halting her fall for only an instant before she dropped to the bottom. But that split second allowed her to brace for impact. She tucked and rolled.

Hot pain shot across her left shoulder as she lay still for a moment. Then she gingerly moved her arms and legs. No broken bones. She pushed herself off the floor and got to her feet. No cuts or other wounds that she could determine, but she was in complete darkness save for a thin tunnel of illumination that shone down through the fractured boards. The light seemed to quiver as if it had a life of its own. The sensation was eerie and disorienting. Addie reached out with one hand and made contact with the wall as she tilted her head to that shimmering light.

"Addie?"

Her eyes fluttered closed before she braced herself yet again. That voice. How many times had she dreamed of it in her ear, imagined his husky whisper in the dark? She shivered now as her name echoed off the walls like a taunt.

"Adaline, can you hear me?"

She peered up into the freaky light. "I can hear you."

"Are you okay?"

"I'm okay. No broken bones or cuts. Where am I?"

"I think you've fallen into an old well or cistern. The porch must have been built over it. Are you in water?"

She shivered again at the echo-like quality of his voice. "No, but the walls are damp. And it smells pretty bad down here. I wonder how far I fell. It looks a long way up there."

"Hard to say. Fifteen, twenty feet maybe. You're lucky you didn't break your neck."

"I grabbed on to a rope. Do you see it?"

"It looks badly frayed. I'm not sure it's strong enough to haul you up."

"Go find Matt. Matt Lepear. He's my partner. He drove his truck out here today. He usually keeps a chain in the back for when he goes off-roading. Someone always gets stuck."

"I'll find him and we'll get you out of there. Just hang tight until I get back."

"Ethan?"

His face appeared back over the opening.

"Someone left a flashlight on the porch railing. I saw it a minute ago. Can you toss it down to me? It's pitch-black and I think I hear rats."

"I see it. I'll tie it off and lower it down. Stand back in case the rope breaks."

She stepped out of the light, allowing the darkness to swallow her. Furtive claws scratched nearby, and she could have sworn something scurried across her feet, but she hoped the sensation wasn't real. She hoped her imagination was getting the better of her because the notion of rats closing in on her—

Ethan cut into her thoughts. "I'm lowering the light down now."

He turned on the bulb so that Addie could track the beam. As the rope spun, the light bounced off the walls, casting giant shadows down into the well. Addie reached eagerly for the flashlight, slipping it free of the knot and then wrapping her fingers tightly around the thick rubber housing.

"I've got it," she said. "Thanks."

"No problem. I'll be right back."

"Ethan?"

"Yes?"

She ran the light up and down the walls and then over the floor, exploring debris that had been abandoned for decades.

"What is it?" he called down to her.

"There's a lot of trash in here." Her voice quivered in spite of her best efforts. "Old blankets. Broken dishes. I think this is where he kept them."

Ethan said something, but she didn't hear his response. She was too caught up in the horror of that place. Too distracted by the image of that wheelchair shoved up under the porch railing. How many times had Gainey rolled across the floorboards, aroused by his memories as he reveled in his secrets?

Addie angled the beam along the crevice where floor met wall. She imagined someone cowering there, but the beady eyes that glinted back at her weren't human.

Repelled by the light, the rat scuttled back to its hidey-hole, leaving Addie alone with the echo of long-dead screams.

ADDIE STOOD WITH her face to the sun, basking in the light as she brushed dust from her hair. Even covered in dirt and grime, she looked good. Ethan was glad for his sunglasses so he could pretend not to stare.

He and some of the officers had easily hauled her up from the well, and she seemed no worse for the wear. But she hadn't lingered, even when her partner had insisted on going down to have a look for himself. Addie had watched for a moment and then, with a shudder, turned and disappeared. Ethan had followed her out into the sun. After the creepy confines of that house, he welcomed the heat, even the trickle of sweat he could feel between his shoulder blades.

"You okay?" he asked.

"I just needed some air. Being down in that well and knowing what he used it for...knowing what he did to all those people...it got to me for a minute."

Ethan nodded. "It gets to all of us now and then, but that's a good thing. You don't ever want to feel numb to what one human being can do to another. You never want to lose your ability to be shocked."

If she thought that sentiment strange coming from him—the son of a profiler who had gone to the dark side—she didn't say so. "You see this sort of thing more than I do. How do you cope?"

"I'd be lying if I said I leave it at the office. But I try to find productive ways to fill up my spare time. I run. I listen to music and read books. Sometimes I visit museums and art galleries just to remind myself that human beings are also capable of creating great beauty."

"That sounds amazingly well adjusted. Right now, I just want a good, stiff drink." She wiped her hands down the sides of her jeans as if trying to cleanse herself of the images.

Ethan found himself checking out her fingers to make sure she hadn't gotten married or engaged since last he'd heard. No diamonds that he could discern, but the sun bouncing off the detective shield she'd clipped to her waist was blinding.

"Congratulations, by the way."

She gave him a suspicious look. "For what?"

He nodded toward her badge. "You made detective in record time, I see."

Her eyes flashed. "I didn't set any records. And there were plenty of times when I never thought I'd make it. This shield didn't just fall into my lap. I worked hard for it."

He'd obviously hit a nerve. Like him, she'd probably battled whispers of nepotism for most of her career. "I never thought otherwise," he said. "My congratulations were sincere."

"Thank you." She glanced away for a moment as if trying to puzzle something out. Her gaze came back to him reluctantly. "You seem different."

"Because I'm happy for your success?"

A frown flitted across her brow. "No. I can't put my finger on it."

"It's been ten years. I expect we're both different people."

"Agreed. At the very least, I like to think I'm a lot less gullible than I used to be."

Their gazes met, clashed again, but behind the glimmer of hostility, Ethan felt a connection, no matter how fleeting. Or maybe the link was nothing more than wishful thinking, but he found himself drifting back, imagining her smile and the spill of blond hair over her shoulders as she stared down at him through hooded eyes. Adaline Kinsella at twenty-two had been something. At thirty-two... Ethan didn't dare let himself go there.

She glanced past him down the road to where the

black Charger had returned to wait him out. "Friends of yours?"

"No."

She lifted a brow at his tone. "Enemies?"

"I don't know."

"But they're here because of you."

"Probably."

"That car looks official. Tinted windows. No identifying tags or marks. I'm guessing feds." Her gaze swung back to him. "Why are *you* here, Ethan? What have you done this time?"

"You don't pull any punches, do you?"

Any hint of a bond melted in the fierceness of her stare. "I've been on the wrong end of your obsession, remember? I recognize the signs. You didn't come all the way from Quantico just to see me."

"Why not? It wouldn't be the first time."

"Okay, stop right there." She gave him a disgusted look. "Don't even think about playing that card. In case you've forgotten, things didn't end well for us. So don't pretend this is a sentimental reunion. Be honest for once in your life and tell me why you're really here."

"It's not an easy explanation."

"It never is with you." She came down the porch steps. "How did you even know where to find me, anyway? I've been away on vacation. I only got back a little while ago, and other than a quick stop at the station, I came straight here." She shot another glance at the Charger. "If those guys are following *me*—"

"They're not. Stop worrying about that car. I'll handle whoever's inside. I knew to find you at this house because I overheard someone at police headquarters mention your whereabouts."

The revelation didn't please her. "You were at head-quarters? Who did you talk to?"

"I didn't talk to anyone about you. I had a meeting with the deputy chief."

She looked even more distressed. "Why?"

"That's for him to say."

Addie shook her head. "This is crazy. I don't want to hear any more. Whatever you're involved in, count me out. Thanks for getting me out of the well. I do appreciate that. But this is the end of the road for us." She turned and headed for her vehicle. "I'm going home and you can go to…" Down the road, a car door slammed, freezing her for a moment as she glanced over her shoulder.

One of the agents had gotten out of the Charger to stretch, apparently now unconcerned about anonymity. Ethan didn't recognize him, but like Addie, he knew the guy was a federal agent.

He returned his focus to Addie. She lifted her chin and turned back to her car. He called after her. "I've found new evidence in your mother's case."

That stopped her again. She turned slowly to face him. "What?"

"I wasn't lying when I said I came to Charleston to see you, but I'm also here pursuing a lead. I wanted you to know before you heard it from someone else."

"Is that why you went to see the deputy chief?"

"Like I said, you need to talk to him about that."

She shoved back a lock of damp hair. "Assuming I believe you, what makes you think I'd ever want any of this dumped on my doorstep?"

"Besides the fact that your mother was murdered? You're a police detective. You must be interested in justice."

She said nothing for the longest time, just stood there staring back at him as he searched her face. Her eyes were so much bluer than he remembered. Softer, too, and liquid. They reminded him of a Monet painting he'd seen in the National Gallery.

But right now, those eyes were narrowed in suspicion. "My mother's case is closed. As far as I'm concerned, justice was served twenty-five years ago when your father was committed to the fourth floor."

"Maybe. Or maybe an innocent man was framed for something he didn't do."

"James Merrick is not an innocent man." She opened her car door. "I've heard enough. I'm not getting sucked back into your delusions. Listening to you almost cost me everything ten years ago."

"If the evidence wasn't compelling, I wouldn't be here."

"Then investigate all you want, but leave me out of it."

"Addie."

She whirled. "Damn it, can't you take a hint? Leave me alone!"

Her tone took him aback. He put up a hand. "Okay. I get it. I'm sorry I bothered you."

She let out a long sigh. "Don't give me that look. Do you think I enjoy acting like a first-class bitch?"

"I would never call you that."

"You didn't have to. I can hear myself. I don't enjoy saying these things to you, Ethan. I'm not an angry person, and I don't like carrying a grudge. But you did lie to me. And worse, you got *me* to lie. That was on me. As a grown woman, I should have known better. I never should have accessed sealed files without authorization, let alone allowed you to leak information to the press.

I shouldn't have done a lot of things I did when I was with you, but that all happened a long time ago. I'm over it. What I can't get past, though, is how you made me doubt myself. How you made me lose faith that I had what it took to be a good cop. I've worked really hard to get my confidence back."

No wonder she was so defensive of her detective's shield. "I'm sorry I lied to you. And I'm sorry about how everything went down."

"I know. That I believe, but it doesn't change anything."

"If you'd just hear me out—"

"I can't."

"Five minutes. That's all I'm asking."

She closed her eyes. "Why are you doing this to me?"

"Because you're the only other person in the world I trust with this information. If anything were to happen to me, I know you'd do the right thing."

Her eyes widened. "What do you mean, if anything were to happen to you?"

He shrugged. "We live in a dangerous world."

Her gaze flicked back to the Charger. "Who are those guys?"

"I don't know."

"They're watching you because of this new information?"

"That would be my guess."

She chewed her bottom lip as she stared down the road at the car. "I can't believe I'm saying this, but fine. Tell me what you've found."

He followed her gaze to the Charger. "I'd rather discuss it somewhere more private. Can I buy you that drink?"

"No," she said bluntly. "When I leave here, I'm going straight home to wash the cobwebs out of my hair."

"Later then. We can meet anywhere you like."

She drew another breath. "I know I'll live to regret this, but I sometimes go for walks on the Battery in the evenings. I'll be there at seven, and I'll wait exactly five minutes. If you don't show, we'll let this drop and you won't ever bother me again."

"Agreed," he said. "But I'll be there."

Nothing short of the apocalypse—or the federal agents inside that black Dodge Charger—could keep him away.

Chapter Four

Addie's house was a modest brick ranch tucked back from the street and shaded by two large live oaks that canopied her whole front yard. Beds of impatiens lined her brick walkway, and hydrangeas grew along the sides of her concrete porch. It was a pleasant place to come home to, a cool and colorful oasis.

Once upon a time, as she'd sanded and refinished the original hardwood floors and painted every wall in the house, she'd had visions of dinner parties and backyard barbecues. But a strange thing happened when she finished her renovations. She became greedy of her privacy and protective of her sanctuary. Most evenings, she was all too content to sit alone in the yard watching hummingbirds fight at her feeders and later, lightning bugs flit through the jasmine.

Today when she turned down her street, she took note of a white panel van parked two doors down from her place. The traditional two-story house was undergoing a gut job, so it wasn't unusual to find any number of vehicles parked at the curb. The side door of the van was open, and Addie glimpsed what looked to be an assortment of tools and lumber inside. The front door to the house was also open, but she saw no signs of life. Addie wasn't alarmed or even that curious; she was merely observant. East Side fixer-uppers had become hot commodities over the past few years, and the heightened activity in the neighborhood sometimes allowed criminals to slip in and out unnoticed. It paid to keep an eye out.

A late-model luxury sedan was parked in her driveway when she got home. This vehicle she recognized. Addie waved to the older woman perched on her porch steps. The woman waved back and called out to her. Just shy of sixty, Dr. Helen Cutler was pleasantly nondescript, neither short nor tall, neither heavy nor thin, but she had an aura of warmth and vitality that drew one in, and her voice was melodic and soothing—desirable attributes for a therapist. She wore her silver hair clipped close to her head, and she favored oversize eyeglasses and knit cotton clothing with a bohemian flare. She sat on the top step with her full skirt flowing around her ankles as she watched Addie cross the yard.

"This is a pleasant surprise. I didn't expect to see you this afternoon," Addie said as she automatically shaded her eyes to check up and down the street. A calico cat rose from the porch, stretched and then sauntered down the steps to greet her at the bottom. She bent to give the feline some attention.

"I didn't expect to see you, either," Helen said. "Not for another two days. As to what *I'm* doing here, did you forget you asked me to feed the strays while you were away?"

"You didn't get my voice mail?"

"I lost my phone," Helen said with a sigh. "Second time this year. One would almost think I'm misplacing them on purpose. Fortunately, my new one arrives tomorrow, although I've rather enjoyed going old-school for the last couple of days."

Addie plopped down on the porch steps beside her. "I'd be lost without my phone."

"Spoken like a true millennial. But David is almost as bad. Sometimes I think he has that thing glued to his ear."

"Your husband is an important man. The department couldn't function without our deputy chief."

"So he tells me," Helen said drily. "But enough about him. Tell me why you're back so early."

Addie pulled her legs up and wrapped her arms around her knees, mimicking Helen's position. The Cutlers weren't blood relatives, but they were closer to Addie than any of her real family. David had been both mentor and taskmaster, and there had been times when Addie had felt he demanded too much of her, that he held her to a higher standard than any of the other detectives. But in the long run, his expectations had served her well, and there was no one in the department she trusted or respected more.

Twenty-five years ago, as a young homicide detective, he'd been the one to find her mother's body. In the painful aftermath of that tragedy, Helen had helped Addie cope with her grief, her night terrors and the confusing notoriety that came from being one of Twilight's Children. The couple had been her lifeline ever since, and Addie knew she would never be able to repay their kindness and support.

"The cabin was wonderful for about three days," she said. "And then I started to go stir-crazy."

Helen glanced at her over the top of her glasses. "With that gorgeous lake right outside your door? All those lovely mountains to explore?"

"What can I say, I'm a city girl at heart. I can only

take so much of communing with nature before I need my morning fix of car horns and exhaust fumes."

"You sound just like David. I've been trying to get him to slow down for the past ten years, but he just gets busier and crankier. Sometimes I think he won't be content until he works himself to death. These days he doesn't get home until well after dark, and he leaves the house before I wake up. And lately—" Helen broke off with a frown.

"Lately what?"

"He seems…distant. Distracted. It's probably nothing."

"Have you talked to him about it?"

"You know he doesn't like to talk about work. Not to me, at least."

"Do you want me to talk to him?"

Helen patted her arm. "I would never put you in that position. You might suggest to him, though, that a vacation with his wife wouldn't be the end of the world."

"I'll do that."

"I can't even remember the last time we went up to the cabin together, much less someplace exotic. We used to love taking cruises in our younger days, but the last one must have been before—" She stopped short and then shrugged. "Before he was appointed deputy chief."

"Were you about to say before my mother died?"

Helen was silent for a moment. "How did you know?"

"Because you always get that look when you're thinking about her."

Helen smiled. "You know me too well. Sandra's been on my mind so much lately. This time of year is always difficult, and now with the twenty-fifth anniversary looming, so many articles are coming out about the Twilight Killer and James Merrick. You can't avoid the subject. Or the memories. I was so glad you decided to take your vacation when you did. I wanted you to have some time away from all that darkness."

"Matt Lepear mentioned he saw a documentary about the Twilight Killer the other night," Addie said.

Helen's expression turned grim. "Yes, I saw it, too. I told myself I wouldn't watch, but I couldn't seem to resist."

"He said they showed a picture of me."

"They had photographs of all the children. It was a where-are-they-now montage." She paused, and her voice softened. "So many lives were torn apart that summer. So many children lost their innocence because of that monster. I'm so thankful you've been able to move beyond it."

"In no small part because of you and David," Addie said.

Helen draped an arm around Addie's shoulders and gave her a quick squeeze. "I'm just happy your grandmother allowed us to remain in your life. Your mother and I were always so close. She was like a younger sister to me. And you're the daughter I never had."

Addie tilted her face to the warm breeze. "What was it like that summer? It's all so hazy to me. Like a dream. Yet I can still remember the dress I wore to my mother's funeral and the songs the choir sang. I even remember hearing you and David talking in the doorway of my bedroom the night she was killed."

Helen glanced at her. "You never told me that."

Addie shrugged. "You always get so sad when we talk about her. I thought it best to keep some things to myself."

Helen regarded her for a moment. "I'm sorry you felt that way. I let you down when you needed me the most."

"That's not true. You *saved* me."

"You saved yourself, Addie. I've never known anyone stronger. Even when you were a child, you were sometimes the one holding me up. I'm glad you don't remember much about those days, but for me, it seems only yesterday. There was a hushed quality to the city after the first body was found, like we were all holding our breath. Like we somehow knew the worst was yet to come. After the second body, fear settled in, and you couldn't walk down the street without glancing over your shoulder."

Addie said, "Was my mother scared?"

"She never let on. But that was our Sandra. She was so full of bluster and bravado. I was scared for her because she fit the profile. Young, single mother living alone with an only child. On some level, she must have been frightened. David and I did our best to keep an eye on you both, but she was stubborn and independent. She refused to change her lifestyle regardless of the warnings. 'If you give in to the fear, you let him in,' she would say. And then she'd laugh and tease me. 'You worry too much, Helen. Only thirty and already you're an old fogey. Come out and have a drink with me.' And I would gently remind her that someone had to stay and watch over you. *Dear Helen. What would I ever do without you?*"

The change in her aunt's voice startled Addie, and a memory flitted. *Sometimes I think you love Helen more than me. I'm glad she's good to you, boo. I'm glad you like going to her house. But don't forget who your real mother is, okay? Don't forget me.*

"Addie?"

The sound of Helen's normal, soothing timbre chased away the memory. "Yes?"

"Where did you go just now?"

"I remembered something Mama said to me once about how much I liked being at your house. Did I stay with you often?"

"Sandra adored going out," Helen said without really answering Addie's question. "She had you when she was so young, barely eighteen, so it was only natural she'd crave a social life."

"You didn't resent having someone else's kid dumped on you? You were young, too. You and David must have had things you'd rather do than babysit me."

"Resent it? The time I spent with you was always the highlight of my week. David felt the same way. He liked having you close so that he could protect you. We were such careful people. We took every precaution. We made sure the doors and windows were locked every night, and we kept an eye out for strangers in the neighborhood. Even so, I never really believed anything could happen to someone so close to us."

"I know."

Helen gazed out toward the street, where the sun hovered just above the treetops. As the shadows grew longer, the perfume from Addie's garden deepened.

Her aunt shivered. "It's been twenty-five years, and I still get anxious this time of day."

Addie followed her gaze to the street. Two doors down, someone had come out of the house and climbed into the white van. She could hear the idle of the engine, but she couldn't make out the driver. Like the Charger she'd seen earlier, the van's windshield was tinted. Why hadn't she noticed that before?

"Do you see that van parked down the street? Was it there when you drove by?"

Helen had been lost in thought, but now she roused

herself. "What? I don't know. I never even noticed it until now. But I've seen a lot of trucks and vans in front of that house since I've been feeding the strays. I'm sure it belongs to one of the workers."

"Probably, but I didn't see any logo on the side."

Helen turned to stare at her. "You're not worried about it, are you? Surely no one would be brazen enough to try to rob the place with so many people out and about."

"It wouldn't be the first time, but I'm not suggesting they're up to no good. I just like to keep an eye on any strange vehicles in the neighborhood."

"David trained you well," Helen said in approval. "He used to make me jot down make, model and license plate number if I saw anything suspicious. Now I just snap a picture with my phone. When I have one on me, that is."

"Good idea," Addie said as she took out her own phone. For the longest time, the driver remained stationary with the motor running. She thought again of that black Charger and Ethan's revelation of new evidence. Of his insistence that if something happened to him, he could trust her to do right thing.

As if drawn by the power of her stare, the van pulled onto the street and slowly came toward them.

The side window was down, but the driver wore a red cap pulled low over his brow so that Addie couldn't get a good look at him.

"That's not at all suspicious," she muttered as she lifted her phone. She zoomed in, trying to capture the rear license plate. "Did you get a glimpse of him?"

Helen didn't answer. She stared after the van for a moment, and then her hand flew to her skirt pocket as if something had suddenly occurred to her. But it was her expression that caught Addie's attention. *Stricken* was the word that came to mind.

"Aunt Helen? Are you okay? You look as if you just saw a ghost."

She turned wide eyes on Addie. "A ghost?"

"You're as white as a sheet. What's wrong? Did you recognize the driver of the van?"

"What? No. Oh, no." She shook her head as if to clear her senses. "Nothing like that. I think I remember where I left my phone."

"Where? Maybe it's still there. We can go look for it if you want."

"It's probably long gone by now, but just in case, I'll have a look on my way home. Speaking of which..." She rose and stood with her back to Addie. "I really should be going."

"I'll walk you to your car."

She seemed so tense and anxious that Addie thought she might decline. Then she relaxed when Addie slipped her arm through hers. Helen patted her hand. "Good to have you home."

"Thank you for looking after the kitties. And for the use of the cabin. It really was good to get away. I hope you and David can make it up there soon. Seems a shame to let it sit empty."

Helen glanced at her. "I'm glad you enjoyed it."

Addie searched her face. "Are you sure you're okay?"

"Yes, I'm just a little tired. I'll call you tomorrow. We'll make dinner plans."

"Just name the date."

"I'll let you get settled with your new assignment first. Addie..." Helen turned back to the street. "Be careful. I know this neighborhood isn't as dangerous as it once was, but there are bad elements everywhere these days. Keep your doors and windows locked, and turn on the alarm even when you're home. Keep your gun nearby when you sleep."

"You don't need to worry about me. As you said, David taught me well."

"Sometimes danger comes from a place you least expect," Helen said as she climbed into her car. She closed the door and lowered the window. "I'll call you about dinner."

Addie watched her back out of the drive and head down the street in the same direction as the white van. The opposite direction from Helen's neighborhood.

TWILIGHT CAME LATE and softly in the summertime. The evening breeze brought a tantalizing mixture of jasmine, moonflowers and the more elusive perfume of the tea olives. Ethan's interest in flowers was limited to his study of Orson Lee Finch. His recognition of the various scents came from Addie. She used to school him as they walked arm in arm through White Point Garden. At twenty-two, Ethan had been more interested in the scent that wafted from her long blond hair. *You're not listening to me*, she would scold him.

I'm hanging on your every word. How could I not when you have me wrapped around your little finger?

And then she would stand on tiptoes to kiss him as he threaded his fingers through that soft, soft hair, turning her face to his, kissing her back with an urgency that surprised even him.

Ethan let the memory fade as he climbed the steps to the Battery. After leaving the Gainey house, he'd gone back to his hotel to shower and change into more casual clothing, but he felt vulnerable out of his G-man uniform. The dark suits gave him a veneer of invincibility, and now in jeans and a cotton shirt, he felt increasingly unsure of himself. He had a feeling Addie would be able to see right through him, but maybe that wasn't a bad thing. He needed her on his side, and complete honesty was the only hope he had.

He trained his gaze on Charleston Harbor, marking the rise and fall of the tide as sailboats floated in the distance. He had always loved this city. His maternal grandparents were native Charlestonians, and despite the publicity surrounding his father's breakdown and arrest, he and his mother had lived here for a time before she'd dated Richard Barrow. After their marriage, his stepfather had moved them to his home in Alexandria. He and Ethan's mother still lived in the same gleaming white colonial. To anyone unaware of the backstory, they seemed an idyllic family, and yet even as a kid, Ethan had felt like an impostor.

Sensing eyes on him, he turned his head, almost expecting to find his counterparts in dark suits and sunglasses watching him. Instead, he saw Addie making her way through the evening crowd. She'd gone home to change and now, in cutoffs and sneakers, she looked more like a college kid than a seasoned police detective. She'd pulled her hair back and tucked it up loosely at her nape. She wore sunglasses, too, so he couldn't see her eyes, but she wasn't smiling. Her sober demeanor took nothing away from her attractiveness. She looked fit, tanned and ready to take on the world. Or him.

Ethan turned back to the water, collecting his thoughts and emotions as he waited for her to approach.

"I wasn't sure you'd come," he said, his gaze still on the distant sails. He turned slowly to face her, eyeing her leisurely from behind his own dark glasses.

"I told you I would. I always try to keep my word."

She moved up beside him at the rail. "You're early, I see."

"I didn't want to take a chance on missing you. I know this can't be easy. The way things went down between us—"

She glanced away. "I don't want to talk about that. That's not why I'm here. You said you had information about my mother's murder. I don't know what you could have possibly dug up after all this time, but here I am, so let's get to it."

He flicked a glance behind her down the crowded walkway. "Not much privacy out here. Are you sure you don't want a drink or a bite to eat? We could go to Pearlz."

"I'm not going to eat or drink with you, Ethan. This isn't a date."

"I didn't mean to imply that it was. Can we at least go across the street to the park and find a quiet bench?"

Her mouth tightened as she reached up to tuck back a strand of hair. "Fine."

They went down the steps and crossed East Bay, keeping a careful distance between them. Ethan could still smell jasmine on the warm breeze that blew across the harbor. The scent and the woman beside him stirred memories he'd tried to keep buried for ten long years, ever since that final showdown when Addie had made it clear she never wanted to see him again. He could still remember the glitter of angry tears in her eyes and the faint quiver of her lip before she'd turned and walked away. They'd both been so young, and Ethan had made so many mistakes. Maybe it was fitting that Orson Lee Finch's words should once again come back to haunt him. *A man like you will always be at war with his emotions. Tormented by what he can't know. Unable to make peace with his past.*

Addie stopped in front of a bench facing the street. "This okay with you?"

Her voice snapped him back to the present. "Yes, fine. The shade feels good."

She waited until he responded before settling herself at one end of the bench. He joined her, draping one arm across the back. Addie took off her sunglasses and laid them on the seat between them as if to create a physical barrier.

For a moment, neither of them spoke. Ethan wondered if she were as lost in the past as he was. If she remembered all those moonlit drives, the walks on the beach, the nights spent in her garage apartment off Morrison Drive. Now she lived in a small East Side house with a mortgage, but she wouldn't like him knowing that.

He felt her gaze on him and turned to find her eyes slightly narrowed as she studied him. Then she glanced at her watch. "I don't have long. We should get started."

He wanted to ask if she had a date later that evening, but instead he nodded. "To explain the new evidence, we'll have to talk about the crime scene. I'm sorry. I know that'll be painful for you."

"And for you," she said, her gaze lifting to meet his. Her expression was not without compassion. "Go on."

"Three DNA samples were collected at that scene. Your mother's, my father's and a third blood sample that was never identified."

"Both the police and FBI concluded the unidentified DNA had been in the alley before the murder."

"A reasonable explanation, but that sample has always tormented me, even though nothing ever turned up in the databases."

"It was your obsession," Addie murmured.

She would remember, because she'd suffered the consequences of that obsession. "My father's erratic behavior at the time of his arrest and his subsequent mental breakdown made it all too easy to accept him as the murderer, especially since his abilities as a profiler enabled him to mimic the Twilight Killer's MO. That MO included things that hadn't been released to the public at the time. The staging of the bodies, for example. But my father wasn't the only one who had access to that information."

"You're leaving out the most damning pieces of evidence," Addie said. "Not only was James Merrick's DNA found at the crime scene, the murder weapon was located two blocks from his hotel and his bloody clothing was found in the hotel dumpster."

"My father was a brilliant man. He knew the criminal mind better than anyone of his time. It's hard to imagine he would make such careless mistakes."

"But that was his whole defense," Addie reminded him. "He wasn't in his right mind. You said yourself his behavior was erratic at the time of his arrest and he subsequently suffered a complete mental breakdown."

An exasperated edge crept into Ethan's tone despite his best efforts at neutrality. "Those discoveries were too convenient. If he still had enough rational thought to remove the murder weapon from the crime scene, why dispose of it in such an obvious location rather than tossing it in the harbor? Why not burn the bloody clothing? None of this has ever made sense to me."

"What puzzles you the most?" Addie demanded.

"That he was careless in disposing of evidence or that he killed my mother in cold blood?"

That was blunt.

Ethan inwardly winced. The meeting wasn't going well. Far from breaking down barriers, he had forced her to put up more walls. She was withdrawn and defensive, and he wondered if he'd made a mistake coming to her with what he'd found. Who else would believe him, though? Whom could he trust to help him dig for the truth if not the victim's child?

"I'm sorry," he said. "I didn't mean to get into any of that. I just wanted to remind you about the third DNA sample."

She made an impatient gesture with her hand. "Got it. Keep going."

"Two weeks ago, I received an email from a genealogist here in Charleston who claimed she'd cross-referenced the third DNA sample against a number of public databases. She got a match."

Addie whirled, her eyes going wide with disbelief. *"What?"*

Ethan nodded. "Thousands of those databases exit, created mostly by people who post their DNA profiles online in the hopes of finding long-lost relatives. Biological mothers and adopted children, for example."

"Now that doesn't make any sense to me," Addie said. "I don't mean the part about the databases or long-lost relatives. I'm talking about the sample itself. How would a genealogist get her hands on DNA evidence that's been in police custody for over twenty-five years?"

"I think she or someone close to her had a connection in the police department."

Addie frowned. "You think a cop gave her the sample?"

"She may have had it for years with no way to check for a match. These public databases are fairly new technology."

"Did you ask her where she got the sample?"

"Yes, but she was guarded. She refused to provide details through email or over the phone. She insisted I come to Charleston to meet with her in person."

"And that didn't set off any alarm bells for you?"

"Her credentials checked out. She said she needed to be discreet because if anyone found out about her research, her life could be in danger."

"And you believed her?"

"I didn't at first. I thought she was exaggerating to coerce my cooperation. We emailed back and forth a few times, and then the correspondence just stopped. I told myself to let it go. No good could come from digging all that up again, but—"

"You couldn't."

He shrugged. "When she didn't answer my emails, I made some inquiries. I found out she'd been killed in a hit-and-run two days after she first made contact with me."

Addie stared at him for the longest moment. Then she asked in a strained tone, "What was her name?"

"Naomi Quinlan. She taught night courses on genealogy research at the community college. She was struck while walking home from class one evening."

"Quinlan, Quinlan," Addie muttered. "I know that name. I remember that hit-and-run. It happened right off King Street. I caught the call, but another detective was already on the scene by the time I got there. It was bad. The impact was so severe the coroner said she probably died instantly. There were no witnesses, nothing at the scene or in the victim's history to support premeditation. We assumed the driver was under the influence and lost control of the vehicle."

"The driver has never been found?"

"Not as far as I know."

"You said you caught the call. Why didn't you lead the investigation?"

"Like I said, another detective was already on the scene, so I backed off because I was being transferred out of the Investigations Bureau, anyway."

"Why?"

"New assignment."

"So you never followed up on the hit-and-run?"

"I had my hands full trying to clear the active cases on my desk." But remorse flashed in her eyes before she turned to stare at the street.

"I understand," Ethan said. "Never enough hours in the day. When I tried to press Naomi for the name of the DNA donor, she reminded me that careers had been built on the Twilight Killer case and on my father's subsequent arrest. If either investigation was discredited by a new piece of evidence, a lot of important reputations would be tarnished."

"That sounds a bit dramatic," Addie said.

"I thought so, too. Right up until the time she turned up dead."

Addie frowned. "You don't know that her death was related to the DNA match. That hit-and-run could have been nothing more than a tragic accident. The driver panicked and fled. Coincidences do happen, you know."

"Are you trying to convince me or yourself?"

She looked annoyed. "Okay, let's break it down. Naomi Quinlan claimed she got a hit from a public database, but she wouldn't provide you with any of the details. She wouldn't tell you how she obtained the DNA sample or the name of the donor match. Isn't it possible she was just messing with you, Ethan? There are a lot of sick people in this world. I still get anonymous letters around this time of year. And now, with all the hoopla surrounding the twenty-fifth anniversary, I expect crackpots will be crawling out of the woodwork."

Ethan's voice sharpened. "You get anonymous letters? What do they say?"

Addie tucked back her hair. "Nothing important. What matters is this woman's motive and her timing. Why now, with the anniversary looming? Is it possible she wanted to inject herself into a famous case for the notoriety? You are James Merrick's son. She wouldn't have had to do much digging to find you, even with the name change. It's just all very curious—convenient, to use your descriptor—that she was able to get a match when CODIS has never turned up a single hit."

"If the unsub doesn't have an arrest record, he or she wouldn't be in any LE database," Ethan said.

"True. But why would someone who left DNA at a murder scene knowingly allow their genetic profile to be publicly cataloged?"

"I've given that a lot of thought," Ethan said. "The unsub may not have realized he'd been wounded. Adrenaline blocks pain, and a thrill kill produces euphoria. Sometimes an almost fugue state of rapture. And remember, the third blood sample was never made public, so the unsub had no reason to believe his DNA could be traced back to the crime scene."

"You have given this thought."

"Yes, and having said all that, I think there's a more

logical explanation. Naomi Quinlan's hit was only a partial match. Familial DNA."

"That's a slippery slope," Addie said.

"For law enforcement, yes. Some states are more stringent about such searches than others. They require that the criminal and the person in the database share an identical Y chromosome, which means the match is limited to men. But a genealogist is under no such constraint. She could have cast a wide net."

"That kind of scattershot approach produces a lot of false positives. You know that as well as I do."

"Depends on how closely the samples matched up."

Addie scowled at him in the fading light. "You're playing with fire, Ethan. This is the kind of thing that got us both into a lot of trouble ten years ago. Some days I feel as if I'm still wading out of that mess. What are the chances you'll forget all about Naomi Quinlan and go back to Quantico?"

"Zero."

She sighed. "I figured. And just what is it you expect me to do?"

"Nothing. I don't expect anything from you. I just wanted you to have this information in case—"

"Nothing is going to happen to you."

She said it so fiercely, he almost believed her. "I know you want to believe that justice was served in your mother's case, but what if it wasn't? What if her killer is still out there somewhere? Can you live with that possibility?"

She turned on him in anger. "That's not a fair question. You've given me nothing but supposition. You have no real proof."

"That's why I'm here in Charleston. If proof exists, I'll find it." He sat back against the bench, casting a wary glance around the park. He couldn't detect surveillance, but that didn't mean they were alone. "I've gone over the emails time and again. Naomi Quinlan had a strange way with words and syntax. It's possible she left clues that I haven't yet been able to decipher."

Addie was still angry. "Do you even realize how that sounds?"

"The Unabomber was caught by the way he turned a phrase."

She merely shook her head and stood. "I've heard you out. Now I need to get back."

Ethan rose, too. He shoved his hands in his pockets as he stood facing her. "Thanks for coming. Thanks for listening."

"Nothing's changed for me. You need to know that."

A breeze blew in from the sea, ruffling her hair as her gaze reluctantly met his. A moment passed, and then another, and still she remained. Ethan's blood quickened, but he didn't move toward her. He knew better. It was too soon. And yet...

"Addie—"

Her voice slipped out on a whisper. "Don't, Ethan." She turned away. "Don't do anything stupid."

Chapter Five

Darkness had fallen by the time Addie got home. She parked in the garage and then let herself out the side door to the backyard. The moment she stepped onto the walkway, a motion-detector light came on to illuminate the space between the garage and the house. She wasn't afraid of the dark. She was a trained LEO, and she was on her home turf. Still, precaution was never a bad thing. Distractions could be deadly. It would be too easy to get preoccupied by Ethan's disclosures—or, if she were honest, by his mere presence—so she needed to be on guard for any lapses.

A decade was a long time, and Addie had been over Ethan for most of those years. How could one cling to something that had never been real? She'd fallen in love with Ethan Barrow, not realizing that Ethan Merrick was part of the package. The son of her mother's killer. Even now their union seemed surreal. How could she not have known what he really wanted from her? How could she not have recognized that his obsession to clear his father's name was so great, he'd wittingly seduced her into his delusions? Not that she was blameless. At twenty-two and freshly graduated from the police academy, she should have been sharper, her radar more finely tuned. She should have seen right through Ethan Barrow's deception, but no. One smile, one brooding look, and she'd been lost.

Everyone's heart got broken sooner or later. Addie forgave herself for falling for the wrong man. She allowed herself a pass for buying into his lies and deceit. What she could never forgive was her own lies. Her betrayal of the one man who had always had her back.

You've let me down, Addie. And worse, you've let yourself down. I can't even begin to tell you how disappointed I am in you. You used my computer, my password to access sealed files, and then you allowed classified information to be leaked to the press, calling this department's integrity into question. If it were anyone else, you would have already been dismissed. But I know your potential and I know, in time, you can be a great asset. I'm willing to look the other way this once, but from now on, your conduct will be exemplary, no exceptions or excuses, and you will work twice as hard as anyone else in your unit. I'm giving you a second chance. The rest is up to you.

From now on, in my office and at this station, I'm Deputy Chief Cutler, even when we're alone. Are we clear?

A hard lesson learned, but Addie had become a better cop, a better person for it. In time, she'd earned the respect of her partner, her captain and the deputy chief, and now she wasn't about to squander their trust, no matter how much Ethan's revelations niggled.

One of the strays she fed stole out of the bushes to greet her, and as Addie bent to pet the still skittish feline, she saw deep red splotches on the walkway. She thought at first one of the cats had been wounded, and her heart catapulted to her throat. In the next instant, she realized the spots were flower petals, crimson and fragrant and every bit as unnerving as drops of blood. She lifted one of the petals to her nose. The scent of magnolia overwhelmed her, and she found herself drowning in dread and old memories.

She rose, still half crouching, and slipped into the shadows. The cat followed her, rubbing against her legs and meowing for more attention.

"Quiet," Addie whispered. She glanced around the yard, senses on full alert. She could hear traffic on a distant street and the trill of some night bird. Sensing her tension, the cat had gone quiet at her feet. Addie remained sequestered for another moment before slipping from the shadows to hurry up the back steps. The door was still locked, and another security light came on, drenching her in illumination. She went back down the steps and circled the house, checking windows along the way until she reached the front entrance. That door was locked as well.

Even so, she remained tense and alert as she entered the house. A lamp in the small foyer was on a timer, and she was grateful for the soft glow that chased away shadows. She hurried over to a small desk, typed in the code on her security console and then unlocked the top drawer, where she kept a gun. Her service weapon was in her bedroom, locked in a nightstand.

Right hand supported with her left, she moved through the house, checking corners and closets, doors and windows until she was satisfied that no one had entered her home.

Grabbing a flashlight from the kitchen, she went out the back door to have another look around. Angling the light along the flagstones, she traced the crimson trail from the steps all the way back to the garage. No way she could have missed those petals, and no doubt they had been left for her to find.

She kept the gun in her right hand while she lifted the flashlight with her left, sweeping the beam back toward the fence where the floodlights didn't reach. A breeze rattled the palmettos, and she could hear the soft mewling of the cat somewhere in the bushes. But all else was quiet. Too quiet.

The hair at the back of Addie's neck lifted as she scanned the shadows. She wanted to believe the petals were nothing but a cruel prank. Like the anonymous letters she received from time to time, the magnolia trail meant nothing. But she couldn't forget Ethan's suggestion that her mother's killer might still be out there. What if he had been keeping tabs on Addie all these years? What if, like Delmar Gainey, he still thrilled to his dark secrets?

The notion of someone deriving pleasure from spying on the daughter of his victim was more than Addie wanted to contemplate at the moment. She'd had enough monsters for one day. Turning, she moved back along the path to the steps, but as the light swung back into the yard, the beam clipped a silhouette against the fence. Just a tree, Addie told herself. *Just a shadow.*

Slowly, she moved the light back over the yard, catching the gleam of human eyes before the figure turned and scrambled over her fence.

"Stop!" Before she had time to consider her actions, Addie sprinted after him, tucking her weapon and flashlight in the waistband of her shorts so that she could hoist herself up and over the fence. She landed with a thud in her neighbor's backyard. Drawing her weapon, she hunkered in the shadows at the fence, peering into the darkness for any sign of her trespasser.

Her neighbor's yard was dark, and only a faint glow emanated from the edges of the closed blinds. Now Addie was the trespasser. She told herself to give up the chase and go home. She could call for a patrol of the street, but the intruder would be long gone by the time a unit was dispatched to the scene. Better she check this out for herself. At the very least, she could give the trespasser second thoughts about invading her turf again.

A dog barked down the street. The same night bird trilled from a treetop. Addie waited. Across the yard came the sound of rustling leaves, followed by a scrape. Heart still thudding, she pinpointed the noise with her flashlight, glimpsing the back of the intruder as he went over the fence into the yard of the house being renovated. No one would be around at this hour. A vacant house would be the perfect place to hide.

Again, Addie told herself to give it up. She'd scared him sufficiently by now. *Go home. Go to bed. Let it go.*

But she couldn't let it go. Her stubbornness propelled her over the second fence, and she dropped to the ground more lightly this time. Hugging the bushes, she took out her phone and texted the address to Matt Lepear.

She slipped the phone back into her pocket and eased across the yard, flashlight over gun. The back door hung open. Not a good sign. Nor were the magnolia petals that had been dropped along the back steps. The intruder was outright taunting her now. Aggressively so.

Protocol and common sense demanded Addie wait for backup. She went up the steps without hesitation, flattening herself against the wall for a moment before proceeding inside. She moved through the open floor plan quickly, clearing each space before entering the next. An empty paint can clanged against her toe, and she crouched as she swept the area with the flashlight.

"I know you're in here," she said. "Show yourself. I just want to talk."

"Adaline." The electronically distorted voice was so low she couldn't tell where the sound came from. Dread descended as she moved through the shadows.

"Who are you?" she demanded.

No answer.

"How do you know me?"

Silence.

"Why did you leave those magnolia petals on my walkway?"

"You know why."

The warped voice echoed through the empty room, sending chills up and down Addie's spine. "Come out now and deal with me, or deal with my backup."

She eased through the plastic partitions, listening for a misplaced step or a telltale breath. All was silent. She had a feeling he could see her, though. That he was watching her every move. She glanced over her shoulder, glanced all around her. He was *there*. She couldn't see him, couldn't hear him, but she sensed his presence. He was close.

Something metallic pinged against the floor, and Addie whirled, moving quickly through the plastic sheets until she realized too late that she'd walked into his trap. She'd let him distract her, and now he'd come up behind her.

She turned, catching only a glimpse of a masked face before the intruder struck her across the forehead with the flat side of a board. The blow dazed her, and she staggered back, dropping the flashlight as she crashed to the floor. The partitions came down on top of her, and for a moment, Addie panicked, clawing like a caged tiger at her plastic prison. She fought her way up and scrambled free, reaching for her weapon as she heard footsteps running from the room, down the hall, out the front door.

Scrambling to her feet, she attempted to pursue, but the blow had stunned her and he had too much of a head start. She trailed him onto the front porch, angling the light over the yard and down the street.

Then she collapsed on the front steps to wait for her partner.

ADDIE SAT ON the edge of the bathtub and winced as Matt Lepear cleaned the cut on her forehead and then applied a butterfly bandage. He was none too gentle about it, either. "You don't need stitches, but that's going to leave an ugly mark. You're lucky he didn't take out an eye."

"I guess this is my day for close calls." She touched the bandage gingerly. "Thanks for doctoring me up. And for getting here so quickly."

"I was at Shorty's," he said, naming a nearby watering hole. "You should have waited until I got here. What you did was really stupid. You know that, right?"

Addie shrugged. "You would have done the same thing."

"I would have had the good sense not to get myself coldcocked before help arrived." He put away the supplies and then rinsed his hands at the sink. "Okay, now that you have my undivided attention, walk me through what happened. Start at the beginning, when you first saw the flower petals."

"Not just any flower petals. Crimson magnolia petals." A shudder went through Addie as she folded her arms around her middle.

"I get the significance," he said with a nod. "The Twilight Killer was a gardener. He studied horticulture in college. They covered all that in the documentary. His schooling. His resentment of the elite and his fixation on single mothers. The particular kind of red magnolia he grew was rare. The crimson petals became his signature. And now someone has left those same magnolia petals on your walkway."

"The same color, at least. We don't know if they're precisely the same. There are dozens of varieties of red magnolias. I admit I was jolted when I saw them—I thought they were drops of blood at first—but now I just think it was someone's idea of a prank. That's why he hung around to witness my reaction. I'm sure he didn't count on my chasing after him."

"He knew your name, though. You said he called you Adaline."

"He would have to know my name to find my address. Maybe he watched the same documentary you did. Saw my picture and decided to have a little sick fun."

"Sick sounds about right."

Addie stood and brushed off her shorts. "You want a beer?"

"I never turn down a cold one. But I have to say, you seem pretty calm about all this."

"It's not even close to the worst thing I've seen today." She checked his handiwork in the mirror before exiting the bathroom behind him. Matt knew her house well enough to take the lead down the hallway and into the kitchen. He sat on a bar stool while she grabbed icy bottles from the refrigerator and uncapped them. Then she went around the bar to join him.

"Do you think this incident could have something to do with why Ethan Barrow's back in town?"

Addie slid over a coaster. "I don't see how."

"It seems a big coincidence, all this happening to you tonight after he showed up today."

"Oh, come on," Addie said. "You don't seriously think he did this."

"Not him personally, no. But he has a way of bringing trouble. Why's he here, anyway?"

"He said he had business with the deputy chief." The half-truth slipped a little too easily through Addie's lips, especially for someone who had always tried to be totally honest with her partner. Matt would see through her, of course, but Addie wasn't sure she was ready to get into the whole Ethan Barrow discussion. The meeting with him had affected her more than she wanted to admit. Memories were stirring, and it was hard enough to keep them at bay without his name popping up all over the place.

Matt eyed her dubiously. "What business?"

"He didn't elaborate. He said it would be up to my uncle to tell me."

"Okay, then. Let me put it another way. Why did he come to see *you*? And how did he know you'd be at the Gainey house?"

"Apparently, he overheard someone at the station mention my whereabouts."

"So he just showed up out of the blue? Without any prior conversations or correspondence? Just boom, he's here." Matt gave her a long scrutiny. "Sorry, Add. Not buying it. You're being cagey as hell. That man's here for a reason, and my guess is, that reason is you."

Addie was quick to dispel him. "He's not here because of me. Not in the way you're implying."

"Then what way is it? I don't mean to get all up in your business, but he caused a lot of trouble for a lot of people. If you've got something going with him—"

"I don't. God, no. Why would you even think that?"

Matt shrugged. "I watched the two of you together earlier. I could be way off, but I'm not so sure all those feelings are dead, at least on his end. I saw the way he looked at you."

"He doesn't still have feelings for me," Addie insisted. "How could he? Until today, he hadn't even seen me in ten years."

"It's called carrying a torch."

"And you would be familiar with that term, since you're dating your ex-wife."

He touched his bottle to hers.

Addie couldn't help but grin. "How is Maggie, by the way?"

"*Amber's* fine. Sends her regards. But let's not change the subject. You say there's nothing romantic between you and Barrow, and I believe you. There's nothing going on *yet*. But you need to watch your back, Addie. He knows how to push your buttons. I don't trust him, and neither should you."

"I will and I don't. No need to worry about me."

"Says the woman who pursued a suspect into an empty building without backup."

"Trespasser. I pursued a trespasser. Not like he shot anyone."

"That you know of. Are you going to file a report?"

"You know how much I hate paperwork," Addie said with a grimace. "Besides, he's long gone, and I doubt he'll be back."

"You never know. Might be a good idea to get proactive." Matt lifted his beer. "Ever think about installing security cameras around the perimeter of your house? If he does come back, you could catch him in the act."

Addie shrugged. "I like the idea, but that's an expense I don't need right now."

"They may not be as pricey as you think. My cousin sells all kinds of security equipment. I can get you a discount. And I have a buddy who owes me a favor. He'll install them for free if you keep the beer flowing."

"That's a nice offer," Addie said. "I'll think about it. It may not be necessary, though. As soon as the anniversary drama dies down, the crazies will crawl back into their basements. At least until next year."

"What do you mean, until next year? This kind of thing has happened before?"

"Not the flower petals, but I've received a few anonymous letters over the years. I blame the media. They're the ones that coined the whole Twilight's Children thing. They created this mystical narrative around the murdered mothers and their surviving offspring, and we became these cultlike figures. You wouldn't believe the weirdos who follow me on social media. Someone even named a rock band after us. It's bizarre and beyond creepy."

Matt scowled in disapproval. "What did the letters say? And why did you never mention them before?"

"I didn't think they were important. Just nonsensical ramblings, usually from someone claiming to be the real Twilight Killer. Or someone claiming to be in love with the Twilight Killer. Strangely, I've never received a letter from anyone claiming to be James Merrick."

"Maybe that's a good thing," Matt said. "Merrick's son did enough damage."

"Dead horse. Let's not go there again." Addie got up and went into the kitchen. "Another round?"

"I'd better finish this one and head home." But he seemed in no hurry to leave. "I'd still like to know what Ethan Barrow is doing in Charleston."

Addie rolled her eyes. "You're really not going to leave this alone, are you? All right, just think about it for a minute. It doesn't take a clairvoyant to figure out Ethan's motives. He's still looking for answers. He's never believed his father was guilty."

Matt studiously picked at the beer label with his thumbnail. "Yeah, I figured. But maybe his concern runs deeper than a desire to clear dear old dad."

"What do you mean?"

His gaze lifted. "*You* think about it, Addie. How would you feel if you were in his position? He's not much younger than his father was when he went off the deep end. With each year that passes, Ethan has to be worried about his genes. He's not just trying to clear his old man. He's trying to convince himself the same thing won't happen to him."

Addie had entertained similar theories over the years, but Matt's ability to cut through the clutter and niceties hit her like a physical blow. She felt stunned, though she did her best to shrug off his reasoning. "I'm the last person to defend James Merrick, but he had a lot of outside stressors. His job, a troubled marriage, childhood abuse. Drug use, too, if the rumors are to be believed. It all came to a head during his investigation of Orson Lee Finch. Somehow he began to identify with the monster he hunted. The experts said he suffered from a kind of trauma bond that compelled him to finish the killer's mission. Ethan has no reason to believe the same thing could happen to him."

"I don't know," Matt said. "Dude's wound pretty tight, if you ask me. Maybe there's more to his behavior than stubbornness or even obsession. Maybe something darker rides along with him."

His words chilled Addie more than she wanted to admit. "And with that, we've officially exhausted the subject of Ethan Barrow." She made a production of stretching. "I think we should call it a night."

"Kicking me out, eh? Did I touch a nerve?"

"No, but you already said you needed to hit the road—"

She broke off as a loud crash sounded outside. They drew their weapons simultaneously. Addie turned off the kitchen light and then trailed Matt to the back door.

"Can you see anything?" she whispered.

"Not much." He opened the door, and they slipped through. "You need better lighting out here."

"The floodlight should have come on," Addie muttered as they went down the steps together.

The breeze had risen while they were inside. Addie thought at first a tree branch had fallen on the garage roof and taken out the security light. But the wind wasn't that strong.

"Matt." She tapped his arm. "Check out the garage. The security light is broken."

He angled his gun and the flashlight in that direction, picking up the trail of crimson petals before shifting the light to the garage door and then up to the eaves, where nothing but a shard of glass protruded from the light socket. He tried the garage door and then shone the light through the glass panel.

While he checked out the garage, Addie hunkered on the walkway to examine the shattered glass. "That bulb didn't break itself."

"Someone deliberately took it out," Matt said. "You still think this is all just a bad joke?"

She glanced up. "How soon can your friend come and install those security cams?"

ETHAN WAS SURPRISED to find Gwen Holloway waiting for him in the lobby of his hotel when he got back from his meeting with Addie. He'd stopped for takeout, and now all he wanted to do was head upstairs, eat his sandwich and go back over Naomi Quinlan's emails, searching for those elusive clues. Maybe Addie was right. Maybe he really was grasping at straws, but it only made sense that the genealogist would have left bread crumbs if she believed her life could be in danger.

He thought about trying to slip past the former agent, but she was planted near the elevators, making avoidance impossible unless he exited the hotel. But that would only postpone the inevitable. She'd wait him out tonight or have her people track him down in the morning. She was that tenacious.

Ethan resolved himself to the confrontation. Gwen Holloway hadn't been on the federal payroll in nearly fifteen years, but she still had powerful connections inside the Bureau and the DOJ. One call and she could make his life uncomfortable if not downright miserable.

These days, she traveled the country teaching and consulting with various law enforcement entities, but she still dressed in the traditional FBI uniform of a plain black suit, white blouse and polished loafers. In her fifties, she'd refused to cut her waist-length brown hair, compromising instead by pulling it back from her face and securing it in a bun at her nape. She wore no makeup, but her nails were always immaculately groomed and her teeth were almost blindingly white, though she rarely smiled.

She came toward Ethan now, her gaze so intently focused she might have been vectoring in on one of the FBI's most wanted. "Hello, Ethan. Do you have time for a chat?"

"Sorry." He held up his takeout bag. "I'm having dinner in my room and calling it a night. Maybe another time."

He might have been addressing a wall. She turned on her heel and said over her shoulder, "There's a coffee shop just down the street. It should be nice and quiet this time of day."

Ethan hesitated for only a moment before he followed her back out into the warm evening air. She was a tall woman, and he matched his stride to hers, the brisk pace drawing a few glances from the strolling tourists. There was still quite a bit of traffic for a Friday night. Delectable aromas wafted from restaurants as laughter and music spilled out from bars. People were in good spirits, anticipating the weekend. The afternoon had been hot and humid, but twilight brought sea breezes and cooling temperatures. This was the time of day that Charleston did best. Good food, strong drinks and interesting company.

Nostalgia stirred, and Ethan found himself once again thinking about Addie. She looked good. The years since their breakup had only enhanced her appeal. She was leaner than he remembered, her toned muscles a testament to the time she dedicated to the track and to the gym. She still wore her blond hair long, though like Gwen Holloway, she pulled it back and up so that her periphery was unimpeded.

Seeing her again had brought back a lot of mixed emotions. Ethan supposed he'd never really gotten over her, though he hadn't pined for her. Pining was an indulgence and a dangerous distraction for someone in his line of work. Yet for the first few months after the breakup, rarely a day had gone by that he hadn't berated himself for what he'd done. Remorse had been an unwelcome companion. But ten years was a long time, and he'd moved on even if those regrets still surfaced now and then. Even if Adaline Kinsella still popped into his head at the most unexpected times.

No, he hadn't pined. He'd thrown himself into his work and recommitted himself to his training. He'd dated. He'd even had a serious relationship, but things had eventually gone flat, and they'd ended things amicably. The romance had never progressed beyond a certain point, and truth be told, she'd never measured up to Addie. In hindsight, Ethan realized that he was the one who hadn't measured up. Comparisons to Addie had been an excuse. Someone like him was probably better off alone.

He hadn't pined for Addie then and he didn't pine for her now, even on a crowded street when loneliness seemed to weigh on him the heaviest.

"Ethan? What's wrong with you? I said your name three times just now and you ignored me."

"Sorry." He shook himself out of his fog as a black Charger came into his line of sight. It was parked at the curb with the windows up and the motor running. "I was just checking out that car across the street. Government issued, looks like. Your people?"

Gwen barely glanced at the car. "What makes you think so?"

"Wild guess." He tossed his unopened sandwich in a nearby trash bin. "Makes me wonder what ordinary citizens would think if they knew certain former federal agents were allowed to call up the FBI and request surveillance on one of their own, all on the taxpayers' dime."

"What makes you think I'm the one who made that call? "

He gave her a sidelong glance. "Who then? My stepfather?"

"There are a lot of powerful people who like to keep tabs on you, Ethan."

"Why? I'm nothing special."

She returned his side-eye. "We both know that's not true."

"I get it. The interest comes from people in the Bureau and the DOJ who don't think of me as Ethan Barrow. To them, I'll always be James Merrick's son. Do you all sit around wondering when I'll crack?"

"If we wondered that, you wouldn't be where you are today. But we do have concerns about your recent behavior. Like it or not, your presence in this city attracts attention. Last time you were here, you compromised the Bureau's relationship with local law enforcement, embarrassed your family and nearly got yourself fired. You leaked information about procedure and blood evidence that allowed the press to question the results of a long and painful investigation. Your stepfather and I went out on a limb for you." She glanced both ways before she stepped into the intersection. "You were given a second chance on our recommendation, so don't act like we're an inconvenience when we expect answers."

"What's the question?"

"Why are you in Charleston?"

He gave a careless shrug. "Just relaxing and taking in the sights."

"I hear you were also taking in the sights in Columbia yesterday." She smoothed back her wind-ruffled hair. "How is James, by the way?"

"About as well as you would expect for someone who has spent the last twenty-five years confined to a psychiatric unit for the criminally insane. But maybe you should go and judge his condition for yourself."

"I have."

He turned. "When?"

"I've gone to see him regularly since the day he was committed." She stopped in front of the coffee shop and waited for Ethan to open the door. For some reason, that surprised him, though he complied without hesitation. Gwen glanced back at him. "You're not the only one who still cares about him, you know."

She stepped inside, holding up two fingers to the barista and then pointing to a table in the back. She slid into the seat facing the door, leaving Ethan to sit with his back exposed. That did not surprise him.

"When was the last time you saw him?" he pressed.

"It's been a while. Almost a year." She shrugged off her jacket and hung it on the back of her chair. She folded her arms on the table and clasped her hands. He could see bits of gold shimmering around her throat and in her ears, but her fingers were bare. She was a handsome, accomplished woman—a successful author and wealthy entrepreneur—but she'd never married. Ethan could understand why. Dating didn't come easy to those who spent their lives hunting monsters.

She gazed at him across the table, silent until their coffee had been served, and then she said, "Are you upset that I still visit him?"

"Why would I be upset?"

"I don't know, Ethan. Why don't you tell me? Maybe

it's a proprietary thing. I can sense your hostility. You used to be better at hiding it."

"I don't know what you mean."

Her hazel eyes watched him closely. "I've known you since you were a child. I've watched you grow up. Your parents graciously included me in the milestones of your life, but you always resented my presence, didn't you?"

"Then why come if you knew you weren't welcome?"

"Because Richard and Karen were my friends and because I cared about you. I still do. I understand the nature of your resentment, even if you don't. Deep down, you blame me for what happened to your father. Rationally, you know that I was just doing my job. That I never wanted any of that for him or for you. But emotionally…" She sighed. "It's still very painful for me, too, Ethan. James was not only my mentor, but also my friend. His absence and his legacy will always be felt in the BAU. And by me."

"You left quite a legacy yourself."

"I like to think so."

Ethan stared back at her. "You were with the FBI for, what? Ten years before you left to write your first book? You were on a fast track. Unit chief, destined to be section chief, maybe even deputy director by now. Everyone must have been stunned when you tendered your resignation."

"Not really. The BAU has a high burnout rate. You should know that better than most. I didn't leave to write a book or even to start my own firm. I wanted to get my life back. And I felt I could be just as effective on the outside as a teacher and consultant, maybe more so. What's your point, anyway?"

"There's no point." Ethan glanced out the window, searching the street for signs of surveillance. The black

Charger was nowhere in sight. He wondered if Gwen had covertly signaled the agents to back off. "It's just something I've thought about over the years. You were my father's protégée. The two of you were very close, and yet you didn't hesitate to profile him."

"He would have done the same to me."

"Not one moment of self-doubt or second thought? Even when you all but led the Charleston PD to his doorstep?"

Something flickered in the green-gold depths of her eyes. Anger, Ethan thought, but not remorse. The Gwen Holloways of the world didn't look back with regret. "I trusted the profile," she said.

"That profile and his arrest made you famous. You became a household name. A Bureau rock star. The young agent who brought down the great James Merrick."

"Again, what's your point?"

"What if your profile was wrong?"

"The evidence wasn't wrong."

"Evidence can be planted."

Ethan could see the wheels turning inside her head as she sifted back through their conversation, deciding on the best way to handle him. She landed on bemused empathy. "You've been holding all this in for a very long time, haven't you? That's not good on any level. You should have come to me instead of letting all this fester." She cupped her hands around her coffee cup, but she didn't drink. "If you've got more to say, now's the time to let it out. Tell me everything. Let's clear the air once and for all."

"You know I can't do that."

"Why hold back now? It's not like I can hurt you. I haven't worked for the government in years. I have no control over your life or your career. You and I are just friends."

Ethan's voice hardened despite his best efforts. He didn't want to reveal any cracks. She would pounce the moment she sensed weakness. "We're not friends," he said. "And we both know you could end my career with one phone call."

"You think I'm that thin-skinned and vindictive?" She lifted her cup with another sigh. "Believe it or not, I've always had your back, Ethan. I've always been your champion, just as James once championed me. I'm giving you a free pass. Speak your mind. You have my guarantee that nothing you say will leave this table or be used against you."

Ethan leaned back in his chair, slipping one hand in his pocket as he regarded her with wary curiosity. What was she up to? "You mean that?"

"I do. I'd really like to explore the origins of your hostility."

"Then instead of talking about the profile and my father's confinement, maybe we should talk about your affair."

Emotion flickered across her face, but to her credit, she never broke eye contact. "That's nonsense."

"I saw the two of you together."

"Of course you did. We worked together."

"No, this was different. I saw you in my grandparents' garden here in Charleston. My mother and I came down one weekend during the Twilight Killer investigation. My father had been gone for weeks, and my mother begged him to have dinner with us on our last night because we wouldn't see him again for a long time. He finally relented and even brought a change of clothing so that he could stay over. I heard him leave in the middle of the night. I got up and followed him out. I wanted to talk him into staying so that my mother wouldn't be so unhappy when she woke up. You were waiting for him in the garden. You tried to kiss him, but he pushed you away. He said it was over. He thought it best that you transfer out of the unit. You got angry, and then you got violent. You slapped him, as I recall. I think you even clawed his face. I didn't understand a lot of what went down between you, but your outburst scared me."

"Why didn't you say anything?"

"I don't know. I just knew that it was a bad thing and that if I told my mother, she would be hurt. It was only when I grew older and looked back on that night that I was able to put it together."

"Yet you still said nothing." Gwen leaned in. "You were a lonely, confused little boy, Ethan. Distressed about your mother's unhappiness and hurt by your father's distance. You misunderstood what you saw. Or maybe you had a dream and convinced yourself it was true in order to rationalize your negative feelings toward me."

"I didn't dream it."

"I remember that night well, too," Gwen said. "I came to your grandparents' home to confront your father about something he'd missed in the profile. He was already making mistakes. I was already seeing signs of his illness. But he never liked to be challenged, and we argued. It had nothing to do with an affair. Our relationship was never anything but professional."

"I know what I saw."

Gwen gave him a slight smile. "You sound so much like James right now. If I close my eyes, I could almost believe I'm sitting across the table from him, conversing the way we used to over a case. I never realized how much alike you are. So focused and single-minded. You don't like to be questioned or challenged, either, do you, Ethan?"

A warning thrill prickled his backbone. She'd laid a trap, and he'd willingly tripped the spring. Already, he could see the beginnings of the case to be made against him. If he overstepped his bounds in Charleston, if he dug up incriminating evidence that threatened the status quo, a subtle campaign would be initiated. This conversation was his warning. Next would come censure, suspension and then a career-killing transfer, if not outright termination, all accompanied by whispers of incompetence, insubordination and insanity.

As if intuiting his train of thought, Gwen said, "What else is on your mind, Ethan?"

"I think we're done."

"Yes, I agree. Time to call it a night. But it's been a most enlightening conversation," she said. "I feel better already now that we've cleared the air. One last thing, though. We still need to talk about Adaline Kinsella."

His gut tightened. "I don't see how she's any of your concern."

Gwen's brow creased as she reached for her jacket. "You caused a lot of trouble for that young woman ten years ago. You nearly derailed her career along with your own. I imagine you broke her heart in the process. I've spoken with Deputy Chief Cutler about my concerns."

"Concerns about me?"

"About Detective Kinsella. Did she tell you that she's been chosen by her department to attend my program? That's quite an honor. A real feather in her cap. But I won't waste my time on someone who isn't one hundred percent committed to the training. It wouldn't be fair to the other enrollees. Detective Kinsella is a promising candidate. She's a good cop—smart, diligent, ambitious. But I worry about outside distractions. It would be a shame if she lost focus and had to be cut from the current session."

Ethan tamped back his anger. "Is that a threat?"

"It's a warning. Leave her alone, Ethan. You screw this up for her, there won't be a second chance for either of you this time."

She stood, slipped on her jacket and left without a backward glance. Ethan paid the bill, and by the time he exited the coffee shop, she'd already crossed the street. The black Charger was nowhere to be seen. Instead, a gleaming Mercedes pulled to the curb, and Gwen got in the back.

Ethan watched as the car turned at the next intersection, and then he removed his cell phone from his pocket and checked his messages. He walked down the street until foot traffic died away. Pretending to tie his shoe, he hunkered at the curb and slipped his phone beneath the front tire of a parked cab.

Tomorrow he would buy a burner phone and turn in his rental car. Small measures that would inconvenience Gwen Holloway, but nothing would stop her once she set her sights on a target.

Chapter Six

The next morning, Addie sat in her parked car with a blueberry scone and iced coffee as she kept an eye on her surroundings. For someone who had a tendency to get bored and restless with too much time on her hands, she'd never minded surveillance. It gave her time to think, and she had plenty on her mind this morning.

Despite her insistence that sometimes a coincidence was just a coincidence, she wondered if the previous evening's events really could be connected to Ethan's arrival in Charleston. Maybe the trespasser hadn't been so much a prankster as a watcher. Someone sent to keep an eye on her. Rattle her cage with those flower petals.

Now she was starting to sound as paranoid and obsessed as Ethan.

Addie shivered despite the heat.

Her initial assumption about the interloper had likely been right. Even as a child, she'd known about that strange breed of spectators who tried to insinuate themselves into a tragedy, or worse, into a victim's life for self-aggrandizement. Her grandmother had tried to protect her from those who would cruelly invade their privacy, but from time to time a "fan" would slip through. Sometimes an aggressive reporter would ambush Addie on the playground or a photographer would hide in the bushes to try to get candid photographs for a story on Twilight's Children. Eventually the personal contact died away, and the letters that came later had never seemed threatening.

Someone creeping onto her property twenty-five years after her mother's death to scatter crimson magnolia petals along her walkway was a deeper kind of stalking. Not to mention the attack upon her person and the distorted murmur of her name, which had come back to haunt her in her sleep.

Addie had awakened in the middle of the night to that same electronic voice, only to realize she'd been dreaming. Unnerved by the nightmare, she'd gone all through the house, making sure nothing was amiss. The security system had still been activated, the doors locked tight, and yet Addie had had the strangest notion that someone had been in her house. Not possible, of course. She was a light sleeper. Even without the blare of an alarm, she would have awakened at the first sounds of an intruder. But that nagging feeling had kept her awake for the rest of the night, and now she struggled with heavy eyelids as the sun beat down through the windshield.

Taking another sip of the iced coffee, she idly tracked the pedestrian traffic as she rolled down the passenger window to get a cross breeze. Then she checked the rearview mirror as she adjusted her sunglasses. She felt confident she hadn't been followed. She knew how to spot and evade a tail. Still, recent events had left her edgy and overcautious. She kept her eyes peeled for a vehicle that made a second pass around the block or a tourist who lingered too long in front of a shop window.

A few minutes later, she spotted a familiar figure as he came around the corner on foot. He had his phone to his ear, walking briskly but not so fast as to attract attention. When he drew even with her car, she said through the open window, "Keep walking."

Ethan's hesitation was almost infinitesimal before he continued up the block and turned at the next intersection. Once she made sure *he* wasn't being followed, she got out of the car, locked the door and headed up the street behind him. He had already disappeared by the time she made the corner. She slowed her steps as if she were out for a morning stroll along the downtown streets.

A wrought iron gate across a narrow alleyway clanged in the breeze. Addie turned at the sound, and Ethan said from the shadows, "I'm in here."

His voice was deep, a little husky—perhaps from his own sleepless night—and as mysterious as the gloom in which he hid. Addie could just make out his silhouette. Tall, lean, head slightly bowed as he observed her.

Watch your back, Addie. Maybe something darker rides along with him.

She suppressed another shiver as she glanced both ways down the street, telling herself she was still being cautious. She was just making sure no one had followed them, but her reaction to that voice, his nearness, the sight of him waiting for her in the shadows provoked an unexpected reaction. For a moment, ten years melted away and she felt hopelessly smitten and dangerously naive. At twenty-two, she hadn't stood a chance against Ethan Barrow's brooding intensity, but she was a decade older and, surely to goodness, wiser. She knew how to protect herself from men like Ethan and, more important, from her own weaknesses.

"Addie?"

"Give me a minute."

She wiped her hands down the sides of her jeans as

she surveyed the traffic. It annoyed her that the mere sight of him could threaten her poise. That the sound of his voice could still catch her off guard. She found herself bombarded with images that were best left in the past. The way he'd looked at her, kissed her, the slow trace of his hands along her quivering body.

"What is it?" he demanded with soft urgency. "Were you followed?"

Addie beat back the images. "I don't think so," she said briskly. "But better safe than sorry." She took off her sunglasses as she stepped through the gate. After the glare of the sun, the deep shade of the alley momentarily blinded her.

Ethan straightened from the wall and came toward her. "Are you all right? What happened to your face?"

Her hand flew to her forehead. She'd forgotten about the bandage since changing it that morning after her shower. She was bruised, too, but the wounds were superficial. "There was an incident at my house last night. It's not important. I'm fine."

"What kind of incident?"

"We can talk about it later. That's not why I'm here."

"Then why are you here?" He searched her features. Her vision was still clouded, but for some reason, she had no trouble at all focusing on his eyes. They were dark and full of concern. "How did you know where to find me, anyway?"

"You aren't that hard to figure out." Her defensiveness made her sound petty, and she winced. She hated that tone. "Naomi Quinlan was killed at the next intersection, and she lived only a few blocks north of here. She would have walked this way to and from her home the night she died. I knew you'd come by sooner or later. I arrived early and waited."

"What makes you think I haven't already been by here?"

"Oh, I'm sure you have. Any number of times. And you'll keep coming back until you're satisfied you haven't missed something."

"That explains how you found me, but you still haven't told me why you're here."

She turned back into the sunlight. "I don't know, Ethan. I've been asking myself that same question for the better part of an hour. A part of me thinks that maybe I can keep you from doing something stupid, and another part of me thinks..." She trailed off. "I don't know what I think."

"Let me give it a go. You're here for the same reason I came back to Charleston." He leaned back against the building, seemingly relaxed, but Addie knew better. He was as anxious as she was about this meeting. "As much as you want to discount the possibility that I could be right, you can't. It's starting to eat at you. You're wondering if the person who murdered your mother could still be out there, and you can't stand the thought that the perpetrator has gotten away with it all these years. Maybe he's long gone or maybe he's still in the city. You're asking yourself, what if he kills again and you do nothing to stop him?"

His assessment was a little too spot-on, and that also annoyed her. "Are you profiling me?"

"You aren't that hard to figure out." Something close to tenderness took the sting out of his taunt. "Come away from the gate," he said. "It's better if we don't attract curious eyes." When she didn't budge, he pushed off the wall. "Addie."

"I heard you. I don't think we can be seen from the street."

Ethan was silent for a moment. "You're not afraid to be alone with me, are you?" His voice was steady, his tone nonjudgmental, but beneath his neutrality, something vulnerable lurked. An unsettling fusion of dread and need.

"If I were afraid, would I have met you last night? Would I have come looking for you this morning?"

His gaze burned into hers. "Maybe not. But sometime during the past ten years, the thought must have crossed your mind—like father, like son."

"I think you're capable of a lot of things, Ethan, but murder isn't one of them."

"Thank you for that."

"Don't thank me." She folded her arms. "I still don't trust you."

"And yet here you are."

She shook her head. "I must be out of my mind."

"Or maybe deep down, you realize that all I've ever wanted is the truth."

"You just didn't care who you took down in the process."

"I never meant to hurt you, Addie. I hope you know that."

She hardened her resolve against his regret. "What I know is that you have a history of deception, so I'll be watching you carefully. I'll take everything you tell me with a grain of salt. But you are right about one thing— I'm curious about that third DNA sample and the possibility of a donor match."

He nodded, his gaze going back to the cut on her forehead. "We can talk about Naomi Quinlan on the way to her house, but I'm not going anywhere until you tell me how you got hurt. Don't say it's not important. It is."

Addie's first inclination was to remind him that she wasn't his business, but all this blatant hostility was unproductive and it went against her nature. She didn't like clinging to her grudges. Her grandmother would be appalled at her comportment. *Be the better person, Addie. Life's too short. Don't let anger and bitterness steal your joy.*

Only her grandmother's memory could prod her into a truce with Ethan Barrow. She would let go of the bitterness, but her guard would remain up, Addie decided. Forgiving was one thing, forgetting quite another. "Someone came into my backyard last night. He was waiting for me when I got home. I gave chase and he ambushed me."

"You went after him alone?"

"I was armed and I wanted to frighten him enough so that he wouldn't be tempted to come back and do it again."

"Do what again?"

She paused. "He scattered crimson magnolia petals on my walkway."

She could sense Ethan's heightened tension even though his expression remained neutral. "When was this?"

"Right after I left you. I found a trail from the garage to my back door. And then I spotted him—or someone—hiding in the shadows near the fence. I figure he'd waited there to witness my reaction. I pursued him through a couple of yards into a gutted house. I let down my guard, and he hit me with a board so that he could get away." She touched the bandage again. "It's not serious. Barely more than a scratch. My ego took a worse beating. I should never have let him get the drop on me. I'm not usually so careless."

"Did you call it in?"

"I called Matt Lepear. He came over, and we both searched the property and the surrounding area, but the suspect was long gone. It's like I told you yesterday. All the publicity surrounding the anniversary is bringing out the crazies."

Ethan wasn't buying her explanation. "This wasn't just a prank. You were assaulted."

"I'll be more careful in the future."

Now it was his turn to glance both ways down the street. "We both need to be more careful. I appreciate that you came here looking for me this morning, but it's probably not a good idea for us to be seen together."

"Why? What happened?"

His gaze whipped back to hers. "I also had a run-in last night. Gwen Holloway was waiting for me when I got back to my hotel."

"*The* Gwen Holloway. What did she want?"

"That's a good question. Gwen says one thing but often means another. She *says* my trip to Charleston has her concerned and, apparently, others are worried as well. According to Gwen, powerful people are keeping tabs on me, one of them possibly my stepfather."

Addie looked at him in alarm. "Why would your stepfather spy on you?"

Ethan shrugged. "To protect his image. He holds an important position in the DOJ. Maybe he's afraid I'll step out of line and embarrass him the way I did ten years ago."

"Seems a bit extreme. Could he have another motive?"

"Unlikely. He wasn't around for the Twilight Killer case or for my father's incarceration. They knew each other, but Richard didn't come into the picture until later. I'd be more inclined to think that Gwen is some-how manipulating him to try to control me."

Addie gave him a look. "That sounds a little para-noid, even for you."

"I know how it sounds. I also know Gwen Holloway has a lot to lose if that third DNA sample pans out. Her whole career was built on my father's downfall. Respect and reputation mean everything to her. Which brings me to another problem. Why didn't you tell me you've been accepted into her program?"

"I didn't think it mattered. And why is it a problem?"

"She's threatening to cut you loose if I don't drop my investigation."

"She said that?" Addie muttered an expletive that drew an amused glance from Ethan. "Sorry for the lan-guage, but the idea that she would even try something like that just pisses me off. I'll tell her to her face what she can do with her program."

Ethan's eyes glinted. "As much as I would pay to see that confrontation, don't give her the ammunition. And don't throw away an important opportunity for pride's sake. You can learn to manipulate her."

"How?"

"There are two kinds of people she routinely drops from her program. Those who can't cut it and those who set out to prove they're smarter than she is. You're smart, but you're also clever. You can make her look good without showing her up. She'll respect that."

"How do you know so much about Gwen Holloway?" Addie asked.

"She's pushed my buttons a few too many times. I've learned from my mistakes. If you can keep your cool, she's not that hard to figure out, either."

"Good to know." Addie slipped her sunglasses back

on. "Should we go take a look at the crime scene? Maybe I'll remember something about that night that we can use."

He looked uneasy. "I know I brought all this to your doorstep, but you don't have to get involved. Things didn't go well for either of us last time, and now you have more to lose."

"Things went south because you lied to me," Addie said. "You didn't even tell me your real name until I was in too deep. Do you have any idea how much that hurt? How humiliating it was to find out who you really are and what you really wanted from me?"

"Addie—"

"Do you seriously think a career is the worst thing a person can lose?"

"Addie."

"Stop saying my name."

"I don't know what else to say. I should have been straight with you from the start. But before I could come clean, I was in too deep, too. I fell for you and then I didn't want you to know the truth."

She looked at the sidewalk, the traffic, anywhere but at him. Anger blossomed, but she pressed it back down. Ten years was a long time to carry the weight of a broken heart. She was fine now. She'd been fine for a very long time. Best to let go of all that negative energy. It would only trip her up. She'd come here to find Ethan of her own accord. No one had twisted her arm. Either she was going to help him get at the truth or she wasn't. No need to keep punishing him for something that was over and done with. Neither of them could change the past.

"Let's just get on with this," she said. "What happened, happened. We're both adults. Let's put it behind us and move on."

"You mean that?"

"I do. But there's something you need to know. It's true I'm curious about that third DNA sample and the possibility of a donor match, and you've raised valid concerns about the hit-and-run that took Naomi Quinlan's life. It does seem a little too convenient. I also don't like being threatened by Gwen Holloway or anyone else, and I'm starting to wonder if she had something to do with what happened at my house last night." Addie held up her hand when Ethan tried to interrupt. "Having said all that, I still think my mother's killer is exactly where he belongs. I still think justice was served twenty-five years ago. But on the slight chance I could be wrong...well, that's why I'm here. That's the *only* reason I'm here."

ADDIE WAS QUIET as they walked along the tree-lined street, and Ethan didn't try to initiate conversation. She appeared deep in thought, and he didn't want to annoy her. She seemed to have a short fuse these days. He could understand that, and he'd gladly give her a pass. Considering everything that had gone down between them, her willingness to put the past behind them was a gracious olive branch.

Addie's interest in the case encouraged him—two pairs of eyes were always better than one when searching for the truth—but he still worried about the consequences of her involvement. Gwen Holloway could cause a lot of trouble for both of them, and Ethan knew only too well that she could be vindictive. She'd already gone to the deputy chief with her concerns, putting Addie in the crosshairs. But Gwen may have underestimated her opponent. Addie was no pushover. She'd made it clear she wouldn't allow anyone to intimidate or manipulate her, and that included Ethan. He respected that. He admired her willingness to fight back. As for him, he would never try to deceive her again. He'd learned his lesson ten years ago. From now on, total honesty. That was the only way their new alliance would work.

He decided it was time to break the awkward silence. "Must be getting close to ninety out here. It's too early to be this hot. Not much of a breeze, either."

Addie gave him a sidelong glance. "Maybe you're too used to sitting in an air-conditioned office. You ought to try walking a beat."

"Detectives don't walk beats, either."

"No, but we canvass," she said. "And before I made detective, I walked my share of foot patrols. You get used to the heat."

She certainly looked cool and relaxed in a white tank, jeans and sockless sneakers. She'd pulled her hair back in a ponytail, and he could see a faint sheen of lip gloss when the sun hit her just right. She smelled good, too, like fresh air and flowers, a clean scent that emanated from her skin and hair when she moved in close. Even off duty and dressed so casually, she exuded confidence and control. She walked along the street, head up, eyes alert, ready to take on the world. He had no doubt she was carrying. The cross-body bag was less conspicuous than a holster and would also contain her keys and cell phone. Ethan was likewise armed, the weapon tucked up under his shirt in the back.

He glanced over his shoulder as they made the next corner. It was still early. The shops hadn't yet opened, and few people were stirring. The sparse traffic would make it easy to spot the black Charger or any other suspicious vehicle.

"Relax," Addie said. "We're not being followed. We would have spotted a tail by now."

"Weren't you the one who just said better safe than sorry?"

"There's careful and there's paranoid." Addie nodded toward a side street. "Naomi's house is just down that way."

"Yes, I know. It's the white one-story on the left."

Addie glanced at him but said nothing. She had been right, of course. He'd already been by Naomi Quinlan's house once and walked the crime scene twice, and he would keep coming back until he had his answers.

The cottage was protected from the street by a fence and a garden of tropical foliage. Morning glories wound around the wrought iron posts and Ethan could smell jasmine, a scent he would always associate with Charleston even though the vine was not uncommon in Prince William County, Virginia, where he now lived.

"Maybe we should have come in the back way," he said. "There's an alley that runs behind the house."

"The problem with coming in through the back is that if you're seen by the neighbors, you look mighty suspicious. Someone could call the police. Or worse, shoot you."

"We could always come back after dark," he suggested.

"And then what? We just break in?"

"What did you think we were going to do?"

Even from behind her sunglasses, he could feel the power of her focus. "I don't know, Ethan. I guess I'm just trying to convince myself there's a line I still won't cross."

That got to him. It brought home all over again what she had risked for him in the past and what he was asking of her now. "Go back to your car," he said. "I'll handle things here."

"Too late. We've been spotted." Addie gave a slight nod to the house next door.

Ethan's gaze swept the neighbor's garden until he spotted an older woman kneeling in front of a flower bed. She was nearly hidden by a thick hedge of rosebushes, but he had no doubt she was thoroughly checking them out beneath the wide brim of her straw hat. After another moment of covert observation, she stood, peeled off her gloves and came over to the fence to call out to them.

"Excuse me! Are you looking for Naomi? I'm afraid she isn't home."

"We were just looking at the house," Ethan said as he shot Addie a glance. They walked down the sidewalk to the neighbor's yard. She came through the gate to meet them, pausing to brush off the knees of her work pants.

"Did one of the agencies send you over? I'm surprised they're showing the place so soon. Naomi's barely cold, poor thing, and no one's been by to clean out her things. But I retired from real estate years ago. Business is done differently these days, I expect." She pushed off her hat, letting it hang down her back by the chin strap. Her face was round and flushed, her eyes beady and avid. "You heard about the accident, no doubt."

"Yes."

"Such a tragedy for someone so young." The woman's birdlike gaze vectored in on Ethan.

"You knew her well?" he asked.

"I don't know about well, but we were neighbors

and I suppose you could say we were friends. I sold her aunt this house years ago, along with a number of rental properties all over the city. But that's neither here nor there. I'm Ida McFall, by the way. I've been keeping an eye on the place ever since the accident. One can't be too careful these days."

"That's smart," Ethan said.

Her head tilted slightly, and the beady eyes deepened with suspicion. "I didn't catch your name."

"Ethan Barrow." He held up his credentials. "I'm with the FBI. This is Detective Kinsella with the Charleston PD."

Ethan didn't know what he had expected in the way of a reaction. A badge and credentials often put people on the defensive even when they had nothing to hide. But Ida McFall's face instantly transformed. Her wariness faded, replaced by a look of genuine incredulity. "Oh, my word, you're *him*, aren't you?"

"I beg your pardon?"

"Naomi's FBI agent." She took off her hat and fanned herself for a moment. "Forgive me, but this is a bit overwhelming. She spoke of you in such glowing terms that I wondered if she'd made you up, especially when you were so conspicuously absent after her death. I'm sorry I doubted you. I blame Naomi's wild imagination and her tendency to exaggerate. Sometimes I couldn't tell her fantasy life from her reality. Writers." She shook her head.

"Naomi told me she was a genealogist."

"She taught genealogy at the community college, but her passion was writing. She gave me the impression you were working on a project together. She implied the two of you had become close." Ida McFall's expression turned coy. "She was certainly taken with you, Agent Barrow, and I can see why."

Ethan exchanged another glance with Addie, who lifted a brow. She had pushed her sunglasses to the top of her head, and even though her expression remained composed, he had an inkling of her thoughts. Had a woman with a secret, perhaps even a fantastical agenda, baited him into coming to Charleston? Was his search for the DNA match nothing more than a wild-goose chase?

"I think you've misconstrued our relationship," he told Ida. "I barely knew Naomi Quinlan."

"And yet here you are," she said. "You came, exactly as Naomi predicted you would. And if she was right about you, I have to believe the other things she told me were true as well."

"What other things?"

"That she was in danger. That powerful people were out to get her because of damaging evidence she'd dug up. She warned me that she was being followed. She said someone watched her house at night, but I thought she was imagining things. I never saw anything suspicious. Even after I learned of her death, I tried to tell myself it was just an accident. Naomi's head was always in the clouds. Perhaps she was distracted that night and didn't see the car coming. Now I know the danger was real. Naomi was murdered. The driver of that car deliberately ran her down. Thank God you've come, Agent Barrow. Someone has to get to the bottom of that poor girl's death."

"I'm sure the police are doing everything they can to find the driver," Addie said.

"I wish I shared your confidence."

"Meaning?"

"It's been two weeks, and as far as I can tell, nothing has been done about Naomi's case. Either she isn't a priority to the Charleston Police Department or something fishy is going on."

"Fishy how?"

"You tell me… Detective Kinsella, was it?"

A frown flitted across Addie's brow at the woman's disapproving tone, but she didn't rise to the bait.

"Detective Kinsella and I will do everything we can to find out what happened to Naomi, but we'll need your help," Ethan said. "Anything you can tell us could be useful. Please don't hold back. Despite what you seem to think, I know virtually nothing about her life. We exchanged a handful of emails, and that was the extent of our interaction."

Ida's assumptions remained steadfast. "Sometimes the most powerful connections are forged through the written word. I corresponded for years with a man I never met. Over time, we developed a bond that became unbreakable. I only mention that relationship because his letters to me inspired Naomi's book. I can't help wondering if there's a connection to her murder."

"What was his name?" Addie asked, with an odd note in her voice.

The older woman's chin came up in defiance. "Orson Lee Finch. Yes, *that* Orson Lee Finch. We shared a love of gardening and rare plants, and I make no apology for our friendship. Mr. Finch was a kind, thoughtful, *gentle* man, and quite refined for someone in his circumstances. I don't believe him capable of the brutal murders they claim he committed. In fact, I would sooner think the FBI profiler killed all those women."

Chapter Seven

Ida McFall's association with the notorious serial killer caught Ethan by surprise, but judging by Addie's satisfied nod, she had already intuited the identity of the woman's pen pal. Ethan gave an answering nod, indicating that she should take the lead while he remained silent. He might feel compelled to defend his father, and the last thing he wanted was to stifle Ida McFall's candor.

He studied the woman surreptitiously while Addie questioned her. Apparently, Naomi had neglected to tell Ida of Ethan's relationship to James Merrick, and he had to wonder if there was a reason for that.

"Do you still have Finch's letters?" Addie asked.

"I gave them to Naomi. I suspect she hid them somewhere in her office, along with all her notes. She wasn't just frightened for her safety. She was paranoid someone might try to steal her work. Dozens of books have been written about the Twilight Killer and his nemesis, James Merrick, but Naomi was certain her new evidence would give the story a twist."

"Did she tell you the nature of this new evidence?"

"Only that she suspected the police had been involved in covering it up."

Addie's voice sharpened. "Covering it up how?"

"I don't know. She never gave me the details. But I know she didn't trust the police. With good reason, it seems."

Addie ignored the inference. "Did she name names?"

"No, but a detective came around asking questions a few days after Naomi's death. He was courteous enough, but there was something about him that made me uneasy." Ida paused thoughtfully. "I couldn't put my finger on it, exactly. All I know is that my instincts are rarely wrong. I think he may have been looking for Naomi's evidence. I'm certain he was fishing for something. He said he would be in touch, but I never heard back from him."

"Did he tell you his name, show you his identification?" Addie asked.

"I remember he had a badge. He was an older gentleman. Around my age, I would guess. Well dressed and handsome with salt-and-pepper hair. He wore those mirrored sunglasses that made him look like a pilot."

"But you didn't catch his name?"

"If he said, I've forgotten. He didn't stay long. He claimed his visit was just a routine follow-up. Wanted to know if anyone had been in and out of Naomi's house. I told him no, not that I'd seen."

"You said Naomi was worried about someone stealing her work," Addie said. "Was there anyone in particular that concerned her?"

"Besides the police? Her aunt, Vivian DuPriest."

Addie looked taken aback. "Wait. Do you mean Vivian DuPriest, the author?"

"Yes, she's the one. Do you know her work?"

"Not personally, but when I was a kid, my grandmother used to read all her books." Addie turned to Ethan. "Years ago she worked the crime beat for the paper, but she was better known for her true-crime page-turners."

"She was very successful," Ida said. "Not that the DuPriests have ever wanted for money. Naomi came from the poor side of the family. Vivian took her in after her parents died and gave her a job as her assistant. Mostly she ran errands. But they had a falling-out sometime back."

"What about?" Addie asked.

"Vivian accused Naomi of trying to ride her coattails to fame and fortune, but I think she was secretly afraid someone younger and more ambitious would overshadow her. Vivian always had a bigger-than-life persona to go with her outsize ego, but after the incident, she wasn't able to produce, and her readers eventually abandoned her. She became a recluse, seemingly content to live off her past glories—until Naomi started to write. That's when the trouble started. There was an ugly dustup, and Vivian kicked the girl out."

"How did she end up next door to you?"

"As I said, Vivian owns the house. Setting her niece up in one of her rentals probably helped assuage her conscience."

"You sound as if you know Vivian DuPriest pretty well," Addie said.

Ida shrugged. "Not that well, but I met her long before I knew Naomi. Vivian is the one who introduced me to Mr. Finch."

"How did that come about?"

"It was happenstance, really. I had an elderly relative who lived across the street from the DuPriest home. When he fell ill, I used to help care for his garden on weekends. Vivian would sometimes stop by to chat about the plants. I was having trouble with the gardenias, and she told me I should write to Mr. Finch and ask for his advice."

Addie glanced at Ethan. "You didn't think that an odd suggestion?"

"I was stunned at first. I could hardly imagine such a thing. But Vivian had been to the prison to speak with him, and she was impressed by his intelligence. Perhaps *intrigued* is a better word. Whether she believed him guilty or not, I couldn't say. She was quite cagey in that regard. After a while, I became excited about the notion of a secret pen pal, and so I sent off a letter before I could change my mind. He answered right away."

"Did you ever go see him in person?"

"No, I never did." She sighed. "I suppose I didn't want the reality of his situation to interfere with our friendship."

Addie flashed Ethan another glance, and he nodded that she should continue. "Did you share the letters with Vivian?"

"At first. Then her parsing became too intrusive. She wanted to dissect his every word."

"But you gave the letters to Naomi."

"By then a lot of time had passed. I was no longer as emotionally connected to our correspondence as I once was."

Ethan had remained quiet for the exchange, but now he said, "You mentioned an incident. What happened to Vivian DuPriest that she was no longer able to write?"

"It was her habit to go out walking alone at night. She called it her thinking time. Someone attacked her near her home and left her for dead. She had a long and painful recovery, both mentally and physically. The assault changed her whole personality. She rarely left her house and was never able to write again. Her last book remains unfinished to this day."

"Was she writing about Orson Lee Finch?" Addie asked.

"About the Twilight Killer case, yes. How did you know?"

"Just a guess."

Ida lowered her voice as she glanced across the garden to Naomi's house. "Do you think there could be a connection between her attack and the hit-and-run that killed Naomi?"

"As you said, a lot of time has passed," Ethan hedged. "Did Naomi have many visitors? Did she ever mention having problems with anyone?"

"Aside from Vivian? She mostly kept to herself."

"What about a boyfriend?"

"No one serious. No one that I knew of, at least."

"Do you think her aunt would allow us inside the house to have a look around?"

"No need to bother Vivian. I can let you in. Naomi gave me a spare key so that I could feed her cat while she was away. Take as much time as you need. All I ask is that you leave everything as you found it. The idea of strangers invading Naomi's privacy makes me uncomfortable." She paused with a smile. "But I don't think she'd mind you going through her things, Agent Barrow."

"TALK ABOUT A TWIST," Addie said as they stepped inside Naomi's foyer.

"The pen pal thing? I didn't see that coming." Ethan closed the front door and took a quick survey of their surroundings. It was an older home, with long windows and walled-off spaces. The foyer led directly into the living area, and through open doorways he glimpsed the dining room and kitchen. The bedrooms would be off the narrow hallway to the left. From what he could see, the furnishings were sparse and serviceable. That was good. The lack of clutter would make their search easier.

He filed away his impressions and turned to glance out the front window. Ida McFall dawdled at the garden gate, staring back at the house. She had her phone to her ear, but the brim of her hat obscured her expression. There was something about her demeanor that niggled. Ethan couldn't shake the notion that the woman wasn't as helpful as she wanted them to think. Like everyone else he had spoken to lately, Ida McFall might have her own agenda.

Addie came up beside him at the window. "Who do you suppose she's talking to?"

"No clue."

"What do you make of her, anyway?" she mused. "She sure was chatty."

"Maybe a little too chatty," Ethan said.

"My thoughts exactly. But it could be a simple case of nerves. People react differently to law enforcement. Some clam up, while others can't spill their guts fast enough. And people her age sometimes get lonely. All they want is a captive audience and a sympathetic ear."

"That's a generous assessment considering her attitude toward cops."

Addie shrugged. "If I took offense every time someone disparaged my job, I wouldn't be able to get out of bed in the mornings." Her gaze narrowed as she stared out the window. "I have to say, though, it does seem awfully convenient that Naomi Quinlan's next-door neighbor once had a direct line of communication to Orson Lee Finch."

"Not really a coincidence if her letters were the inspiration for Naomi's book. Sounds like all three women had a connection to Finch."

Addie folded her arms. "About that book. She never mentioned to you that she was writing about Finch or your father?"

"Not once. She always presented herself as a genealogist."

"Would it have changed anything had you known? Would it have made you more suspect of her motives?"

Ethan thought about that for a minute. "Probably. But I would have come, anyway."

Addie nodded. "I figured."

"Does it change anything for you?" he asked.

She gave his query the same consideration. "Not really. Because no matter what her motive was in contacting you, we're still looking for the same thing."

"The truth?"

"The truth, yes, but more specifically, that DNA match. If it exists." She turned back to the foyer. "Where do you want to start?"

"We should split up to cover more ground. If Naomi went to the trouble of hiding Finch's letters and her notes, we can assume she concealed the DNA results as well. My hunch is, she put everything on a thumb drive."

"The proverbial needle in a haystack then." Addie moved to the glass door to the right of the foyer. "I'll start in her office. You can search her bedroom, seeing as how she wouldn't have minded you going through her things." Her blue eyes glinted as she glanced over her shoulder. "What was the word Ida used? *Taken*. Naomi was *taken* with you. Those emails must have really been something."

He gave her a warning look. "You just couldn't help yourself, could you?"

"Sadly, no. But don't begrudge me. I've waited a long time for this."

"I can tell."

The banter helped relieve a lingering tension, but Ethan reminded himself that one playful moment meant nothing. A few throwaway lines didn't erase years of anger and resentment. Still, he hadn't seen Addie so unguarded since his return, and his mind wandered into places he had no business going. They had always worked well together whether she wanted to admit it or not. It was their personal relationship that had come undone. What would their lives be like now if things had gone differently ten years ago? If he had been honest with her from the start? Would they still be together, married maybe, with a kid or two?

Funny that he should even have such a thought. Ethan had never considered himself a family man. He was too much of a loner, too intensely focused on his career and in righting the wrongs of the past. Now he felt keenly the loss of something that was never meant to be. He carried too much baggage to ever have a chance with Addie again. He accepted the inevitable, but the thought of missing that smile every morning for the rest his life was a pain that had started to gnaw at his soul.

"Ethan? Did you hear me?"

He pulled himself out of his reverie. "I'm sorry?"

She gave him a curious glance. "I said holler if you find anything." She handed him a pair of disposable gloves from her bag.

He snapped them on as she opened the office door. She stopped short, stared into the room for a moment and then said, "Looks like someone beat us to the punch."

He followed her into the office, and they both stood gazing around. The room had apparently been tossed and put back together in haste. Desk drawers were only partially closed, and books had been haphazardly returned to the shelves. A corner of the rug had been turned back. A piece of artwork hung askew.

"There's no computer," Ethan said as he walked over to the desk. "Unusual for a writer. Unless someone took her laptop." He opened drawers, searched through the contents and then checked for false bottoms.

"Maybe she had it with her the night she was hit. I can check the list of personal effects when I go back to HQ." Addie moved around the room, peering behind paintings and underneath seat cushions. "Do you know if she told anyone else about her DNA database searches?"

"I doubt she did. She seemed extremely cautious and secretive about what she'd found. But she also never mentioned that her aunt was the reporter assigned to my father's case or that her neighbor once wrote love letters to Orson Lee Finch."

"Maybe she didn't *tell* anyone. Maybe she started asking questions and someone took notice of her interest. Hold that thought." Addie left the room and came back a few minutes later. "No sign of a forced entry front or back. Both doors have dead bolts, and the windows in the rear have burglar bars. Whoever searched this office likely had a key. Or else Ida let someone else in."

Ethan hunkered down and looked underneath the desk, then ran his hand all along the bottom. "Maybe the driver removed Naomi's key from her body before he fled the scene."

"He could have taken her laptop, too." Addie sifted through the contents of the bookshelves. "The owner of the house would also have a key, wouldn't she? Maybe we should pay Vivian DuPriest a visit. If she'll see us, that is."

"Oh, I'm pretty sure she'll see us," Ethan said. "I'm James Merrick's son and you're the daughter of his victim. She won't be able to resist."

"One way to find out."

"Agreed." Ethan walked across the floor, testing for loose boards.

"I find it curious that Naomi kept all her aunt's best-sellers on display even though they had a falling-out. Most of them are autographed, too. *To Naomi with greatest affection.* She even has a picture of the two of them together. They looked pretty chummy when this shot was taken." Addie studied the photograph. "She was pretty. Naomi. I couldn't tell much about her appearance that night on the street."

Ethan understood the insinuation. A moving vehicle could do a lot of damage to the human body. He came over to check out the photograph. "I see now why Ida said Vivian DuPriest had a larger-than-life personality. I don't think I've ever met anyone with hair quite that shade of red."

"She was always something of a character, the best I remember. A bohemian socialite, if there is such a thing. A local celebrity, for sure. Used to make all the morning talk-show rounds." Addie returned the frame to the shelf. "You never answered Ida when she asked if you thought there could be a connection between Naomi's death and Vivian's attack."

"You may not like what I think."

Addie shrugged. "Let's hear it."

"Crime-beat reporters cultivate sources in police departments. If someone leaked information about a cover-up to Vivian, she could have become a target."

Addie looked annoyed. "Nice theory, but no one has yet explained what this alleged cover-up entailed."

"I keep coming back to Naomi's last email," Ethan said. "She seemed certain the results of her DNA search could damage reputations."

"Like Gwen Holloway's."

He eyed her uneasily. "Gwen Holloway wasn't the only one who built a career on my father's case. David Cutler became a local hero after he made the arrest."

Addie's irritation quickened. "But unlike Gwen Holloway, he never cashed in on his notoriety. He stayed on the force as a detective and worked his way up through the ranks. He earned every promotion he got the hard way, and there is no one in the department with more integrity."

"People make mistakes. Even David Cutler. I know you consider him family, but no one's infallible."

Her eyes glittered a warning. "David Cutler's reputation isn't up for debate or discussion. Let's just get on with the search."

So much for an open mind, Ethan thought. He wasn't as convinced of the deputy chief's unimpeachable honor as she was, but for now he let the matter drop. Their alliance was still too tenuous to test the boundaries.

A car door sounded, and Addie went over to the window to glance out. "We've got company."

Ethan moved up beside her. A patrol car had pulled up to the curb directly in front of the house. Two uniformed officers got out and converged on the sidewalk outside the gate.

"What are they doing here?" Addie muttered. "Do you think Ida ratted us out?"

"I think we shouldn't stick around to find out." Ethan cast a glance around the room to make sure they hadn't left a trace of their visit. "Come on, let's go."

Addie was still at the window watching the officers. "We can't just run from the police. How do you think it'll look if Ida mentions my name? Maybe I should go out there and talk to them."

"And say what? We don't have a plausible excuse for being inside Naomi Quinlan's house unless you tell them about the DNA results. And that would open a can of worms I'd rather you not have to deal with. It's best if we avoid a confrontation."

"You're forgetting that I have a vested interest in Naomi's case. I was at the scene the night she died," Addie said. "I could say I'm here on a follow-up, which I am, in a way."

"Is that a story you really want to try to sell to the deputy chief? Why borrow trouble?" He took her arm. "Let's just get out of here."

She turned with a reluctant nod and followed him through the house to a small sun porch at the back. She went out first and paused on the steps to glance around while Ethan locked the door with Ida's key. Then she nodded an all clear.

They hurried through the garden in a half crouch, using the back gate to escape from the premises. A dog barked from one of the enclosed yards as they jogged down the alley away from Naomi's house. When they came to the end, they slowed to a walk and crossed the street, taking refuge behind the wrought iron gates of one the city's oldest churchyards. No one was about, but the bells that tolled from the belfry seemed ominous.

"Do you think we were spotted?" Addie asked.

"No, we're good for now."

"I don't know if I would put it that optimistically. We did just run from the police."

"We avoided unnecessary contact."

She tucked back her hair. "You really are good with semantics, aren't you? Not to mention justification."

"Addie—"

She lifted her hand to silence his protest. "I know. No one twisted my arm."

He watched her for a moment. "We didn't break any laws."

"Not yet. But you've only been in town a couple of days. Give it time." There was no humor in her voice now. Not the slightest hint of her earlier teasing.

She stepped back into the shade, taking a moment to cool down and catch her breath. The light slanting down through the trees picked up the gold flecks in her blue eyes. Her lips were slightly parted as she stared up at him, and for a moment, Ethan had to fight the urge to weave his fingers through her hair, pull her close and kiss her as he'd wanted to do since their first meeting at the Gainey house.

Had that only been yesterday? Seemed like a lifetime ago, and yet in some ways, it felt as if they'd never been apart. Same old arguments. Same intense attraction. Memories flooded Ethan's head. Desire clouded his good sense. Before he could stop himself, he lifted a hand to smooth back her hair.

She caught her breath at his touch.

"Addie." He murmured her name as he wound a soft tendril around his finger.

Sunlight danced like fire in her eyes. "You keep saying my name as if you expect me to just fall back under your spell. It won't work, Ethan. You and I are not going to happen. We've established a temporary truce, but I still don't trust you. You're on a mission and I know how you get when you're obsessed. Nothing else matters. Not food, not sleep. Not even the law."

"At least you didn't say sex."

She rolled her eyes. "Oh, sex always mattered to you."

"And to you."

Their glazes clung for a moment, his hot and testing, hers fierce and defiant. He could see her now the way she'd looked at twenty-two. Naked in the moonlight as she ran toward the sea. Proudly uninhibited and breathtakingly beautiful. *Come in with me, Ethan. The water feels like silk.* Her skin wet, warm to his touch. Her legs wrapped around him as the waves gently rocked them.

His pulse thudded at the memory. "Is it so inconceivable that I might have changed in ten years?"

"We've both changed, Ethan. And yet here we are, right back where we left off. Running away from the police. Sneaking into places we have no business. Crossing fine lines. Risking everything for a case that was closed twenty-five years ago. I don't blame you for any of that. You've made no pretense about your intentions. This time, it's all on me. My choices, my consequences." She moved up to the entrance, surveying the street before she turned back to him. "Did you ever ask yourself why we bring out the worst in each other? That maybe, just maybe, what happened to my mother at the hands of your father is a barrier too high for us to scale? That maybe we shouldn't even try?"

"All the time," he said softly.

He saw a shiver go through her as she wrapped her arms around her middle. Defensive. Uncertain. And angry with herself for feeling that way.

"Addie…"

"Say my name like that one more time and I swear—"

He held up a hand to cut her off as the rumble of a powerful engine sounded nearby. He took a position on the opposite side of the gates.

"False alarm," he said.

"We should get moving."

"Not yet. If anyone comes looking for us, we'll be harder to spot in here than out on the street."

Her eyes glittered with frustration. "Who would come looking for us, Ethan?"

"I told you earlier, Gwen Holloway is already gunning for us both."

"You seriously think she would hunt us down on the street?"

His voice hardened. "She would do that and more if she considered either of us a threat. You need to at least trust me on that."

"Still a tall order," Addie said bluntly. "Are you sure you've told me everything?"

"You know as much as I do."

She paused as another car went by. She tracked the blue sedan until it turned at the next corner. "Now you've got me acting all paranoid."

"You know what they say. It's not paranoid if someone is really out to get you."

Addie returned her focus to the street. She kept watch in one direction, Ethan the other. "You think Gwen had us followed to Naomi's and then called the police on us? Why would she do that?"

"To get us out of the house would be my guess."

Addie pondered that scenario for a moment. "For the sake of argument, let's assume Gwen is behind everything. Let's say she sent someone to search Naomi's office to look for the DNA results. If she or her people called the cops to get us out of the house, then that likely means they didn't find what they were looking for." She spoke in a low, pensive tone, and Ethan didn't interrupt her. He kept his gaze peeled while she sifted through her thoughts. "From everything I know about Gwen Holloway, she's methodical and meticulous and she demands the same of her subordinates. How does that square with the sloppy search of Naomi's office?"

"They were in a hurry. They got interrupted."

"By us?" That possibility seemed to unnerve her. She glanced around anxiously. "We can't hide in here forever. Let's just go back to my car."

"You're right," he said. "You should go."

"What about you?"

"I'd like another crack at finding that thumb drive."

Addie stared at him in alarm. "You don't even know you're looking for a thumb drive. Those DNA results could be hidden anywhere. And if Gwen is as dangerous and desperate as you seem to think, she's bound to have someone watching the house. She won't risk letting you inside again."

"I'll be fine. Go out the main entrance of the churchyard and keep to the alleys as much as you can. You should be able to make it to your vehicle undetected."

Addie's chin came up. "Don't worry about me. I know all about the secret backstreets in this city."

He nodded. "I'm sure you do, but be careful anyway, okay?"

The fire seemed to drain out of her then. She held his gaze for the longest moment before glancing away.

"You're the one who needs to be careful. Trouble always follows wherever you go."

"This is a dangerous time for both of us," he said. "We're shaking things up while we're still in the dark. We don't yet know who all the bad actors are."

Addie gave him a sidelong glance. "It's always dangerous when you don't know who you can trust."

"I trust you."

She fell silent. "Maybe you shouldn't. I'm not as committed to this as you are. I have my own responsibilities and my own loyalties."

"Even so, you still came looking for me this morning."

"Don't read too much into that," she warned. "I'm only here because I want to put the past to rest for both of us. But you should know that if push comes to shove, I intend to protect myself this time."

"I wouldn't have it any other way."

Still she lingered, her gaze dark and watchful. "Ethan?"

"What is it, Addie?"

"You shouldn't have come back."

"Are you sorry I did?"

She closed her eyes on a deep sigh. "No. And that worries me most of all."

He leaned back against the wall and watched her stride away, ponytail swinging, hips subtly swaying. Ethan had always admired her walk. Not cocky, not coy, just straight-up confident.

He reluctantly turned away, moving through the gates and onto the sidewalk. The morning light hit him in the eyes, and he slipped his sunglasses back on, taking note of his surroundings—delivery trucks, parked cars, nearby businesses. A man crossing the street.

Other than the one lone pedestrian, the area was quiet. Too quiet. The calm before the storm, Ethan thought as he headed back to Naomi Quinlan's house.

Chapter Eight

Addie berated herself as she made her way across the churchyard, resisting the urge to glance over her shoulder to see if Ethan watched her. She'd felt his gaze on her back when she walked away, but maybe that had only been her imagination. Maybe the dark heat in his eyes and that knowing smile had only been wishful thinking.

Addie, Addie, what are you doing?

Was she really going down this road again when her future in the department had never looked brighter? Was she once more willing to risk it all because she couldn't smother the embers of an old attraction?

Ten years. *Ten years* and she still hadn't gotten Ethan Barrow out of her system. What was it about him that could tie her in knots with nothing more than a fleeting smile or a lingering stare? Addie had convinced herself she was smarter than that. Tougher than that. *And yet here you are.*

She shook off her doom and gloom as she left the churchyard and walked two blocks before ducking into another alley. She had other things to focus on at the moment. Like Naomi Quinlan's hit-and-run. Like a possible match to the third DNA sample found at her mother's murder scene.

Addie had just turned seven when Sandra Kinsella had been killed. Some days, she could barely recall what her mother looked like, and then there were times, especially in the dead of night when she lay awake staring at the ceiling, that she not only remembered her mother's features, but the scent of her perfume and the deep red of her favorite lipstick. Addie had bought that same classic shade for herself, though she rarely wore it. The color reminded her too much of a crimson magnolia.

Besides, red lipstick didn't really suit her. She wasn't her mother's daughter. Sandra Kinsella had been capricious and bold, a woman who gleefully embraced her darkest emotions and deepest desires. Addie wasn't like that. She was cautious and serious. Or at least…she had been until Ethan Barrow had come into her life.

Him again.

Addie frowned.

Put him out of your mind and focus.

Her mother's face wasn't the one she saw now in the back of her mind, nor was it her mother's whiskey-smooth voice she heard in her ear. The imagined reproach came from Helen Cutler, a woman who had been there for Addie through thick and thin, who had been both confidante and guardian. Helen had encouraged Addie to reach for the stars even as David Cutler had held her feet to the ground.

Was it at all conceivable that the deputy chief had been involved in a police cover-up twenty-five years ago, one involving her mother's murder and that third DNA sample? Addie didn't think such a thing possible. David Cutler was as straight an arrow as one could find in the police department, and he'd earned the respect and admiration of every man and woman who served under his command. And yet his promotion had allowed him to seal some of her mother's case files that remained out of Addie's reach to this day. She hadn't questioned his action, because she thought she knew the answer. He'd done it to protect her mother's reputation and to inoculate Addie from gossip. But doubts were starting to niggle, and Addie had to decide how far down the rabbit hole she was willing to go to placate Ethan Barrow's obsession.

She hurried along the cobblestone lane, impatient to get back to her vehicle. So deep in thought, she'd lost track of time and her surroundings when she needed to remain focused and vigilant.

Lined with brick walls and lush plantings, the alley lay in deep shade, but a sunlit street glimmered just ahead, like a light at the end of a tunnel. Somewhere behind her, a dog barked. The guttural bay sounded primal and fierce, an animal protecting its turf. Addie registered the commotion but she wasn't concerned. The dog was safely contained within the brick wall, doing what came naturally to a canine guardian. Still, the hair at the back of her neck lifted as the barking dropped to a menacing growl, and for a moment she had visions of gleaming eyes and a predatory prowl.

The barking ceased abruptly. In the eerie quiet, Addie heard the rustle of bushes and the soft thud of what might have been footsteps.

She whirled, hoping to find Ethan trying to catch up with her, but the lane was empty for as far back as she could see. She scanned the shadows, peering into the deepest part of the shade along the wall as her hand went to her bag. She'd heard *something*. The stealthy sound hadn't been her imagination. Had someone disappeared inside a gate?

Farther down the alley, the dog came back to life.

The throaty snarls unnerved her as she took a few steps toward the sound.

"Hello? Is someone there?"

She saw him then, a man slipping along the top of the brick wall, crouched and almost hidden from her view by a silvery cascade of Spanish moss. Even after she'd spotted him, she wondered if her eyes were playing tricks on her. His movements were so fluid and furtive, he might have been nothing more than a figment of her imagination. Yet he was right there, hidden in plain sight, and she could have sworn the scent of magnolias emanated from his presence as he drew close.

The perfume overwhelmed her. The whole tableau seemed so dreamlike that she felt disoriented and dazzled from the sunlight shimmering down through a live oak. "I see you on the wall," she called out. "I'm a police detective. Come down with your hands where I can see them."

He remained where he was, shoulders slouched and head bowed so that the hood he'd pulled over his head obscured his features. But Addie knew that he watched her. The power of his gaze was a tangible shiver down her backbone.

She kept a safe distance as she drew her weapon. "I said come down!" When he still didn't comply, she hardened her commands. "Who are you? Why are you following me?"

"Adaline…"

The distorted singsong was identical to the disguised voice she'd heard in the gutted house the night before. He was the same intruder who had left a trail of crimson magnolia petals on her walkway.

She took out her phone to call for backup.

"Adaline…" the altered voice rasped.

"Who are you? What do you want?"

A long pause. Then, "It's time you learn the truth."

She squinted into the light. "What truth?"

"The truth about your mother."

He burst out of the Spanish moss with the shock of a shotgun blast. His speed and agility startled Addie and she stumbled back as he dropped down on the cobblestones in front of her. Her phone clattered to the ground as she clung to her weapon.

He didn't attack even though he momentarily had the advantage. Instead, he turned and dashed back down the alley.

His features had remained hidden, but Addie took note of his size. He wasn't a big man. Average height, average build. She'd faced more physically imposing suspects, but none that had unnerved her more.

She picked up her phone and took off after him. "Police! Stop right there! I said *stop*!"

As abruptly as he'd fled, he halted. His hands came up as he stood with his back to her. Then slowly he turned, head still bowed, but now Addie could see the lower part of his face. Mouth, chin, part of his jawline. His grinning countenance seemed both feral and cunning, and her blood ran cold with dread.

The dog was still barking, louder, closer, a frenetic counterpoint to the man's silent sneer. The sunlight streaming through the oak canopy elongated his shadow, and for a moment, it almost seemed to Addie that something evil crawled along the ground toward her. She inadvertently took a step back as the dog grew more frenzied. Nails pawed at the wooden gate. The latch and hinges rattled.

Too late, Addie realized she had been lured to this particular spot for a reason. The scent of magnolia seemed to intensify as her fingers tightened on the grip of her weapon.

"Who are you?" she demanded yet again.

His hands were still in the air. Slowly, he unfurled his arms as if he were reaching for the edges of the alley. He opened his hands, and scarlet petals rained down upon the cobblestones. Addie wasn't surprised. She'd known he was her assailant, and yet for one split second, she froze in shock.

His fingertips raked against the brick wall, drawing a deep shudder as Addie tried to intuit his next move. With a flex of his hand, he released the wrought iron latch, and the gate flew open.

Addie saw nothing more than a dark blur with bared teeth and gleaming eyes before she was knocked off her feet. She landed hard on the cobblestones, and the dog was on her in a flash. Instinctively, she lifted her arms to stave off the attack, but a sharp command from behind the wall saved her.

"Thor! Come!"

The German shepherd hovered over her, growling and drooling, and then he turned with a defeated whimper and trotted back through the gate.

The owner came rushing out, effusive with apologies and explanations as she closed the gate behind her. "Oh, my God, are you okay?"

"Yes, I think so. He didn't bite me. Just knocked me down."

The woman hurried over to offer a hand as Addie scrambled to her feet. "I'm so sorry. Nothing like this has ever happened. He's a good dog, well behaved and obedient. But he's very protective of his turf. If anyone tries to come onto the property, he lets me know." Her tone held a subtle accusation.

"It wasn't his fault." Addie inspected the scrapes on her palms. "I suspect someone provoked him before they let him out."

"Provoked him?" The woman looked outraged. "How?"

"I don't know. Maybe he was goaded through the gate or from over the wall. He may even have been physically incited."

"Why would someone do such a thing?" The woman was clearly upset, so much so that she'd failed to notice Addie's gun. Her eyes widened as Addie slipped the weapon into her bag. She backed away. "What are you doing back here, anyway? Who are you?"

"Detective Adaline Kinsella." Addie presented her shield and ID. "Someone was here a minute ago, a man wearing a hoodie. Average height, average build. You didn't see him when you came through the gate?"

"There was no one back here but you." The woman glanced around uneasily. "Was he the one who tormented my dog? Should I be worried?"

"You've got Thor. You should be fine," Addie said. "Just be on the lookout for any suspicious activity." She handed the woman her card. "Give me a call if you see or hear anything."

The woman hurried back through the gate, leaving Addie alone in the alley. The man in the hood was long gone. Nothing remained of their strange encounter but a trail of crimson magnolia petals.

THE SQUAD CAR had already departed by the time Ethan returned to Naomi Quinlan's house, but he wanted to make certain the black Charger wasn't lurking somewhere nearby. He took a position down the street where he could watch the house without being detected.

After several minutes went by with no sign of countersurveillance, he circled the block and came in through the alley, using Ida's key to let himself in. He went through the house quickly, clearing each room before he returned to the office for a more thorough search. Then he headed down the hallway to the bedroom. He'd just opened a nightstand drawer when a sound checked him. He turned his ear to the hallway, listening for the click of a closing door or the telltale creak of a floorboard. Nothing else came to him, but he had the strongest premonition that he was no longer alone in the house.

Drawing his weapon, he moved silently across the room, flattening himself against the wall as he peered out the door. He listened for a moment longer before slipping down the hallway to inspect the rest of the house. He checked the rear rooms first, easing through the kitchen and onto the sun porch. The windows were closed and the dead bolt on the back door was still engaged. Nothing seemed amiss, and yet Ethan couldn't shake the notion that he had company, well hidden and malevolent.

He opened the door and went down the steps, lingering at the bottom as his gaze moved along the fence line. A mild breeze blew across the garden, rustling the banana trees and stirring a distant wind chime. The sky was clear, the sun warm and bright. Perfect weather to be lying on the beach or drifting on a lake. Not a good day to be searching a dead woman's house.

He went back inside and retraced his steps, examining the windows and doors at the front of the house. Another sound propelled him back into Naomi's office. A black-and-white cat sat atop the desk, cleaning his paws. Ethan's sudden appearance startled him. The cat paused midgrooming, ears back, fur puffed.

Ethan looked around the room and then glanced over his shoulder into the foyer. Then he moved to the desk. The cat hissed and backed away from him.

"Ferocious, aren't you?" Ethan examined the window locks. "How did you get in here, anyway?" Ida had said something about feeding Naomi's cat, but surely the animal hadn't been locked up in the house since the hit-and-run. He looked healthy enough. Had someone let him in after Ethan and Addie fled earlier?

Ethan went back into the foyer and opened the front door. The cat shot out of the house like a rocket, lunging off the porch and sprinting across the yard to Ida's garden.

Glancing both ways down the street, Ethan closed the door and made his way back down the hallway to Naomi's bedroom. He stood on the threshold, his senses still on alert as he waited for another giveaway sound. When nothing came to him, he set to work, finishing his search of the nightstands and then turning to the dresser. He put away his weapon, but he kept an eye on the door and an ear tuned to the hallway just in case.

After several minutes of intense riffling, he sat back on his heels as he cast his gaze around the room, looking for less obvious hiding places. Then his gaze came back to the dresser. He had a view of the closet in the mirror. The door was ajar. Had it been that way earlier?

He rose silently and moved across the room to throw back the door. Stepping inside, he parted hangers until he was certain the closet was clear. Then his gaze lifted to the ceiling, where a thick cord hung down from the attic door. He released the folding stairs and climbed up, each step creaking and shifting beneath his weight.

Another string hung from a light socket attached to a rafter. Ethan clicked on the bulb, but the anemic light chased away only the nearest of shadows.

He hoisted himself up through the opening, hunching his shoulders to avoid the rafters. The area was larger than he would have imagined and partially finished with floors and walls. The space on either side of the furnace accommodated several storage boxes, and someone had created a desk using an old wooden door and two small file cabinets. Colored folders were stacked on top of the desk, and photographs had been thumbtacked to a corkboard wall behind it. For whatever reason, Naomi Quinlan had outfitted a secret office in her attic.

Ethan's impulse was to go straight for those files, but instead he turned to survey the rest of the attic. At the fringes of illumination, he could just make out an old wicker chair and a myriad of plastic lawn ornaments. A one-armed mannequin lay discarded on the floorboards. Someone had tucked a red flower in the nylon strands of her hair and posed her remaining arm across her chest. The staged tableau looked eerily familiar, and a shiver crept up Ethan's spine as he moved in closer.

The mannequin's eyes were glass rather than painted, and the reflection of light gave life to the frozen face. Ethan knelt to touch a finger to the crimson flower petal that had been placed over the molded lips. The dried botanical crumbled at even so light a contact, releasing a musty, funereal scent into the attic.

There was no mistaking the intent. The mannequin had been displayed like a Twilight Killer victim and left for someone to find.

Or was this a private exhibition, a macabre showing for one?

Ethan had only known Naomi Quinlan through her emails, but nothing she had written suggested this kind of ghoulish fascination. He used his phone to snap a few shots before he moved to the other side of the attic. Here, the boxes and forgotten keepsakes had been shoved aside to accommodate a narrow mattress beneath the eaves. Apples and potato chip bags littered the floor around the makeshift bed and a hardback lay open on the pillow. Ethan recognized the title. It was one of the dozens of books that had been written in the aftermath of his father's confinement. He'd read them all in the hope of finding a clue or even flawed logic in the telling of his father's story.

Unlike the dried magnolia petal, the apples appeared fresh. Someone had been here recently.

Using the flashlight app on his phone, Ethan scanned the attic. Satisfied that he hadn't overlooked anything significant—another clue or someone lurking in the shadows—he carried his phone to the desk, angling the beam over the folders before zeroing in on the photographs.

The corkboard had been divided into three sections. The first was comprised of images that had been clipped from newspapers and magazines of Twilight's Children. The second section was all about the killers—newspaper accounts of Orson Lee Finch's arrest and trial, courtroom sketches and even a grainy shot of Ethan's father captured inside the state psychiatric hospital.

The third section contained crime scene and autopsy photographs arranged in chronological order by victim. Ethan was no stranger to gruesome imagery, but the display in Naomi Quinlan's attic took him aback. The photographs could only have come from the official murder files, reinforcing his belief that Naomi or someone close to her had had an important contact in the police department.

Ethan took his time studying the images before turning his attention to the folders. He found more newspaper clippings, manuscript pages and hundreds of handwritten notes and interviews, but no DNA results.

Returning to the corkboard, he scoured the crime-scene photographs with a magnifying glass he found on the desk. The bodies had all been displayed in an identical manner. Arms folded over chest, legs straight, hair fanned about the face.

Ethan's gaze shot to the mannequin. He wanted to believe she was nothing more than a visual inspiration for Naomi's writing, but the mattress shoved up underneath the rafters suggested a darker stimulation.

A sound at the top of the steps caught him off guard, and he whirled as he reached for his weapon. He caught only a glimpse of black-and-white fur before the cat clambered down the stairs and bolted to safety.

Ethan stared down the open hatch into the closet. He heard nothing, saw nothing out of place, but someone had let that cat back in the house.

Possibly the same person who had been living in Naomi Quinlan's attic. An unsub with an unnatural fixation on the Twilight Killer case.

Chapter Nine

Addie walked up and down the alley and then circled the block, looking for the man in the hoodie. She'd never had a good view of his face—probably couldn't pick him out of a lineup—but the disguised voice and the trail of crimson magnolia petals left no doubt that he was the same man who had assaulted her the night before.

What she couldn't figure out was how he'd managed to follow her to and from Naomi Quinlan's house without her or Ethan spotting him. Addie had been careful leaving home that morning, taking a circuitous route out of the neighborhood and then cruising through the downtown streets at a sedate pace while she kept an eye on her rearview mirror.

She was certain she hadn't picked up a tail, and yet someone had managed to track her and Ethan's whereabouts. The police hadn't arrived at Naomi's house out of the blue. Someone had known they were there. If Gwen Holloway was responsible for alerting the cops, had she also sent someone to attack Addie?

Ethan's paranoia was starting to rub off on her, she decided. More likely, her initial assessment had been correct. The man in the alley was one of those fanatical people who did creepy things like write letters to a dead woman's daughter. Only he'd taken the fixation a step further. His behavior had everything to do with Twilight's Children and nothing at all to do with Gwen Holloway. Addie and the other victims' children had always attracted their share of crazies. People were fascinated by serial killers and had been since the term was first coined. That same grisly captivation had propelled profilers like James Merrick to near rock-star status until his downfall had blighted the unit.

Addie paused on the street to glance behind her. She didn't notice anything out of the ordinary. No covert stares or sidelong glances. The pedestrians on the street paid her no attention at all, and yet she couldn't shake the notion that her stalker—as she had now come to think of him—was nearby. That he watched her in amusement from the safety of a shop window or from a shady park bench.

The day was steamy, and yet Addie's blood ran cold. She felt exposed on the street and vulnerable in a way she couldn't explain. It wasn't so much that she feared for her physical safety. She knew how to handle herself. But she experienced a deeper dread. A festering premonition that old secrets were about to be exposed and her life might never be the same.

A breeze rippled through the leaves, sounding like whispers.

It's time you learn the truth.

The truth about your mother.

A squad car cruised by, and Addie turned her face away, pretending to study a clothing display in a window. Once the car was out of sight, she left the shade of the awning and crossed the intersection at the light. The streets were quickly filling up. Tourists meandered while locals bustled to work or to brunch. Addie kept to the fringes of a sightseeing group, breaking off at the next corner to head back to her vehicle.

She drove straight to police headquarters and entered through the public door, sending her bag and weapon through the metal detector as she presented her ID.

The place was quiet for a weekend morning. She said hello to another detective as she made her way to her desk. He glanced up from his paperwork, bored and eager for a distraction. "Thought you were on vacation, Kinsella."

"I was. Came back early to clear a few things off my desk before Monday morning."

She kept her gaze averted as she sat down at her desk. The last thing she wanted was aimless chitchat. She waited for the detective to return to his work, and then she turned on her computer and entered her password at the prompt. She typed Naomi Quinlan's name in the search bar and glanced around anxiously as she waited for the file to load. The phone on her desk rang, and something—maybe intuition, maybe a movement at the corner of her eye—drew her gaze to the second floor as she picked up the receiver.

She spotted the deputy director gazing down at her as she identified herself to the caller.

He had a cell phone to his ear and nodded when he saw that he had her attention. "Come up," he said into the phone. Then the line went dead.

Addie replaced the receiver, turned off her computer and stood. The detective watched her curiously as she walked past his desk. By the time she'd climbed the stairs, David Cutler had disappeared into his office. He stood at the window, a tall, proud man who had devoted his life to public service. Addie had always thought of him as ageless, but now she noticed a slight stoop to his shoulders and the shimmer of more silver in his hair. Little wonder, she thought. The job eventually took a toll on all of them.

He didn't turn as she hovered in his doorway. He seemed so deep in thought, Addie was reluctant to interrupt him, but finally she said, "You wanted to see me?"

He motioned her in but remained at the window for another moment before he took his place behind his desk. "Have a seat."

Addie told herself she had no reason to feel anxious. She'd done nothing wrong, and she'd known the deputy chief for longer than she could remember. He had been there for her when her mother was murdered, when her grandmother had died of natural causes and all the years in between. He'd been guardian, mentor and champion all rolled into one. That he matched the description of the detective who had gone to see Ida McFall meant nothing. The very idea that he might be responsible for a police cover-up was ludicrous. David Cutler remained the finest man Addie had ever known, and she suddenly felt fiercely protective of him.

He sat back in his chair and rubbed the bridge of his nose. "I'm getting too old for these hours."

"It's the weekend," Addie said. "Why aren't you home cutting the grass or watching a ball game?"

He placed his palm on a stack of paperwork and lifted his hand. "The reports were this high when I came in earlier. Can you imagine what that pile would look like if I waited until Monday?"

"There's always going to be paperwork," Addie said. "You look tired. You should think about taking some time off. Maybe go up to the cabin. The lake is beautiful right now."

He gave her a pained smile. "You've been talking to

Helen. Not that either of you has any room to criticize. Her hours are as long as mine, and here you are back from your vacation early. What are you doing here, anyway?"

"I had some loose ends to tie up before Monday. Nothing that can't wait, though, if you'd like to grab lunch."

"Another time," he said with sigh. "I'm glad you came in today. Gives us a chance to talk."

"What's on your mind?"

A frown flicked across his brow as he picked up a pen from his desk, absently weaving it through his fingers. "Did you know Ethan Barrow is in Charleston?"

"He came by the Gainey house yesterday. I was surprised to see him. Actually, *stunned* might be a better word."

"You didn't know he was coming?"

"Not a clue. I hadn't seen or heard from him in ten years."

"No phone calls, no email? No correspondence at all?"

Addie cocked her head. "None of the above. Why the third degree?"

"He came to see me, too." He cast her a glance before returning his attention to the pen. "It was a strange meeting, to say the least."

"Why? What did he say?"

He hesitated. "He wanted to talk about the night your mother died."

Addie sat up in her chair. "What about that night?"

Another frowned flickered as he contemplated her question. "I don't think we need to get into that right now. I thought you should know that he's in town and apparently still laboring under the misconception, or outright delusion, that James Merrick is an innocent man."

Addie tucked back her hair. "You don't think there's a slight possibility he could be right?"

"Don't tell me he's suckered you back in already." He gave her the longest stare, one of those censuring looks that made Addie feel like a guilty teenager. "Let me guess. He's found new evidence."

Addie tried not to fidget under the spotlight of his glare. "He did mention something to that effect."

"Did he also mention the nature of this new evidence?"

She opened her mouth to answer, but something in David Cutler's eyes—a cold, hard gleam—reminded her of Ida McFall's misgivings about the detective who had come to see her. *I think he may have been looking for Naomi's evidence. I'm certain he was fishing for something.*

What if the man Ida had spoken to was no longer a detective, but the deputy chief? Her description matched. It might also explain why he hadn't given her a name. But why would the deputy chief take an interest in Naomi Quinlan's hit-and-run?

Addie didn't like the direction of her thoughts. She didn't like the worrisome doubts that were starting to burrow beneath her affection for David Cutler and undermine her faith in him.

"You should probably talk to him about it," Addie said.

"I'm asking you."

She shrugged. "All I know is that a local woman contacted him. Apparently, she was writing a book about the Twilight Killer case and had turned up something in the course of her research. Before he could come to

Charleston to meet with her in person, she was killed in a hit-and-run. Could be just a coincidence. Or maybe she really was onto something. We may never know. Anyway, her name was Naomi Quinlan. I caught the call the night she died, but by the time I arrived on the scene, Detective Yates had assumed control. Since I was in the middle of a transfer, I didn't raise a stink about turf. But the timing of her death is curious, to say the least."

"I hope you're not implying that Detective Yates or anyone else in this department had something to do with that woman's death."

His conclusion surprised Addie. "I'm not saying anything of the sort. I meant just what I said. Naomi Quinlan contacted Ethan about her research, and then she turned up dead before he could meet with her in person. The timing *is* curious."

"Does any of this really surprise you, Addie? Ethan Barrow has a nose for trouble."

"I know that. But he only arrived in town two days ago. He can hardly be blamed for Naomi Quinlan's hit-and-run. And even though I may not agree with his methods, I can't fault him for wanting to clear his father's name."

"You're still defending him."

His accusatory tone rankled. Addie waited a beat before she responded. "Seeing his side of things doesn't equate with defending him. A child, no matter the age, needs to believe the best about a parent. I'm no different. I know my mother wasn't perfect, but I still like to think that she loved me more than anything. That I was the most important person in her life."

"She did. You were."

Addie smiled. "I may remember more about my mother than you think."

His expression darkened. "What's that supposed to mean?"

"Nothing." She paused with another shrug. "Funny thing about those memories. Most days I can barely recall what she looked like, and then I'll smell a flower or hear a song and it's like she's right there with me. Helen and I were talking about this just yesterday. Out of the blue, I remembered a whole conversation from the night my mother died."

His demeanor never changed, but Addie sensed a sudden tension. "What conversation?"

"I overheard you and Helen talking in the hallway outside my bedroom. She was very upset. She wondered how she would tell me what happened. You told her to let me sleep, that the news could wait until morning."

"You talked to Helen about this?"

Addie nodded. "I'm afraid I upset her. She always looks so sad when my mother's name is brought up."

"She was very fond of Sandra. We both were. I don't think either of us has ever really gotten over the loss. She was such a vibrant person. A big believer in living life to the fullest. I still think of her as a bright star gone dark too soon."

"That's a lovely sentiment." Addie studied his expression. Despite his gracious words about her mother, he suddenly seemed pensive and unsettled.

"It's true," he said with a sigh. "Sandy could walk through a door and light up a room."

Sandy. Something in his voice shifted when he said her mother's name. Addie hadn't heard anyone refer to Sandra Kinsella by her nickname in a very long time. "Tell me about the night she died."

He flicked her a troubled glance. "So you can convey whatever I say to Ethan Barrow?"

His rebuke stung, although Addie supposed she deserved it. She'd thought—hoped—they'd long ago moved past her betrayal. "I would never do that, but you only have my word. If I haven't proved my loyalty and dedication to you by now, I guess I never will."

"I'm sorry," he said. "That was a cheap shot."

She nodded her acceptance. "I understand why you have reservations about Ethan Barrow, but this isn't about him. What happened to my mother changed my life. Her murder changed us all. You said yourself you and Helen have never gotten over it. Hearing about that night might help me understand some of my unresolved issues."

He stared down at his desk, looking as if he would rather be anywhere at that moment than in his office with Addie. She understood what she was asking. Digging up the past pained her, too, but too much had been swept under the rug for the sake of sparing her feelings. She needed to hear a firsthand account of that night.

He glanced up with a deep scowl. "This won't be easy to hear."

"I know."

"You're sure you want this?"

"Yes."

His gaze dropped back to the desk. "I worked late that night. Not unusual back in those days. These days, either, for that matter. My partner and I had gone out for a beer and a bite to eat after our watch. He went home to his family, but I came back here to have another look at a case file. You always think you've missed something. Just one more glance at the crime-scene photos or another reading of the eyewitness statements and you'll find that elusive piece of the puzzle."

Addie nodded, though he barely seemed aware of her presence now. She studied him furtively, wondering what had caused the deep furrows in his brow and the new creases around his mouth and eyes.

"Helen called around two in the morning. I'd fallen asleep at my desk, and the phone woke me up. She was very upset. Almost hysterical. She said that Sandra had promised to pick you up before ten. You had a doctor's appointment first thing the next morning, and she didn't want to have to come by our place to get you. When she didn't show, Helen was certain something had happened. I reminded her that your mother wasn't always the most reliable, that she was probably out with friends and time got away from her, but Helen wouldn't be calmed."

"Why did she wait so long to call you?"

"We were both burning the candle at both ends. Helen had just started her practice, and she was under a lot of stress. She'd fallen asleep on the couch watching the news. When she woke up and realized she hadn't heard from Sandra, she became frantic."

"And I slept through it all," Addie murmured.

"She had no reason to wake you. We were still hoping for the best. Helen stayed with you while I went out looking for Sandra. I can still remember how quiet the streets seemed that night. Almost ghostly. The clouds had moved out, and the moon was up. It cast the strangest glow over the city. Not soft and misty as one tends to think of moonlight, but cold and harsh and so brilliant it seemed as if you could peer into the darkest corners and find evil staring back at you."

Addie shivered at his description, at the distant look

in his eyes and the tinge of dread in his voice. She could almost imagine herself in the car with him, riding shotgun as they searched for her murdered mother.

"You and Sandy lived in a little house just north of Calhoun. Your grandmother had bought the place after you were born so that you could have a proper home. That same house on that same street would cost a small fortune these days, but back then, people like us could still afford to buy downtown. Helen and I lived only a few blocks over."

"I remember that house," Addie said. "I still drive by now and then."

"It was dark when I arrived. I got out of the car and knocked on the door. When no one answered, I circled around to the back and searched the yard. I kept telling myself there was no reason to worry. Sandy always lost track of time. She was out having fun and would apologize profusely in the morning when she came to pick you up. But deep down I knew something was wrong. I could feel it in my gut. You work cases for as long as I have, you develop a sixth sense."

Even though Addie knew how the story ended, she found herself pressing forward, gripping the armrests of her chair as she shivered. "What did you do?"

"I got back in the car and drove through the neighborhood looking for her. I found her two blocks over. She was in a narrow alley that ran between two streets. You may remember it. Your mother always loved taking those shortcuts. She said those alleys were Charleston's secret passageways. Not everyone knew about them."

"We used to go out on Sunday afternoons looking for them," Addie said.

He gave a vague nod. "If I hadn't already been on alert, I might not have seen her. She was just a shadow within a deeper shadow. When I moved in closer, though, I saw the blood. The puddle had already started to congeal. She had been there for a while." He seemed to catch himself then and glanced up to gauge her reaction.

"Go on," Addie said. "I want to hear the rest."

"It's not something a daughter needs to hear about her mother."

"Tell me anyway."

"She was posed. Arms folded over her chest, hair fanned out around her face, clothing arranged just so. That kind of attention to detail takes time, and yet no one had come out to investigate or called the police. No one saw or heard anything. I still ask myself how that could be. Not a single witness saw her die. Not a single person heard her scream."

"It was late. You said yourself the streets were empty."

"Yes. When I realized *how* she was posed, my first thought was that we'd made a terrible mistake. We'd arrested the wrong man. Orson Lee Finch was in jail awaiting trial, but how could he be guilty of all those other murders when the Twilight Killer had struck again? Then I noticed subtle differences in the way the body had been laid out. Sandy's left arm was folded over her right instead of the other way around. The hair was different, too, and the clothing. Discrepancies so slight only someone who had spent hours scrutinizing crime-scene photos from Finch's spree would have picked up on them. It was like the killer wanted me to find them. Like those clues had been left just for me."

"Gwen Holloway noticed the clues, too, didn't she? You helped her write the profile."

That roused him from the spell, and his frown deepened. "I gave her my input, sure. But that night, even after I noticed the inconsistencies, I couldn't process what it all meant. In the back of my mind, I was already thinking copycat, but I couldn't formulate a coherent theory. I was still in shock when the first patrol car arrived. Then the detectives came, forensics, the coroner. At some point, I drove home. Helen waited at the window. She met me at the door. I didn't have to say a word because she already knew."

"You've never told me any of this," Addie said.

"I couldn't bring myself to tell you, even after you became a cop. I didn't want those terrible images to sully your mother's memory. I wanted you to remember Sandy as she was. Maybe I wanted to remember her that way, too. A free spirit, infuriatingly irresponsible at times, but beautiful inside and out. She loved you, Addie."

"I loved her, too. She was a complicated woman. Secretive and oftentimes selfish. I'm not sure I ever really knew her, but I did love her. I understand why you've always tried to protect me, but sometimes the truth is the only thing that can heal old wounds."

A bitter edge crept into his voice. "And sometimes the truth just rips them wide-open again."

"So you had her case files sealed," Addie said. "You knew as soon as I joined the department that I would go looking for them."

"The case files have always been available to you," he said.

"Not all of them."

"You didn't need to see the photographs."

"Or the autopsy report?" She clasped her hands in her lap. "I know why you did what you did."

His gaze shot to her. He seemed on the verge of a

denial and then thought better of it. "What are you talking about?"

"You didn't want me to find out that my mother was pregnant."

His eyes closed briefly. "What purpose would that knowledge have served? It only made the tragedy that much harder to accept."

"But I already knew. The autopsy report was merely confirmation."

His head came up. "Before you accessed the files? How?"

"She told me."

Her simple statement seemed to stun him anew. "But you were just a child. She shouldn't have put that burden on you. Why did you never say anything?"

Now it was Addie who grew pensive and hesitant. Twenty-five years after her mother's murder, and she still felt as if she were betraying a confidence. "She told me not to tell anyone, even my grandmother. She said it had to be our secret. People would be hurt when they found out, and she needed to decide how best to deal with the fallout."

He rubbed a hand across his eyes. "I wish you would have come to me."

"There were times when I wanted to, but my mother's secret was the last thing I had of her. It bonded us. And whether I realized it or not, I needed to protect her."

His gaze softened. "You understand, then, why I wanted to do the same."

She nodded. "I do. You were worried what people would say about her and how that gossip would affect me. But she died twenty-five years ago. Hardly the Dark Ages. No one would have cared about her pregnancy."

"Don't kid yourself, Addie. The more things change, the more they stay the same. People will always judge."

She wanted to argue his point, but deep down, she knew he was right. "Is that why you're worried about Ethan Barrow? Are you afraid he'll rip open all those old wounds?"

"I worry about your wounds, Addie."

"I can take care of myself."

"Under other circumstances, I would agree, but that man caused a lot of damage ten years ago. Not just to this department but to you personally. He coerced you into accessing those sealed files, and to what end? So that he could cherry-pick information to feed to the press in order to taint the investigation. He tried to free his father by jeopardizing this department's reputation and Finch's conviction. He was devious and manipulative, and I don't see that he's changed much in that regard. But you have, Addie. You've grown into a damn fine investigator. You earned your detective shield and the respect of your peers the hard way. Everyone in this department recognizes your talent and dedication. You may be interested to know that your selection to Gwen Holloway's program came as a unanimous decision." He sat back in his chair and folded his arms. "You've worked too hard to throw it all away on another bad decision. Think before you act."

"I will. I always do."

"I hope so," he said, but his tone sounded doubtful. He picked up his pen and opened a folder in dismissal. Addie got up and walked to the door, turning to study his bowed head before she went back downstairs to continue her work. The conversation left her sad and unsettled. It wasn't so much his account of her mother's murder scene that upset her. Addie had known the basic facts for years. It was the look in his eyes, the odd note in his voice. She tried to shake off her uneasiness, but she'd never seen David Cutler look so worn-out, and she wondered if Helen had been right to worry about his health.

Or was it something other than the job that had hollowed his cheeks and shadowed his eyes?

Addie looked up to find him watching her from the second-story railing. Their gazes clung for a moment before she turned back to her computer with a shiver.

Chapter Ten

Ethan waited on the porch steps when Addie got home late that afternoon. She pulled into the driveway and parked, taking her time to gather her things before exiting the vehicle.

Her conversation with David Cutler still lingered, and his warning had not fallen on deaf ears. Ethan Barrow was trouble, but Addie couldn't put all the blame on his shoulders. She had free will. She was the one who had allowed herself to be drawn back into an ill-advised investigation, but it wasn't too late to right things. All she had to do was get out of the car and send Ethan packing. Come Monday morning, she could start her training with a clear head and enjoy this new phase of her career. She could seize the opportunity and run with it. Get on with her life as if the past two days had been nothing more than a glitch.

But that wasn't going to happen, and Addie knew it. From the moment she'd agreed to hear Ethan out, her course had been charted, and now things were moving too quickly to turn back. Someone had assaulted her, stalked her and loosed a dog on her. She wasn't convinced those incidents were connected to Ethan's investigation or to Naomi Quinlan's DNA evidence, but at the very least, questions had been raised. Doubts were stirring. What if her mother's killer was still out there somewhere? What if the murderer was someone close to her, someone she knew, respected, someone she would least expect? If she walked away now, would she be able to live with those uncertainties?

Addie had been so young when her mother died and so devastated by the loss that she'd never thought to question the official investigation. As she grew older, certain things had crossed her mind—the paternity of her mother's baby, for one thing. Even now, she had no idea who the father was. She barely knew her own dad. Her mother had kept her social life completely separate from their home life. All Addie had ever been told about the pregnancy was to say nothing.

It has to be our little secret for now, Addie. Do you understand what that means?

I can't tell anyone.

No one. Not even Grandma. People would be upset if they knew.

Why?

It's grown-up stuff. You don't need to worry about it.

Mama?

Yes, Addie?

Will the baby live with us?

Would you like that?

I wouldn't mind. She could stay in my room and I could take care of her like Aunt Helen takes care of me.

Is that what you think? That Helen is the one who takes care of you?

Don't be mad, Mama. What did I do?

You didn't do anything, sweet girl. And I'm not mad. I just wish... Never mind what I wish. Actions speak louder than words. Things are going to change around here, Addie. That's a promise. From now on, I'm going to be the best mother I can be to you.

And to the baby?

We'll see.

Addie hadn't thought about that conversation in years. She hadn't let herself dwell on the consequences of her mother's pregnancy, hadn't dared to acknowledge the suspicions that had glimmered at the edge of her subconscious since childhood. Those doubts threatened her peace of mind now, but she ruthlessly cut them out before they could take root. But as her mother's voice flitted away, another, more sinister one took its place.

It's time you learn the truth.

The truth about your mother.

She glanced across the yard at Ethan. He stared back at her. The power of his gaze penetrated the car window, and Addie shivered. His father had killed her mother. As much as Ethan want to clear James Merrick's name, Addie needed to believe in his guilt. Because the alternative was unfathomable.

She got out of the car and started across the grass toward him. He rose to greet her. "What's wrong?"

"Who said anything's wrong?" Her retort sounded sharper than she meant it. She took a breath and tried to relax, but his insight grated. She didn't like that he could read her so easily.

His gaze turned mildly reproachful. "I know you, Addie. I can tell when something is bothering you."

"No, you used to know me, but that was a long time ago."

"Or maybe I still know you better than you'd like to admit."

She sighed. "It's been a long day. Let's just leave it at that." She sat down on the porch. "I won't ask how you found out where I live, but I am curious how you got here. I don't see a vehicle anywhere."

"I took a cab to the neighborhood entrance and then walked the rest of the way." He sat down beside her. "I thought it was safer that way."

"You're still that certain Gwen Holloway is having you followed?"

"I'm that certain someone has eyes on me, yes. The cops showing up at Naomi Quinlan's house proved that."

"Ida could have called them."

"Why would she do that?"

Addie turned to give him a measuring look. "I don't know, Ethan. I don't know about a lot of things lately. You don't just bring trouble. You bring confusion. Chaos. You're exhausting. I feel worn-out already."

"Is that your way of asking me to leave?"

"No, sit down. It's my way of venting."

He sat back down. "I understand your frustration, but we're getting close. We're rattling cages, and someone is getting nervous."

"It says a lot that you think that's a good thing."

"How else will we find the truth?"

She could sense a nervous tension in him, an excitement that bubbled and brewed just below the surface. His anticipation was almost a tangible thing and more than a little infectious. Addie's heart thudded as she studied his profile. She couldn't help but admire the curl of his lashes, the straight line of his nose, the curvature of his lips. He was a very attractive man, more so now than a decade ago, because all those years on the job had seasoned and hardened him while all his secrets and obsessions kept him vulnerable. Addie found herself irrevocably drawn to him, even though he had once been her downfall and could be again if she wasn't careful. She supposed that said a lot about her.

He turned to her then, his expression inscrutable. If he had an inkling of her thoughts, his demeanor didn't betray him. "I found something at Naomi Quinlan's house that you should know about."

She drew a quick breath. "The DNA results?"

"No, not that, unfortunately. But I did stumble across an interesting cache in the attic. I found notes and manuscript pages from her book project and some of the police reports and crime-scene photos from the Twilight Killer case files. Given Naomi's age and her aunt's connection to the case, I think we can safely assume that Vivian DuPriest is the one who had the police contact. We should go talk to her. She may know about the DNA results. It's possible she acquired a portion of the original sample twenty-five years ago."

"I agree we should talk to her, but the leaker may not have been a cop," Addie said. "Vivian probably had sources in the coroner's office as well as the lab."

"I'm sure she did, but regardless of the original source, the material ended up in Naomi's possession. She's the one who ran the sample through the databases. From what I saw in the attic, her research was well organized. The photos and newspaper clippings were arranged in three distinct categories—Twilight's Children, the killers and the victims."

Addie was horrified. "She had pictures of me in her attic?"

"She had images of all the children. You should see that place. It was like she—or someone—had set up a hidden office. I saw a mattress up there, too. The area was littered with fruit and soft drink cans. Someone has been staying up there since her death."

"This just gets better and better," Addie said with a shiver. The scenario sounded straight out of a scary movie. Someone taking up residence in a dead woman's attic.

Dark scenes bombarded Addie, but she tried to corral her imagination. "What makes you think Naomi didn't set up the bed? If she thought her DNA discovery had put her in danger, she may have felt the need for a hiding place in case someone came looking for the results."

"Anything's possible, but some of the apples looked fresh. I noticed other odd things, too. A cat got inside the house twice after I locked the doors. And an old mannequin had been placed on the floor and posed like one of Finch's victims."

That stopped Addie cold. She stared at him for another long moment as she hugged her arms around her middle. "Posed...how?"

"She was missing an arm, but the other one was crossed over her chest. Her hair was fanned out around her head, and a dried flower petal had been placed over her lips."

"A crimson magnolia petal." It wasn't a question.

He nodded. "I had the crime-scene photos right in front of me. There was no mistaking the pose."

"This is starting to freak me out a little," Addie admitted. "We're not the only ones rattling cages."

"Apparently not."

"What's this about a cat getting inside the house?"

"Yeah, that was strange." Ethan's hand rested on the step between them. Addie had the strongest urge to link her fingers through his and hold on tight, because this was getting to be a very bumpy—not to mention, creepy—ride. "I first saw the cat in Naomi's office. When I opened the front door, it ran outside, and then a little while later, I saw the same cat at the top of the attic steps."

"How do you know it was the same cat?"

"It was black and white just like the one in the office. If you think back, Ida McFall said Naomi gave her a house key so that she could feed the cat. As in a singular feline. Either the cat has a secret way in and out of the house, or someone let it back in."

"Someone with a key."

"Exactly."

"Which means that person was in the house with you."

"It's possible."

Addie glanced around the neighborhood and then stood abruptly. The streets were still sunlit, the lawns green and dotted with color. But a pall had been cast, and now Addie found herself peering around corners in search of sinister silhouettes. "Let's go inside. I could use a drink."

Ethan followed her up the steps and into the tiny foyer. She punched in the security code and then turned to survey the entrance with a frown.

"What is it?" he asked.

She opened the door and examined the lock. "I don't know. I just had the strangest sensation. Maybe it's all our talk about keys and someone being in the house, but..." She glanced over her shoulder as she closed the door. "Have you ever had the feeling when you go home at night that someone has been in your house? It's nothing concrete. Nothing has gone missing. Everything is in its proper place, but the air just feels different."

He walked over and glanced out the window before turning to scan the living area. "You think someone was here while you were out? Who else knows your security code?"

"Helen and David Cutler. Matt Lepear. A cleaning service I use occasionally. I can't think of anyone else other than the security company where I purchased the system."

"Why does your partner know your security code?"

She gave him an exasperated glance. "That's your takeaway?" She shook her head. "He crashed here for a while after his second wife kicked him out. I never got around to changing the code. Not that I need to. I've trusted him with my life for the past ten years." The comment hung like an uneasy accusation between them. Addie had never consciously compared the two men. Matt was her partner. Of course she trusted him. Ethan continued to be both a frustration and a mistake, but there was no denying their chemistry. There seemed to be no dousing that spark.

Ethan watched her curiously. "Is there any reason one of the Cutlers would come by while you were out?"

"I was with the deputy chief earlier after I left you. Helen came over yesterday to feed the stray cats that hang around the backyard, but I can't think of any reason she would have been here today. She knows I'm home from vacation." They walked through the living area and into the kitchen. Addie opened the refrigerator and took out two icy bottles of beer. "You know what else is odd? I woke up last night with the same feeling. I was certain someone had been in the house. I even got up to look around. It turned out to be nothing. The alarm was set, the doors all locked. I was probably still wound up from finding those flower petals on my walkway. Not to mention being coldcocked." She touched the bandage at her temple. "My anxiety spilled over into my sleep."

"Anyone would be on edge after all that." He took the opener from her hand and uncapped the bottles.

"And I haven't even told you everything." Addie went around and perched on a bar stool. "The guy who hit me? I saw him again today."

Ethan sat down beside her. "Where? When?"

"After I left the churchyard this morning. I took a shortcut through an alley like you suggested, and he came up behind me."

"Why didn't you call me?"

"It happened so fast, I didn't even have time to call for backup. But there's no doubt in my mind he was the guy. Same height, same build. And he used a voice disguiser like he did last night. You can get those everywhere these days for less than twenty bucks. He probably clipped the microphone inside his hoodie so that I couldn't see it."

"Could you tell what he looked like?"

"No, he kept that hood pulled around his face so that I never got a good look at him."

Ethan frowned. "You said he used a voice disguiser. What did he say?"

Addie hesitated. "The whole encounter was pretty unnerving. When I said he came up behind me, he was actually on top of a brick wall, almost hidden by foliage. I'm not sure I would have seen him at all except for a dog behind the wall that kept going crazy. I knew something was wrong. Even after I spotted him up there, I thought I might be imagining things. It was just so bizarre to see him creeping along that wall, and I've seen a lot of weird things in this city. He called out my name.

Adaline. Adaline. Just like that." She ran a hand up and down her chilled arm. "So creepy."

"That's all he said? Just your name?"

"He said it was time I learn the truth about my mother." She kept rubbing at the goose bumps as if she could scrub away the memory of his taunt.

Ethan lifted his beer and then set it back down. "What do you think he meant by that?"

"Who knows? He jumped off the wall, startled me, and then he fled. I gave chase, but…he got away."

Ethan searched her face. "Why do I have a feeling there's more to the story than you're telling me?"

"I've given you the highlights. Anyway, what I'd like to know is how he found me in the first place. He must have followed us to Naomi's house and then he tailed me from the churchyard. Maybe he's the one who called the cops." She paused in alarm. "You don't think he's the one who's been staying in the attic, do you?"

"He's a person of interest, to say the least."

Addie let out a breath. "I've tried to write him off as just another weirdo who's latched onto one of Twilight's Children—me—but I can't forget what you said about that mannequin and how she was posed with a magnolia petal on her lips. What if whoever is staying in Naomi's attic isn't just someone fascinated with the Twilight Killer case? What if he's practicing to *be* the Twilight Killer?"

"It's a leap, but the thought has crossed my mind."

That Ethan didn't immediately dismiss her theory worried Addie even more.

The house suddenly seemed unnaturally quiet. Even the hum of the refrigerator sounded menacing. Was her stalker out there right now watching her place? Was he imagining her prone and posed, gushing blood from a fatal stab wound to her heart as he placed a magnolia petal upon her frozen lips?

Addie shook herself and glanced at Ethan. "Maybe we're both letting our imaginations get the better of us."

"Maybe we are. We need to remain objective. We don't know enough to draw any conclusions at this point, but the hoodie guy bears finding and watching."

"Right now, he's the one who keeps finding me," Addie said. "I'm certain I wasn't tailed when I left the neighborhood this morning, and we were both careful when we walked to Naomi's house. So how did he know we would be there? How did he know I would be in the alley at that precise time?"

"If he's the one staying in the attic, he could have followed us out of the house when the police showed up. Did you have your phone with you this morning?"

"Yes, of course. I always do."

"That's another possible explanation. GPS has opened doors for law enforcement and criminals alike. It doesn't take much sophistication for either to track a cell phone. All anyone would need is your number, and not even that with the right equipment and know-how. You should probably use a burner until we resolve this."

"You know I can't do that. I'm a cop. I can't go off the grid because some sicko has decided to play mind games with me."

"Gwen Holloway's program starts on Monday, right? Your whereabouts won't be a secret, anyway. Use a burner when you're off the clock and when you're working on our investigation."

Our investigation. Addie inwardly winced.

"What else did you have in your bag this morning besides your phone and your gun?"

She thought for a moment. "My shield and ID. My car key. A tube of lip gloss."

"Have you had your car worked on lately? Used a car wash or a valet service? A tracker or transmitter can be powered using the battery in a key fob. If you've got a spare, switch it out. Change the code on your security system, too. Do it now before you forget. Then get the locks on your doors changed as soon as possible."

"Changing the locks is no small expense," she said. "Maybe we're overreacting."

"Come on, Addie. You know better than to take chances."

"Okay. I'll call a locksmith in the morning."

Ethan sat drinking his beer while she returned to the foyer to reprogram the security panel. She came back with cell phone in hand. "I don't care if this guy is tracking my number. I'm starving and I'm using this phone to order a pizza. Any objections or requests?"

"No objections. Your vehicle is parked in the driveway. Anyone watching the house would already know you're home."

"Requests?"

"Are you inviting me to dinner?"

Something in his voice, a quiet intimacy, quickened Addie's pulse, but she tried to downplay her reaction with a shrug. "We both have to eat. No anchovies or olives, correct?"

"You remembered."

"Don't be flattered. No anchovies is a given, and I don't like olives, either."

"I remember."

She started to retort, needed to retort so that her defenses remained fortified. Instead, she went into the kitchen to call the neighborhood pizzeria, keeping her back to Ethan while she gathered her poise. When she turned, he was at the kitchen door staring out into the backyard.

"Mind if I have a look around?" he asked.

"Knock yourself out."

Addie didn't follow him. She needed another beat to collect her thoughts. She tried to tell herself she was tired and on edge, but spending so much time with Ethan had made her feel things she hadn't experienced in a very long time. The flutter of her heart at his nearness. Her keen awareness of his heated gaze. She'd forgotten what it was like—the thrill and the terror—to be in those first throes of sexual attraction.

Addie had dated enough after their breakup to know the kind of connection she'd felt with Ethan was rare. He wasn't like any man she'd ever known. He was intense and introspective, someone she knew she should run from. But Addie had discovered that with all those dark emotions came deep passion, the kind that had made her lose coherent thought and good sense. She'd known using David Cutler's computer to open sealed files was morally wrong and professionally indefensible, but she hadn't cared. Not in that moment. One touch, one kiss, one whisper in her ear and she would have done anything for Ethan Barrow.

She was older now, wiser, harder and a lot more jaded. Because of Ethan, she didn't trust easily, and she'd vowed to never again be taken in by a pair of dark eyes and knowing hands. And yet when she watched him now as he moved about her backyard, all she could think about were those eyes staring down at her in a dim room, his hands sliding slowly up her thighs, parting her, teasing her until the only thing she cared about was having him inside her.

She picked up her beer, gulped it down and then, squaring her shoulders, she opened the door and went outside to join him.

He was hunkered on the walkway staring up at the broken security light. He glanced her way when he heard the door. "When did this happen?"

"Last night."

"Before or after you tangled with the suspect?"

"After. Actually, it happened while Matt was still here. We heard a crash and came out to investigate. I think someone threw a rock and took it out."

"Someone?"

"Most likely the same suspect." Addie sat down on the porch steps. The sun was just sinking below the tree-tops, but the air was still hot. She peeled her ponytail off the back of her neck as she tracked Ethan's move-ments. He'd changed his clothes since last she'd seen him. By comparison, she felt grungy, cranky and in bad need of a shower. The day seemed never ending. All the angst over the stalker and her unfinished business with Ethan…the conversation with David Cutler that still niggled at the back of her mind. It all took a toll.

She got up and brushed her hands on the sides of her jeans. "I'm going in to take a shower," she said. "I'll leave money on the bar for the pizza. Can you listen for the doorbell?"

"Yes, don't worry. I'll take care of it."

Addie went back inside and headed down the hall-way to the bathroom. She started the shower, and while the water heated, she went into the bedroom to lay out clean clothes. Tossing fresh underwear on the bed, she opened the top drawer of her chest and removed her picture box.

After her grandmother died, Addie had become the

keeper of the family photographs. She opened the lid and riffled through the cherished images until she found the picture that she wanted. It was a shot of her mother with David and Helen Cutler.

Addie had always loved the photograph, but now as she stared down at their smiling faces, the unlikeliness of their friendship struck her. Their disparate personalities were reflected in the way they each presented themselves. Addie's mother wore a halter top, shorts and her signature red lipstick, her overt sexiness a stark contract to Helen's earth-mother persona and David's stoicism. Sandra stood in the middle—always the center of attention—with her arm linked through Helen's, but she stared up at David. He looked straight into the camera, not smiling, not scowling, but something about his posture, an almost infinitesimal lean toward Addie's mother, reminded her of the way he'd said her mother's nickname. *Sandy.* A bright star gone dark too soon.

Had her mother known she was pregnant when that photo was taken? Had David Cutler?

Addie put the picture box away, but she propped the photograph against her mirror so that she could study it later. So that she could dissect her mother's catlike smile and that dark glint in David Cutler's eyes.

And the faint worry lines etched in Helen Cutler's brow.

Chapter Eleven

A few hours later, Ethan stood at Addie's front window staring out at the dark street. They'd spent a pleasant evening over beer and pizza, and when it had come time for him to head back to his hotel, she'd stunned him by suggesting that he spend the night.

"It's late and I have a spare bedroom, extra tooth-brush, everything you need. What's the point in calling a cab at this hour?"

"Are you sure?"

"It's no big deal. The most that will happen is that we'll both get a good night's sleep and then tomorrow morning, we can go see Vivienne DuPriest together."

But it was a very big deal to Ethan. Addie could have sent him away the moment she saw him on her front steps. He was certain that had been her first inclination. Instead, she'd invited him in for drinks, dinner and a sleepover. If that didn't constitute a major step forward in their relationship, he didn't know what would.

Still, he knew better than to get ahead of himself or to read too much into a gesture too soon. The worst thing he could possibly do was push Addie in a direc-tion she didn't want to go, and Ethan was more than a little gun-shy himself. What if instead of proving his father's innocence he only cemented his guilt? How would Addie feel about him then? How would he feel about himself?

For years, Ethan had lived in the shadow of James Merrick's dark deed. For years, he'd tried to tell himself the sins of his father had no power over him. Unlike James, Ethan had grown up in a stable home with a mother he loved and a stepfather he respected. He'd had all the advantages, gone to all the right schools, had companionship whenever he craved it. He was a loner by choice, not necessity. He was dedicated and persistent, not obsessive. He wasn't his father's son.

But there was no fooling DNA. Ethan supposed it was ironic that in a very real sense, his future now hinged on someone else's DNA.

There was no fooling chemistry, either. The more time he spent in Addie's company, the deeper his attraction. Whether she wanted to admit it or not, she felt something for him, too. He saw a glimmer in her eyes now and then, heard a certain timbre in her voice on those rare occasions when she let down her guard. But Ethan wouldn't let himself revel in her lapses, and he certainly had no intention of taking advantage of her confusion. If anything, he wanted to protect her.

Leaving the window, he made the rounds through the house. Addie had turned in some time ago. Her door was closed, and Ethan stood for a moment listening to the quiet before he went into the bathroom to brush his teeth and wash up.

In the guest room, he peeled off his clothes and climbed under the covers in his boxers. The bed was comfortable and the temperature pleasant, but he couldn't fall asleep for a long time. He watched the rotation of the ceiling fan until he finally grew drowsy.

The shrill blast of the security alarm woke him some time later.

He bolted upright while simultaneously reaching for his weapon. Rising, he moved silently across the floor and stepped into the hallway just as Addie came out of her room. She wore a T-shirt that hit her midthigh, and her hair flowed loosely about her shoulders and down her back. She took aim when she first saw him and then instantly refocused. They went down the hallway together. The front door stood open.

Clearing the immediate area, Ethan went out on the porch. Addie came up behind him after she'd turned off the alarm. "What's going on? Do you see anything?"

"There!" He pointed to a darting silhouette a few houses down. "He's cutting through your neighbor's backyard. Get in the car and see if you can head him off at the next street."

Ethan was down the steps and on the sidewalk before he remembered that he was barefoot and in his underwear. Propriety didn't stop him, nor did the bite of cracked concrete as he pounded after his quarry. He sprinted for the bushes, lifting himself easily over the fence and then pausing to listen for footfalls. He heard Addie's car start up behind him. The engine faded as she made the block.

He moved through the yard, weapon ready, senses alert. A dog barked nearby, and as he turned toward the sound, he glimpsed the interloper from the corner of his eye. The man wore a dark hoodie that blended almost seamlessly with the shadows. Ethan whirled, but before he could close in, the suspect disappeared. Just…vanished.

Ethan wondered if his eyes were playing tricks on him, but as he cautiously approached the back of the fence, he realized an opening had been created in the slats through which the man had slipped.

Easing through, Ethan hugged the side of the house as he made his way out to the sidewalk. The suspect was nowhere to be seen.

A vehicle came toward him without lights. Ethan recognized the car. He stepped off the curb into the street, forcing the Charger to stop. Then he rapped on the glass until the driver lowered the window.

Ethan ducked his head so that he could see both agents. The driver stared up at him while the passenger kept his head turned toward the side window. "Let me guess. You just happened to be in the neighborhood."

The driver shrugged. "Why not? Last time I checked, it's still a free country."

"I would think the FBI could find a better use of your time," Ethan said. "You're not denying you're federal agents, are you?"

"Not denying or confirming anything. Just minding our business."

"Minding your own business, huh?" Ethan glanced at the passenger. His face remained suspiciously averted. "I'd like to see some ID."

"Show us yours first." The driver looked to be in his mid-to late thirties, with dark hair and a cocky attitude.

"You know who I am," Ethan said. "And we all know why you're here. Is this a sanctioned surveillance?"

"I don't know what you're talking about."

"Someone broke into Detective Kinsella's house just now. I don't suppose you know anything about that, either."

"We don't break into houses, Special Agent Barrow. That's more your thing."

"So you do know who I am."

"Let's just say your reputation precedes you."

"Oh, I'm sure Gwen Holloway has briefed you well." Ethan glanced at the second agent, trying to get a sense of his age and body type. "The suspect was on foot and wearing a dark hoodie. Average height, average build. You're certain you didn't catch a glimpse of him?"

"We didn't see anything." The driver paused. "But let's say, hypothetically speaking, that we *were* watching Detective Kinsella's house tonight. You know how surveillance works. We would have maintained a discreet distance. Anyone approaching or fleeing her house on foot would have gone undetected if he knew what he was doing."

"Mind turning on your dome light?" Ethan asked.

"What for?" the agent asked in surprise.

"Your partner has kept his face hidden this whole time. Makes me wonder."

"Nothing to wonder about. He's just shy."

"Is that why you refuse to show me your credentials?" Ethan pressed. "Not that I'll have a hard time figuring out who you are."

"You go right ahead and try, Agent Barrow."

Ethan's hand shot through the window to manually release the lock, and then he opened the door before the driver had time to do much more than swear under his breath.

"Hey, you," he said to the second agent.

The man turned, giving Ethan full view of his features. He, too, looked to be in his thirties, but his hair was lighter than his partner's, and his expression was more flinty than arrogant. "Satisfied?"

The driver closed the door, snuffing out the interior light. "If I were you, I'd be careful who I piss off. Your visit to Charleston hasn't exactly endeared you to the powers that be."

"Do I look worried?"

Addie's SUV pulled up just then. She got out of her vehicle and hurried over to the car. She was barefoot, too, and still dressed for bed except for the weapon she held at her side. She looked incredibly appealing in the moonlight, hair all tangled and eyes flashing with excitement. "What's going on?"

"These guys are federal agents. They've been watching your house tonight," Ethan said.

Her brows lifted. "Well, that's interesting."

"They claim they don't know anything about the break-in. Didn't see a thing."

"How convenient for them." She leaned in. "What's in the back seat?"

"Nothing, as far as I can tell."

She made sure the agents were aware of her weapon. "Think we can convince them to pop the trunk?"

"Doubtful," Ethan said. "They haven't been very cooperative."

Addie straightened. "Feds." She made it sound like the lowest form of indictment. She turned to Ethan. "How do we know they didn't do more than just watch my house? We only have their word for it."

The driver shifted his gaze to Addie. "Trust me, Detective, if we wanted to enter your house, you'd never know we were there. We sure as hell wouldn't set off the alarm."

Addie pounced. "Who said anything about an alarm?"

"Good question," Ethan said.

The driver glanced at him. "Still hypothetically speaking?"

"Sure."

"It's a hot night. If we'd been watching Detective Kinsella's house for any length of time, we would have had the windows down to get a cross breeze. We could have heard an alarm without actually seeing anything until the two of you came flying off the porch, armed and in your underwear. Being the conscientious types, we would have circled the block to see if we could figure out what was going on."

"So your hearing is fine, it's just your other senses that are lacking," Addie said.

The agent's gaze dropped appreciatively. "Nothing wrong with my eyesight."

"Hey, eyes up here." Ethan rapped on the hood to attract the agent's attention. "You can tell Gwen Holloway if she wants to keep track of my whereabouts, she can come find me herself."

"We're not your messengers, Agent Barrow."

"Just beat it," Addie said wearily. "Your surveillance has been busted. If you insist on hanging around my neighborhood, I'll be forced to haul you in on suspicion."

"That would be a big mistake."

"We'll see, I guess."

"Yes, we will. In the meantime, you two have a good night." The Charger peeled away from the curb, swerving so sharply that Addie and Ethan had to jump back.

Addie swore as they stood, gazing after the car. At the end of the street, the brake lights flashed, and then the driver gunned the engine as he shot around the corner.

She said in awe, "Are you sure those clowns are federal agents? Who teaches you people to drive, anyway?"

"Always a few bad apples," he said.

"No kidding." She pushed back her tousled hair. "You really think they're working for Gwen Holloway? How the hell does she still have the kind of clout that she can call up the FBI and order surveillance on another agent?"

"Profiling wasn't her only talent at the Bureau," Ethan said. "She excelled at politics. She made sure that people in power owe her."

Addie shook her head. "I understand how the system works, but dedicating resources and manpower to protect her reputation seems like overkill. And I thought I'd seen egos in the police department."

"You have to take into account the current atmosphere at headquarters. The FBI is still reeling from corruption and bribery charges, and the last thing the brass needs is publicity from a botched investigation and cover-up that wrongly indicted one of the most celebrated profilers since the inception of the BAU. Given all that, it's an easy sale for Gwen. One phone call and she's provided all the technical and logistical support she needs to shut us down. But beyond the Bureau's reputation and Gwen's ego, something else may be at play here. There's still a lot about Gwen you don't know."

"Then tell me."

He gave her a skeptical look as he rubbed the back of his neck. "Not sure this is the time or place."

"Oh, after that little confrontation, I think this is exactly the time and place."

Ethan glanced around uneasily. "Let's go back to your house, then. I feel like an idiot standing out here in my underwear."

"We need to check the neighborhood first. You can talk while I drive."

He followed her back to the SUV, and they climbed

in. Addie started the engine and pulled away from the curb. "Maybe we'll get lucky. Our suspect can't have gotten far on foot."

Ethan nodded, turning to search the shadowy yards as they made the block.

"So tell me about Gwen Holloway," Addie said.

"In a nutshell, she may have more than ego and reputation riding on our investigation."

"So you implied, but that doesn't really tell me anything."

"I think this is personal for her. She has an ax to grind."

"With you?"

"With me, with my father. I never told you this, but he wanted her transferred out of the BAU."

"So she's taking it out on you? Twenty-five years is a long time to carry a secondary grudge," Addie said. "You were just a little kid back then."

He turned to study her profile. "Same age as you when you lost your mother."

She scowled out the windshield. "We both lost a lot. That was a seriously messed-up time."

"Understatement."

She glanced at him before returning her attention to the road. "Go back to Gwen Holloway. How do you know your father wanted her transferred?"

"I overheard an argument between them. My mother and I had come down one weekend to stay with my grandparents. It was in the middle of the Twilight Killer case, and my father had been in Charleston for weeks. That was unusual for a profiler. Despite what you see on TV, they're deskbound most of the time. But for whatever reason, my father wanted to be in on the action, and he worked closely with the task force. He became so consumed with the investigation that he rarely called, let alone visited. I didn't realize until later that my parents' marriage was falling apart. I guess that time was a trial separation. I only knew that things weren't right and that my mother cried a lot. Anyway, on our last night in Charleston, my father left the house to meet Gwen in the garden, and I followed him."

Addie turned a corner and drove half a block before commenting. "You saw them together? *Together*, together?"

"She tried to kiss him. When he pushed her away, she attacked him."

Addie fell silent for another long moment. "Ethan, what are you saying here?"

He scanned the shadows, still searching. "There's a reason Gwen Holloway shut me down ten years ago and why she's still trying to control the narrative even today. Yes, it's about reputation and ego and protecting her business interests, but it's more than that. Like I said, for her, it's personal."

"I get that, but you're still beating around the bush. If you think she had something to do with my mother's murder, just say so."

"All I can tell you is that Gwen was as familiar with the Twilight Killer case as my father. They worked on it together for months. She knew Orson Lee Finch's MO, his signature, his kill list. Everything. She helped develop the profile."

"Means and motive, but what about opportunity?"

"My father was already showing signs of a breakdown. Disorientation, blackouts…" Ethan trailed off as a cloud descended, the same darkness he often experienced when he thought about his father's illness.

"So you think it's possible Gwen killed my mother

during one of your father's blackouts and planted his DNA at the crime scene? Then planted his bloody clothing and the murder weapon near his hotel? Just to be clear, that is what you're suggesting, isn't it?"

"It's a theory, nothing more."

Addie made another turn. "The other day, you said the match from Naomi's database search might have been the result of familial DNA. Do you know anything about Gwen's family?"

"She doesn't have any."

"No living parents or siblings?"

"No."

"What about distant relatives? Cousins, aunts, uncles…?"

"I don't know of any."

Addie checked the rearview mirror. "There is another possibility."

"I'm listening."

"Don't tell me you haven't already thought of it," she said. "What if Gwen's relationship with your father resulted in a baby? Could she have kept something like that a secret?"

"It would be difficult for someone in her position, but not impossible."

"She didn't take a leave of absence after your father's incarceration? No hospitals stays or transfers to remote field offices?"

"None that I've been able to uncover."

"Did you ever consider submitting her DNA to see if you get the same match that Naomi did?"

"I've considered it," he admitted. "But even if I managed to get a sample of Gwen's DNA, there are thousands of public databases. I don't know which one Naomi used."

Addie sighed. "It always comes back to her, doesn't it? She was the catalyst for everything that's happened. And we still don't know how any of this connects to the guy who just broke into my house."

"If it connects at all."

She shot him a glance. "I can't decide which is more unsettling—the possibility that Gwen Holloway sent him to harass me or that he's just some random dude with a fixation. Did you get a look at him?"

"He's too smart for that," Ethan said. "He knows enough to keep his face protected. I chased him into your neighbor's backyard, and then he slipped through a hole in the fence and disappeared. Which tells me he's familiarized himself with your neighborhood. He may even live nearby."

"That's a cheery thought." She eased around another corner. The houses in the neighborhood remained dark, the occupants oblivious to their search. "This is a waste of time," she said in frustration. "He's long gone. Or else he found a place to lie low. Not much more we can do tonight. Tomorrow I'll take a look through some of the empty houses. See if he's holed up in one of them. You're right. That could be how he's able to move through the neighborhood so easily." She pulled into her driveway. The front door stood open.

"Did you close the door before you left?" Ethan asked.

"Yes."

"Are you sure?"

"Yes. I remember closing it after I grabbed my car key."

"But you didn't lock it?"

"Not the dead bolt."

They got out and met in the driveway. "I'll take the back," Ethan said.

ADDIE WAITED UNTIL he'd gone through the gate, and then she crossed the yard and went up the front steps, flattening herself against the wall to listen before she stepped into the foyer. The security system was still disarmed. The blinking message seemed to taunt her as she moved across the foyer into the living area. She cleared the kitchen and then moved down the hallway.

A light flickered from the open door of her bedroom. Her hand tightened on the grip of her weapon as she moved steadily forward, clearing the bathroom and then the guest room before she approached her room.

She paused for only a second to listen before she went in, flipping on the light switch so that she could scan every corner. A candle had been lit and placed on her dresser, along with the photo of Sandra Kinsella and the Cutlers. Someone had scrawled *whore* across her mother's face in red marker.

Addie heard a sound in the hall and spun. When Ethan appeared in the doorway, she dropped her weapon to her side. "All clear outside," he said and then noticed the candle. He came into the room and set his gun aside. "What's this?"

"He must have doubled back while we were circling the neighborhood. He came into the house, lit the candle and defaced my mother's photograph." Addie's gaze lifted in frustration. "Who the hell is this guy, Ethan? How can he come and go from my house so easily?"

"That's what we have to find out."

Addie turned back to the dresser and stared into the candle flame with a brooding frown. "I really wanted to believe he was just another fanatic, but the timing can't be coincidental. He first appeared in my backyard right after I met you in White Point Garden. Do you think he was watching me even then?"

"I don't know, Addie."

She picked up the photograph and ran her finger over the ugly word. "If he's connected to the DNA evidence and Naomi's research, then why is he coming after me specifically? Naomi contacted you. You're the one who instigated a new investigation. Not that I want him coming after you," she quickly added. She stared down at her mother's marred face and then handed the photograph to Ethan.

"I recognize the deputy chief," he said. "The other woman is his wife?"

"Yes. You met Helen once years ago."

"Now I remember. It was an awkward encounter. She seemed to be evaluating my every word."

"She's a shrink. Comes with the territory. Plus, she's very protective of me."

Ethan glanced up from the photograph. "The Cutlers and your mother were close?"

"Helen and David have always been like family. I called them aunt and uncle when I was little. I spent more time at their house than I did my own. My mother was a party girl. She had me when she was young, and I guess she never really grew up."

"She was a beautiful woman," Ethan said.

"Yes, she was." Addie took the photo and propped it against the mirror. All those dear faces seemed almost sinister in the candlelight. "Helen had a really hard time after my mother's death. She not only lost her best friend, but also in a way, she lost me, too. I went to live with my grandmother, and I didn't see her and David as much. My grandmother was protective of me, too. The Cutlers could visit me whenever they liked, but it was a long time before Grandmother would let me spend the night at their house. She never wanted to let me out of her sight."

"Understandable after what happened to her daughter."

At the hands of your father, Addie thought. Or maybe not. "Helen and David did everything they could to stay in touch, but it wasn't the same. Not for a long time."

"You seem close now."

"When my grandmother died, they were there for me. I had no one else. My father was never in the picture. I don't know him or his family. We're strangers that happen to share DNA. I still consider the Cutlers my family. I'm lucky to have them."

"It's interesting how different they all seem," he said with a pensive frown.

"I was just thinking about that earlier. My mother was like a younger, wilder sister to Helen. In some ways, I think Helen lived vicariously through her. Helen was always so down-to-earth. I suppose that's why they got on so well. Opposites attract. She kept my mother grounded." Addie folded her arms around her middle. "That was my favorite photograph of the three of them. Why would someone spoil her image that way?"

"Assuming whoever did this is the same guy you saw earlier, he said that it was time you learn the truth about your mother. Are you sure you don't know what he meant?"

"My mother's past is no secret." Addie bent and blew out the candle. "You say Gwen Holloway's motives are personal—well, so is this. Intensely personal. I hate what he's doing, coming in here and violating my home. This is supposed to be my safe place, my sanctuary, and now I can't even stand to be in my own bedroom."

"You're a cop, Addie. You've seen this before. He's taunting you. Don't let him get under your skin."

"Easier said than done. I'm a cop, yes, but I'm also human. The thought of him going through my things makes my skin crawl. I'm not sleeping in here tonight," she said with a defiant glower.

"You don't have to. Take the spare bedroom. I'll sleep on the couch."

"I'll take the couch, but we can argue over sleeping arrangements later." She moved to the door. "I could use another drink. Something stronger than beer this time."

"You go ahead," he said. "I'll process the scene. Do you have a print kit in your car?"

"Yes, but you won't find anything. You can bet he wore gloves."

"Probably, but it's worth a shot."

Addie paused in the doorway to glance back at him. "I don't like being on the other side of things."

"I know you don't. But it's okay. We'll figure it out."

Funny how capable and comforting he could seem standing there in nothing but his boxers. Maybe it was the ripple of all those muscles or the memories that were suddenly storming through Addie's head. She felt weak in the knees and tried to convince herself it was nothing but aftershock.

She glanced away then brought her gaze back to him. "It helps that you're here tonight. Thank you for that."

"You don't need to thank me. I'm the one who got you into this."

She shrugged. "Maybe, maybe not. We still don't know if this guy has anything to do with you."

"Regardless, I think we can both agree that I owe you. I made a lot of mistakes ten years ago. I'll always regret how things ended between us."

She rubbed a hand up and down her arm as she scowled into the bedroom. "I don't want to talk about that right now."

"There are still things you need to know about me," he said.

Addie leaned back against the door frame and sighed. "Not now, Ethan, please. It's been a long day. I'm done in. And besides, do you really want to have a serious conversation in your underwear?"

"Not like you have any room to talk."

She smiled. "We must have looked like a pair of lunatics running around the neighborhood like this. Good thing no one saw us. Except for those two idiots in the Charger."

"Yes, they certainly got an eyeful," Ethan agreed. His gazed dropped and lingered admiringly.

"Hey," she said softly. "Eyes up here."

"Can't help myself. You've always had great legs."

"And I thought you were only interested in my mind."

"That, too."

Their gazes locked, and Addie's breath quickened. Strange that the man who had betrayed her and left her brokenhearted could stand half-naked before her and the last thing she wanted was to send him away.

Something must have shifted in her eyes or in her smile. She hadn't said or done anything, and yet Ethan had picked up on a vibe. His gaze deepened. She could almost hear the throb of his pulse, the sudden rush of his blood. He said nothing, either. Didn't move so much as an inch toward her, and yet Addie was suddenly trembling. Her heart flailed as images bombarded her once more. All those hot nights locked together in the bedroom of her tiny apartment. The long, soulful kisses.

The groans and soft cries as he devoured her and then she him.

"I remember how it was, too," he said. "I remember every inch of that little garage apartment. And of you."

"That was a long time ago," Addie felt compelled to remind him.

"You really were something," he said in a hushed voice. "Like a wild colt. All legs and untamed excitement."

"That's how you remember me?" She laughed. "I was a mess. Right out of the academy, uncertain and untested, but trying desperately to prove myself. The best that can be said is that I was exuberantly green."

"You always struck me as supremely confident."

"You took care of that."

He stared at her for the longest moment. "I'm sorry."

She shook her head and turned away. "No, I'm sorry. I don't know why I said that. I don't know why I keep picking at you." She paused and glanced back at him. "It's easier to guilt someone else than to admit your own screwups."

"You've every right to blame me."

She closed her eyes on a breath. "We've both paid our dues. Anyway, I didn't want to get into anything heavy tonight. We've been through the wringer already. We can talk in the morning."

"If that's what you want."

"Ethan?" She bit her lip. "I'm glad you're here tonight. I said that already, didn't I?"

"I'm not tired of hearing it." He stared at her so intently, Addie felt as if she'd had the wind knocked from her lungs.

She said on a whisper, "Ethan."

"If you keep saying my name like that, I swear I'll—"

"Ethan."

He was across the room in a flash, pulling her against him, pushing up her shirt so that he could splay his hands across her bare skin. Addie returned his kiss with a pent-up ardor that stunned her. She'd been alone and celibate for far too long, and common sense deserted her like a caged bird released unexpectedly into the wild. Her heart pounded. Her blood heated. She didn't know what to do with herself. She didn't know what Ethan expected of her.

Wrapping one arm around his neck, she steadied herself with the other hand flattened against the wall. She pressed into him, needy and demanding and feeling more reckless than she had in years. It was heady, that don't-give-a-damn feeling. An intoxicating mix of lust and freedom.

He kissed her, broke away to nuzzle her neck and then kissed her again. Addie drank him in like a cool glass of water on a hot summer's day. She savored but was nowhere near sated.

"I'd rip your clothes off if you were wearing any," she murmured against his lips.

He laughed softly.

"Kiss me again," she demanded.

He willingly complied, and when he finally drew away, she tried to pull him back to her. "No. Don't go away."

"I think I have to."

She sighed. "Why?"

"Addie, you know why."

"No, I don't. I want this. See? Eyes wide-open."

He cupped her face and dropped his forehead to hers. "What am I going to do with you?"

"Nothing, apparently."

He drew away once more. "You think I like being the spoiler? I want this, too. But those unresolved issues don't just magically go away. You'll regret this in the morning."

"There you go again, thinking you still know me."

"I do know you. No matter how much you try to pretend otherwise, you haven't forgiven me yet. I don't blame you. I haven't earned back your trust. Maybe I never will. The last thing I ever want to do is hurt you again."

She tugged down her shirt with brisk efficiency. "You're assuming that I'm emotionally invested. People can sleep together just because they want to, you know. It doesn't have to be a big deal."

"For us it does."

"If you say so." She moved toward the hallway. "You go ahead and process the crime scene, Ethan. Take all the time you need. I'll just go have that drink now."

"Addie."

She put up a hand. "Nope. Discussion's over," she said without glancing back.

ADDIE COULDN'T SLEEP. She threw off the covers and rose, treading softly down the hallway so as not to awaken Ethan on the couch. She moved to the window and stared out into the night, her gaze moving from house to house as she searched the shadowy yards.

Ethan stirred behind her. Then he bolted upright as he grabbed for his gun.

"It's just me," she said.

"Addie? What's the matter?"

"I couldn't sleep."

He rose and came over to the window to join her, peering out at the night just as she was.

"He's out there," Addie murmured. "I can feel him watching me."

"We can fix that." Ethan reached over to close the blinds, but she stopped him.

"No, don't. I want him to see me. I want him to know that I'm not scared of him."

"You're taunting him," Ethan said. "Not a good idea."

Addie shrugged. "Drawing him out is the only way we can catch him."

"So you're using yourself as bait."

"Wouldn't be the first time."

He was silent for a moment. "I don't like to think about that."

"Why? We both have dangerous jobs. Don't go all caveman on me, Ethan. I know how to take care of myself."

"I never doubted it. I can still be concerned, can't I?"

"I guess I did give you reason to worry earlier," she admitted grudgingly. "I let him drive me out of my own bedroom. A momentary weakness."

"You're entitled."

"Ethan?"

He turned to study her profile. "What is it, Addie?"

"Do you ever think about what it might have been like if things hadn't ended the way they did for us?"

"That's an abrupt change of topic," he said in surprise. "I thought you didn't want to get into anything heavy."

She shrugged again. "Just answer the question."

He seemed to consider his response. "What you're really asking is how things might have been different if I hadn't lied to you. I used to think about it all the time."

"And now?"

He stared out the window with a brooding frown.

"At some point, I had to move on. But being here with you has brought back a lot of memories."

"For me, too," she admitted. "I think we had something special. Or was I just kidding myself? Was that a lie, too? I never could figure out where your deception began and ended."

"What I felt for you was never a lie. If you believe nothing else, please trust me on that one."

"Maybe it doesn't matter anymore," she said on a wistful note.

"And maybe it does." He put a tentative hand to her cheek. "Addie."

She closed her eyes on a breath. Then tilted her face to his.

The kiss was gentle at first, almost sweetly hesitant. And then as she responded, he threaded his hands through her hair and drew her to him. Addie clung to him, willing away the past, willing away any negative thought that might once again kill the moment.

She reached up and closed the blinds. Without the soft glow of the security lights, the room fell into darkness. Ethan was barely more than a silhouette as he walked her slowly back to the couch. She sank into the cushions and he hovered over her, staring at her intently before slowly moving down her body, kissing and stroking with fingers and tongue until those ripples of pleasure exploded and she thrust her hands in his hair, tugging him up and over her once more.

She wrapped her legs around him, drawing him in as her eyes closed and her head fell back in ecstasy.

Chapter Twelve

Ethan was already up and dressed the next morning by the time Addie got around. She told him to help himself to anything in the kitchen while she stumbled groggily to the bathroom to shower. When she came out a few minutes later, dressed in her usual jeans and tank, she avoided his gaze as she went about the business of gathering her keys and weapon.

"Are you ready?" she asked as she headed for the door. "I'll take you by your hotel so you can change and then we can go see Vivian DuPriest. If you're still up for it, that is."

"Just drop in on her?"

"Unless you have a better idea. I don't have a phone number, but I know where she lives. My grandmother and I used to walk by her house sometimes. Besides, if we just show up at her door, she'll be less likely to turn us down."

"Then I guess I'm ready."

He went out the front door and waited on the porch while Addie set the alarm and locked up. "For all the good that dead bolt will do," she muttered. "I'll look for a locksmith this afternoon."

"Addie," Ethan said as they climbed into her vehicle. She could feel the intensity of his gaze through the lenses of his sunglasses. She pretended to adjust the rearview mirror to escape the impact. "What is it?"

"Should we talk about last night? I don't like this awkwardness between us."

"We'll get over it." She dropped her hand from the mirror and turned to face him. "For what it's worth, you were right about us. I don't have regrets, but maybe it would have been best to keep things professional. We do still have issues, and maybe I haven't forgiven you. I want to. I know it's petty of me to keep harping on the past."

"It's not petty. It's self-preservation. I get it."

She shrugged. "Still, it doesn't say much for my character. This may be presumptuous, but I'm going to say it, anyway. Where can this ever go, Ethan? You live and work in Virginia, and my home is in Charleston. I don't see myself ever leaving this city. I belong here."

"I know that."

"And what I said about hooking up being fine with me...sometimes it is. Sometimes a casual relationship is all I want. But not with you. You were right about that, too. Nothing about us has ever been casual. Or easy, for that matter."

He smiled. "No."

"Things are really complicated right now. The investigation is heating up. Maybe we should just concentrate on that."

"Maybe we should."

She nodded. "We're cool then? Truce still on?"

"Truce is still on."

"Okay. Let's get to work." She started the engine and backed out of the driveway. The neighborhood was just coming awake. She waved to a couple she recognized as they pushed a stroller down the sidewalk. For one split second, she let herself go there. She imagined a different life, one with a husband and kids, playdates and soccer games and noisy evening meals eaten in the dining room rather than at her solitary perch at the bar. She imagined someone to wake up to in the morning and someone to come home to at night. Addie liked her life just fine. She really did. But sometimes she had the passing thought that more might be better.

Shaking off her momentary discontent, she pulled onto King Street, heading south toward the water.

She parked in a lot across the street from Ethan's hotel and got out with him.

"You want to come up?" he asked.

"No, thanks. There's a coffee shop just down that way. I'll get caffeinated while you change. Take your time, though. I'm in no hurry."

"I know the one you mean. I'll meet you there and grab a cup to go," he said.

He leaned in, and despite their previous conversation about keeping things professional, Addie thought he meant to kiss her, just a peck goodbye as if they were an old married couple. Instead, he brushed a leaf from her hair and then he was gone. She watched in bemusement as he crossed the street and disappeared inside the hotel. How could such a light touch electrify so many butterflies in her stomach? How could her world have gone so crazy so quickly?

She turned and headed down the sidewalk toward the coffee shop. The morning was already hot and steamy. She tucked back her damp hair and kept her eyes peeled as she walked along. She didn't want to be caught unaware as she had been the day before. The image of her stalker slipping up behind her flashed in her head, and she turned to glance over her shoulder. Traffic was sparse on the street, and only a few pedestrians were out and about. Addie stopped beneath an awning on the pretext of adjusting her sandal strap. Across the street, someone lurked in a recessed doorway. She could see little more than a silhouette, but she could feel eyes on her. Or was that her imagination?

She continued down the street to the coffee shop, pausing to glance in the plateglass window before entering. If someone had followed her, she couldn't detect him.

Placing her order at the register, she sat down at a window table and faced the door. Her iced coffee arrived a few minutes later, along with a raspberry muffin. She nibbled and sipped as she stared out the window. A tall woman in aviator sunglasses caught her attention. She wore a dark suit and polished loafers, a somber outfit for a summer morning. She'd never met Gwen Holloway in person, but Addie recognized the former profiler from her book jackets and program materials.

She halted on the sidewalk when she saw Addie staring at her through the window. A chill shot through Addie even as she braced herself for the coming confrontation. It was no accident that Gwen Holloway had picked the same coffee shop. She had tailed Addie here, may even have orchestrated the break-in at her home last night. What else did the woman have up her sleeve?

As if sensing and relishing Addie's trepidation, Gwen Holloway smiled and removed her dark glasses as she came into the shop.

Like Addie, she placed her order at the counter. Then she turned and swept her gaze across the tables before lighting once again on Addie. She lingered near the register, but Addie knew it was too much to hope that she'd ordered her coffee to go. Once she had her cup in hand, she made a beeline for Addie's table.

"Detective Kinsella, isn't it? I'm Gwen Holloway." Addie rose and they shook hands. "Mind if I join you?" Before Addie could protest, Gwen pulled out the chair across from her and sat down.

"Of course," Addie said after the fact. "How did you know who I am?"

"I recognized you from the photograph that accompanied your program application. You aroused my curiosity early on."

"How come?"

"It seems you have a lot of fans in the Charleston Police Department. They couldn't say enough good things about you. So I dug a little deeper to see if all the hype was warranted."

"And?"

Gwen gave her a long assessment. "You and your partner have an impressive record. More closed cases than any detectives in your department. You're an impressive team. I'm sure he'll miss you over the next few weeks, but his loss will be this city's gain. The insight and tools you'll acquire from my program will change how you approach police work. You'll be a different investigator by the time the course is concluded. But I warn you, Detective, it won't be a cakewalk. The schedule is demanding."

"I look forward to the challenge."

Gwen smiled as she picked up her coffee. "So do I." She turned to scan the street before refocusing on Addie. She had something on her mind. That much was obvious. Addie thought about the two agents sent to watch her house last night and Ethan's speculation that

Gwen Holloway's interest in their investigation might be motivated by something darker than ego.

Addie had seen photographs of James Merrick. Ethan bore a slight resemblance to his father, but not so much that alarm bells had gone off when she'd first met him or even after she'd fallen in love with him. The truth of his identity had hit her like a sledgehammer blow. But the shock of that revelation was all in the past. Now when she conjured an image of James Merrick, Gwen Holloway was at his side, perhaps plotting his demise. Addie imagined the profiler's growing disenchantment with his protégée, and her rage that everything she'd worked for could so easily be tossed aside. In some ways, Addie sympathized. Times hadn't changed in that regard. Women in law enforcement were still held to a higher standard. They still had to work twice as hard to prove themselves to their male superiors, and second chances came few and far between.

But Addie doubted that Gwen Holloway would appreciate her empathy.

"It's nice to have this chance to chat," Gwen said. "We'll be spending a lot of time together for the next few weeks. It's always good to break the ice."

"How did you know where to find me?" Addie asked.

"I dropped by Ethan's hotel to see him. I saw the two of you drive up."

"So you followed me here?"

"Yes. Is that a problem?"

"It's not a problem. I don't mind breaking the ice," Addie said. "We can chat for as long as you like. But I don't think that's the real reason you're here."

Gwen's eyes glittered with an emotion Addie couldn't define and didn't trust. "You're both perceptive and blunt. I like that."

Addie said nothing.

"Since we both favor the direct approach, I won't beat about the bush. I'm concerned about Ethan's presence here in Charleston. I'm even more worried about his frame of mind."

Addie was immediately on guard. "Why?"

Gwen cradled her cup in both hands as she leaned in. "I know all about your past with Ethan. I know what he did to you. You're more aware than anyone how obsessed he is with clearing his father's name. The evidence against James remains damning, and yet Ethan has convinced himself of his father's innocence. He dragged you into his delusion once before, and it didn't end well for either of you."

Addie took a moment before responding. "With all due respect, how is any of that your concern?"

"I'm concerned for a multitude of reasons."

"Why? As I understand it, Ethan is here on his own time. He's not utilizing FBI resources or manpower to further a personal investigation. He's working alone with a little help from me. But even if that wasn't the case, you don't work for the Bureau. Why do you care what he does?"

Annoyance flashed across Gwen's features before she shrugged it away. "I don't know how much Ethan has told you about our background, but we go way back. I knew him when he was just a little boy."

"Yes, I know. His father was your mentor," Addie said. "I've read all your books. I found them fascinating, and I don't say that to suck up."

"That's not your style, is it, Detective Kinsella? You're fiercely independent. You don't like giving or receiving favors, and as I noted earlier, you're blunt. I appreciate that. So let me be straight with you. Unless you cut Ethan Barrow off at the knees, that man will be your downfall. I know what I'm talking about."

Addie frowned. "What do you think he'll do to me?"

"The same thing he did before, only worse. The same thing his father tried to do to me."

"Which was…?"

Gwen glanced around, automatically scoping out their surroundings. "It may surprise you to know that I've remained good friends with Ethan's mother and stepfather over the years. And with Ethan when he would allow it. I've watched his career successes—and his failures—with great interest. I've always known he had something special—intelligence, talent, dedication, but also that indefinable quality that sets certain agents apart from the pack. He's like his father in that respect. He has James's insight and instincts. His single-mindedness. He could truly be one of the greats. The powers-that-be want him in the BAU, but Ethan is nothing if not stubborn. His resistance hasn't gone unnoticed."

"What does that have to do with my downfall?" Addie asked.

"If he's so careless with his own career, I can't imagine that he'll have much regard for yours. He's a man on a mission, Detective Kinsella, and he won't stop until he takes you down with him. He reminds me more and more of James with each passing day."

"From what I've read, a lot of factors contributed to James Merrick's breakdown. Ethan may be driven, but there is nothing wrong with his head."

An unpleasant smile flitted. "Are you sure about that? When I first knew James, I would have sworn he was as steady as you or I. There were aspects of his personality and behavior that troubled me, but I told myself he was just unconventional, as so many brilliant people are. I tried to convince myself of his eccentricity right up until the moment your mother was murdered because James Merrick could no longer distinguish between fantasy and reality. He became Orson Lee Finch that night, the killer he had hunted so intently for months. Looking back, I saw the signs. I've always wondered, if I'd spoken up earlier, could I have stopped him? Maybe your mother would still be alive."

Oh, she was good, Addie thought. So good that she could almost make Addie believe she had her best interests at heart. Gwen Holloway spoke as if they were confidantes. A sage imparting her wisdom. *Listen to me. Learn from my mistakes with Ethan's father.*

Addie knew exactly what the woman was doing. She recognized Gwen's cunning and manipulation, and yet a part of her couldn't help asking, "What signs?"

"I don't know if I can explain it so that you'll understand, but James became someone else when he worked a case. He was obsessed, yes. We all were. But it was more than that. He lived and breathed the kills until he became the shadow of whatever monster we hunted. He had instincts and insight like no one I've ever seen before or since, although Ethan comes close. When James lost himself in the hunt, nothing else mattered to him. Not rules, not protocol, not even his family. Does that sound like anyone else you know?"

Addie's hackles rose in defense. "It sounds nothing like Ethan."

"Then you're lying to yourself just as I did all those years ago."

"You underestimate me." Addie scooted back her chair and stood. "My eyes are wide-open. I know exactly what I'm getting into. I'll help Ethan for as long and as much as I want and then I'll walk away."

"Easier said than done, Detective."

"Maybe. But here's where you and I differ. I don't expect anything in return. I certainly would never want anyone to leave a wife and child for me."

Fire flashed in Gwen Holloway's eyes, a quick, violent flare that took Addie's breath away. Then just like that, the blaze went out and the woman stared up at Addie with cool resolve. "You're out of line, Detective."

"Then I apologize. But you're the one who followed me in here. You're the one who started this conversation. You said you appreciate my candor, so here it is. My relationship with Ethan is none of your business. What we do on our own time is none of your business. I realize that speaking my mind will likely jeopardize my standing in your program, but I won't be manipulated. And I won't be used as a weapon against Ethan." Addie started to walk away and then turned back to the table. "Oh. And tell those two agents you sent to watch my house last night to knock it off. All you're doing is making me wonder why you're so desperate to stop Ethan's investigation."

Gwen rose. "You don't want me for an enemy."

"No, I don't," Addie agreed. "But if you start a war, you'll find I'm no pushover. Unless I get word that I've been dismissed from your program, I'll see you first thing tomorrow morning."

She walked outside and put on her sunglasses. Ethan was just crossing the street. She strode over to him. His gaze went past her to the coffee shop, and he muttered something under his breath.

"What happened in there?"

Addie shrugged. "You were right about her. She's manipulative and vindictive. And unless I miss my guess, she's hiding something."

"What did she say to you? Or maybe I should ask what you said to her."

Addie shrugged again. "Suffice to say, she's not my biggest fan."

Ethan grinned. "That's okay. I am."

Chapter Thirteen

Addie parked near Waterfront Park, and they walked down the Battery to the farthest point of the peninsula. Crossing East Bay, they lingered in the gardens while she recounted her conversation with Gwen Holloway and the insinuation that Ethan might be following in his father's tragic footsteps. He didn't seem at all surprised. "That sounds like her," he said with a shrug and then wondered aloud about the best way of approaching Vivian DuPriest. In the end he agreed that showing up at her house was their only recourse. Addie wasn't surprised by the leap. Changing the subject kept them both from dwelling on Gwen's insidious implications.

"Remember, we've got history and name recognition on our side," she said. "Vivian was a reporter assigned to the Twilight Killer investigation, and she planned to write a book about the case. She may be a recluse now, but I don't think she'll be able to resist seeing us."

They walked through the park, past the cannons and gazebo to Meeting Street, and then cut over to Tradd. The houses here were centuries old with hidden court-yards tucked away behind wrought iron gates and lay-ers of shady piazzas overlooking lavish gardens. For the longest time, they strolled in silence, watching their step on the cracked sidewalks. The morning was quiet and peaceful. A breeze stirred luscious perfumes from behind brick walls. A horse-drawn carriage clopped by on the street.

Addie told herself not to be lulled. Even in paradise, danger lurked. The historic district had been Orson Lee Finch's hunting ground. Most of his victims had come from South of Broad, though Addie's mother had grown up north of Calhoun. Ethan's grandparents had lived only a few blocks away. It seemed strange to think that their paths may have crossed when they were children.

"What's the house number?" Ethan asked. "We must be getting close."

"Yes, this is it." She pointed across the street to a three-story dark brick home with hunter green shutters.

Ethan whistled. "Ida McFall wasn't kidding about old money."

"The DuPriests go back a long way in this city," Addie said. "My grandmother knew the family slightly, though they hardly moved in the same circles. And of course, she became one of Vivian's most avid readers." They crossed the street, and Addie tried the gate. It swung inward with barely a squeak. "Must be a sign. Maybe she'll see us, after all."

The scent of jasmine trailed them to a side door, which was the main entrance on many of the old homes. Ethan rang the bell, and after a moment, a twentysomething man in khakis and a blue knit shirt the exact shade of his eyes answered. Their appearance seemed to confuse him. He glanced past them to the street as if he had been expecting someone else.

"Can I help y'all?" he drawled.

"We'd like to see Vivian DuPriest," Addie said.

"Honey, you and a few dozen other people." He gave them a reproving once-over. "I handle her schedule, so

I know she's not expecting anyone. If y'all are here to get a book signed or you want an interview, I'm afraid you're barking up the wrong tree. She doesn't do speaking engagements, either, nor is she interested in joining your book club. If you have other business, then I suggest you make an appointment."

Ethan took out his credentials. "I'm Special Agent Ethan Barrow with the FBI, and this is Detective Adaline Kinsella with the Charleston PD. We're here on a matter of some urgency."

The man scanned their IDs and then glanced up with a puzzled frown. "I don't understand. Is this about her niece's accident? She's already spoken to the police."

Ethan put away his credentials. "Tell her James Merrick's son would like to speak with her."

"And Sandra Kinsella's daughter," Addie said. "Please make sure you get those names right. Trust me, she'll want to see us."

The young man looked simultaneously annoyed and intrigued by their insistence. "Wait here."

He closed the door in their faces, and Addie exchanged a glance with Ethan. "He'll be back."

"We'll see."

The man returned a few minutes later and motioned them into a spacious foyer with paneled walls and marble floors. From there he led them down a wide hallway lined with gilt mirrors and family portraits. The house was beautifully appointed but dark and oppressive. Addie was glad when they were ushered into a garden room, where sunlight poured in through skylights. The effect was almost blinding after the dim hallway, and it took a moment to adjust to the brilliance. A wall of French doors looked out on a tropical wonderland of hibiscus, ginger and hummingbird trees.

Vivian DuPriest looked anything but traditional. Little wonder she had gravitated to the most dazzling room in the house, Addie thought. Her vivid red hair and turquoise kimono rivaled the showiness of her garden. She looked to be in her early sixties, petite but hardly fragile. She watched with avid curiosity as they came into the room, but she didn't rise to greet them.

"Thank you for agreeing to see us," Addie said.

The woman looked her up and down. "So you're Sandra Kinsella's daughter." She turned her attention to Ethan. "And you're James Merrick's son. You were children the last time I saw you. And look at you now. A police detective and an FBI agent. How interesting that you've both chosen careers in law enforcement. How intriguing that you've come here together. Would you like tea?"

Addie exchanged another glance with Ethan. "We're fine, thank you."

Vivian waved to a pair of wicker chairs with high backs and curved arms. "At least sit. I don't like lurkers."

They sat across from the sofa where she perched.

She picked up a floral teacup and sipped delicately as her gaze vectored back in on Ethan. "You look like James. I can see his kindness in your smile and his drive in your eyes. I sense something darker there, too, I think." She took another sip of her tea. "Your father was a very brilliant man."

"Did you know him well?" Ethan asked.

"Well enough, I suppose. I had the distinction of being the only reporter ever allowed to interview the great James Merrick. We got along well. I respected his boundaries, and he appreciated my discretion. And we both enjoyed a good scotch. I rarely leave my home these days, but when I still had a license, I would drive to the state capital to visit him now and then." She smiled as she regarded Ethan thoughtfully. "I see that surprises you."

"It does," he admitted. "Until recently, I was under the impression that I was my father's only visitor."

"Oh, I'm sure a great many people have gone to see James over the years. He is still a source of endless fascination. Whether he received any of those visitors is another question."

"But he agreed to see you," Ethan said.

"Yes. As I said, we always got on. I even tried to smuggle in a bottle of Johnnie Walker Blue once, but it was confiscated at the desk, more's the pity."

"Was he responsive when you saw him?"

"I suppose that depends on your definition."

Addie turned to glance at Ethan's profile. His arms rested on the curve of the chair, and he leaned forward slightly as if he were hanging on Vivian DuPriest's every word. She would appreciate that, but he wasn't faking interest to flatter her. He was hungry to hear about his father.

Something in his voice, the barest hint of hope, made Addie want to reach out to him. Not for the first time, she wondered what it must have been like for him as a child and then as an adolescent, living in the shadow of his father's guilt and desperately wanting to believe in his innocence. Addie's own childhood had been tragic. Losing her mother so violently had been devastating, and it had changed her in ways she would never fully understand. But Ethan's loss might have been harder to accept. Harder to live with, too.

Her gaze shifted to Vivian DuPriest. The woman was something of an enigma. On the surface, she seemed like an aging, eccentric Southern belle, but Addie suspected that was only one of her many personae. Beneath the rouged cheeks and ruby lips, the hardness of a once crack reporter still glimmered through.

Idly, she stirred her tea as she continued to ponder Ethan's question. "James never spoke to me when we visited. I did all the talking. He spent most of our time together looking out the window. He didn't have much of a view, but he seemed captivated by it nonetheless. I used to wonder what he was thinking. His eyes even then were so expressive. Was he responsive?" she mused to herself. "No, not in the way you mean. But I always had the sense that he knew who I was. And I think there was a part of him, some small corner of his consciousness, that remained fully engaged in my chitchat."

"When was the last time you saw him?" Ethan asked.

"Oh, it's been years. I can't even remember the last time. So many things have happened..." She trailed away on a wistful note. "It may sound strange considering his situation, but I wouldn't want him to see me as I am now. I was always so strong and resourceful. He admired that about me."

"I'm sure he did."

"I admired him, too. Such an intensely complicated man, your father. Handsome, too, and surprisingly charming when he wanted to be. It pains me the way we are now. Each of us a mere shell of our former self." She sighed. "I always wondered about his breakdown."

Ethan's voice sharpened. "What was there to wonder about?"

Vivian turned to stare out at the garden. A butterfly flitted over a yellow hibiscus, and she seemed momentarily transfixed. Then she rallied with a shrug. "I always prided myself on my perception. That was one of the things that set me apart as a reporter. I could read people so well. James's illness happened suddenly, and it manifested so violently. I never saw it coming."

"I don't know about sudden," Ethan said. "My mother told me that he had been seeing a therapist. He never told anyone else because of his job. He also consulted a neurologist, but no one could find the cause of his headaches and blackouts."

"You never told me that," Addie said.

Ethan glanced at her. "I only found out recently. But it doesn't change anything."

Addie lifted a brow. "I disagree, but we can discuss it later."

Vivian DuPriest watched them curiously, her gaze going from one to the other. "Oh, don't mind me. I'm just sitting here wondering what brought the two of you together. And why you've really come to see me."

"We'd like to talk to you about your niece," Addie said. "Naomi Quinlan."

Vivian leaned forward and topped off her teacup. "I've already spoken to the police. I don't know what more I can tell you."

"Detective Yates came to see you?"

"I don't know any Detective Yates," she said with a dismissive wave. "The deputy chief came to see me."

Addie stared at her for a moment. "David Cutler came to interview you?"

"*Interview* sounds too official. He came to pay me a courtesy call. Now you seem surprised, Detective Kinsella, but I don't know why you would be. Charleston is like a small town. Everyone knows everyone. The deputy chief and I go back a long way. Why wouldn't he come to see me in person rather than send one of his detectives?"

Something in the woman's tone, a flicker in her eyes brought Addie to the edge of her seat. Like Gwen Holloway earlier, what Vivian DuPriest said was not precisely what she meant.

Ethan must have caught the inflection, too. "You say you go back a long way. Did you become acquainted during the Twilight Killer case?"

"We go back even further than that, if you can imagine such a thing. I knew David Cutler when he was still a rookie. He was a good-looking young man and so very ambitious." She eyed them sagely over the rim of her cup. "He went out of his way to assure me that Naomi's death was a tragic accident, so I can't imagine why you would need to talk to me again. Unless, of course, the driver of the car that struck her has been found."

Addie shook her head. "No, not yet, I'm afraid."

Vivian's gaze flicked from one to the other. "Then why don't you tell me what this is really about?"

"We just want to ask you a few questions," Addie said. "We're trying to tie up some loose ends. Naomi's neighbor told us that you and your niece recently had a falling-out."

"By neighbor, I assume you mean Ida McFall. That woman is a terrible busybody, always has been. What else has she told you about me?"

"She said the two of you also go way back."

"Ah, did she? I suppose she mentioned the letters."

"She did, and we would love to hear more about them, but right now we're interested in your relationship with your niece. Ida implied you were upset with Naomi because of a book she was writing."

"I was upset with Naomi because she stole from me. The girl was a thief, plain and simple. I caught her red-handed, so I kicked her out."

"What did she steal?" Addie asked.

"Notes, interviews, research materials. She even pilfered the first draft of my manuscript. She planned to tweak it a bit and pass it off as her own. And after everything I did for her. I brought her into my home when she had nowhere else to go, gave her work, a purpose in life, and that's how she planned to repay me. By stealing my legacy."

"You obviously have strong feelings about Naomi," Addie said.

"Why wouldn't I? I inherited money, but I earned my writing credentials by working hard and paying my dues. And yes, I do realize that my passion makes me somewhat suspect, but I didn't run down poor Naomi. As I said, I rarely leave my house these days, and the deputy chief *assured* me that her death was an accident. But your visit suggests otherwise."

"It's an ongoing investigation," Addie said.

"I see."

"Could you tell us what was included in your research materials?" Ethan asked. "Crime-scene photos, autopsy reports…?" He left the question hanging.

"All of the above. Back in those days, I was well connected. I would sometimes receive a copy of the autopsy report and toxicology screen before they were even sent to the detective on the case. I know what you're thinking," she said as she settled more deeply into the sofa. "But I never betrayed my sources, nor did I use information until I was authorized to do so. Despite my extensive contacts, I never compromised a single investigation."

"Were you assigned to my mother's case?" Addie asked.

"I was assigned to all the major cases. The Twilight

Killer investigation took a toll, but your mother's murder was especially troubling. We all thought the killings were over, and then another victim turned up. And to later find out that someone I admired and respected had been accused of such a gruesome crime. I can't imagine what your family went through," she said to Addie. "I knew your grandmother in passing. We belonged to the same garden club for a time. A lovely woman. I was sorry to come across her obituary in the paper."

"Thank you," Addie said. "Were you given a copy of my mother's autopsy report?"

"No, and that was unusual. My contacts knew they could trust me, but from the start, that investigation took a strange turn. There was a complete information blackout. It was as if my sources were afraid to talk me."

"Why would they be afraid?"

"Perhaps their jobs had been threatened. I don't know. I was never given or shown a copy of your mother's autopsy report, but I was fed certain tidbits under the table." She spoke carefully, as if she were gauging Addie's reaction.

"Someone told you that she was pregnant, didn't they?"

Her brow furrowed. "It was only a rumor. I didn't print it because I couldn't corroborate the information. No one would comment on the record. I could barely get anyone to talk off the record. I always wondered why the investigation operated in such secrecy. And why so many of the case files were sealed so quickly."

"You must have a theory," Ethan said.

Vivian glanced at him. "I never thought James committed that murder. No matter his frame of mind, violence wasn't in him." She turned back to Addie. "I've always believed the key to solving your mother's murder was hidden in her unborn baby's DNA. Find the father, find the killer."

Addie's heart thudded. She had the sudden urge to rush out of the room and leave the rest of Vivian Du-Priest's story untold. "I don't know what to say to that. I don't know if I believe it."

Vivian's gaze darkened. "Why do you think I was attacked and beaten so viciously? I was on the trail of the truth. I would have uncovered everything eventually. But my recovery took a toll, physically and mentally. For nearly a year, I couldn't walk. I couldn't feed or bathe myself. It was a humbling and humiliating experience."

"You don't know who attacked you?" Addie asked.

"I was completely blindsided. Knocked unconscious and left for dead. It's a miracle I'm alive. Like your mother's murder, the investigation surrounding my attack was shrouded in secrecy. I always felt someone with clout was pulling strings. Maybe in the police department, maybe in the FBI. I had enemies in both camps. After James was sent away, no one wanted the truth to come out."

"A third person's DNA was found at the scene of Sandra Kinsella's murder," Ethan said. "That person was never identified. Two weeks before your niece's death, she emailed me to say that she'd sent a sample of that DNA to a public database and had gotten a hit. She insisted that I come to Charleston so that we could speak in person. But before I could arrange my schedule, she was killed in the hit-and-run."

"You don't say," Vivian said.

Ethan watched her for a moment. "So you already knew about the DNA results. Naomi stole that sample from you, didn't she?"

"I won't comment about the sample or how and when it was acquired. Naomi was a genealogist. Naturally such a mystery would appeal to her. She came to me with the results. I'm sure I must have been a last resort after everything she'd done, but she was stymied. She'd made contact, she said. She and the donor had emailed back and forth, and she'd found out his name and address, but she couldn't connect him to the murder or even to the Twilight Killer case in general. I did some digging and called in a few favors, but the man was a ghost."

"Could you share his name with us?" Addie asked. "Maybe the two of us can find out something."

Vivian hesitated. "You should know that Naomi was struck down by that car only a few days after she came to see me."

"You don't think the hit-and-run was an accident, do you?" Ethan asked.

"I was *assured* that it was."

He glanced at Addie even as he addressed his question to Vivian. "Did you tell David Cutler about Naomi's research?"

Vivian leaned forward and removed the lid from a porcelain box on the coffee table. She took out a slip of paper and handed it to Addie. "I told the deputy chief what he wanted to hear. What I needed him to hear. Naomi led a quiet, mundane life. There was no reason in the world that anyone would want to harm her. Or me, for that matter."

Chapter Fourteen

"That was an interesting visit," Addie said as they headed back to her car. She handed Ethan the folded paper. "We now have a name and address, which is a lot more than we had an hour ago. Although according to Vivian, he's a ghost, so we'll have to do some digging."

"I'll run the name through our databases and see what I can come up with," Ethan said as he glanced down at the name and address. "Daniel Roby. Doesn't ring a bell for me."

"For me, either. Let's go check out that address. Maybe after we talk to him, we'll have some answers."

"I appreciate your enthusiasm, but we need to play this smart," Ethan said. "If we barge in and start asking a lot of questions, we could spook him. I'm guessing the reason he's a ghost is because he has something to hide. Whether it has anything to do with the DNA results remains to be seen, but anyone that low profile usually has a sketchy background. Daniel Roby may not even be his real name."

"What do you suggest we do then?"

"We watch him. We stake out his place. See where he goes, where he works, if he has any visitors. We find out all we can about him before we tip our hand."

Addie glanced up with a frown. "Stake out his place for how long?"

"For as long as it takes. A few days. A week, maybe."

She grimaced. "A week? Ugh. No. I don't have that kind of time to devote to a stakeout, and besides, I hate surveillance. I vote the direct approach."

"Let's compromise," Ethan said. "We watch his place for the rest of the day and then we play it by ear."

"Agreed." She used her remote to unlock her vehicle and then slid behind the wheel while Ethan went around to climb in on the other side. "Let me see that address again." He handed her the paper and she nodded. "Yeah, I know where that street is. It's in Westside before you get to the Citadel." She glanced up at the buzzing vibration of a cell phone.

"Not mine," Ethan said.

"I didn't have time to get a burner, so I left mine in the glove box." She leaned over and extracted the phone, then frowned as she checked her missed calls. "Helen called three times while we were gone." Alarmed, she pressed the play button on her messages and lifted the phone to her ear. "Oh, no."

"What is it?"

She glanced at him as she listened. "David was rushed to the hospital this morning. They think he had a heart attack."

"What's his condition?"

Addie shook her head. "I don't know. Helen says they're running tests." She listened to another message before putting the phone away. "She sounds frantic. I'm sorry, but I have to get to the hospital."

"Yeah, of course. You need me to drive you?"

"No, I'm fine. Sorry about bailing on our surveillance."

"Don't worry about it. I turned in my rental, but I can get another. It's better if we don't use your vehicle for surveillance, anyway."

She nodded. "You'll call me if you find out anything?"

"I'll keep you posted. And you call me if there's any news, okay?"

"I will."

He opened the door to get out and then glanced back. "It'll be okay, Addie. He's a strong guy. Stubborn, too."

"I know. It's just…when I saw him yesterday, I remember thinking how old he looked, and that surprised me. I'd never thought so before. He always seemed so timeless. I never expected this."

"You'll feel better after you see him," Ethan said. "Just be careful, okay? Keep your guard up even while you're at the hospital."

"You, too. Ethan?"

"Yes?"

She bit her lip. "Nothing. I'll see you soon."

She watched him in the rearview mirror as she pulled away from the curb. He kept his gaze on her, too. It was as if neither of them wanted to be the first to break eye contact. As if this might be the last time they were together.

Which was crazy. These were dangerous times, but she and Ethan knew how to take care of themselves. Everything would be fine.

She repeated that sentiment as she drove to the hospital and then as she rode the elevator up to the sixth floor. She exited the lift and glanced around for a moment to get her bearings. A man came down the hallway toward her. He was dressed casually in jeans and a

T-shirt with a baseball cap pulled low over his features. He was average height, average build…

Addie was so preoccupied with worry that she barely paid him any mind. Only after he had passed her in they hallway did she turn for a second glance. He had stepped onto the elevator, and his head was bowed as he pushed the button. She could only see the lower part of his face, but Addie could have sworn she saw a grin flash.

Her mind went back to the alley and to the moment when she and her stalker had come face-to-face. Then as now she'd only glimpsed his lower face, but she couldn't forget that sneer.

Her heart thudded and she stood staring at the closed elevator doors for the longest time until she heard someone call her name. She turned to find Helen hurrying toward her.

"Thank goodness you're here, Addie. I was so worried when I couldn't reach you."

"I'm sorry. I didn't have my phone with me. I only got your messages a few minutes ago."

"That's not like you," Helen said. "I'm the one who misplaces phones."

"I didn't misplace it. I just didn't have it with me. Not that it matters. How's David?"

"They've taken him downstairs for more tests." She looped her arm through Addie's and guided her to a quiet bench. "His room is just down that way. We'll see them when they bring him back up."

"Have they told you anything?"

"The preliminary tests look good. They don't think it's his heart, after all. It's more than likely stress related. He may have had a panic attack."

"That doesn't sound like David. He's usually a rock."

Helen frowned. "He's so strong that I sometimes think we forget he's human. So does he. He just keeps pushing himself. He refuses to acknowledge that we're not as young as we used to be. When this is all over, we're making some changes. I know people always say that in a crisis, but I mean it. I won't lose him," she said fiercely.

"You're not going to lose him," Addie said. "If it's stress related, then maybe this will turn out to be a blessing in disguise. You've wanted him to cut back his hours for ages. Maybe this will finally be the catalyst."

"I'll need you on my side," Helen said.

"I'm always on your side."

She let out a long breath. "Do you have any idea how glad I am to see you?"

"I'm sorry I wasn't here earlier. And I'm sorry if I caused *you* stress."

"You're here now. That's all that matters." Helen studied her for a moment. "Are you okay?"

"Yes, of course. Why wouldn't I be?"

"I can always tell when something is bothering you."

"It's not important."

"If it's bothering you, then it's important," Helen said. "What's going on?"

Addie hesitated. "I really didn't want to get into this right now. You've enough on your mind. But I know you'll keep badgering me until I tell you, so..." She trailed off. "Someone tried to break into my house last night."

Helen stared at her in shock. "What? Did you call the police?"

"I am the police, remember?"

Helen's tone turned reproachful. "You know what I mean. Did you file an official report?"

"I haven't had a chance. I've been busy with other things, but we don't need to worry about that right now. I would like to ask you something, though."

"Of course. Anything."

"Remember the other day when you told me you'd lost your phone? Did you ever find it?"

Something flickered in Helen's eyes before she glanced away. "Yes, as a matter of fact, it was underneath the desk in my office. I must have knocked it off without realizing it."

"Is it possible someone took it without you knowing and then returned it?"

"I can't imagine such a thing. Who would steal a phone and then return it?"

"Someone who wanted to get information from it," Addie said.

"What information?"

"You and I texted back and forth before I left on vacation. I reminded you of the alarm code and where you could find the extra key. All of that information was right there in our text messages."

"How would anyone else know about that? And besides, I keep my phone locked just as a precaution against that very thing." Her gaze met Addie's. "There's something you're not telling me. Why on earth would you think someone had gotten your information from my phone?"

"I'm just trying to figure out how this person came by a key to my front door and possibly the code to my security system. The alarm went off last night after I'd changed the code. But night before last, I could have sworn someone had been in my house without setting off the alarm. That would only be possible if the person knew the code."

Helen put a hand on Addie's arm. "You're scaring me with all this talk. Someone came into your house while you were asleep? Are you sure?"

"I'm sure about last night. We caught a glimpse of the suspect as he cut through my neighbor's backyard."

"We?"

"Ethan Barrow was there."

"Oh, Addie."

"I know what you're thinking, but you don't need to worry about me," Addie said. "I know how to take care of myself."

Helen lifted her hand to Addie's cheek. "I know you do, but I'll always worry about you, sweet girl."

"Let's just focus on David right now."

Helen tensed. "We don't need to mention this to him. You know how he feels about Ethan. His blood pressure is through the roof as it is."

"I won't say anything."

"There he is." Helen rose and squared her shoulders. She took a breath and pasted a smile on her face. "How do I look?"

"Beautiful," Addie said.

But her mind was still on their conversation and the term of endearment that Helen had used. No one but Sandra Kinsella had ever called Addie *sweet girl*.

ADDIE SPENT MOST of the day at the hospital, only leaving for a short time to have the locks changed on her doors and then returning to relieve Helen while she went home to rest. David dozed for most of the day. When he awakened, he stared out the window, saying very little to Helen or Addie, but he looked as if he had the weight of the world on his shoulders.

Intermittently, Addie received text messages from

Ethan. He had parked down the street from the subject's house but hadn't seen anyone coming or going for hours.

How are things at the hospital?

Fine. David is sleeping. Helen is reading. I may slip out of here soon. I hate hospitals. Even a stakeout is preferable.

Let me know if you're coming. I'll watch for you.

Okay.

Have to go now. Someone just pulled up in the driveway. I'll see if I can get a closer look.

Be careful, Ethan.

"Who are you texting?" Helen asked.

Addie slipped the phone in her pocket as she glanced up. "A friend."

Helen's lips thinned. "A friend, huh? I'll bet."

David said weakly, "Did I miss something? What is going on with you two?"

"Nothing, dear. I'm just giving Addie a hard time."

"Well, don't," he said. "What would our lives be without her?"

"I shudder to think," Helen murmured.

Addie went to his bedside. "How are you feeling?"

He tried to muster a smile. "Cranky. I hate hospitals."

"I know. So do I."

"Then go home," he said firmly. "You've got a big day tomorrow, and there's no point in both of you staying. I wish Helen would go home, too. I don't need a babysitter."

"Well, that's too bad, because you're stuck with me." Helen moved to the other side of his bed. "So long as you're in here, I'm not leaving your side. Not tonight, not ever."

David's gaze turned solemn. "We've been through a lot together, Helen."

"Yes, we have, dear."

He took her hand, entwining his fingers with hers. "I thought I was going to die this morning. So many things went through my head. There's so much I need to say to both of you."

"Shush. We don't need to talk about any of that right now," Helen said.

"Helen—"

"Please, David, not now." Her voice came out sharper than she had undoubtedly meant it. "You need your rest, and we don't need to upset Addie with all this talk about dying."

"Addie?" He said her name as if he'd forgotten about her presence.

"I'm right here, David."

"Your mother loved you very much. You need to know that."

"David, *hush*. You're working yourself up into a state, and the doctor said you need to remain calm." Helen glanced across the bed at Addie. "Would you mind giving us a moment alone?"

"No, of course not. I'll be right outside if you need me."

She moved toward the door, pausing for a moment to glance back over her shoulder. Helen was leaning over the bed, speaking to David in a low voice as she gripped his hand. He turned his head, and for one brief moment, his gaze met Addie's before she slipped out the door.

Her phone rang as she headed down the hallway toward the waiting room. She glanced around as she answered. "Hello?"

"It's Ethan."

"Are you okay? What's going on?"

"I'm sending you a photo I just snapped of Daniel Roby. At least I think that's who he is. He went inside the house about an hour ago, and now he's just come back out again. I'm going to have a look around."

"I don't think that's a good idea," Addie said. "What did you tell me earlier? We need to gather as much information as we can on this guy before we tip our hand."

"I'll be in and out before anyone knows I'm around."

"Ethan, don't do that. I'm just down the street from you. I can be there in ten minutes. Don't do anything without backup. You know that's what you'd tell me."

He laughed softly. "Probably. And you'd do exactly as I'm doing. Don't worry, Addie. I'll be careful. Did the text come through?"

"I'm looking at the photo now." She switched to the text window. "His head is turned away from the camera. I can barely see him."

"Sorry. That was the best I could do. Hang on. I think I've found a way in. I'll call you back in a minute."

"No, Ethan! Wait for me."

The call went dead. She swore under her breath as she walked over to the window to study the photo. She couldn't see the man's features, but she recognized the clothing and the ball cap pulled over his face. He was the man who had gotten on the elevator behind her.

The phone buzzed, and she jumped. "Ethan?"

"Addie?" His voice sounded strained. "You have to

see this place. He's blown up the crime-scene photos and plastered them all over his walls. And there's trash all over the place just like in Naomi's attic. He must have felt the need to hide out there for a while. Or else he was looking for something. The DNA sample most likely."

"If that's true, you need to get out of there before he comes back," Addie said.

"He's got pictures of you, too, Addie. He's your stalker."

Her heart thudded. "Who is he? How does he know me?"

"Whoever he is, he's obviously been watching you for a long time. I'm sending you more images."

"Ethan, the first photograph you sent me. I think I saw him at the hospital this morning. I was just getting off the elevator. But that doesn't make any sense. How would he know I would be here?"

She heard a muffled voice in the background, a crash, and then the call dropped.

"Ethan? Are you there? What happened? Ethan?"

"Is something wrong?" Helen had come up behind her.

Addie whirled. "I don't know. I lost the connection."

Helen frowned. "Was that Ethan Barrow on the phone just now? Where is he? Did something happen?"

"That's what I'm trying to find out. I have to go, Helen. I'll be back as quickly as I can."

"Yes, of course," Helen said. "I'll take care of everything here."

Chapter Fifteen

Addie parked down the street from the address that Vivian DuPriest had given them. Since she didn't know what kind of car Ethan had rented, she had no way of knowing whether his was among the vehicles lined up along the curb. She sat for a moment taking stock of her surroundings. The houses in the neighborhood were small, single-story cottages that had seen better days. College students gravitated to the area because of the rent and the proximity to MUSC. Someone wanting to keep a low profile wouldn't attract much attention with the high turnover in renters.

Addie hoped that she had overreacted to Ethan's dropped call, but she'd tried to reach him a half dozen times on the short trip from the hospital. Something was wrong. She could feel it in her gut.

Exiting the vehicle, she slipped her weapon in the small bag she wore across her body. Then she headed down the sidewalk, glancing over her shoulder to make certain she wasn't followed. She'd texted the address to Matt, and common sense told her she should wait for her partner. But if Ethan was in trouble, timing could be everything.

She checked the front entrance and then circled the house. The back door stood ajar. She went up the steps and glanced through the crack. Drawing her weapon, she toed open the door and entered quickly, clearing each room before moving on to the next.

As she eased into the front room, her gaze lit on the giant photographs pinned to the walls. Slowly, she moved about the room scanning the macabre gallery. Her gaze went to the crime-scene photos first and then to the wall that had been devoted exclusively to her. She had been captured at the lake, at police headquarters, even coming out of her house. Every facet of her life displayed on a madman's canvas.

The creak of a floorboard alerted her to danger, and she whirled. Helen had come in the back way behind her. She stood just inside the room gazing at the disturbing images.

"My God," she whispered.

Addie lowered her weapon. "Helen, what are you doing here?"

"I knew you were in trouble, so I followed you."

Addie started across the room toward her. "That was a foolish thing to do. We need to get you out of here."

"What is this place?" Helen moved to the wall of crime-scene photos, lifting a hand to her heart as she took in the image of Addie's mother lying in a pool of blood. "I've never seen this before."

"Neither had I."

Helen glanced over her shoulder. "Oh, Addie, she was so young and so beautiful even in death. How it must hurt you to see her like this."

"It does hurt, but I can't dwell on that now. It's not safe for you to be in this house. The man who lives here could be back any minute, and he's obviously unstable. Please, Helen, just go back to the hospital. I don't want to have to worry about you, too."

Helen seemed not to hear her. Her gaze was still on the grisly images. "She was beautiful, Addie, I admit it. But she was also selfish. You can't imagine. She could be cruel, too. I need you to know that."

Addie's heart fluttered in alarm. "Helen? What are you talking about?"

She turned and met Addie's gaze. Something in her eyes…in her voice…

"She didn't deserve you."

Addie took a step back, her blood icy with shock. "No. Helen, not you…"

"David was wrong earlier. She didn't love you. Not really. She only cared about herself. The last thing she needed was another baby."

"You knew she was pregnant?"

Helen nodded. "I guessed. She didn't deny it."

Addie's hands trembled as she lifted the weapon. "So you killed her? That doesn't even make sense, Helen." Her gaze went to the photographs. "None of this makes any sense."

"It does if you look at it from my point of view." Helen's voice was soft and smooth and deceptively persuasive. "I loved you like my very own daughter. Cared for you when she didn't have the time or the inclination. She wanted to take you away from me. She wanted you and David all to herself. She was going to give him the family that I never could."

Addie's hand tightened on the weapon. "How could you do such a thing? If you loved me, how could you take my mother away from me?"

"I never wanted to hurt you, sweet girl."

"Don't call me that."

"I don't want to hurt you now. I just want you to understand. I want you to hear my story."

"I'll listen to whatever you have to say, but I'll never understand how you could kill my mother in cold blood. How you could pretend to love me after what you did. You're sick, Helen. You must know that."

Helen's gaze hardened. "A mother does what she has to in order to protect her family."

"You're not my mother."

"I was in all the ways that mattered. You were the child I always wanted and could never have again."

"Again?"

"I had a baby once. I was young and just out of high school. The father left town when he found about the pregnancy. I made the decision to give my son up for adoption. It was the hardest thing I've ever had to do, and I never got over the loss. They say you still feel pain in a severed limb. It's the same with a missing child. Your arms never stop aching. Until you have a baby of your own, you'll never be able to fathom my torment."

"I'm sure it must have been difficult for you," Addie said, willing to placate Helen while she waited for backup.

"Difficult? You've no idea. I told myself I'd done the right thing. He was better off in a good home with two loving parents who could give him everything he needed. But I never forgot him. I never stopped looking for him. And then I met David. He became my whole world, and I thought when we had a child together that I would finally be able to put the past behind me. But years went by, and it never happened for us.

"Then one day I saw you, Addie. I used to walk past your little house on my way to work. Sometimes you would be in the yard playing by yourself or looking out the window at passersby. You were always alone. You seemed so forlorn to me. So starved for a mother's love, and I had so much love to give."

"I had a mother," Addie said. "And she did love me."

"But she loved herself more. She wasn't fit to call herself a mother. I saw how much needed me, so I started stopping by just to say hi. Sandra would sometimes invite me in for a chat. We became friends. She loved that I was so willing to look after you whenever she wanted to go out. She thought I was doing her a favor, but it was the other way around." Helen smiled dreamily. "Our arrangement worked out well for a time. We were all happy. I enjoyed her company, and I came to love you as if you were my own. I couldn't bear the thought of anyone taking you away from me."

"What happened that night?" Addie asked.

"She came to get you at ten, just as she said she would. She was acting very strange that night. Mysterious. She said the two of you might be moving away soon. She was sorry because she knew that I would miss you. The last thing she ever wanted to do was hurt me, but sometimes life happened. That's how she put it. *Life happened*. So cavalier and self-centered. After everything I'd done for her."

"So you lost your temper," Addie said. "It was a crime of passion. I'm just trying to understand how someone I've looked up to and admired, someone I've thought of as family all these years, could do something so unspeakable. You must have been out of your mind with rage."

"Actually, I was calm and resolved," Helen said. "I knew what I had to do. I'd been thinking about it for a while, longer even than I wanted to admit. As it happened, James Merrick was a patient of mine. He'd been coming to see me ever since he arrived in Charleston. I knew about his blackouts, the memory loss, the disorientation. Do you know why memory-regression hypnosis is so unreliable? The subject is completely malleable. Completely susceptible to false memory implantation."

Addie stared at her in horror. "You made him think he killed my mother? You did that to a man who already thought he was losing his mind? You deliberately pushed him over the edge. And then you planted his DNA at the crime scene."

"I did what I had to do," Helen said simply.

"But you overlooked one thing, didn't you? You left your own DNA. What happened? Did you cut yourself in the attack?"

"It wasn't very deep. I never gave it a second thought. The data banks were never going to find a match, because I'd never committed any crimes."

"And then Naomi Quinlan submitted that sample to a public database. And she got a hit." Addie glanced around. "Who lives here, Helen? Who is Daniel Roby?"

"He's my son."

Addie shuddered as she lifted her gaze to the crime-scene photos. "Where is he now?"

Helen's expression turned dreamy again. "I located him some time ago. I didn't know if he'd want to see me, but it turned out that he'd been looking for me, too."

"He sent a sample of his DNA to one of the databases," Addie said.

"Yes. We became close very quickly. It was as if we'd never been apart. He needed me, you see. And I needed him."

Addie lifted her gaze to the photographs. "You told him about my mother?"

"I told him everything. He needed to know that there were people who would try to keep us apart. He came to me as soon as Naomi made contact. We knew she would discover the truth sooner or later, and we'd already lost so much time together. We didn't want to lose each other again."

"So you manipulated him into running her over with his car. Your own son."

Helen's eyes glittered. "My son would do anything for me as I would for him. I won't let anyone take him from me again. Not Naomi Quinlan. Not Ethan Barrow. Not even you, Addie." She turned her head toward the hall but kept her gaze on Addie. "Where are you, Danny?"

A disembodied voice said softly, "I'm here, Mother."

THE GUN IN his back prodded Ethan forward. Hands clasped behind his head, he moved down the hallway and into the front room. Addie's eyes widened at the blood on the side of his face, but the raised weapon in her hand never wavered.

"Drop your gun," Ethan's captor told her. "Do it now or your boyfriend gets a bullet in the brain."

"Don't do it, Addie," Ethan warned. "He'll kill us, anyway."

The man clipped him in the back of his head with the gun so hard Ethan stumbled forward. His captor pushed him to his knees and aimed the barrel at his skull.

"Okay, okay." Addie's gaze was still on Ethan as she bent and placed the gun on the floor.

"Slide it away," the man ordered.

Addie did as she was told. When she straightened, her gaze flicked to Helen. "Does David know you're here? Is he in on this?"

"I don't want to talk about David," she said. "I didn't want any of this to happen. You have to know that. But you left me no choice. You couldn't leave well enough alone."

"So he doesn't know," Addie said. "But he must suspect. That's why he sealed the case files. That's why he questioned Naomi's neighbor about the comings and goings from her house. The weight of those suspicions is what put him in the hospital."

"David is going to be fine," Helen insisted. "I'll find a way to make it up to him."

"Just as you plan to make up all those missing years with your son?" Ethan said as his gaze met Addie's. "You want to know why he's been following you? All those years of love and attention that Helen lavished on you should have been his. That's why he follows you. That's why he torments you. He's just a jealous little boy."

Roby pressed the gun into Ethan's nape. "Stop talking."

"You're too jealous to realize that your own mother is manipulating you," Ethan taunted. "You think she cares about you? She doesn't. She'll throw you away as soon as you've done her dirty work."

Helen stepped forward, eyes blazing. "That's not true, Danny. Don't listen to him. This is all for you. Everything we're doing is so we can finally be together. Please, son. Stick to the plan. It'll all be over soon."

"Who came up with this plan?" Addie asked as her gaze shifted to Daniel Roby. "Make no mistake, she's already thought this through. She'll put all the blame on you, Danny. Getting rid of Naomi, getting rid of us... it's all part of *her* plan. She'll convince people you're crazy. She'll have you put away just like she did James Merrick."

Helen must have sensed a weakening in her son, because she said quickly, "Just do it. Don't think about it, sweet boy. Just do what has to be done and then set this place on fire. Burn it to the ground so that nothing can be traced back to us. Afterward, go to the cabin and wait for me just as we planned. Do it, Danny. Do it for your mother—"

Her plea was cut off by a loud crash. The front door flew open and Matt Lepear, flanked by two officers, stood with his weapon at the ready as he quickly sized up the situation. Ethan used the diversion to grab Daniel's arm and bring him to the floor. Seizing the gun, he put a foot against Daniel's throat as he took aim.

Meanwhile, Addie lunged for her weapon and then for Helen. The woman collapsed to the floor and buried her face in her hands. "What have I done? Oh, Addie, what have I done?"

"It's a little late to worry about that now." Addie was numb to Helen's remorse. The pain would come later when the dust had settled and yet another loss set in. She turned to Matt. "I see you got my text."

"Yeah, you okay?"

"I'm fine, but Ethan needs the EMTs."

"No, I'm good." He jerked Daniel Roby to his feet and turned him over to one of the officers. Then he crossed the room to Addie. His eyes were dark and deep as he gazed down at her. "Thanks for coming to my rescue."

"Always." For a moment she was mesmerized by that stare. "But we should both thank Matt."

"Damn right," Matt agreed. His gaze went back to the images on the wall. Then he took in Helen's huddled form on the floor. "Is that—"

"Yes."

He shook his head. "What have you gotten yourself into this time?"

"It's a long story," Addie said. "Twenty-five years in the making."

Matt's gaze shifted to Ethan and then back to Addie. "How about you give me the short version."

"In a minute," she murmured as Ethan pulled her into his arms and kissed her.

[faint mirrored text visible at top of page, illegible]

Chapter Sixteen

The next day, Addie stood on the Battery watching the waves roll in. Behind her, the sun was just setting over the Ashley River, casting a gilded glow over the cityscape. A breeze blew gently across the water, stirring the scent of jasmine from the walled gardens along East Bay. It was the perfect time of day, when shadows lengthened and anticipation settled like a velvety whisper.

She felt his presence before she heard her name. She turned to search the walkway, her gaze moving quickly through the tourists until she found him. He was dressed in his usual dark suit, but he'd taken off his jacket and tie, loosened his collar and rolled up his sleeves. Addie's heart quickened at the sight of him. Like her, he still wore the cuts and bruises that punctuated the end of their investigation. Addie wanted to go to him, to wrap her arms around his waist and lay her head against his shoulder, but she held back. If he was coming to tell her goodbye, she needed to be stoic.

"Thanks for meeting me," he said.

"Of course. I've plenty of time on my hands. You heard Gwen canceled the training session?" When he nodded, Addie said, "I guess she needs time to process everything that's happened."

"I'm sure she's concerned how all this will affect her bottom line, which is probably why she worked so hard to get us to back off the investigation in the first place."

"Do you think she knew your dad was innocent?"

He shrugged. "I don't know. Her ego may not have let her entertain doubts about her profile. In any case, it's over now."

Addie paused. "Did you see your father today?"

"Yes."

"How did it go?"

Ethan stared out over the water for the longest moment. "I knew what to expect. I knew nothing had changed for *him*, and yet a part of me—the kid who watched his hero disintegrate twenty-five years ago—hoped that the truth would somehow set him free."

"You're free," Addie said. "You always believed in his innocence. You never gave up. All those years I thought your father killed my mother. And then to find out that the woman I trusted more than anyone in this world did what she did to your father. Helen and David Cutler were everything to me after my mother died. They helped raised me. It's because of David that I became a cop. And now I know that he helped cover up Helen's crimes. Out of loyalty and guilt and maybe love, but..." She broke off. "His reasons don't matter. I'm sorry, Ethan. I'm so sorry."

He took her face in his hands. "You've nothing to be sorry about. None of this is on you or me. We were both collateral damage."

"It's a lot to process. I feel like I've lost my family all over again."

He gazed down into her eyes. "You're not alone, Addie."

Her heart started to pound. "I don't want you to worry about me, okay? I'll be fine."

"What if I want to worry about you? What if I don't want to be alone?" He dropped his hands to his sides and turned back to the water as if were suddenly unsure of himself. "There's an opening in the field office here in Charleston. I'm considering putting in for a transfer."

Addie laid her hand on his arm. "Don't do that. Not for me. You'd kill your career with that transfer."

"Someone wise once told me that a career is not the worst thing a person can lose." He turned back to her, his gaze earnest. "I'm not asking for a commitment. I'm just asking for another chance."

She closed her eyes and let the breeze and his voice wash over her. "Welcome home, Ethan."

* * * * *

A COLTON TARGET

BEVERLY LONG

To the many women in my family who are moms and teachers and handle both roles so skillfully. You're making a difference and I thank you for that.

Chapter One

Blaine Colton woke up in a strange bed. Which wasn't that unusual, given how he'd spent the last thirteen years. But the fact that he was at Colton Manor, in one of its many guest rooms, made it not all that great.

His parents' home was big enough that a map would be helpful. And built soundly, with well-insulated walls, making it difficult to tell if anyone else in the house was yet awake. But just in case they were, he stayed right where he was.

He'd arrived too late last night for any real conversation. Had made small talk with his mom and been relieved to learn that his dad was at a late-evening meeting. Then he'd looked in on his grandfather Earl, who had his own suite within Colton Manor, and had apologized for missing the man's ninety-fourth birthday celebration. Although he wasn't sure the old man had fully grasped who he was, Blaine had thought he seemed happy enough.

Perhaps happier than he was. Generally, upon waking, he had a purpose. Lives depended upon it. Now, he turned his head, stared at the wallpaper with its pale green background and tan vertical stripes, and started counting. When he got to the corner of the room, he turned his head again, and did the opposite wall.

Forty-two stripes on each side. A big room.

He had not been raised in this showplace, aka home. It had been built long after he'd moved away. Enlisted in the army. The organization where he'd served with pride.

Before he'd thrown it all away.

And had to come back, in disgrace. Well, almost. Unbeknownst to him, his father, the powerful Russ Colton, had asked a favor of his even-more powerful cousin, former president Joe Colton, and with a wave of a wand or some greasing of palms, depending on your perspective of government, his discharge paperwork had been altered.

Honorable was a much nicer word.

Blaine owed his father—never a comfortable position to be in. *I want you to come home.* That's what his father had said.

It wasn't as if he had anyplace else to go. His friend Rylan Bennet, who'd fallen hard and fast for Blaine's cousin Bree, had offered to put a good word in for him with Rylan's old security company. But he'd passed on that. Couldn't really think about anything permanent until he did what he needed to do here.

He'd express his gratitude to his father. But so help him, if Russ even hinted that Blaine had made worse choices than he'd made over the course of his own lifetime, it wasn't going to be pretty. That man was the reason he'd left Roaring Springs some thirteen years ago. The reason he'd returned only sporadically, until now.

To be a stranger in a strange house.

Who had nothing but time on his hands. Hiding in his bed, counting stripes.

He threw back the covers. The hell with that.

FORTY MINUTES LATER, Blaine stood outside his brother Decker's office, located in the far corner of the top floor of The Lodge. While he'd never been inside it before, he knew, from a photo that Decker had once shared, that his two walls of mostly windows offered magnificent views of both the Rocky Mountains and, in the distance, the town of Roaring Springs.

He opened the heavy door, and a woman sitting behind a desk, her hands on a computer keyboard, looked up. She had very short dark hair and was dressed in a black business suit. Maybe midforties. He was confident that this was Penny. Decker had mentioned his administrative assistant a few times over the years. Always favorably.

"Good morning," she said politely. "How may I help you?"

She probably thought he was a lost guest, looking for his way to the coffee shop. He flashed a smile. "I'm here to see Decker."

"Do you have an appointment, sir?"

He shook his head. "I'm his brother."

He could see the wheels turning in her head. She thought she knew Decker's family. After all, most of them worked in some way for the Colton Empire, as his father liked to call it.

"Blaine Colton," he added for clarity. It wasn't as if he expected that Decker had spent much time talking about him in the office. And he'd been gone for years. In places doing things he couldn't talk about. Ever.

She picked up her phone. "Your brother Blaine is here to see you," she said. Then she listened. "Of course," she murmured before hanging up. Now she was eyeing him with some speculation. "He'll be right out. And he asked me to cancel his nine o'clock."

Decker wanted some time. Probably didn't want him to have to hurry his explanation. Blaine owed him that. Might owe him a lot more before their meeting was over because he was here to ask a favor.

Another debt of gratitude. He was going to have a pile at the rate he was going.

Not a comfortable situation for a man who'd spent more than thirteen years never asking for or expecting any favors from anyone.

He sank down into a chair, but his brother didn't keep him waiting long. In less than two minutes, he was striding through a connecting door, his face showing very little emotion. But the rough hug and the solid pat in the middle of his back said enough. Decker was happy to have him home. Over the years, he likely had envisioned that when this moment came, Blaine might be in a casket with a flag draped over it.

"I was going to come by the house tonight," Decker said, pulling back.

Blaine had suspected as much. But this wasn't the kind of conversation one had over cocktails. Or in front of an administrative assistant, regardless of how loyal she might be. "Can we talk?" he asked.

"Of course."

Decker's office was big but not fancy. Polished wood floor and a nice rug that he suspected his brother had had some help picking out. There was a big desk, maybe cherry, and a black leather chair, placed so that Decker could work and enjoy the view the windows offered. Two comfortable-looking tan leather chairs sat in front of the desk. But Decker didn't lead him there. Instead, he headed for a round table in the corner. Four more leather chairs. They took seats across from one another.

Blaine glanced over his shoulder at one of the ski pictures that hung on the wall. "Nice," he said.

"Taken on Wicked."

"I love that run."

"All the daredevils do."

"Speaking of daredevils, congrats on the wedding," Blaine said.

Decker flashed a wide smile. "Nothing daring about it. Most rock-solid decision I ever made. Kendall is great. Can't wait for you to meet her."

"Looking forward to it. I was sorry to hear that she'd been injured." He'd heard there had been some doubt that they might save her eye.

"Yeah. Bad days. But she's rallied like a champ," Decker said. "And doing well."

There was an awkward silence. Neither of the brothers excelled at small talk. Finally, Decker leaned forward. "What happened?" he asked quietly.

"I got stupid." That was the simple explanation. But his brother deserved more. "I met a woman. Honor Shayne. Very bright, hardworking, fun."

"Doesn't sound all bad," Decker said.

"We were both officers. Normally, a consensual relationship would have flown under the radar. Unfortunately, my commanding officer was old-school and, given that I was leading a team that Honor was assigned to, he'd made it very clear that he wouldn't view *dalliances*—" he emphasized the word because in the last several weeks, after hearing it over and over again, he'd begun to hate it "—favorably."

"You didn't listen, and he tossed you to the curb."

"Kicked. *Tossed* is too nice of a word."

"Did you love her? Do you?" Decker said, amending his question for present tense.

"Didn't and don't. I liked her. I respected her. I'm sorry that she got caught up in this mess. But she's moving on. Has already landed on her feet, teaching at West Point."

He'd never been in love. Had maybe come close before he'd left Roaring Springs at age eighteen. That is, if a kid that age could know what love was. He'd known that he cared for Matilda Deeds. Cared enough that for the last thirteen years he'd been carrying around a picture of them at prom. Him in his dark suit. Her in her pretty red dress that had accented her dark hair and unusual, dark gray eyes. Her sexy, curvy shape had seemed to be poured into her dress that night, likely making every teenage boy that saw her unable to think of much else.

He'd been mostly thinking about how to get his hand under the slit that ended midthigh. And, later that night, had figured out how.

Yeah, he'd cared. Enough that he would have married her if she hadn't lost the baby that they'd conceived that prom night on the couch in her parents' basement.

"You'll land on your feet, too," Decker said confidently, bringing Blaine back to the present.

"Dad called in a favor with Uncle Joe. Got my dishonorable discharge changed to *honorable*."

The other man shrugged. "You were a Green Beret and served with distinction for more than a decade. You earned a chest full of medals. You made a mistake, one that shouldn't have cost you everything. I think our uncle simply gave the army a chance to get it right."

For the first time since he'd opened his eyes that morning, Blaine felt his chest relax. The Coltons were a complex bunch, but when push came to shove, they were family, and he could count on them.

"What's Dad saying now?" Decker asked.

"We haven't talked yet. Not looking forward to that," Blaine added. "I was hoping you could help me with that."

"What can I do?"

"I need a job. I'll do anything."

Decker turned his head, looked out the window. "We've had late snow this year. Great for business. But the director of my Extreme Sports division broke his leg a week ago. It—"

"I'll do it," Blaine said, sitting forward in his chair.

"I was going to say it's going to require you to strap on the equipment. We're also short on instructors, and the demand for skiing and snowboarding lessons has never been higher."

The Colton property was a popular winter destination for many reasons. But for the true sports aficionado, it had always been because of the diversity of runs that were offered. Everything from the bunny hill to the super challenging, including two terrain parks, filled to the brim with opportunities for snowboarders to strut their stuff. Serious winter-sports fanatics came from all over to test themselves. "Sure. I can do that."

"Okay," Decker said. "You'd be doing me a favor."

Nice of Decker to frame it that way.

"You'll need to swing by Curtis Shruggs's office to fill out some paper work," his brother continued. "He's our director of personnel."

He thought he'd met Shruggs once before, on one of his brief trips back to Roaring Springs. His parents had been hosting a party for managers at Colton Manor. Blaine had been hiding out in one of the libraries, and the man had wandered in. "The guy with the blue eyes?"

"Yeah."

He could still remember a couple of his female cousins, and maybe even one of his sisters, going on about the man's eyes. *So gorgeous.* For his part, he'd thought the guy was nice enough and his eyes were fine. The brief encounter *had* left him thinking that there was something about the man that hadn't seemed quite right. He'd not said anything to his family, realizing that in all likelihood, it hadn't been Shruggs who was off-kilter that night, but rather, it had been him. Coming back to Roaring Springs had always been difficult for him.

But now, if Shruggs could get Blaine set up with a job, Blaine was only too happy to go see him. "One more favor?" he said, smiling at his brother.

"What?" Decker asked.

"I want to move into staff housing."

Decker rocked back in his chair. "Wow. You must really want to avoid Dad."

TWO DAYS LATER, Blaine had his hands full, corralling a group of six middle-school boys who'd signed up for the intermediate snowboarding class. They were in the larger park, the sky was a brilliant blue, with the temperature hovering around twenty-eight degrees, and there was two inches of fresh powder from the night before.

"Let's go," a blond kid yelled. Blaine thought his name was Isaac. "I am ready to shred the gnar," the boy added, invoking some favorite snowboarding lingo.

"Yeah, well, before any of you conquer this mountain, you're going to show me that you know the basics." He suspected they did. Kids in this area of the country were snowboarding in preschool. But he also understood boys and young men—having been one and having led a fair number of brand-new recruits over the years. Sometimes skills were exaggerated to keep up with the rest of the group. "Let's quickly run through a few things." He wanted to make sure they all knew how to stop and turn, both sharp and wide, gracefully fall and get up by themselves, and walk their boards back up the hill.

He ignored the moaning and groaning, and when he was confident that they were all more or less ready, he motioned for them to follow him.

"Where are the jumps?" a smaller kid named Tommy asked.

"Just over that hill," he said. That's where they would also find a pristine bowl. Its shape, with its steep sides and narrow gut—similar to the cement structures that skateboarders salivated over—would keep them busy for hours. "I'll demonstrate, and then you'll all get your chance. You don't have to feel pressured to do anything you're not comfortable with, okay?"

"Sounds like sex ed class." This again from Isaac.

That cracked the group up. A good-looking kid in the front named Josh looked at Blaine rather sheepishly. "Just ignore Isaac."

"You ready for this?" Blaine asked him.

"I'm going to do them all," Josh answered, his voice cracking at the end.

Blaine appreciated his attitude. He'd been like that as a kid. "All right," he said. "Let's go."

MATILDA DEEDS GLANCED at her watch. She'd arrived too early to pick Josh up from his lesson. But it had given her a chance to grab a latte at the coffee shop.

She'd been at The Lodge a few times over the years. One could hardly live in Roaring Springs and not have been. Every time, she'd carefully checked her surroundings, anxious about running into Russ Colton, but thankfully she had never encountered him. In recent years, she'd heard that Decker was taking on a bigger role in the day-to-day operation of The Lodge, which made it even less likely that she'd see the elder Colton, but she remained vigilant.

There was no sign of either Russ or Decker Colton today. This part of The Lodge was crazy busy with skiing and snowboarding enthusiasts trying to take advantage of the late-season snow. She took her coffee and settled at a small table in the corner of the room where the students would return following their class. About half of the other twenty tables were occupied, and conversation hummed in the air. A fire burned in the big stone fireplace at the far end of the room, and there was a tray of freshly baked cinnamon donuts on a table.

She resisted, not wanting the extra ten pounds that she carried to turn into fifteen or twenty. Sighing, she leaned forward, resting her elbow on the table and her chin in the palm of her hand.

Tilda supposed it was natural that she would think of Blaine Colton in this place. Not that she'd ever been here with him. The year they'd started dating, just weeks before prom night, there had been no late-season snow. And by the next fall, when the slopes were once again covered, Blaine had been long gone. Already done with basic training by that time. Happy to already go off to some dangerous, far off place, to serve his country.

And she'd been dealing with her own issues. Alone.

She'd done okay by most anyone's standards. Her parents had helped, of course, once they'd come to terms with her situation. Both unskilled workers, they'd clung on to the dream of having their daughter become the first college graduate in the family. They hadn't let her give up or give in. And Dorian Stoll had been a true friend.

She checked her watch again and looked out the big window, searching the slopes. There he was. Her son, her pride and joy, all long legs and gangly arms. He was taller than many of the kids in his class but thin enough that he looked as if a good, strong wind might blow him away. He was with five other kids. They'd taken off their helmets and goggles and were carrying their snowboards under their arms. She recognized his best friend, Isaac.

And there was a man, much taller, much broader, his head thrown back, as if he was laughing at something one of the kids had said. There was something so familiar about that motion, so unconsciously sexy, that she could feel her body heat up.

Jeez. What the heck?

She stood up but stayed where she was. At thirteen, Josh didn't want his mother running up to him. When the door opened, in came a whiff of cold air, laughter and young excited voices. Another voice. Deeper.

And she knew. Her knees felt weak.

Josh turned to search the room. She managed to wave at him.

The man turned. Followed Josh's gaze. Settled on her.

Blaine Colton. Still as handsome as ever. With that bold, confident look on his face, like he could take on the world. His dark brown hair was short, certainly shorter than he'd worn it in high school. It showed off his lean, strong features.

His smile faded as he followed Josh across the room.

"Tilda?" he said. His light brown eyes were very serious.

She nodded. Wet her lips with her tongue. "I hadn't heard that you were back." If she had, there'd been no way that she'd have brought Josh to The Lodge.

"Been in town just days," he told her. He stood very still, very straight, his impossibly broad shoulders filling the space.

She said nothing. Every word was potentially filled with peril.

"Hey, you know my mom?" Josh asked, looking at Blaine. He sounded as if he thought that was cool.

"Your mom," Blaine repeated.

She put her hand on Josh's arm. "We need to get going." She looked briefly at Blaine before turning to leave. "Good…uh…good to see you again."

"But—" Josh protested.

She pulled him along with her, away from Blaine. "Don't argue, Josh," she said under her breath. "Just keep walking."

Blaine made sure all the other kids got picked up, but he was moving on automatic. Tilda Deeds. What were the chances that he'd run into her here?

He guessed it wasn't all that odd. Had heard on one of his rare visits back to Roaring Springs over the past years that she'd married and had a child. He hadn't asked for details. At the time, he'd told himself that it was because he didn't care. But the news had unsettled him, and he'd never asked about her again. The idea of Tilda in bed with someone else, loving someone else, wasn't a comfortable one.

Was she still married? Somebody in his family would know.

Her kid was cool. He'd said he was going to try everything, and he'd been true to his word. Funny, too.

Once they were on the slope, he'd sparred back and forth with his friend Isaac and landed a couple zingers.

In those few seconds that he'd seen mom and son side by side, he'd noticed the resemblance. Still thinking about Tilda, he walked to his brother's office. Penny, now used to him, waved him in. He knocked sharply on Decker's door.

"Come in," Decker said, still staring at his computer screen. But when he saw it was Blaine, he pushed his chair back and took a breath. "Hey, how's it going?"

"Good. Just did a snowboarding class. Middle schoolers. All terrific kids and pretty darn good on their boards." Blaine took a breath. "And crazy as it sounds, one of them was Tilda Deeds's boy."

"That's not so crazy. She's a teacher at Roaring Springs High. English, I think."

They'd been in the same English class when they were seniors. She'd been smart. Always had a book with her, too. "What's her husband do?"

"He's dead," Decker said. "It's been years. Shame. Dorian Stoll was a nice guy. He didn't grow up in Roaring Springs but he always seemed to fit in."

"She's a widow," Blaine breathed, trying to get his head around that. She was so young. But then again, being in the military, he'd quickly learned that young people died, too.

Decker stared at him, considering. "As I recall, you had a thing for her in high school. You wanted to marry her."

He'd told Decker but no one else. Had sworn his brother to secrecy. And had only given Decker half the story, leaving out the part that Tilda was pregnant because the two of them had agreed that was their secret for the time being. As he recalled, Decker had initially laughed at him for mentioning marriage but, once he'd realized Blaine was serious, had switched tactics, telling him he was a fool, that he needed to go to college and prepare himself to someday take his rightful place in the Colton Empire.

Blaine had known even then that was an okay path for Decker but not for him.

And when Tilda had lost the baby, and he'd been at loose ends, wanting only to leave Roaring Springs and the dysfunctional relationship between his parents and the incessant pressure from his father to join the family business, the army had offered endless possibilities. He'd left quickly, before anyone could stop him. And almost from the very beginning had realized that it had been a very good decision.

"How old is her son?" he asked.

"I have no idea," Decker said.

There was no reason for Decker to know. And no real reason for Blaine to care. But the question nagged at him. How soon after he'd left had she jumped into another relationship? Had they dated for a long time before getting married?

Had she been happy?

Had she ever thought about Blaine and that, if things had gone differently, she'd have married him?

He shook his head. Water. Over the bridge.

"How's staff housing?" Decker asked. "Missing Mom's thousand-thread sheets?"

Blaine smiled. "I'm just happy to have a bed, bro. Didn't always have one of those, these last thirteen years."

"It's good to have you back," Decker said. "I worried..."

His voice trailed off. Blaine knew what he'd fretted

about. It was always harder on the ones left behind. That's one of the reasons he'd been right to leave Tilda and to never look back. It had given her the freedom she deserved.

And apparently, she'd run with it.

Chapter Two

Josh could not stop talking about his snowboarding lesson. He was thrilled that there was a teacher's planning day on Tuesday, and he and his friends had already arranged to go back.

There was no way that she wanted him to spend more time with Blaine. But she couldn't say they didn't have the money. Josh might have bought that excuse under other circumstances because he knew that their finances were sometimes tight, but the lessons had been a Christmas gift from her parents. They'd already been paid for.

She could always tell him that there was no way to get him there because, as a teacher, she had to be at school that day even if he didn't. But she knew that he'd get a ride with one of his many friends. Everybody liked Josh.

He was outgoing and made friends easily.

Like Blaine. Who had been one of the most popular kids in the senior class. Rich. Good-looking. Funny. Confident. She'd been over the moon when they'd started dating.

And she'd been quite happy to lose her virginity to him on prom night.

The surprise had been that he had also still been a virgin. And while it might not have been the smoothest of couplings, she'd felt that she could stay in his arms, against his warm, muscular body, forever. When he'd left her that night, she'd dreamed of all the possibilities.

And then her dreams had turned into a nightmare when she'd missed her next period. Had waited ten days, never saying a word to anyone, before she went and purchased a home pregnancy test. She recalled sitting on the toilet, early on a Monday morning, both of her parents at work, and how she had cried and cried when she'd seen the positive result.

Hadn't told Blaine for another week, even though they'd had two more dates during that time. She could still remember his face when she finally worked up the courage.

Disbelief.

Sadness.

And he'd left her house, offering no promises, only to return an hour later. They would get married, he told her. His child would have a father. He hadn't told her that he loved her. Hadn't said any of the words that might have reassured her that it was going to be okay. Instead, he'd been resolute, stone-faced.

Accepting of the inevitable. But terribly disheartened by it.

And then, a week later, she'd started spotting…

"Mom!" Josh yelled.

Jarred from her thoughts, she jumped, her hands briefly coming off the wheel. "What?" she asked.

"You aren't listening to a word I'm saying."

"I'm sorry," she said. "Really, honey. I'm glad you had a good time."

"What was he like in high school?" he asked.

She turned to look at her son, her bright, fun-loving son. "You know, I don't really remember. But hey, let's talk about the pizza we're having tonight. Pepperoni or sausage?"

"Pepperoni. You can get mushrooms on your half," he added grudgingly.

She and Josh had been sharing pizzas for a long time. Just the two of them, since Dorian's death four years earlier. And they were doing just fine. Blaine Colton wasn't going to mess that up.

TILDA KNEW THAT she wasn't at her best the next day at school. She'd barely slept and had a nightmare where Josh had fallen into a cave and, when she tried to pull him out, his hands kept slipping away from hers. Until finally he disappeared altogether. She'd awakened at 3:00 a.m. and had never gotten back to sleep. Now, almost twelve hours later, facing her last class of the day, she was barely able to keep her head up.

But she couldn't let the students know that. This was senior English, and her most challenging student, Toby Turner, would sense her weakness. In that way, he was a bit like a predatory animal. In another way, he was simply an obnoxious eighteen-year-old who appeared to hate authority of any kind.

"Hand forward your assignments," she said, standing in front of the room. She waited as the students unzipped backpacks and rustled through papers, pulling out the three-page, double-spaced book report on George Orwell's *1984*. As papers started coming forward, she stood at the front of each row and collected them. It did not escape her attention that Toby Turner didn't turn one in. She said nothing.

When she dismissed class, she made sure she was standing near the front of Toby's row. As he walked by, she quietly said, "Please stay for a minute." She half expected that he might simply ignore the request, but once the room emptied, he was still there, leaning insolently against the chalkboard.

"I didn't see a paper from you," she said.

He shrugged.

It drove her crazy. He had the ability. She was sure of that. But he was putting forth no effort. "You're going to fail this class if you don't turn in the work."

Now she didn't even get a shrug. Just a blank stare.

She took a breath. "Is there a reason that you didn't turn in your assignment?"

"Not any particular one," he muttered.

This behavior had started in mid-February, about five weeks into the semester. Here they were almost two months later, and he was running out of time to pull the grade up to passing. She'd taken the usual route. First she had posted a note to his parents on the school portal. When there had been no response, she'd tried to call the contact number in the school database. But it wasn't correct—assuming, that is, that Toby wasn't living in a Walmart in Denver. She'd then consulted with the school guidance counselor who, in turn, had met with Toby. The behavior hadn't improved. Finally, after too many weeks had gone by, Tilda had gotten desperate enough to resort to old-school methodology and had mailed a hard-copy progress report to his home address, asking his parents to sign it and to contact her for a conference. The progress report had come back signed, but there'd been no effort on the part of his parents to meet with her.

"I'll accept it until the end of this week, knocking off a half letter grade for each day that it's late," she said.

"Whatever. Are we done?"

She held on to her temper. Barely. "Yes. You are excused."

He left, and she started gathering up her things. Her head was down when she heard her door open. She looked up and smiled when she saw her friend from the classroom next door. Fellow teacher Raeann Johnson sank into a desk, her legs sprawled out, her head hanging back. "How many more days of school are there?" she asked.

"Twenty-nine, but who's counting?" Tilda said, doing her best to sound bored. She had a calendar at home, and every morning, she and Josh put an *X* through another day. She loved her job and he liked school well enough, but by this time of year, everybody was anxious for summer break.

"What are you doing tonight? There's no kids tomorrow. We could come in hungover." Raeann was a big talker and a small drinker. One glass of wine put her over the edge.

"Josh needs new jeans. I swear, he's grown three inches this year."

"He's such a cute kid. I hope mine grow up as nice."

Even though she and Raeann were the same age, both thirty-one, she had a thirteen-year-old and Raeann had twin boys who were nineteen months. Raeann had done everything the right way. Gone to college full-time, graduating in four years. Met a man there. Dated for three years before they got married. Bought a house with money they'd saved. Then had her kids.

Tilda had done it all backwards. Had Josh, gotten married, gone to college part-time, finishing in six years, gotten a teaching job, and at the ripe old age of twenty-seven, become a widow.

Raeann pushed herself out of the desk. "Okay. No

wine for us. You go shopping, and I'll try to keep my two from falling down the stairs or painting the walls with markers."

Tilda smiled, remembering those days. She'd loved it when Josh was a baby. He'd been such a happy kid, and she could hardly even remember him crying. Dorian had been super with him, too. Sometimes, Josh, just nine when Dorian had died, would mention something that he remembered doing with Dorian, but she never prompted those conversations. Didn't want him thinking about the fact that he didn't have a dad.

She pressed her fingers against her forehead. She had a splitting headache. Always did when she didn't get enough sleep.

She knew what had awakened her at three. Memories.

Of the relief on Blaine Colton's face when she'd told him that she'd lost the baby. It had been crystal clear in that moment that he felt as if he'd been given a second chance to get it right.

And *get it right* really meant get the heck out of Roaring Springs. He'd left in less than a week. And in the months that followed, when he'd taken the time to send a quick email, it had been easy to see that he was terribly happy with the ways things had turned out.

Every time she'd gotten one of those messages, she'd cried for days.

Over the years, she'd heard a few things. War hero. Promoted over and over again. A freakin' Green Beret. She might even have been happy for him. Had told herself that things certainly had worked out for the best.

Tilda said goodbye to Raeann, walked out of the school and into the parking lot. Teachers parked in the front two rows. She got into her SUV, fastened her seatbelt and drove. Her house was less than ten minutes west of the school. Josh went to the middle school that was seven blocks east of their house and had permission to walk home. They generally arrived within minutes of one another. If he beat her, he'd have the television on and the chips already open. But if she got there first, she'd insist upon cutting up some apple slices and cheddar cheese instead.

The house was blessedly quiet when she walked in. She hung up her coat and tossed her briefcase onto the counter. Normally, she graded papers at night, while Josh was doing his homework. But tonight, because there was no school tomorrow, she'd be hard-pressed to get him to focus on doing anything. Instead, they would shop for an hour or so, grab dinner at the food court, and come home and watch a movie.

And tomorrow, he'd be back at The Lodge. She'd spoken to Isaac's parents early this morning. They offered to do drop-off if she could pick the boys up. She'd readily agreed, knowing that she needed to be smarter now that Blaine was back and apparently teaching snowboarding classes. She'd arrange to meet the kids outside the main lobby, a five-minute walk from where she'd seen Blaine yesterday. The Lodge was huge. They didn't need to run into each other.

She heard Josh outside the front door. He walked in, half dragging his backpack, leaving the heavy wooden door open behind him.

"Close the door," she reminded him. "And lock it." Roaring Springs was a safe place. It was one of the reasons that she'd stayed here to raise her son when there had been many reasons to go. But the world was changing and, like any parent, she wanted her child to always be safe. The recent discovery of a dead body on

Blaine's brother Wyatt Colton's land had been terribly upsetting. Tilda had thought about the young woman for days and had been relieved when the newspaper had finally reported that the killer had committed suicide.

Josh went right for the cupboard, grabbing a bag of trail mix that they'd made on Saturday. "We still going shopping?" he asked, his mouth full.

"Chew, swallow, then talk," she reminded him. "And, yes. How was your day?"

He made a production out of chewing and swallowing, looking and sounding a bit like a skinny cow. "Pretty good. Mrs. Armstrong is losing it, though. In history, she went over the same stuff that she did last Friday. We were halfway through class before she realized it. Then she started making all kinds of lame excuses."

Helen Armstrong was nearing retirement age and, quite frankly, probably should have quit at the end of the previous year. But she was delightful and was still able to control her classroom. "You know what they say," Tilda deadpanned. "History repeats itself."

Josh groaned. "Oh, Mom. Please do not try to be funny. It's too painful."

She swatted his arm. "I'll show you what's painful. You wearing pants that are too small. We leave here in five minutes. Get going."

WHEN TILDA WOKE up on Tuesday morning, she could already hear Josh moving around in his room. Any other day, she'd have to wake him up at least three times before he stumbled out of bed to go to school.

He was so excited about going back to The Lodge. Conversation during last night's dinner at his favorite hamburger joint had been all about bowls, jigs and half-pipes. A few times, he mentioned Blaine and how cool he was.

"That's *Mr. Colton* to you, right?" she said. There needed to be some formality between Blaine and her son.

"He said we could call him Blaine," Josh told her. "You know, one of the other guys in our group said he was some kind of war hero. That's pretty cool."

With that, she'd put a hand on his arm. "You know, Josh. War is never cool. It's not fun."

"I know that," he said. "But if we have to have them, then I'm glad there are people like Blaine Colton, if it's true that he was a hero."

She didn't doubt it for a minute. Even in high school, he'd taken a stand, even when it put him crossways with his friends. He ran with a bunch of other rich kids, who had nice clothes and new cars, and life seemed to generally just go their way. Everybody else who wasn't in their crowd really wanted to be. But that kind of social power went to some of the kids' heads, and they could cross the line at times, both in and out of school. And they generally had each other's backs.

However, one time, just days before prom, when somebody in his group was picking on one of the underclassmen who walked with leg braces, she'd seen Blaine get in his friend's face. For a minute, it had looked like it might erupt into a fight, but Blaine hadn't backed down. And pretty soon, his friend had been offering up an apology to the younger kid.

That's why she hadn't been all that surprised when he'd pretty quickly gotten over his shock that she was pregnant and had been back at her house, offering up a marriage proposal. He was determined to do right by her.

She got out of bed, stretched and headed for the

kitchen. On the way, she knocked on Josh's door. She waited for the *Come in* before she opened the door. "Good morning," she said.

He was sitting on the floor, his snowboard next to him. "I started the coffee," he said.

He'd been eleven when she'd taught him how to do that. With just the two of them in the house, they needed to watch out for one another. "Bless you, my son," she said.

He smiled, a grin that lit up his whole face. "I felt sorry for you because you have to go to school today and I don't."

She raised a corner of her mouth in a sneer, gathered her long hair up in her hand and rubbed the back of her neck. She yawned. "More proof that it's not always great to be the adult. Enjoy being a kid." She'd had to grow up so fast. Didn't regret any of the decisions she'd made, but man, it hadn't been easy. She wanted something different for Josh. "Want some breakfast?"

"Sure. Scrambled eggs and bacon?" he asked, sounding hopeful.

"Because you made the coffee," she said agreeably. "Ten minutes." She went to the kitchen, poured herself some java and sipped it while she pulled eggs and bacon from the refrigerator. Josh was skinny as a rail, even though he seemed to always be eating. With that in mind, she cooked him three eggs to her two and three slices of bacon while she skipped that altogether. He got two pieces of sourdough toast to her one. The last thing she did was pour him a big glass of milk and put an orange next to his plate.

"It's ready," she yelled.

A few moments later, he slid into his chair and attacked his food.

"Breathe," she reminded him.

He loudly blew out a puff of air. "This is going to be the best day! There was more snow last night."

"Just be careful," she said. Two years ago, he'd broken his collarbone at a friend's house. Somehow they'd managed to fall off a garage roof. She could still remember getting that call from the friend's mom, saying they were on their way to the emergency room.

It had been a relatively minor injury that could have been much worse. That realization had given her a few nightmares. Josh was everything she had. She couldn't bear the thought of losing him.

"Josh," she said.

The seriousness of her tone caught his attention. "Yeah, Mom?"

She wanted to warn him to stay away from Blaine. To not give him any details about their lives. But there was no way she could do that without sounding crazy. "You're going to need some lunch money," she said instead.

"Yeah, I guess," he replied, sounding puzzled.

She got up fast, fumbled around in her purse and handed him a twenty. Then wrapped her arms around him and hugged him tight. "Be safe, my boy," she said. "And have fun," she added. Then she turned and hurried back to her bedroom before he could see the tears in her eyes.

Teenage boys simply didn't know what to do with crying moms. Wasn't in their wheelhouse. And she didn't want to do anything to spoil his day. He was such a good, hardworking kid, and he deserved to have a fun day off from school.

And Blaine would have lots of other kids on the slopes today to worry about. There was no reason to focus on her son.

Chapter Three

Blaine had three instructors in various areas of the mountain, and he was going to take three classes himself. He told himself that it meant nothing, absolutely nothing, that he took the time to preview the list of class participants in advance and then *just so happened* to pick the class that Josh Stoll was in.

At precisely one o'clock, he met the same group of six kids that he'd had that previous Sunday. Isaac and Josh were side by side, laughing, as he approached. They had not yet put their helmets on. He slowed, studying Josh's face.

And felt his heart start to beat a little faster. Because, crazy as it seemed, in those few seconds, he'd seen a glimpse of something that reminded him very much of his brother Decker when he'd been a kid.

He tore his eyes away, trying to make sense of everything. It was probably just being back in Roaring Springs that was messing with his head. Making him think about paths not taken when he should be thinking about what came next for him. He wasn't going to stay in Roaring Springs, that was for sure. He had other options. With his skills, he could join any number of firms that provided services to the government. He could get right back into the thick of things, fighting for his country, only this time, as a private citizen as opposed to being in the military. It would be different, but that didn't necessarily mean bad.

"Afternoon, gentlemen," he said to the boys.

"Hey, Mr. Colton," Josh replied.

On Sunday, the kid had called him Blaine. But that was before the brief, but oddly tense, interaction with Tilda when she'd come to pick Josh up. Had Tilda said something afterwards to make Josh think of him in a less friendly way? "Just Blaine is fine," he told him.

"My mom said I should call you Mr. Colton. That it was more respectful."

"His mom's a teacher. A cool one, but still, things like that are important to her," Isaac said, as if that explained it.

Maybe that was it. Or was it even possible that she was somehow angry with him for what had happened? Hell, they'd both just been kids. And it seemed as if her life had worked out okay. "Whatever works for you," he conceded, smiling at Josh. He didn't want to get between the kid and his mom. "Get your helmets on. Let's hit the slopes."

And for the next two hours, tasked with the responsibility of watching six kids who had various levels of proficiency, he was too busy to dwell on Tilda Deeds. At the end of the lesson, he started to walk the group back to The Lodge. "Your mom picking you up?" he asked, turning to Josh.

"She has to be at school until four. So we've got another couple hours. We're going to rent some skis for the rest of the day."

In the old days, when he'd been Josh's age, it was an *us versus them* kind of mentality between snowboarders and skiers. Kids were generally in one camp or another. But Decker had told him on his first day that had changed in the last five years. Now, it wasn't unusual for guests at The Lodge to do both. In fact, to encourage it, participants in either a snowboarding or skiing class could rent both types of equipment at a steep discount on that same day. "Okay," Blaine said. "Be careful," he added as he watched Josh and Isaac veer off toward the ski-rental area.

He murmured goodbye to the other kids in the group, telling them that he'd be offering another class on Sunday if they were still interested. He'd looked ahead at the weather, and there was every indication that the snow would continue to be good for at least another week.

Then he crossed the room and headed for his office. There was always paperwork to push through at the end of a busy day. And he wanted to check tomorrow's schedule to make sure he had everything covered. After stripping off his outerwear and making himself a cup of coffee, he sat at his desk, opened his laptop and found the spreadsheet he was looking for. Clicked a key to pull in new data.

And thought about Josh and his friend on the slope. They would be fine. He'd certainly skied by himself when he was a kid. He glanced out his window, across the wide expanse of mountain.

Beautiful.

But even beauty could be dangerous.

Surely they were smart enough to pay attention to any warning signs that were posted. There were a couple areas that were closed due to avalanche risk.

He shut his laptop and pushed back from the desk. In another minute, he had his ski clothes back on. Then opened his corner closet and pulled out his skis, boots and poles.

There was no reason why he couldn't spend a little time on the slopes. If, in the process, he made sure that Josh and his friend didn't do anything stupid, that would be okay. He told himself that his motivation was to prevent anything that would put him at odds with Tilda Deeds. They had history, if nothing else. But, in truth, he felt a need to watch over Josh. Couldn't explain it. But had learned a long time ago not to ignore his gut.

In less than five minutes, he was outside with his ski boots on. He got in line for the chairlift and, when it swung up behind him, sat down fast. As it rose in the air, he scanned the slopes, looking for Josh's bright red coat. He didn't see him but wasn't surprised. From where the chairlift dumped out, there were four different paths that a skier could take. Only one of those paths ran under this particular lift.

When he got to the top, he considered the remaining three options. River Bend, which was a nice, relatively easy path, with smooth curves reminiscent of a winding river. Tree Glory, which was exactly what it sounded like—a challenging path with large scatterings of pines along the way. And finally, Devil's Leap, a steep decline with a fair number of moguls.

And he knew, without a doubt, that Josh and Isaac had likely looked at their choices and decided that Devil's Leap was the one. Unfortunately, it was also the closest to Wicked, a slope that had been closed due to avalanche risk.

If they were careful and stayed on the path, they would be fine.

Blaine set off, aggressively banking his skis every so often to slow down his speed. He kept his eyes peeled. About a third of the way down, he saw them. They were another four hundred yards down, but he was confident it was them. Two bodies, one in red, the other in black, moving in tandem.

The black coat was in the lead, straying very close to an area they had no business going.

He pushed off, tucked in and flew down the slope. He made a sharp turn, sending up a shower of powder.

"Hey," Josh shouted, sounding mad. "Mr. Colton?" His tone had changed from anger to surprise.

He'd surprised them. Good. "What are you two doing?"

"We're going to ski Wicked," Isaac said. "It's got some super-cool moguls. I skied it a couple weeks ago."

That was before several of the recent snowstorms that had led them to close the trail due to avalanche risk. "Those warning signs aren't up for decoration," he admonished.

Josh looked uncomfortable.

"We're not going to do anything to start an avalanche," Isaac said.

They could. Without a doubt. A person's body weight was enough to set it off. "How fast have you ever gone in a car?" he asked.

Josh looked surprised at the question. "Maybe eighty miles an hour. That's the speed on the interstate, right?"

"Yeah. Imagine going that speed without the benefit of a car frame and air bags. Because that's how fast an avalanche of fresh powder can go. People are buried by the snow in seconds. And then you know what happens? The snow settles around them, just like concrete, making it almost impossible for a person to dig themselves out. And your only hope is that someone comes along and rescues you." Pausing briefly to let his words sink in, he went on to say, "If that doesn't happen, you've got about fifteen minutes before it all goes south fast."

"We studied avalanches in science class," Josh said. "Our teacher said to swim with the snow."

"Good advice." A person's body weight would pull them down into the snow, making it impossible to find them. If they could swim to the snow's surface and get a hand up in the air, their chances of being located were better. "Better advice is to pay attention to the warning signs and to stay in bounds. If you're going to be doing anything off-trail, make sure that you're wearing a transponder and that everybody is carrying a probe and a shovel in their packs."

"Sorry, Mr. Colton," Josh said.

"No problem," he answered. His goal was not to bust the kids' chops but to make sure they stayed safe. "I'll see you at the bottom." He took off, leaving the boys where they were, demonstrating that he had faith that they would heed his warning. And sure enough, by the time he reached the end of the slope and turned, he could easily see them coming his way.

Once back inside The Lodge, he decided to check in with his cousin Molly Gilford, who was the director of guest services for The Lodge. He stopped for two coffees on his way.

"How's it going?" he asked, handing her a cup. She sat behind her desk that had three very orderly piles.

The ever-efficient, pretty blonde waved a hand. "Today's crisis was missing jewelry, which had a frantic guest throwing around ugly accusations, frightening the staff. Also one very naughty twenty-two-month-old who was hiding it all in a deep pocket of her stroller. All's well that ends well. How was your day?"

"Good. Had a full slate of classes because it was a teachers' planning day. Took a couple of classes myself."

"I think you were born on skis."

"If that was true, I think my mom might have mentioned it," he said easily. He'd come to pick Molly's brain about Tilda but thought he better make a little small talk first. Didn't want to appear to be too obvious. "Have you seen my friend Max Hollick lately?"

"Uh…no. Why?"

The question seemed to startle her. He'd served with Max, who was now putting his heart and soul into raising service dogs for veterans. "Just wondering. The last time I spoke with him, he mentioned that he'd stopped here a couple times over the last few years."

"It's been a few months since he was here," she said, looking down at something on her desk. "We barely saw each other. So how are things in the Extreme Sports division?" she asked, switching topics fast.

"Good. It's just temporary," he said.

"I know, I know. Living in Roaring Springs isn't your thing. You do realize that the rest of the family misses you?"

"I promise that regardless of where I end up, I won't stay away as much as I have in the past thirteen—well, I guess, almost fourteen—years. Speaking of people who stuck around, I ran into Tilda Deeds the other day."

"She's still as pretty as ever, isn't she?" Molly said. "When you guys were seniors, I was a sophomore, and I thought you were the cutest couple." She winked at him. "Maybe you could start something up again."

He shook his head. "I don't think so. Her son was in one of my classes on Sunday, and when she picked him up, she was as frosty as a north ridge on a January day." He said it lightly but in truth, it had bothered him more than he was letting on. He'd really liked Tilda and on prom night, when they'd had sex, it had been the most amazing night of his life. He'd left her house in the wee hours of the morning feeling like a different person, somehow more whole.

She'd been so beautiful, with her flowing, dark hair and her flashing eyes. So damn sexy. So damn sweet as their bodies had joined.

"Frosty doesn't sound like Tilda," Molly said thoughtfully. "People love her. Especially her students. So sad that her husband died."

Blaine managed a nod. What did it say about him that he was envious of a dead man that he'd never met?

"She's too young to be alone," Molly added.

"I suppose that could apply to any one of us," he said. Molly. Tilda. Himself.

"I'm much younger," she said. "Still in my twenties."

"Barely," he teased her, wanting to lighten the mood. He stood up. "I'll see you later."

He got to her office door before he turned around. "You don't happen to know how old Tilda's son is, do you?" He tried for casual.

"Let me think. I guess he's probably about thirteen. His best friend is Isaac Trammell, and his mom buys groceries where I do. I saw her last week, and she mentioned that she was getting stuff for Isaac's thirteenth-birthday party."

Thirteen. The space between his ears was buzzing. Of course, just because Josh and Isaac were friends, it didn't mean that they were the same age. But on Sunday, they'd been talking about a teacher, and it had sounded very much like they were in the same class.

Molly smiled at him. "Have a good night."

"Right. You, too," he said automatically. If Josh was also just thirteen, then Tilda must have gotten pregnant again right away.

Which was kind of weird, given that she hadn't seemed all that happy about being pregnant the first time. He'd have assumed she might be super careful about preventing pregnancy, sort of like he'd been after that.

He remembered glancing at Josh, catching a fleeting glance of something so familiar.

A dark suspicion threatened to overtake him. But, like the soldier he'd been, he forced himself to clear his head and not jump to conclusions. When people did that in war, they sometimes made mistakes that had very serious consequences. This situation might not be all that different.

He turned the corner and almost bumped into Seth Harris. He was a manager at The Lodge and also his cousin Remy Colton's maternal half-brother. "Sorry," Blaine said, stepping aside.

"Nice to see you, Blaine. I'd heard that you were working at The Lodge," Seth said.

Blaine wasn't in a mood to make small talk, but from what he'd heard about Seth's life, before Remy had taken him in when the kid was fifteen and Remy just twenty, he'd been dealt a bad hand. Remy and Seth shared a mother, Cordelia Ripley, who was never going to win Parent of the Year. Seth wasn't a Colton, but he was obviously important to Remy, and once Seth finished business school, Remy had secured a job for his half brother at The Lodge. And based on what Blaine had heard, Seth did pretty good work. He dressed a little too trendy for Blaine's taste, but then again, Blaine's wardrobe for the last thirteen years had primarily been desert khaki. "Yeah, the late snow is keeping us all busy for a while."

"Good to have family to come back to, right? You

know, when things get tough," Seth added. "Not every-body has that kind of safety net."

There was an undertone to the remarks that bristled Blaine's already stretched nerves. On another day, he might have been willing to push back, to remind Seth that the Coltons had been a safety net for him, too. But today, he had other things on his mind. "You bet," he said. "I'll see you later, Seth."

He walked past the man. Josh had said that Tilda had to work until four. That meant that she'd probably arrive at The Lodge by four fifteen. He made a sharp right turn at the next hallway, and with ten minutes to spare, he was standing in the spot where he'd seen her on Sunday. But no sign of her. He didn't see Josh or Isaac, either. He moved to a place where he could see the door where the kids would enter and also the hall-way that Tilda would come from.

And he tried to breathe deep, to slow his heart rate.

At four twenty, when he was about to jump out of his skin, he saw Josh's bright red coat outside. He and Isaac were taking a path that would lead them toward another door. He ran outside, ignoring that he didn't have a coat on. He quickly caught up with the boys.

"Hey, Mr. Colton," Josh said. "Didn't expect to see you again."

"On your way home?" he asked.

"Yeah. My mom said she'd meet us outside the main lobby."

Because she was trying to avoid him? He fell into step with the boys. "Hey, I have some paper work I need to fill out about class participants. I need your ages."

"Thirteen," they both said at the same time. "Well, I'm almost thirteen," Isaac corrected. "In a week. Josh already had his birthday a couple weeks ago."

Blaine stared at Josh. Again, he thought of how the boy had reminded him of Decker. But what had everyone always said? That he and Decker had almost looked like twins when they were young.

Was it even *possible*?

They were within a hundred yards of the door that led to the main lobby. He could see Tilda standing outside, wearing the same bright blue coat that she'd had on before. As they got closer, he could tell that her eyes were fixed on him before she shifted them to her son.

She reached for Josh, like she was going to hug him, but instead, patted his back. "How was your day?"

"Great," Josh said. "Best day ever."

She smiled, looking so much like the girl that he'd left all those years ago. But if his suspicions were right, then she wasn't sweet and nice or any of the good things he'd always thought.

"Hello, Blaine," she said.

"Afternoon," he responded, working hard to keep his tone even.

"In the car, boys. We need to get going." She took a step.

"Can I have a word, Tilda?"

She stopped, looking as if she wanted to make a run for it. Instead, she handed Josh the key fob. "Go ahead and get in. Do not start it," she warned him.

She watched the two boys until they got to a tan SUV. Then turned to look at him. Her pretty eyes were wary.

He didn't know what to say. Didn't know how to ask her about something so important. "Josh is thirteen."

"Just," she said.

"When did you and Dorian get married?"

"Around the time that Josh was born."

"Before or after?" he pressed.

She wet her lips with her tongue. "A couple weeks after."

He let the words settle. "Does that mean…" Again, he was at a loss for words.

She stepped away from him as a large group of people came out the door. "I can't have this discussion here," she hissed.

She didn't have to say the words. He knew the truth. "What the hell have you done, Tilda?" he asked. He felt a raging pain tear through him. How could she have deceived him so? How could she have let him leave Roaring Springs? How could she not have said a damn word all these years?

"Come to the house tonight," she said. "Nine o'clock. The ranch at the very end of Dale Drive."

"Tilda," he gritted out. He reached for her and saw that his arm was shaking.

But she was already moving away from him. Not running, but walking very fast.

He could catch her. And then what? Have Josh and Isaac and many other guests witness what should be a very private conversation?

He lowered his arm, tucking it tight to his side. Then he didn't move.

He had a son. Josh was his.

Chapter Four

He knows. It was the only thought running through Tilda's head as she drove. And she was filled with a bone-chilling combination of relief and fear. The two emotions ebbed and flowed as her thoughts cascaded.

It's time for the truth to come out.

He'll try to take Josh from me.

Josh will have the father he deserves.

My son will hate me for what I've done.

Back and forth her mind zipped. She dropped Isaac off. Maybe she said goodbye, she couldn't remember by the time she turned the corner. At home, she walked inside the house, dropped her purse on the table and went directly to her room. She lay on the bed, listening to the too-loud television that Josh had immediately turned on.

She should be grateful that thirteen-year-old boys were not always attuned to their mothers' moods. But eventually, he'd seek her out. If for no other reason than to see what was for dinner. And how was she going to tell him that the conversation that would occur between her and Blaine tonight was going to change everything?

She could lie to Blaine, try to convince him that he was seeing something that just wasn't there. She dismissed the idea immediately. Not only would a DNA test prove her wrong, but there had been too many lies already.

She'd had her reasons. Good reasons. But would Blaine understand?

Josh could not be here for the conversation. She hadn't been thinking when she'd told Blaine to come to the house. But nor did she want to meet in a public place where someone might overhear. She reached for her cell phone. When her mom answered, she made her voice bright. "Hi. How's it going?"

"Good. Your dad and I are just watching some television."

"I know it's last minute, but do you think that Josh could come over and spend the night? And you could take him to school tomorrow?"

"Well…of course, honey. Is there something wrong?" Her mom, always supportive, was clearly puzzled by the unexpected request.

"No. Nothing's wrong," she lied. Her parents worried about her and Josh enough as it was. "I just have something that I need to take care of tonight. I can pick up some dinner for the three of you on the way."

"Don't worry about that. I made a lasagna, so there's plenty. Can you join us for dinner, too?"

She wasn't sure she could keep anything down. And it was hard enough to keep up the *Everything is fine* facade on the phone. In person, it would be impossible. "Not this time," she said. "I'll have Josh there in a half hour or so."

She hung up and walked out to the living room. Josh was sprawled across the couch, an open bag of corn chips next to him. She walked over, picked it up and closed it. "New plan, sport," she said. As a single working mom, she'd sometimes had to do some just-in-time juggling to get both her and Josh where they needed to be on any given day. Whenever there was an unexpected change, *New plan, sport* had become their official signal.

"What?" he asked.

"You're going to have dinner with your grandparents and spend the night. They'll take you to school."

He frowned at her. It wasn't the idea of going to her parents' house…he loved spending time with them. But clearly he was surprised. "I have homework," he said.

"And you'll need to do it there."

"Are you sleeping over, too?"

"Nope. I've got something that I need to take care of, so you're going solo."

He shrugged. "Okay. What's Grandma making for dinner?"

She let out a breath, grateful that these days Josh mostly thought about his next meal. After tonight, would that be true?

"It's a surprise," she said, swallowing hard. "But it's one of your favorites."

AN HOUR LATER, Tilda was back home, anxiously wandering from room to room. What would Blaine think of her home? She and Dorian had built it just two years after they'd been married. Three bedrooms. One for the two of them, one for Josh, and she'd hoped, at the time, that there might be another baby to fill the third.

But that had never happened and, after Dorian had gotten sick and died, she'd been grateful that she'd never gotten pregnant. She wasn't sure she'd have been able to handle two children by herself.

She stopped wandering long enough to sanitize the bathroom that Josh used. Then she scrubbed the kitchen sink, cleaned out her refrigerator and, finally, tackled the mess inside her microwave.

She should have a crisis more often, she thought wryly. Her house would be neater.

But still, by eight forty-five, she was sitting on the couch, hands clasped together in her lap. Waiting.

At 8:57 p.m., there was a knock on her door. She took a deep breath, said a quick prayer and opened it. "Hi," she said.

He nodded at her. His handsome face was a blank canvas, telling her nothing.

"Come in," she said, standing back.

He walked in, stood, his shoulders back, his posture soldier-perfect. It made her stomach tighten. "Let me take your coat," she offered.

He shrugged it off. "Where's Josh?" he asked.

"Not here. I… I thought that might be better." She motioned him toward the couch. Waited until he took a seat before taking the chair opposite him.

"I—"

"What the hell did you do?" he barked, interrupting her.

And just like that, she could feel her good intentions to have a reasonable conversation desert her. "I did what I had to do, Blaine. Because I was alone," she added bitterly.

"He's my son," he said hoarsely.

"Yes," she whispered.

Blaine closed his eyes. Drew in deep breaths. When he opened his eyes, she could see bitterness. "Did your husband know, or did you lie to him, too?" he asked.

It was harsh. She probably deserved it, but still, it stung. "He knew. From the beginning. That's why he married me."

"Who else? Who else knows this big secret?"

"My parents may suspect that the baby wasn't Dorian's. I never explicitly told them one way or another. But they don't know…about you."

"Josh thinks that Dorian was his father?"

"Yes."

"You told me that you lost the baby. That you had a miscarriage."

"I thought I did. I was spotting. I didn't know anything about being pregnant. You were already gone before I learned the truth."

He stared at her. "There's this thing called the telephone. There's email. Not impossible to send a quick Hey, by the way, I guess I am still pregnant."

He was very angry with her. She understood. But he needed to also understand something. "I was scared. Petrified, really." For so many reasons. But did she dare tell him the whole truth? Would he believe her? She'd been warned at the time to never tell anyone. And she hadn't. "And you didn't want him."

Her words hung in the air. Seemed to vibrate off the walls. *And you didn't want him.* Could he deny it? But he wasn't on trial here. He wasn't the one who'd lied about a huge thing. "I didn't *know* about him," Blaine said, his voice hard.

There was nothing to be gained by reliving the past. "I intended to give the baby up for adoption. That was my plan."

"What happened?"

"I couldn't do it. He was my son, and I already loved him. Dorian, who'd been a family friend for years, offered to marry me. Told me that he'd always cared for me. Told me that he hoped that one day we'd be more than friends."

"And were you?"

She wasn't going to lie anymore. "Yes."

He stared at her. The tension was so thick in the room that it felt heavy on her chest.

"Then, I'm sorry for your loss," he said finally.

She nodded, her throat closing up.

"But you're not the only one here who lost something," he added, all signs of compassion gone.

She knew that. But did he even understand that once a path was chosen, it was very difficult to change course? "Now what?"

"We have to tell Josh."

She couldn't even imagine that conversation.

"Tilda," he prompted.

She nodded. "You're right. He deserves to know. You deserve to have him know."

"Tonight?" Blaine prodded.

She shook her head. "He's at my parents' house. It would be better if we waited until school was out tomorrow. We can tell him together. Here."

She could tell he was frustrated with having to wait one more night. But he finally nodded and settled back onto the couch. He looked around. "What's he like to do?" he asked. "Besides snowboard and ski."

"He plays baseball in the summer. Second base. And he's a good swimmer. Likes to camp and fish. He's a good student, usually A's and B's. Plays the trombone in the school band."

Blaine nodded. "Can I see his room?"

"Sure." She stood up and led him back. He stood in the doorway, looked at the hockey posters on the walls and the chess set on his desk. He smiled. "Chess?"

"He loves it."

"He gets his brains from you," he said quietly.

She felt her stomach relax. They could get through this.

Then Blaine's eyes settled on the picture next to Josh's bed. It was Dorian and Josh, with Josh proudly holding a fish that he'd caught. He said nothing, but his whole body stiffened up, and he turned on his heel.

Didn't look at her again until he had his coat on and the door open.

"What time does he get home from school?"

"By four usually," she said.

"I'll be here. You better be, too."

He turned and walked away. Closing the door behind him, she sank down onto the couch and forced herself to take several deep, calming breaths. She didn't blame him for hating her, but she'd made the best decision under the circumstances. He hadn't wanted a baby and would have felt as if she'd trapped him.

Now, he simply felt deceived.

BLAINE LOOKED AT the clock a hundred times the next day. The hours dragged on. Because the local kids were back in school, classes were more limited, and there was no need for him to instruct. That meant he could hide in his office. It gave him too much time to think.

A son.

A thirteen-year-old son.

He'd missed so much. Because Tilda had lied, he'd missed thirteen years that he could never get back. He understood that she might have initially made the wrong assumption about having a miscarriage. They were both so young, trying to navigate something they knew nothing about. But then later, when she learned the truth, why the hell hadn't she reached out to him?

He wouldn't have been able to leave the army right away. That wasn't how it worked. But he could have come back on his leave, would definitely not have re-enlisted when the opportunity came.

He'd have come back to Roaring Springs years ago. That thought made him swallow hard.

But he'd have done it. For his son.

Who would know the truth in about an hour. His heart ached for the kid who was right now sitting in some middle-school classroom blissfully unaware that his life was about to radically change due to no fault of his own.

Josh was a Colton and with that name came the privileges that wealth and power could buy. That had never been terribly important to Blaine. Maybe because he knew that the Coltons had worked hard to prosper. Maybe because he knew, all too well, the family had troubles even though they were rich. Others, outside the family, didn't see that. And they didn't like the Coltons because all they saw was the advantages of being a Colton.

When it became public that Josh was a Colton, his world would be very different. He might lose friends over it. Some people in the Roaring Springs community would delight in seeing a Colton fall from grace and would take every opportunity to point out a Colton's shortcomings.

Was Josh up to that?

Because of the choices that Tilda had made, the boy wasn't going to get any ramp-up time. He wasn't going to *grow into* being a Colton. It was going to be thrust upon him.

How could she have done it? That had been the question that had been running through his head since the moment that she'd almost run away from him at The Lodge. How could she have hidden such a vitally important thing?

Yes, he'd left abruptly for the army, with barely enough time to say goodbye to his family or friends. Yes, he'd rarely come home, but he had his reasons for that—his father's infidelity was something that he simply hadn't been able to get past. He didn't understand his parents' marriage. Never had, probably never would.

But he understood a couple things. Truth. Honor. Those things mattered. His father had failed him there. Now…well, so had Tilda. It was… He drew in a breath, not wanting to overdramatize the situation. After all, he'd seen a lot of bad things in the world in the last thirteen years. Things that most people could likely not even imagine. And he knew that he had the resilience to bounce back from a lot of adversity. But still, Tilda's deception seemed mean-spirited to him, and he was having a hard time getting his head around that because that was not the girl that he'd cared about at one time. Not the girl that he would have married, and would have been faithful to, had it come to that.

But he had to own some of this as well. Because Tilda had been right. He *had* been relieved when she'd said that she'd had a miscarriage. Now, thinking about Josh, that made him feel guilty. But he could still remember the feeling, as if a giant boulder had been lifted from his chest, and he'd been able to finally take a deep breath. And, damn him, but he could still remember his initial exclamation, upon hearing Tilda say that she'd miscarried: *Oh, thank God.*

He wondered if she remembered it. Would she use it against him? Would she tell Josh that he'd been happy that there wasn't going to be a baby?

Would the boy understand that he'd been eighteen, just five years older than Josh was now, and not mature enough to respond in a better way? Would Josh think that Tilda had done the right thing to pass him off as another man's son because his own father hadn't wanted him?

This was a damn mess. No other way to describe it.

He looked at his watch again. It was time.

He closed his office door behind him and walked to his vehicle in the parking lot. The drive to Tilda's house took twenty minutes, and he waited at the curb for another ten before he saw her drive into her garage. He gave her two minutes to get inside the house, then walked up to her front door and rang the bell.

"Hello, Blaine," she said, when she opened the door. She stood back and motioned him in.

She looked tired. There were shadows under her pretty dark eyes, suggesting that her sleep may have been as disturbed as his. She wore a royal blue sweater and a black skirt that hugged her curves and made him too easily remember a dark basement and the feel of her round bottom in his hands and then later, as they lay together, the warmth of said bottom pressed up against him.

"Josh should be here in just a few minutes," she informed him. "Do you want something to drink?"

"Water might be good," he said. Perhaps in a pail that he could dunk his head in.

She got two glasses and handed him one. Then they sat in silence, her on the couch, him in the chair. They had history; they had been as close as two people could be. Still, it felt as if they were strangers. And it was absolutely absurd that in minutes they would attempt to create something akin to a family for their son.

"What comes after this?" he said finally. "After we tell him?"

"I don't know," she answered. "I think all we can do is try to understand his feelings and answer his questions as truthfully as we can."

As truthfully as we can. That was an odd way to put it. Why hadn't she simply said that they needed to answer his questions truthfully? But before he could drill her on it, he heard a key in the front door. He stood up, then sat down quickly. He didn't want to loom over Josh.

The boy saw his mom first, and there was genuine affection in his smile. Then he saw him in the chair.

"Mr. Colton?"

"Hi, Josh," he said.

"What's going on?" he asked, his tone puzzled.

Tilda patted the couch. "Come sit with us," she said. "We have something that we want to talk to you about."

She sounded pretty calm, but he could tell that Josh was already thinking that something strange was going on. But the boy sat, saying nothing.

Tilda drew in a breath. Let it out. She had her hands folded in her lap, and her fingers were pressing into her flesh. "Josh, I...we have something to tell you. And it's going to come as a pretty big shock to you. You're going to have lots of questions, I'm sure. We will answer every one of them."

As truthfully as we can, Blaine added silently in his head.

"Okay," Josh said. "Did I do something wrong?" Now the kid looked nervous.

"Absolutely not," he said emphatically. Then looked at Tilda. "Let's get on with it."

"Of course," she said softly. Then she turned so that she could look her son in the eye. "Josh, a long time ago, I got pregnant with you. And I wasn't married yet."

"I know that," Josh said. "You and Dad got married a couple weeks after I was born. You have the wedding announcement from the newspaper in your jewelry box."

"You're right," Tilda replied. "Partially. I married Dorian Stoll a few weeks after I gave birth to you. But he wasn't the father of my baby. Wasn't your father," she added, probably trying to be crystal clear.

Josh said nothing.

Blaine could feel his empty stomach cramp. This was going to be really hard on the boy. Everything he'd thought was true for thirteen years was going to be exposed as one big lie.

"Your father...is Blaine."

"Mr. Colton?" Josh turned to look at him with something in his eyes that could have been horror or fright or just plain disbelief.

"Yes. Blaine Colton is your father."

"But...but why did you marry Dorian?"

"Because I wanted you to have a father," she said.

Josh turned to him. Now there was no mistaking the look in his eyes. Hate. "You didn't want to marry her? Didn't want a kid?"

He tensed up. What was Tilda going to say? He watched as she reached out her hand and put it on her son's knee. "No, Josh. It wasn't like that. When I found out that I was pregnant, Blaine and I were going to get married. He wanted you. But then, I thought I had a miscarriage. There are signs in a woman's body that tell her that." She stopped. Swallowed hard. "It was only after we thought that there wasn't going to be a baby that he enlisted in the army. But then I found out that I hadn't miscarried, that I was still pregnant. I didn't tell Blaine. He never knew about you. Not until yesterday."

She'd chosen not to paint him badly. He supposed he should be grateful.

"Did Dad...did Dorian know that I wasn't his son?" Josh asked, his voice cracking.

"He did. But he loved you from the minute you were

born," she said. "He could not have loved you more if you'd been his."

Blaine supposed he should also be grateful for that. But right now, he wasn't feeling grateful about much. In military terms, this was a snafu of epic proportions.

"All this time, you lied to me," Josh accused, staring at his mom.

The words were a spike in Tilda's heart—that was obvious by the distress in her eyes, the tight set of her lips. "Decisions were made, Josh," she said. "And actions were taken. Decisions and actions that you may or may not agree with. The one thing that is for certain, that always has been and always will be, is that I love you. And I only ever want the best for you."

Josh said nothing. But his eyes were bright with unshed tears. He stared down at his hands that were braced on his knees, as if he was physically holding himself together.

Blaine wanted to make it better for him immediately but knew that this would be a process, likely full of starts and stops and maybe even a few wrong turns. "I know this is a lot to take in, Josh," he said quietly.

"Is this why you were nice to me at The Lodge?" His voice broke halfway through the sentence.

Blaine shook his head. "I was nice to you because you're a cool kid. I didn't realize that you were *my* cool kid until after you'd left yesterday. I'm hoping that now that you know, that it's out in the open, that we can move forward, get to know one another."

"Who else knows?" Josh asked.

"Just us," Tilda said. "But people are going to find out. I'm sure Blaine wants to tell his family about you."

He supposed he did. Hadn't really thought about it.

What the hell were Mara and Russ going to say about suddenly having another grandchild?

"Do I have to change my name?" Josh asked.

For the first time, Tilda looked to Blaine for the answer. Of course he wanted his son to carry his name. But now wasn't the time to draw hard lines in the sand. "You don't have to do anything you don't want to do," Blaine said.

No one said anything for a long moment. Finally, Josh took his hands off his knees and appeared to take in a deep breath. "Now what?" he asked.

"I thought maybe you and I could go get an early dinner. I know how hungry I was when I got home from school."

"Just you and me?" Josh asked. "What about Mom?"

Blaine said nothing. Tilda had had Josh for thirteen years. Was it too much to ask for one night?

Tilda stood up. "You know, it would probably be great if the two of you got better acquainted. You go without me. Just remember, it's a school night, and I'm sure there's some homework, so home by eight."

Blaine relaxed. She was okay with it, and her approval seemed to go a long way with Josh, who also was now standing. "I guess I could go," his son said. "I am hungry."

Tilda smiled. "Of course you are. You're breathing, right?" She reached out to hug her son but he shied away.

Tilda wrapped her arms around herself.

Blaine opened the door and motioned for Josh to precede him. As he was pulling the door shut, he took one more look at Tilda. She was still standing with her arms wrapped around herself. Her lips were pressed together. She looked smaller. Beaten.

As angry as he had been, still was, he didn't want that. She'd done a good job with the discussion. Had been straightforward and factual. Had gone as far as to say that he'd wanted the baby. That certainly wasn't true.

It couldn't have been easy for her. On the tip of his tongue was a reassurance that they would get through this. But then he reminded himself that none of this would have been necessary if she'd simply told the truth years ago.

"I'll have him home by eight," he said and pulled the door shut.

Chapter Five

Tilda's knees gave out, and she sank to the floor. And the sobs that she'd managed to hold back burst from her chest, like hot lava, too long trapped. Josh had pulled away from her. And the look in his eyes when he'd accused her of lying had been so full of hurt that it had almost taken her breath away.

When Blaine had suggested that the two of them go for dinner, she'd wanted to grab her son and run. But common sense and…well, perhaps a shred of decency had prevailed, and she'd managed to put up a brave front long enough to get them out the door.

Now she felt as if she might never catch her breath again.

Everything was going to unravel. Tonight they'd pulled a thread, and the tightly knit family that she and Dorian had started and she'd continued with on her own was going to come undone. Could she lose her son?

It was really everything she'd been afraid of in the hours after Russ Colton had come to see her all those years ago. He'd threatened her, said she wasn't good enough for his son. Threatened her family. Had had the power to hurt them all terribly. Of course, he hadn't known about the baby, and she'd decided that day that no one in the Colton family was ever going to know that her baby was a Colton. They played by rules that Tilda didn't even understand.

She'd been afraid then, and she was afraid now.

All she'd done was delay the inevitable.

And rob Blaine of years of getting to know his son.

She also couldn't forget about the harm that she'd caused Josh—who was her everything. He'd been without a father for years, and now he was going to realize that the man he'd loved and mourned had simply been filling in.

Tilda pressed the heels of her hands against her eyes, willing the tears to stop. She would not let Josh see her like this. He could not know that she was dying a slow death. Her son was going to have all he could deal with in the coming weeks, getting to know Blaine, and coming to terms with being a Colton and what that meant in this community. People were going to talk, and everyone would have an opinion.

She finally summoned the strength to pull herself up from the floor. Then she walked into the bathroom and rinsed her face for five minutes, doing the best job that she could to erase the tears. She was going to have to tell her parents. They absolutely could not hear this news from anybody but her. And then she'd tell Raeann. The woman had been her best friend for years.

She picked up her phone. Her mom answered on the third ring. "Hi, honey. How are you?"

"I'm okay," she said. How many times was she going to say that over the next few weeks and not mean it? "Are you and Dad busy?"

"No. Just watching television."

"Can I come over?"

"Of course. Josh, too?"

"No, just me." Josh might never want to get into a car with her again. "See you in ten."

When her mother opened the door and frowned, Tilda realized that she hadn't been a hundred percent successful in erasing the signs of her crying jag.

"What's happened?" her mother asked.

Tilda didn't answer. She simply walked in, took a seat on the couch, picked up the remote to turn down the television and looked at her parents. "I have something to tell you."

"You're scaring us," her mom said.

"I don't mean to." Her parents had been absolutely wonderful. Sure, there had been some initial shock when she'd told them she was pregnant, as well as some irritation when she'd refused to tell them who the father was. But they'd vowed to be there for her no matter what. And when she'd been confident that adoption was the answer, they'd been nothing but supportive. But as the pregnancy had progressed and she'd fallen more and more in love with the baby she carried, they'd also promised to help her in any way they could if she decided to keep the child.

Then she'd thrown them for another loop when she'd quickly married Dorian after Josh's birth. She'd never told them that Dorian was the baby's father, but by not denying it outright, she'd let them think that was possibly the truth.

Over the years, they'd been her constant rock.

And she was about to hit them with a sledgehammer.

"Thirteen years ago, when I got pregnant with Josh, I hid the fact that Blaine Colton was his father."

There. It was out.

"Blaine Colton," her mom repeated, no doubt trying

to remember the young man who'd been around those few months of her senior year.

Her dad said nothing. He knew the power of the Coltons in Roaring Springs. Was likely already thinking of the problems this news might unleash.

"Blaine recently returned from the army," she said. "We told Josh the truth tonight." There was no need for them to know the gritty details of how they'd gotten to that conversation.

"How did he take it?" her mom asked.

"He was surprised, of course. But he and Blaine are out having a quick dinner, starting to get to know one another."

"You knew it was Blaine Colton's baby?" her dad asked.

"I did."

"But never told him?" he continued.

"That's right."

Her dad considered her. "Then, I'm guessing you had a pretty good reason."

The tears that she'd managed to get in front of threatened again. As always, her parents were in her corner. "I did," she sniffled. "At least, I thought I did." She wasn't going to give details. Her parents, along with Russ and Mara Colton, were Josh's grandparents. If she told her parents the full truth, they would be very angry with Russ Colton and likely not be able to hide that fact from others. Again, it would only be Josh who would suffer if he had to choose between the grandparents he'd always known and the very rich and powerful Coltons.

"What do you need from us?" her mom asked, her tone kind.

"Nothing. I just needed you to hear it from me. To be prepared. There's going to be talk."

"I imagine so," her mom said. "Roaring Springs can be a bit of a gossip mill at times. But here's what I know for sure. You've been a great mom, honey. You've raised an amazing son. No one can say different."

Would it be enough? For Blaine? For Josh? "Thank you," she whispered. Then she got up, hugged each of them and walked out the door. She wanted to be home when her son got there.

BLAINE TOOK JOSH to a local sports bar and grill, thinking the casual atmosphere might be helpful. The Rockies were playing, and the two of them settled in a booth to watch the baseball game.

"Your mom says that you play second base. You like it?"

"I guess."

"You must have a pretty good arm. Got to get those double plays off fast, right?"

Josh stared at him. "This is weird," he said finally.

"Yeah, Josh," he admitted. "It is. But it's going to get easier. The more that you and I get to know each other, the easier it's going to get."

"Mom said you enlisted in the army. Did you ever shoot anyone?"

He had. Green Berets were called upon to complete some of the most dangerous assignments. And he'd done it very well.

And would have had none of it if he'd known the truth all those years ago. Tilda's lie had allowed him to pursue a career that he'd excelled at. But that didn't mean that he was happy that he'd been in the dark. "I did what was necessary," he said. "But if I'd have known about you," he said, "I would have come home much sooner. Would have been part of your life."

"I guess I'm glad that my real dad isn't dead," Josh said.

"I… I'm glad that you loved Dorian. I'm glad that he was a good father to you. I don't ever want you to feel weird about the fact that you loved him."

Josh swallowed so hard that Blaine could clearly see the movement. Neither of them said anything else until the pizza was delivered. When it arrived, Josh dug in. Blaine picked up a slice. His first meal with his son. He felt as if he should memorialize it in some way, maybe stand up and make an announcement. He glanced around, realizing that the people at the other tables were oblivious to the importance of the moment.

But word was going to get out. How long it took for the news to reach his parents would represent the quality of the Roaring Springs grapevine.

He would go see Russ and Mara tonight, once he dropped off Josh. After moving into staff housing, he'd been successfully able to limit his interactions with both of his parents. But it was time to talk to his dad. To offer up a sincere thank-you for whatever favors he'd had to call in to get someone to take another look at Blaine's discharge status. And then he'd tell them about Josh.

They chatted during dinner, mostly about the baseball game, but at the end of it, he felt okay about it. For a first time, it had gone pretty smoothly. He paid the bill and then drove Josh back home. He pulled up in front of Tilda's house at 7:57 p.m.

"Are you coming in?" Josh asked.

"I don't think so," Blaine said. Several times during dinner he'd thought of Tilda, how she'd looked standing in her doorway, and it had pulled at his gut. He'd had to remind himself that everyone, Josh included, was suffering. "Tell your mom that I'll call her tomorrow." They were going to need to work out a schedule for him to see Josh.

"Okay." Josh opened his door. "Uh…thanks for dinner."

"You're welcome."

His son made no move to get out. His young face, illuminated by the streetlights, was tight with concern.

"Is there a question I can answer for you?" Blaine asked softly.

"Not exactly a question. I guess I just don't know what to call you," he said. "*Dad* feels weird."

Blaine nodded contemplatively, not letting the boy know how hard it was to hear those words. It should not be weird in any way for his son to call him Dad. That was Tilda's doing. "This is all pretty new," he agreed. "Why don't you just call me Blaine for now."

Josh nodded, looking relieved. "I think that would be good."

Blaine smiled. "This is going to get easier, Josh. I promise."

"Right. I've got to go." Josh got out and practically ran into the house.

Blaine waited until he was inside and then pulled away from the curb, thinking once again about Tilda. Would she quiz Josh about what he and Blaine had talked about? Would she try to turn his son away from him?

He didn't think so. Was confident that Tilda wasn't that type.

Then he gave himself a mental head slap. If anyone had asked him, he'd have been confident in saying that the girl he'd once adored would never hide the fact that he had a son. Look how wrong he'd been about that.

He drove to Colton Manor and parked near the front

door. As family, he should feel comfortable just walking in. But he'd been gone a long time, and he felt better about ringing the doorbell. He waited. Finally, the door opened. It was his father.

"Blaine?"

"Hi, Dad. Can I come in?"

His father stepped back, motioning him in. "We weren't expecting you."

"I know. I just need a few minutes. Is Mom here?"

"I imagine she's reading upstairs. I'll go get her."

"I'm right here." Mara stood off to his right. In a nightgown and robe. Even in that, she managed to look elegant.

She led them to one of the many sitting areas in the main living space. Blaine wasn't familiar enough with the house to know exactly what they used this room for, but it didn't appear that the furniture had ever been sat on. It still looked showroom-perfect. He sat on a chestnut-colored leather couch. His mom took a chair on his right, his dad took one on his left.

He focused on Russ first. "I want to thank you for helping me with my discharge status. I appreciate it." Short, succinct. Earlier tonight, he'd appreciated it when Tilda's explanation had been the same. Maybe his dad would react similarly. And really, what else was there to say?

"Coltons do not get dishonorably discharged," his dad said.

Of course not. Blaine had known from the beginning that his father's help had been more about protecting the family name than about genuine concern for Blaine. At one time, that might have made him angry. But his years in the service had given him a broader perspective on many things. And the truth of it was that, regardless of the motive, his dad's help had pushed the process forward faster than he could have reasonably hoped for.

Blaine leaned forward. "I need to talk to the both of you about something else. Something that I've recently learned." He cleared his throat. "I'm not sure if you remember Tilda Deeds. She and I dated at the end of my senior year."

A look passed between his parents. It was brief and indecipherable but definitely there. And it made the hair on the back of his neck stand up. "What?" he asked.

Neither of them said anything. Fine. Whatever. He was never going to really understand his parents. "Anyway, Tilda has a thirteen-year-old son. Joshua. She calls him Josh. He's…he's my son."

"What?" his father barked.

"Josh is my son. I didn't know about it until yesterday. Tonight, Tilda and I told Josh."

"How do you know that she… Tilda…is telling you the truth?" This from his mom. "There are women who would find it very convenient to have a Colton child. Have you had a blood test?"

He didn't need a blood test. He could look at Josh and tell. "I think Tilda would have preferred it if I hadn't guessed the truth," he admitted. "She didn't tell me to lure me into any trap or to get financial security for her child."

"You should get medical proof," his father said.

"Maybe we will," Blaine hedged. "But for now, work off the assumption that I'm right. Josh Stoll is your grandchild."

The words seemed to echo in the quiet room. Finally, Mara leaned forward in her chair. "I want to meet him."

"Of course. But in due time. This has been a big

shock to him." Blaine turned to his father who was being uncharacteristically quiet. "Dad?"

"I guess it would be appropriate to offer congratulations. It's not every day that a man finds out he has a son."

"Or a grandson."

"That's true," Russ said contemplatively.

Blaine stood up. "I wanted you both to hear it from me. I'm sure word will get around town quickly enough." He could see his mom's jaw tighten. Gossip about the family always made her uncomfortable. Unless, of course, there was a way to spin it into more business.

"Good night," Blaine said.

He walked out the door, feeling very, very weary.

Chapter Six

Tilda slept fitfully and then slept through her alarm. She was trying to brush her hair and eat a piece of toast when her cell phone rang. Since she did not recognize the number, she considered letting it go to voice mail but ended up answering it, thinking it might be a parent of a student.

"Hello."

"Tilda?"

"Yes."

"This is Mara Colton."

Tilda put down her toast and her brush. She steadied herself with one hand on the bathroom vanity. "Yes."

"I'd like to meet my grandson."

Well, that answered the question of how long it was going to take for word to spread. "I..." She stopped to take a breath. "I'm sorry. I wasn't expecting your call."

"On Saturday. I want him to come to the house for lunch."

She wanted to say *Hell no*. But knew she had no right to do that. But she didn't trust the Coltons. "Not alone," she said. "I need to be with him."

"That's fine," Mara replied. "I'll expect you both at one."

The woman hung up. And Tilda picked up her toast

and tossed it into the bathroom garbage. There was no way she could eat now.

She wouldn't tell Josh. Not right now. She'd find a better time to break the news.

She walked out of the bathroom. "Are you ready?" she asked. When it was cold, she dropped Josh off at his school in the mornings before going on to the high school.

"I'm walking today."

He was avoiding her. But it was slowly getting warmer and safe enough. There was no reason to say no. She'd been hoping that this morning things would be better. He'd returned from his dinner with Blaine and mumbled something about homework and retreated to his room. When she'd knocked on his door before she went to bed, he hadn't answered. As was her custom, she'd opened the door. His light was off and he was asleep. Or at least pretending to be asleep.

"Okay," she said. "Don't say I didn't offer," she added lightly.

He didn't respond. Just grabbed his backpack and walked out the door.

It wasn't as if he'd never been mad at her before. One couldn't parent for thirteen years and not have a few slammed doors and some angry shouting. But those had been kid tantrums—little bouts of adolescent independence rearing up. His demeanor now was far different.

And it scared her.

What if they couldn't ever get back to the loving and trusting relationship they'd had? The thought of that just made her sick. And she considered whether she should call in to work. But knew she couldn't. Subs were hard to find, and she didn't want to put her principal in the bad position of having no one to cover her classes. She was not irresponsible, not thoughtless. To be fair, though, Blaine might want to debate that right now. She wasn't sure. He was being rather circumspect about his thoughts.

He'd been easier to read at eighteen. He'd liked her. A whole lot, it had seemed. And she'd felt the same.

Now, it all seemed a lifetime ago.

Sad, perhaps sadder than she'd ever been, she drove to school on autopilot and parked in her assigned space. However, when she walked into the building, she had a smile on her face. Her students deserved a hundred percent effort from her. No one needed to know that her heart was breaking.

By noon, she felt as if she'd run twenty miles. She stayed at her desk and tried to eat the tuna salad sandwich that she'd packed. But it felt as if it might get caught in her throat. She was halfway done when Raeann poked her head in the door.

"I was worried when I didn't see you in the lounge," her friend said. "Everything okay?"

Tilda shook her head. "Come in," she said. "I need to tell you something."

Raeann shut the door behind her. "What?"

"You know that I was married. That my husband died." That had been before she and Raeann had met but they'd had more than one discussion about it.

"Yes."

"I let you think that Dorian was Josh's father."

"I suppose you did. I mean, I never really thought about it. I guess I just assumed."

"Well, he wasn't. And the biological father has returned to Roaring Springs after being away for all these years. He knows about Josh. And Josh knows the truth, too."

Raeann's mouth made the shape of a circle but she said nothing. "Now I understand why you look as if a truck has run you over," she said finally.

"It's stalled on top of me, pressing on my chest, cutting off my breath."

"Oh, honey," Raeann said. She came around the desk to give her a hug. "I'm so sorry. But it's going to be okay. I know it will be."

"I don't know. I may have really screwed up this time. I didn't tell the biological father the truth. He left town more than thirteen years ago thinking that I'd miscarried. Because I'd *thought* I'd miscarried," she added. "When I found out the truth, I… I didn't tell him. He's pretty angry about that right now."

Raeann studied her. "You were so young. Just eighteen, right? And you and I both know, better than most, that eighteen-year-old kids can do adult things, but they aren't even close to being adults. Knowing you the way I do, I'm confident that you had a reason, a good reason, to do what you did."

Tilda's eyes filled with tears. Not everyone was going to feel the same way as Raeann. Many others were going to assume that she'd had bad motives and had been deliberately cruel. But having her best friend in her corner meant a lot. "Thank you," she said. "For believing me. For believing *in* me."

"Who's the father?" Raeann asked.

"Blaine Colton." Raeann had not gone to high school with them.

"As in Colton of the Coltons?"

"Yes. He's a middle brother. Wyatt and Decker are older. The twins, Skye and Phoebe, are younger. There's also Fox and Sloane, who are actually cousins but were raised alongside Blaine and his brothers and sisters after their parents died."

"I follow Skye on social media," Raeann said. "It's some family!"

That was one way to put it. One need not have grown up in Roaring Springs to realize the power that came along with the Colton name. Power to crush an adversary. Power to…oh, God…take a child away from a loving mother.

The five-minute bell rang, warning kids that lunch was almost over. She had three more hours to get through before she could go home and cry.

"How do you feel about Blaine after all these years?" Raeann asked.

That was a complicated question. "He evidently did really well in the military."

"Good for Blaine," Raeann said. "How do you feel about him?" She'd never been one to let her questions be pushed aside.

Tilda swallowed hard. "He's a man who has seen things. Been tested. Hardened. I see that in him. But when I look into his eyes, I see the boy I fell for, the boy who could make me laugh and even make me watch scary movies because he was there to protect me. The boy I might even have loved." There. She'd said it. Out loud. "But I suspect he's not reflecting quite the same way on our shared past."

"You don't know that, Tilda, But the one thing I do know is that once Blaine Colton realizes what a good person you are and what a great mom you've always been, he'll come around."

Raeann hadn't seen the look in Blaine's eyes. He despised her for what she'd done.

BLAINE WAS IN his office, looking at spreadsheets, when there was a knock on his door. He looked up to see Decker.

"Penny said you stopped by earlier. Did you need something?" his brother asked.

Blaine waved him in, toward a seat at the table in the corner. He joined Decker there. "I wanted to tell you something."

"Okay."

"This is going to come out of left field, but I'm just going to say it. I mentioned seeing Tilda Deeds the other day. And her son. Well, it turns out that he's mine. My biological child."

Decker said nothing for a minute. Finally, he offered up a smile. "Congratulations?"

Blaine nodded. "Yeah, it's a good thing. I mean, I'm still getting my head around it, but yes, I'm a father."

"You had no idea."

"I thought Tilda had miscarried the child. That was before I left for the army."

Decker leaned back in his chair. "Was that why you were going to marry her? You never said anything about a child."

"I know I didn't. We were keeping it to ourselves." In any other circumstance, he'd have told Decker the full truth. But Tilda hadn't been ready for that and he'd never considered going against her wishes. She was his future. They were linked in all things going forward. At least it had seemed that way to him. In retrospect, perhaps his thinking had been a little one-sided. "That was certainly a big reason. I would never have walked away from my child."

Decker held up a hand. "Of course," he said, as if

there was never a question about that. "Wow. Have you told Mom and Dad?"

"Yes. Last night."

"What did they say?"

"Mom was immediately suspicious of her motives," Blaine said. "But suffice it to say, if Tilda had her way, she'd have probably continued to keep it a secret."

"I guess Tilda's not as nice as she wants everybody to think," Decker said.

"Maybe not," Blaine said. It was nice to have Decker solidly in his corner. "It does seem as if she's done a good job with Josh," he added…well, because it was true. She'd certainly done a commendable job with the conversation with Josh. Hadn't made a lot of excuses.

"Josh knows?"

"Yeah. We went out for dinner last night, just him and me. He said it felt weird to call me Dad. We settled on Blaine for now."

"Probably a good idea not to get hung up on the small stuff. I know you mentioned the other day that he seemed like a good kid, but something like this could throw the most stable of kids off their stride."

The idea of that made him feel ill. He recalled vividly having conversations with men in his unit who were married and had kids at home. They would get a letter, some kind of news, and it would take their heads out of the game for days. Now he understood that a little better. Worrying about a kid was all-consuming.

"Can I tell Kendall?" Decker asked.

"Of course. Even if I said no, you probably would, right?"

"Yeah," Decker admitted. "No secrets."

Blaine was a little envious. That clearly wasn't the

relationship that he and Tilda shared. Had ever really shared.

As if reading his mind, Decker asked, "Has she given you an explanation for why she did this? Why she hid the fact that you have a son for thirteen years?"

Blaine shook his head. He stood up to go. They both had work to do.

"It better have been a damn good reason," Decker said.

"To be honest, I can't think of any reason that would be good enough," Blaine gritted out.

Decker stood up and walked to the door. "I understand. But I think you're going to have to find a way to get past your feelings. For the sake of your son."

Two hours later, Blaine tried to remember Decker's advice as he called Tilda's cell phone for the second time in ten minutes and it went straight to voice mail again. He glanced at his watch. The school day was over. There was no reason for her not to answer her phone. Unless she was avoiding him.

The hell with that. He closed down his laptop and was fast getting to the parking lot. Then drove down the mountain and was parked in front of the school in fifteen minutes. They'd added a wing since he and Tilda had been students there. But beyond that, it looked remarkably the same.

He'd been a good athlete and a pretty good student, with enough money to do the things he'd wanted to do. His girlfriend had been the prettiest in the whole school. But still, he had very eagerly anticipated graduation. Because that meant that he could get away. From Roaring Springs, where everybody had an opinion of the Coltons. From his father and his constant insistence that Blaine would join the family business. From everybody who didn't understand that he wanted to serve his country.

With the optimism of youth, he'd seen endless possibilities. Until his world had come crashing down in the form of a positive pregnancy test.

When that problem had seemingly gone away, he'd left Roaring Springs, never anticipating that he'd set foot in the school again. But here he was. And likely would be again, he realized, because in two years, Josh would be a student here. Blaine would be coming to parent–teacher conferences, athletic events, school plays. The whole deal.

He'd do better than his own dad. Of that, he was confident. He would never put any business interest ahead of Josh. His son would know how much he was loved.

He walked up the steps and tried the front door. It was locked. Not surprising, considering the violence that had occurred in so many high schools. He was glad to see it. He rang the bell next to the door and looked up into the camera.

"May I help you?" the voice over the intercom asked.

"Blaine Colton to see Tilda Deeds."

"Do you have an appointment?"

"Yes," he lied.

The buzzer sounded, and he reached for the door. Blaine didn't know the number of Tilda's classroom, but he could still remember the hallway where most of the English classes had been taught. He headed in that direction.

Twenty feet away from room 230, he heard a raised voice. Male. Then a softer one. Tilda. He picked up his pace. Edged around the corner to see a teenage boy standing in front of a teacher's desk. Behind the desk, standing, but still several inches shorter than the boy, was Tilda. She had her hands on the back of her chair, and she looked very serious.

"I was hoping to see a paper from you today, Toby. As I said, I'm going to fail you if you don't do the work," she said, her voice soft, yet still firm. "You won't graduate with your class."

"I don't care," the young man said. He said it easily enough, but Blaine wasn't confident that the kid was telling the truth.

"You should. And I know you have the ability to be successful. That's the part I can't understand. Tomorrow is the last day I will accept the paper. I've got a note here for you to take home. One of your parents needs to sign it acknowledging that they are aware that you're in jeopardy of failing this class and failing to graduate. I expect it to also be returned by the end of the day tomorrow."

"My parents are out of town," Toby said, sounding bored.

"Will they be back this weekend?"

"I guess," he muttered.

"Then bring it Monday. You are excused." She slid the paper in her hand across the desk.

When the kid made no effort to move, Blaine swung around the corner. "Ms. Deeds, I think I'm your next appointment." He offered up a smile in her direction while he sized up the teenager.

Toby was staring at Tilda, animosity in his eyes. When he leaned towards Tilda, putting himself within arm's reach, every protective instinct Blaine had surged upward. The kid had big hands, hands that could do damage.

Blaine took three steps and got close to Tilda. Close enough that his body edged hers back.

Toby said nothing and after a long minute, he picked up the paper on the desk and shoved it into the zipper compartment of his backpack. Then he left without another word. Tilda pulled back her chair and sank into it, head forward, chin down.

She seemed worn out. And fragile. Her long hair fell over her face and it was a startling reminder of when he'd pulled out her hair pins on prom night and let down the wild mass, letting it flow over her naked breasts.

He'd thought her fragile that night, too. Until she'd taken him into her body and then he'd thought her a warrior.

He took a step back, feeling unsure. "Are you okay?" he asked, his voice sounding rough.

"Just tired of fighting the same battle," she said, looking up.

"What's his story?" Blaine asked.

"Decent kid who has fallen off the rails in the last couple of months. Doesn't turn in assignments. Is failing most of the tests."

"In just your class or every class?"

"Most of his classes," she said. "I'm afraid that his other teachers have written him off."

"But you haven't. Are you sure he's a good kid?" He was having a hard time forgetting the look in Toby's eyes.

"I think so." Turning to him, she arched a brow. "We did not have an appointment."

"No, we didn't. And you should tell whoever it was that buzzed me in that they should verify the person has an appointment before letting them wander through the school."

"We have a temp in the office. Our regular secretary is on medical leave. She would have known to do that.

I'll make sure I say something. Unfortunately, we're all too familiar with the need to be more vigilant with security."

He'd not given much thought to the dangers in Tilda's job, but they were definitely there. "I called you," he said. "You didn't answer. I thought you might be avoiding me."

She rolled her eyes. "Would that be a good long-term strategy?"

"No."

"I wouldn't have thought so," she said. "Your mother called me."

Wow. That had been fast. "She's always been very efficient."

"She wants Josh to come for lunch on Saturday. I told her that I wouldn't let him come by himself, and she did extend the invitation to me, too."

More than he'd done the previous night. "I'll let her know that I'll attend, as well."

"Fine," she said, as if she could not care less. "Josh might need some time to come to terms with being a Colton. I don't want your parents heaping a bunch of expectations on him."

He knew all about Colton expectations. His father had expected him to join the business, and that had been the furthest thing from his mind. It was kind of ironic now that he was working at The Lodge, but that was just temporary. "I'll handle my parents. We need to work out a schedule for when I can see Josh."

She picked up her bag and slung it over her shoulder. "I'll talk to Josh tonight."

"You will?" he prodded.

"I said I would."

Now she sounded irritated. Well, that made two of

them. He was irritated beyond measure that he was having to ask to see his son. "How was he when he got home last night from our dinner?"

"Fine. He didn't say much."

"Is that normal?"

"Not really," she said. There was something in her tone that wasn't right. She sounded…hurt.

"He's a smart, funny kid. He's going to be able to handle this," he said, not sure if he was assuring her or himself.

"I hope so," she said. "He has to come first, Blaine."

"I don't disagree."

She stared at him. "Then, please, for his sake, don't get him all excited about having a father again if you're planning on leaving again."

He *had* been planning on leaving. This was only supposed to be a temporary stop. "Even if I…" He stopped. Even if he did leave, there was no reason that Josh couldn't come with him. But he didn't want to have that discussion and inevitable argument right now.

"Even if you what?" she asked.

"Even if I get him all excited, I imagine that you'll be able to temper his enthusiasm." His comment came out as a little mean-spirited, and he wasn't happy with that, but she'd pushed him into a corner.

She sighed. "I need to lock my classroom. You need to go."

He should apologize. "I—"

"Good night, Blaine," she interrupted him, looking pointedly at the door.

He walked out without another word.

WHEN TILDA GOT HOME, Josh and his friend Isaac were on the couch, along with two open bags of chips and a package of chocolate chip cookies. "Hey, guys," she said. "How's it going?"

Josh said nothing.

"You know, the usual Mrs. D.," Isaac said. "School is a bore, and Josh has a new dad."

She was glad that Josh had confided in his best friend. He needed somebody to talk to since he obviously wasn't talking to her. "Exciting news, huh?" she murmured, keeping a smile on her face.

"I'll say. You guys are rich now."

"Then, why is there only forty dollars in my billfold?" she said, keeping her tone light. She wasn't going to let her son's friend throw her off her game. If she allowed that, she'd better just give up teaching high school right now.

"I told Josh he should ask for free lessons at The Lodge. For both of us."

"I don't think so," she said, then turned to her son. "Good day at school?"

"Fine," he muttered, not even taking his eyes off the television. "Let's go to my room," he told Isaac.

"Okay. I'll bring the chips. You get the cookies."

Tilda should probably warn them about ruining their dinner, but right now, she just couldn't muster the energy. She waited until she heard Josh's door shut, then sank down onto the couch, where her son had been. She let her head fall back, then turned her face to rest her cheek against the cushion.

It was still warm from his body.

As a baby, how many nights had she held him close, his body warm and soft in her arms? In the early days, she'd agonized over the decision to pass him off to others as Dorian's son. But she had eventually come to terms with the deception, especially since Dorian had known the truth and it hadn't mattered to him. And, ultimately, what truly mattered was that Josh had a dad who wanted him. A dad who was around for his first words, his first steps. A dad who wanted to be in Roaring Springs, to raise a family here.

A dad whose family didn't scare the hell out of her.

Saturday's lunch with Mara Colton loomed large. She could probably back out, ask Blaine to accompany Josh. Remove herself from any possible confrontation.

But the idea that her son would meet his new *grandparents* without her there to run interference was simply not an option. He likely wouldn't be happy that she was going. After all, right now, he didn't seem to want her around at all. But Josh didn't understand these people like she did. And if they thought that they were simply going to push her aside, they had better think again.

Chapter Seven

On Friday, Blaine was eating lunch at his desk when there was a light knock on the door. It was his cousin Sloane.

He got up, walked around his desk and hugged her. "Oh, man. Good to see you. I'm sorry I missed your and Liam's wedding."

She smiled. "It was small, just at the courthouse."

"You've taken on a lot. New job. New marriage."

"Don't forget I'm raising a two-year-old," she said teasingly, as if she wanted full credit. "And if the grapevine is correct, Chloe is not the only Colton grandchild."

He pretended to frown. "Well, let me think. Wyatt and Bailey are pregnant."

She shoved the heel of her hand into his chest. "Don't play dumb."

He motioned for her to take a chair, and he returned to his. "Yes, I have a son. Joshua. I guess everybody calls him Josh."

"And you had no idea?" she asked.

That didn't sit well. "You think I would have stayed away for thirteen years if I'd known?"

"Of course not," she said. "I said that poorly. It's just that you and Tilda didn't date all that long."

"Only takes once," he replied. "Prom."

She rolled her eyes. "Chloe is never going to a school dance."

"She found out right before graduation. I'll admit, I was pretty shook up. But then she told me she lost the baby. She says that she thought she did and didn't realize she was still pregnant until several weeks later."

"And you were already gone."

"Yeah."

"How's it going between the two of you?" Sloane asked.

"It's…" He stopped. He'd been about to say that it was fine. But this was Sloane. He could be honest with her. "It's really hard. I'm angry with her. With what she did."

"I get that. But you were gone, and you'd told most everybody that you couldn't wait to leave Roaring Springs, that you didn't intend to come back. She had to have heard that. And have you considered that she might not have told you because she didn't want you to come back because she and the baby were an obligation?"

"She said that she intended to give the baby up for adoption but couldn't once he was born."

Sloane's face softened. "The first time I held Chloe, my heart was so full of love I thought it was going to burst. I would have never been able to give her away, so I get that Tilda would have changed her mind."

"She could have told me then."

"I suspect she thought she was doing what was best for her child. I had to do the same thing when I left Chloe's father and got a divorce. It was hard. But I did it for Chloe. And I never regretted it for one single moment."

What she said made sense, and it wasn't all that different than what Tilda had already told him. But still, he'd missed thirteen years. "I don't know if I'm going to be able to get past it."

She stood up. "I hope you can. My divorce was a messy one, and I lived in the shadows for a long time. And until I met Liam, I think I forgot that happiness is a choice. Don't make a bad choice and hang on to the anger. You're too good a person for that."

He stared at the door of his office long after she'd walked away. She made it sound easy. But he knew the truth. There was nothing easy about this situation with Tilda and Josh.

But then again, he wasn't exactly known for running away from hard things. As a Green Beret, he was one of the people called in when it got especially difficult.

And speaking of difficult, there was lunch at Colton Manor tomorrow. Tilda hadn't seemed to care one way or the other if he attended. But he wasn't going for her. He was going for Josh.

TILDA TRIED TO FOCUS on teaching but couldn't get past wondering if Blaine might show up again at the end of the day. Was it dread or anticipation in her stomach? Hard to know.

There was no paper from Toby and no explanation. Raeann came in just as she was packing her bag. "Yay, it's the weekend," she said. She propped herself on the edge of Tilda's desk and let her feet hang. "What are your plans?"

"I'm having lunch at Colton Manor. With Mara Colton. And Josh and Blaine," she added.

"Oh my God. I want to hear everything about that house. It looks so gorgeous from the outside. Can you take some pictures?"

"We'll see," Tilda said. "They'll probably be pretty blurry because I'm pretty sure my hand will be shaking."

"Don't be nervous. My mother used to say that the rich put on their pants the same way as the rest of us, one leg at a time."

"I'll try to remember that," Tilda said wryly.

"I've seen Mara Colton at events in town. She always looks perfect. Her hair is perfect, her clothes are perfect. She smells good. Or at least that's what somebody told me once."

"Not making me feel any better," Tilda said. She was feeling rather like a hot mess right now.

"What are you taking for a hostess gift?" her friend asked.

"Ugh… I haven't exactly been focused on hostess gifts these last couple days."

"You have to take something. Something cool, yet classy. Probably not wine since it's a lunch date."

The perfect hostess gift. More things to worry about. She was going to have a permanent wrinkle in her forehead if this continued. "I'll think of something," Tilda said. Probably not, but really, it likely wasn't going to be the deciding factor whether Mara Colton approved of her. "What are you doing this weekend?"

"Painting the laundry room," Raeann said.

That sounded heavenly. "Want to switch?" Tilda asked lightly.

"Is Blaine Colton included in the deal? I saw him in the hallway outside my room yesterday, and he is a fine example of a man. If I wasn't happily married most days, I'd have found a reason to casually bump into him. Maybe I could have pretended to be lost, and he could have helped me find my way."

"And then when he found out your classroom was next door?" Tilda asked dryly.

"By then he'd be so enamored that he wouldn't care. Of course, once he found out about the twins, probably not so much."

Tilda shrugged. "I don't know about that. He's good with Josh."

Raeann looked at her. "You're not unhappy about that, are you? I mean, that's a good thing."

"Of course. I already had this conversation with myself," Tilda admitted. "The first night that Blaine and Josh went to dinner by themselves. I was...a little jealous that Blaine seemed so easy with it all. I was being stupid."

Raeann shook her head. "You're never stupid, Tilda. You're thoughtful and self-aware, and you just need to accept that this has been a pretty significant change in your life and that you might need more than a minute to get used to it."

Tilda hugged her friend. "Does your laundry room really need to be painted? Because it would be very helpful if you could come home with me so that you're available when I need the next pep talk."

"Call me if you need me. I can paint and talk. I can pretty much do anything and talk at the same time."

TWO HOURS LATER, Tilda and Josh were at her parents' house. There was pizza and salad and absolutely no discussion about the Coltons. Either her parents wanted to give Josh a chance to bring it up or they'd decided that they were simply going to ignore this most recent development. Given that her parents were not the stick-your-head-in-the-sand kind of people, she thought it was the former.

She was grateful for the interlude. It offered a brief respite when she could stop thinking about their mandatory appearance at Colton Manor and simply enjoy life as it had been for so many years. She and Josh were getting ready to drive home when she heard the ping of an incoming text. She glanced down at the open purse at her feet. Could see the screen. It was Blaine. And for just one sweet second she allowed herself to hope that he had reconsidered how they'd ended their conversation the previous afternoon and he wanted to apologize.

She reached for her cell and quickly realized that she'd been foolishly optimistic. He was simply confirming that he'd meet her at his parents' house at 1:00 pm. With a heavy heart, she acknowledged his text with a quick Thank you.

Her mom saw her on her phone and asked, "Everything okay?"

She wanted to tell her mom the truth. That Blaine's return had stirred up feelings that she'd thought were wrapped up and put on a shelf a long time ago. That she didn't know what to do about the attraction she still felt for him. That…that she wasn't sure she could bear it if he never forgave her. But her mom didn't need to be carrying around those kind of worries. "Yes. All good. Josh and I are going to Colton Manor tomorrow to have lunch with Mara Colton. Blaine will be there, too. My friend said I should take a hostess gift."

"A nice box of chocolates," her mom said.

"I don't know. Mara Colton is super thin."

"Super thin. Super rich. Doesn't matter. Even if she doesn't eat them herself, she can always take them to work and share them."

Tilda smiled at her mom. "Why am I not surprised

to know that you have an answer for every one of my problems?"

"I'm your mother, darling. That's my job." She leaned in to hug Tilda and whispered in her ear. "You're every bit as good as any one of the Coltons. Don't you forget it."

Tilda drove home, her mom's words reverberating in her head. She went to bed and there was no relief. She dreamed that she was standing outside Russ and Mara Colton's house, her fist raised in the air, shouting, "I am as good as any one of the Coltons." On Saturday morning, she woke up with a dull headache. She could hear Josh already up in his room and figured he was too excited or maybe too nervous to sleep in like he would on a usual weekend during the school year.

Nothing usual about their lives right now.

Now, she walked into the kitchen and saw that Josh had not started the coffee. It was just one more way of showing her that he was seriously unhappy with her. She pulled out a filter from the cupboard, tossed some grounds in, and added water. Then stood there while she waited for it to brew.

Finally, cup in one hand and two pieces of peanut butter toast in another, she walked back to Josh's room. Kicked gently at the door with her foot.

"Yeah," he said.

"Good morning," she said through the door.

"Good morning," he answered.

That was progress. "You're up early."

"Not every day a guy gets to meet grandparents that he knew nothing about."

He said it sarcastically, a bite in his tone, not at all in the easy, teasing manner that had been a hallmark of his usual communication with her. She was grateful that she was still in the hallway, where he couldn't see her face, couldn't see the hurt. "We leave at noon," she said. "Don't wear jeans."

The Coltons needed to understand that she'd done just fine raising Josh. That he had good manners. Was respectful of others. In the car ride there, they'd have a short conversation about all those things.

Tilda took two steps before stopping, remembering her mother's parting words. She had nothing to prove to the Coltons. Turning, she walked back to Josh's door and set her coffee cup on the floor so that she could knock properly.

"Yeah," he answered.

"May I come in?"

"I guess."

She opened the door. He was sitting on his bed, still in his pajamas. His laptop was open, on the bed next to him. His hair was rumpled, and he looked like the young and sweet kid who'd lived in her house for all these years.

Because he was.

"Actually, Josh, you can wear whatever you want. And for the record, I'm sorry. Sorry that I wasn't more forthcoming with the truth. Sorry that all of this just got sprung on you. You didn't deserve this. And believe me, if there was anything I could do to make it better, I would. Because I love you. More than you will ever know. Well, at least until you have a child of your own."

He stared at her. "I think I just want to know why."

She could not tell him. It would influence how he felt about the Coltons, and maybe even about Blaine. "It's complicated, Josh. But believe me when I say that I had very good reasons. And trust me, as well, when I say that we're going to get through this."

He stared at her. "I told… Blaine that it didn't feel right calling him Dad."

"How did he take that?"

"He said that it was okay, that maybe for now I could just call him Blaine."

She sat down on the edge of the bed. "Here's what I believe to be true. Blaine very much wants to have a relationship with you, to be your dad. But as an adult, he also realizes that this is all pretty new and strange."

"And do I call her Grandma?"

It was hard to think of the very stylish and chic Mara Colton as *Grandma*. "Not if you're not comfortable with it." And if Mara insisted or made a big deal out of it, she would simply pull her aside and explain that now wasn't the time to push it. "We're just going for lunch. We'll stay an hour or so and be on our way."

"I heard that their house was so big that people get lost in it."

She smiled at her son. "Nobody is getting lost today. And look at the bright side. You'll have a good story to tell Isaac."

He chewed on the side of his mouth. "I'm sorry that I've been a brat."

"You are never a brat," she said. "You're a champ. Always have been, and always will be." She leaned in and gave him a quick hug. "Now I'm going to go take a shower."

"Are you wearing jeans?"

"I don't know. I just might."

IN THE END, neither of them wore jeans. Josh put on the blue dress pants she'd bought for him to wear to church on Christmas Eve along with a blue and white button-down shirt. Tilda chose a long black skirt with short black boots and a white loosely knitted sweater. She put on makeup and jewelry and even a little perfume. Then she took an extra fifteen minutes to put hot rollers in her hair.

Who was she trying to impress? Mara Colton? Russ, if he happened to be there?

Blaine?

He used to tell her that she was the prettiest girl in high school. That her mouth was made for kissing and that her breasts were a perfect fit for his hands. It wasn't poetic, but it got the point across. And more than one night, before that fateful prom night, she'd felt him press up against her, hard. Wanting. But he'd never pushed her.

But just her luck, she'd gotten pregnant the one and only time they'd had sex. On prom night.

She was such a cliché.

They, she supposed, was a better pronoun. After all, while she'd been the one with a baby in her belly, he'd been every bit as responsible. And had been willing to assume it. Had not been happy about it, that was for sure. And the relief in his eyes, upon hearing the news that she'd miscarried, had been sincere.

They left early enough that she had time to stop at one of the small shops in town, and she got a box of expensive chocolates. They wrapped it up really pretty, too. She and Josh did not talk for most of the drive. Six blocks out, he turned to her. "What if she has something fancy for lunch, something that I hate? You know, you can only push it around your plate for so long."

She turned to give him a look. "Like delicately sautéed pigs' feet in lavender-infused butter."

"Or sheep brains over pasta with smelly cheese," he countered.

It was an old game they played on Wednesday nights when her favorite cooking show was on. Most weeks, instead of retreating to his room, he'd curl up next to her on the couch and try to come up with the most outlandish, foul-sounding recipe he could.

"I'm hoping for cow intestines in a simmering broth of snails and caviar," she said.

He waved a hand. "Fish eggs. You can do better."

She laughed. "If there's caviar, I am so going to enjoy watching you eat it."

He laughed, too. "I can push that around my plate all day if I have to."

BLAINE KNOCKED ON his parents' door. His mother answered, wearing a turquoise pantsuit, looking lovely as usual. She leaned in for a quick hug. "Good to see you," she said.

When he'd found out about the luncheon from Tilda, he'd immediately sent Mara a text, telling her that he'd be attending, too. She'd replied quickly, You know that you're always welcome.

He supposed he was.

Now, she stepped back to consider him. "You look as if you might be anticipating a trip to the dentist."

He knew there was a good chance that this lunch could be more painful than that. "I want you to meet Josh," he assured her. "He's a great kid."

"I'm sure he is. I've done a little research."

"On kids?" She'd had five of her own and mostly raised Fox and Sloane, too, after the death of her sister and her husband, but then again, she'd never really embraced motherhood.

"On Tilda. And Josh."

That didn't thrill him. But it also didn't surprise him.

Mara Colton prepared and planned for every event and any eventuality. She would not want to be surprised in any way. "And you discovered?" he asked.

"Tilda is the teacher everybody wants to have. Her students love her. Their parents respect her. Got the Teacher of the Year award two years ago."

He'd not heard that last little tidbit. "What else?"

"She lost her husband to throat cancer. Very rarely dates."

Very rarely meant that she did date once in a while. The thought of that made his stomach turn. Told himself that the only reason it bothered him was that these men had access to Josh. "What did you learn about Josh?" he asked.

"Good student. Good athlete. Makes excellent farting noises in social studies." She smiled at him. "That comes from Stella Witman, who works with me at The Chateau, who has a daughter in Josh's class."

"Good to know he has talents," he deadpanned. His mother had raised boys. She was no stranger to farting noises.

"Yes, it is," she said.

"Mom, I want this to go well," he said. Since seeing Tilda at her school on Thursday afternoon, he'd done nothing but think about her and about Josh. She'd seemed so tense. Maybe that had to do with the student that she'd been dealing with, but he was fairly certain that it also had something to do with him. He'd wanted to call Josh on Friday but decided not to press too hard too fast. His son needed a minute to catch his breath.

He was a happy kid. That was good.

It wasn't Blaine's intent to screw that up.

He also wasn't giving up. He'd missed thirteen years

through no fault of his own. He wasn't missing any more.

"I want the same thing," she said. "I don't see any reason why it won't."

"Is Dad joining us?"

"Not this time," she said. Her tone was carefully neutral, giving him no indication if there had been words about that or not. Perhaps Russ was simply otherwise engaged. Perhaps his parents no longer ate meals together. Perhaps he didn't care about meeting Blaine's son.

He couldn't worry about any of that now.

"We're going to eat in the sunroom. A little less formal than the dining room, don't you think?"

He wasn't sure he knew exactly where the sunroom was. "Yeah, that's fine. I think I'll just hang out here and watch for them."

"Of course," she said.

She left the foyer, and he started pacing. Since waking up this morning, he'd been worried that they might not show. Had considered sending a text, just to verify that they were on their way. But had managed not to. He and Tilda were never going to have the romantic relationship they'd once enjoyed. But they needed to get to a point where they trusted each other, especially when it came to Josh.

He saw her SUV turn into the drive. Let out a breath that he hadn't realized he was holding. Was this how new parents felt when they brought their baby home from the hospital to meet the extended family? Proud. Anxious for no defined reason. Sensitive to the potential of the slightest criticism.

They were out of the car. Tilda looked beautiful, he realized. She had curves, and he very much liked that on a woman. And Josh…well, that was his boy. He couldn't be more perfect.

He opened the door. Waved.

"Hi," Tilda said softly.

"Good to see you," he said. "Hey, Josh."

"Hello," Josh replied.

"Looks as if we're only going to get one more lesson in," he said, falling back to what they had in common. "Winter is finally moving on." The days were warming up, especially in the valley. It was still cold enough on the mountain to maintain snow cover, but that wasn't going to last.

The Lodge, which continued to attract guests all through the summer, would switch over to warm-weather mode. He'd spent the last couple of days at work laying the groundwork for a series of rock-climbing adventures, overnight hiking trips and an ATV off-roading camp.

"I'm so ready for spring," Tilda said. "And the month of summer that we get."

Colorado got more than a month of summer. But he understood what she meant. Summer in the mountains was a glorious time, with beautiful blue skies and temperatures in the mideighties. Just weeks ago, he'd assumed that he'd be somewhere else by summer, but now the season beckoned.

He and Josh could fish. Camp. Hang out.

"I thought I heard voices."

He turned to see his mom approaching. She had a smile on her face. First, she extended a hand in Tilda's direction. "It's nice to see you again, Tilda."

"Thank you for the lunch invitation," Tilda said, returning the handshake. She handed his mother a pretty package.

"Bethel's candy. How wonderful. Maybe we can all have a piece later." Then his mom turned toward his son. "Hello, Josh." She kept her arms at her sides.

And for the first time, Blaine realized that, as cool and collected as his mom had pretended to be earlier, she was also a little nervous.

"Hi," Josh said, his voice barely audible.

"I'll bet you're hungry," Mara said, already turning. She pointed towards the back of the house. "Blaine was always hungry when he was your age. Follow me."

She led, Josh followed, and he and Tilda brought up the rear. "How's he doing?" he whispered, leaning close. He caught a whiff of her perfume. Understated. But sexy. Like Tilda.

"Okay," she said. "A little nervous about this."

"Aren't we all?" he said, rolling his eyes.

She laughed, then caught herself when his mother looked over her shoulder. When his mother turned forward once again, she swung her head toward him. "You're not helping," she mouthed.

"Sorry," he said. But he wasn't. Tilda always did have a great laugh. Deep, a little throaty. And it felt good to make her laugh. Certainly better than it felt to argue with her.

When they got to the small square table on the porch, Mara stopped at one end, then motioned for Josh to take the spot on her right. Tilda took the chair to his mother's left and he took the other end.

"Pretty table," Tilda said.

He supposed it was. There were tulips in a vase in the middle. The place mats were a blue and white checkered print and the dishes a pale yellow. Starched white napkins had been carefully folded, and the silverware was shiny enough that he could see his reflection in the knife.

"Thank you," his mother said. She was still standing. "A touch of spring."

"We need that," Tilda responded warmly.

He appreciated that they were both trying with the small talk. Josh was looking around the room, his eyes stopping when he got to the cabinet at the far side. Blaine knew immediately what had drawn his attention. He got up and retrieved the eight-by-ten photo that sat on the third shelf.

"Is that you?" his son asked.

"Yeah. I was just a couple years older than you. Played shortstop. We won State my junior year." Not only that, he'd also been voted Most Valuable Player for the final game.

"You didn't say anything the other night," Josh said.

He hadn't. "Wasn't important. We were talking about your game." He sure as hell wasn't going to be one of those dads where the kid had to live up to some legacy.

There was an awkward silence at the table, and he glanced at his mother. She was staring at him, a very odd look in her eyes. Suddenly, she smiled brightly. "I hope you like Thai food," she said, looking at Josh. "I ordered lunch from AppeThaizer."

Josh nodded and looked at Tilda. "I love that place."

"AppeThaizer?" Blaine asked.

"Cool restaurant in the Diamond," Tilda explained, mentioning a trendy part of downtown. "Everything is homemade and delicious. It just might be Josh's favorite place to eat."

Now his mother was practically beaming. "I'm glad I guessed right, then. Blaine, would you help me carry things in?" She headed for the kitchen.

He pushed his chair back. But before he could leave the table, Josh leaned across it, towards Tilda. "No cow intestines."

She shrugged, looking innocent. "Or sheep brains? Who knew?"

"Huh?" he asked.

"Just something Mom and I do," Josh said. He added no further explanation.

What Blaine heard was clear enough. *The two of us already have our own little world. You're the outsider.*

But he wasn't going to get discouraged. He was just going to have to try harder. "Sounds kind of fun and gross," he mused. "Be right back."

When he got to the kitchen, his mother was loading up two serving trays with rice and what appeared to be cashew chicken and pad thai. "Good job on the food, Mom," he said.

"I had help. Stella asked her daughter if she knew what kind of food Josh liked. Evidently, in health class he told the teacher that fried rice should be on the basic food pyramid because he couldn't live without it. And everybody in town knows that AppeThaizer is the best."

Mara had a better spy network than some small countries. "Thanks for making an effort to have this go well," he said.

She stared at him. "Blaine, I could have done a better job at motherhood. I'd like to think that I've learned a few things along the way about what's most important in life. I don't want to make the same mistakes with my grandchildren."

He wanted to assure her that she'd done a fine job, that he had no complaints. But he could tell that she wasn't interested in platitudes. She was very serious about this, and when his mother put her mind to something, experience told him to *watch out*. She could be a force to be reckoned with.

"What do you think of Josh?" That was the question he couldn't help asking.

"He reminds me a great deal of you at that age."

He didn't see the resemblance so much. But it pleased him to know that others might. How crazy was that?

You didn't want him. When would Tilda's words stop echoing in his head?

"I want to be a good dad," he admitted to his mom as she pointed to a pan of egg rolls. They both knew that he hadn't had the best of role models. But there was no need to say it.

"You will be, Blaine. You're good at everything you do."

This mattered more than most things. "I hope you're right, Mom. I really do."

Chapter Eight

Lunch went better than Tilda had expected. Although, to be fair, she hadn't been exactly sure what she expected. The Coltons' grandiose world was very different from her own simple existence. She taught, she loved her son and she tried to be a good mom, daughter and friend.

And she'd been satisfied with that.

But now, as she lay awake in her bed, she felt needy. It had been so long since she'd felt the warmth of a man next to her. Felt the strength of his body, the heat of his desire.

Damn Blaine Colton for coming back. Now it seemed as if that was all she could think about.

Mara had talked directly to Josh for much of the lunch. Had inquired about school and extracurricular activities. When she'd found out that he'd be playing baseball, she'd asked for a schedule. Tilda had struggled for a minute to get her head around the idea of Mara, in her six-hundred-dollar designer suits, sitting on wooden bleachers in the rain, but she'd been grateful that the interest had seemed genuine.

She'd even talked about her work a bit at The Chateau, as if it was important that Josh had some understanding of her world and her interests as well. When they'd left, there'd been no demands for a repeat performance. Mara had simply thanked them both for coming.

Blaine had walked her out to her vehicle, grabbing her arm when she'd slipped on an icy spot on the driveway. He'd let go quickly enough once she was steady, but it was that touch that had ignited the need that was keeping her awake tonight. She was swamped by memories of his touch, his tremendous want. It had been... powerful to know that she was the one causing that.

He'd reminded Josh that he'd see him tomorrow at The Lodge for what would likely be the last snowboarding lesson of the season. Josh had said that he'd be there, and he and Tilda had driven home. Once there, it had been a fairly quiet day. Isaac had come over midafternoon and stayed for dinner. The boys ate chicken fingers and French fries in Josh's room, something that Tilda rarely allowed, but she'd had the feeling that her son needed some time to relax and decompress. If he'd been anywhere as nervous as her about the luncheon, then he was still likely wound tight.

She'd cleaned the house and tried to watch television but, in truth, she'd mostly worried. Where did she and Blaine stand? It was hard to tell from the mostly stony silence and distant looks he gave her. Although, for a minute, as they'd been following Mara to the sunroom, he'd actually seemed to tease her. Aside from that, he appeared to reserve his easy-going attitude for Josh.

The worst thing for Josh was to feel torn between his parents. Which meant that she and Blaine were going to have to figure this out.

TILDA WOKE UP before Josh on Sunday morning. She made herself coffee and a piece of toast and sat in her sunlit kitchen. Twenty minutes later, Josh wandered in, his feet bare, even though the floor was very cold. He wore sweats and a T-shirt that should have found the trash bin some time ago.

"Good morning," she said.

"Morning," he mumbled. He pulled out a new box of cereal from the cupboard, poured about half of it into a deep bowl and added enough milk that it almost overflowed the rim. And, by some small miracle, managed to get the bowl to the table without spilling it.

"Put the box away, please," she said.

He rolled his eyes but did it. Then returned to the table and started shoveling it in.

"Do we have to go to church?" he asked.

They went through this every Sunday. "Yes," she said. "And then lunch with Grandma and Grandpa. Then I'll drop you off at The Lodge for your two o'clock class with Blaine."

"I'm having a hard time figuring the two of you out."

Tilda put down her cup. "Why's that?" she asked carefully.

"Well, you both talk to me, but you don't talk to each other very much. I mean, at one time, you must have liked each other, right?"

She could feel her face grow warm. Josh knew that babies didn't come from the cabbage patch. And, while he was just thirteen and not interested in girls yet, at least she didn't think so, she'd had several conversations about the importance of safe sex and preventing teenage pregnancy. Every time they'd had one of those conversations, it hadn't been easy or fun, but she'd felt good afterwards.

"Of course we liked each other," she said. Like she'd told Raeann, maybe she'd even fancied herself in love. But that had changed when it had become obvious that

Blaine thought he'd escaped a bullet when she'd miscarried.

"I don't want you to be concerned about your dad and me. We're going to get along just fine," she promised, hoping that it was true.

Josh ate his cereal. When he was finished, he pushed the bowl aside. "Mom, if Blaine hadn't come back, would you have ever told me the truth?"

It was a very grown-up question coming from somebody that she still considered her little boy. "I don't know," she answered honestly.

She couldn't have told Josh and expected him to keep it a secret, as if she was ashamed of it. At the very least, she'd have had to tell her parents and Russ and Mara Colton. Would she voluntarily have given that much power to Russ Colton? It would have been a huge risk that could have destroyed both her and Josh. "Dorian may not have been your biological father, but he was a very good dad to you. And he loved you very much. He was taken from us way too early. I'm sorry about that."

"They're pretty different, you know, Dad and Blaine," Josh said.

Dorian Stoll had had a kind heart. He'd offered her marriage and the chance of a family. Had helped her in so many ways and had been behind her a hundred percent of the time. But he had never stirred her blood the way that Blaine Colton had. While they'd never discussed it, he'd probably known. But he had never held it against her.

"Different, yes, but both fine men. I hope that, in the days to come, you'll realize that you benefited in some way from your relationship with both of them." The sentiment was perhaps too advanced for him, but then again, he was surprising her a lot lately. "While it may not seem that way to you, I'm grateful that I ran into Blaine again, and I knew that I was going to tell him about you—way before he asked me. There was no way that I could not. He deserved to know the truth. You both did."

"Everything feels different," Josh admitted.

She knew what he meant. "I think it is. But different isn't necessarily bad."

An hour later, she was wondering if that was really true. She and Josh were in a pew, waiting for church to begin, when Blaine slid in beside her. He leaned forward, caught Josh's eye and smiled. Then he settled back in the pew, arms folded across his chest. He was big and solid and smelled so good. She wanted to lean closer.

"Good morning," she said, staying perfectly upright. She was surprised but determined not to show it. The man could go to church if he wanted to. But she had a feeling that this might be less about communing with God and more about letting the good people of Roaring Springs know that the gossip they might have heard about Josh being his son was true.

"Morning, Tilda," he said.

"I thought you would be working. After all, probably only a couple good snow days left, right?"

"I can take a few hours for myself," he told her.

She quirked a brow. "How did you know that we'd be here?"

"This is the church you went to as a kid."

"I'm surprised you remembered that."

"I remember a lot of things," he said, right before the pianist launched into a song and the minister came down the middle aisle.

Like what? she wanted to demand. But given that

they were likely already attracting enough attention, she kept her mouth shut. And forty-five minutes later, when the service ended, she had absolutely no recollection of anything the minister might have said.

As they walked out of church, Blaine fell back to walk next to Josh, leaving Tilda to lead the way. As she walked down the church's front steps, she saw her parents waiting down the sidewalk. Somewhat dreading the meeting but knowing it needed to happen, she led Blaine and Josh to her parents.

"Hi, Dad. Mom."

"Hello, honey," her dad said, his tone considering.

Tilda waved in Blaine's direction. "You remember Blaine, right?"

Blaine stepped forward, his posture absolutely straight. Stuck out his hand. "Mr. Deeds," he said, his tone respectful.

"I think, under the circumstances, you ought to call me Howard."

"All right, sir," Blaine said.

"This is my wife, Janell."

"Ma'am," Blaine murmured.

The army had taught him respect, that was for sure. But now that the introductions were over, it seemed as if nobody knew what to say next. It was too much for Tilda to take. "We should be going," she said. "Lunch plans," she added, looking at Blaine.

"Would you like to join us?" her mother asked.

Traitor. "Blaine's teaching some classes this afternoon at The Lodge. I'm sure he has to get ready…"

Blaine looked at her, then at her parents. "Tilda's right," he said. "Perhaps next Sunday?"

"We'll plan on it. You can come to the house," her

mom told him. "It's…good to see you again, Blaine. Really."

"Thank you," he said.

Then, without another look at Tilda, he tousled Josh's hair. "See you in a little while, Josh." Then he walked away.

"That was kind of rude, Mom," Josh said.

Her parents said nothing. Which suited her fine because she sure as hell didn't want to talk about it. He'd surprised her, and she hadn't been at her best.

"Let's just go," she said. "You need to eat before you hit the slopes."

"HOW WAS LUNCH?" Blaine asked.

"Good. Pot roast, with apple pie for dessert," Josh said.

It sounded delicious. He'd grabbed a burger and fries after he'd left Josh, Tilda and her parents standing on the sidewalk. Her parents had been decent, very decent, given that there was no telling what Tilda might have told them about him.

Howard and Janell Deeds had stuck by their daughter. Josh had grown up with a loving extended family, one that had now increased in size exponentially. The Colton clan was big and, because of the reach and influence that wealth provided, sometimes seemed even bigger than it actually was. He'd have to start introducing Josh to more of the family. But he wouldn't push that too soon.

"There's Isaac," Josh said. He waved his friend over.

"Hi, Josh's dad," Isaac said.

"Afternoon, Josh's friend," Blaine replied dryly.

Isaac's face split into a smile. "All about Josh, right?"

It was. Almost as if a switch had been thrown, his

perspective had changed. But he wasn't getting sentimental in front of a group of middle schoolers. "It's all about hitting the slopes for one last time this year. Come on. Let's go."

Twenty minutes later, they were in the snowboarding park. "Half-pipe, half-pipe," the group started chanting. Josh was right with them.

It was today or wait for another year. And he was glad that his kid was the type to want to spread his wings, try something new. But there was another new emotion, one that he was pretty sure was worry.

He suddenly remembered the conversation he'd had with his mother on one of the rare visits back to Roaring Springs when he'd been on active duty. She'd said that she worried about him every day. He'd said that wasn't necessary, that he was as careful as he could be. She'd told him it didn't matter. That she was a parent. Therefore she worried.

Crystal clear now.

But he held his concerns back. After all, he didn't want to raise a kid who was afraid to try things. He led the way and, as he'd done the day before, demonstrated some technique. Then the kids practiced with varying degrees of proficiency. Josh, he noted, was perhaps not the most skilled but seemed to have the most natural athletic ability among the group. He couldn't help but be proud.

A chip off the old block.

Good God, was he a hundred years old?

After an hour, he waved to the group, letting them know that they were free to make their way down the slope. When they got to the bottom, he came up next to Josh. "Is your mom picking you up?" he asked.

Josh shook his head. "Nope. She has a date."

"What?" Blaine sputtered, almost tripping over his own board. "I didn't know your mom was dating anyone."

"Chuck Pearce," Josh supplied.

"Have you met him?"

The kid shrugged. "We went to his house for hamburgers one night. He has a cool aquarium."

Did you stay over? Did your mom? He managed to keep those questions inside. "What's he do for a living?"

"Works at our bank. I think that's how they met."

He wanted to ask if it was serious but didn't want to put Josh on the spot and, quite frankly, wouldn't have trusted a thirteen-year-old boy's assessment, anyway. "So, you're going to be home alone tonight?"

"Nope. I'm going to Isaac's. Mom said she'd pick me up there at eight. Tomorrow's a school day," he added, mimicking Tilda. "See you later," he said, before he walked off to get in a green van with Isaac.

It took Blaine about five seconds to find Chuck Pearce online. His social media posts didn't mention Tilda or Josh, but they were full of glorious recollections of the *most amazing ten-day hike on the Appalachian Trail ever.* Based on his photos, he was tall and thin and looked to be in his midthirties.

So the guy could strap on a backpack and some hiking boots. Big deal. Blaine had done that, along with about forty more pounds of equipment and weapons and walked across most of Afghanistan, trying to avoid hostiles hoping for a clear shot.

There was also a picture of him with his sister Anniston and his parents, celebrating his parents' fortieth anniversary. One big happy family.

Was he hoping to add to it? Hoping to have a wife and a son, maybe a new baby in a year or two?

He realized he was getting a little ahead of himself, but he couldn't keep his head from going there. Josh was *his* son. Not Chuck Pearce's.

He needed to find out how serious the relationship was. Which is why, four hours later, he was waiting in his vehicle, watching Tilda's house, when he saw her pull into her driveway at 8:12 p.m. The garage door opened, and he gave them five minutes to get into the house. Then he was ringing the doorbell.

TILDA HEARD THE bell and grabbed a towel to dry her hands. It was an old habit to wash her hands immediately upon coming home from anywhere. Schools were germ factories, and now spring colds were going around. The last thing she needed was to get sick.

She was not expecting anyone, and she looked through the peephole before opening the door. Blaine. Why was he standing on her porch?

She opened the door. "Hello," she said.

He stared at her, almost as if he was inspecting her. There wasn't much to see. She'd dressed casually, in jeans and a sweater, for the movie. He was dressed similarly, looking very handsome in his insulated vest, flannel shirt and jeans. He wore cowboy boots. He did not have a coat on, and it couldn't be more than thirty degrees.

Maybe he ran hot.

He made her feel the same. But no way was she admitting that. To anyone.

"May I come in?" he asked.

She stepped back. "Of course." Josh was in his bedroom, probably with his earphones on. He wouldn't have heard the door. "Did you need to speak with Josh?" she asked.

He shook his head.

They were standing, rather awkwardly she thought, by the door. "Would you like to sit down?" Had something happened at today's lesson? She'd tried to grill Josh as delicately as she could after she'd picked him up from Isaac's house, but he'd offered up nothing that seemed concerning. It had been another *super cool* day.

She'd been a little jealous. Her date, which she had belatedly remembered during lunch with her parents, was the fourth one she'd had with Chuck Pearce. It had been *fine*. Like the previous three. She'd enjoyed her salmon at dinner, and the movie had been pretty amusing. But when Chuck had kissed her, she'd thought about garlic, because his pasta had clearly been loaded with it.

And damn her, she'd known in the pit of her stomach that if Blaine had kissed her, she wouldn't be thinking about anything but how good it was. And then later, when Josh had described his day, all she'd been able to think about was that *fine* was actually pretty damn boring and would never be confused with *super cool.*

Blaine sat on the couch.

"Would you like coffee or tea?" she asked.

He shook his head. "Josh mentioned that you had a date tonight."

He'd not told her that. "That's true," she confirmed.

"Is this a serious relationship?" he asked.

What? Four dates was definitely not serious. If it was serious, she probably wouldn't have forgotten about it. But it irritated her that she was suddenly having to explain herself. "Why the question, Blaine? You haven't exactly been interested in what I've been doing for the last thirteen years."

"I was pretty much otherwise occupied," he said. His words were clipped. "And I think I have a right to be interested. Any man you get involved with becomes a part of my son's life. I don't like it when he gets shuffled off to his friend's house. I guess it would have been too much to have expected him to be your priority."

Shuffled off. His words hurt more than a physical blow. Nothing had been more important to her than Josh. Nothing.

"You don't know what you're talking about," Tilda said, working hard to keep her tone even.

"Enlighten me," he demanded.

No. She would not. Granted, she'd not been forthcoming about Josh's existence, but quite frankly, it wasn't as if Blaine had made any effort to reach out to her these last thirteen years. He'd screwed her and then taken the first bus out of town when it seemed as if that night wasn't going to come back to haunt him.

"What I do and who I do it with are none of your damn business," she said. It made it seem as if her relationship with Chuck was more serious than it was. But that couldn't be helped.

"You're wrong," he bit out. "I don't want him here with Josh."

Chuck had never been to her house. She wasn't a fool; she'd always met him somewhere. Tonight had been no different. "I get to decide who comes to my home. Not you."

"You know what, Tilda? I used to think you were a reasonable person."

"I'm no longer an eighteen-year-old girl who is easily bullied."

"Bullied?" he spit out the word. "When did I ever bully you?"

"Prom night."

His jaw tightened. "We had consensual sex, as I recall. *Very* consensual."

Yes, it had been. But he didn't understand what it meant to have the most handsome, most athletic, richest boy in town pay attention to you. It had been overwhelming. So, while the bullying hadn't been overt in any manner and he certainly hadn't forced himself on her, there'd been a little voice in her head that had told her she'd be an idiot if she said no.

Turns out, she'd been a bigger idiot for saying yes.

But Josh was the result. Sweet, sweet Josh. "I'm sorry," she said softly. "I shouldn't have said that. But you also have no right to barge in here, to demand explanations about what I'm doing."

"Did you tell your new boyfriend about me?"

She had. Because she'd figured it was just a matter of time before he heard the story. His response had been somewhat predictable. *The Coltons. Wow. They're the bank's biggest customer.* "I did."

Blaine nodded. "Good."

"*Good* what?" she asked, pushing her hair away from her face. She was so tired. It felt as if she hadn't slept in days.

"*Good* as in I want him to know that Josh has somebody in his corner. Somebody who is going to look out for him."

Again the words cut into her. All she'd been doing for the past thirteen years was watching out for Josh. It filled her every waking moment. "I've been looking out for him."

He shrugged. "Maybe that's true. But maybe you were really looking out for yourself more. I think that you're selfish, Tilda. And that you did a very selfish thing by keeping Josh a secret."

Tears of outrage filled her eyes, and she wanted to hit him. He knew nothing. "I think it's time for you to leave, Blaine." She got up, walked over to the door and jerked it opened.

He got up slowly. "I'm taking Josh out to dinner tomorrow night. I'll be here at six."

He wasn't asking. He was telling. "Six thirty," she said. "He'll have homework that he'll need to do first."

"Fine."

"And there's school the next day," she added.

"I'll have him home by eight." He stepped out onto the porch.

He had all the answers. "Make sure that you do," she said before she shut the door.

Chapter Nine

Tilda was eating her turkey and cheese sandwich at her desk when Raeann poked her head in the door of her classroom. "Your room is going to have ants, big, ugly ones that bite, if you continue to eat in here," her friend said, by way of greeting.

"I'm not eight," Tilda replied, giving her friend a tired smile. "You can't scare me with that."

"So, tell me about the lunch," Raeann said, walking over to look out the windows. The weather had warmed significantly, and any snow that had been piled was slowly melting from the edges. If this kept up, it would disappear in the valley quickly, although it would take longer at higher elevations. "Keep in mind that most of my lunches involve boxed macaroni and cheese and hot dogs, so I'm going to need details."

"I did not choke or otherwise embarrass myself too much," Tilda began. "I took chocolates from Bethel's as a hostess gift. We had Thai food that she ordered in, and to the best of my knowledge, I chewed with my mouth closed and nothing remained stuck in my teeth. All in all, I'd have given myself a solid B," she added, with a smile. Despite her heated confrontation with Blaine the night before, she'd woken up this morning with new resolve. She was going to stay positive. Be positive.

"I heard that Blaine was in church with you and Josh," Raeann said. "My sister saw you. I gave her enough of the facts so that she could stop any weird gossip about you."

And that was how it was going to go. When people heard the truth, they'd likely pick sides, choosing either Tilda or Blaine, depending on where their loyalties had previously been. If people didn't get the facts, they'd make up something, on that same basis.

"I don't really care what people say, as long as Josh isn't hurt by it," she admitted. She'd come to terms with her decision. The hell with everybody else.

Everybody else, she knew, didn't include Blaine. But given that he acted as if he could barely stand to be in the same room as her, she guessed it didn't matter that she'd believed at the time that her decision was the best for both of them.

"Best attitude to have," Raeann said. "Have I told you how much I'm dreading this Saturday night?"

Teachers at the high school rotated the responsibility of chaperoning the senior prom. This year, both she and Raeann were on the hook for it. In her day, prom had been in the gym, decorated with streamers and Christmas lights. Now, it was held in one of the ballrooms at The Chateau. Parents dropped way too much money on the event, but there was no momentum to get it back to the high school gym, even though the teachers would have preferred that. "Did I mention that it was prom night that I got pregnant with Josh?" Tilda asked.

"You did not," Raeann said, her eyes big. "We're passing out condoms at the door."

She was pretty sure her friend was teasing. "Hm. Perhaps I could give a first-person testimonial."

Raeann smiled. "That's the spirit. Go with what you've got."

She had wisdom gained from the school of hard knocks. "Blaine is taking Josh out for dinner tonight."

"Date night for you, then?"

"I don't think so. I told Chuck the truth about Josh last night. I got the impression that he didn't think it would help his career to be involved in any situation that might alienate the Coltons or their money."

"Weasel," Raeann said.

"It wasn't going anywhere," Tilda admitted.

"Go online tonight. Create a profile. Don't let any grass grow under your feet."

"We'll see," Tilda said, noncommittally. She knew she wasn't going to do that but really didn't want to defend her decision. With Blaine back in town, she had enough to worry about without having to focus on a romantic relationship. And given the way he'd responded to her date with Chuck, she didn't even want to contemplate his reaction if she found a stranger online.

Her cell phone buzzed. She fished it out of her bag. Josh: Extra band practice tonight. Be home late.

She texted back. Okay. Thank you. The middle-school band was supposed to play for the eighth-grade graduation ceremonies in a couple weeks. Clearly, the band director thought they needed work.

The five-minute warning bell rang. Raeann grimaced. "Back to work. Let's hope nobody sets the chemistry lab on fire this afternoon."

Tilda watched her friend leave. At least in English class she didn't have to worry about those things. But an hour later, she realized that she did have to worry about underperforming students when Toby Turner failed the quiz. At the end of class, she again asked him to stay behind. "Do you have your signed progress report?" she asked.

"I gave it to my parents," he said. "They must have forgotten to give it back."

He was running out of time. "Do you not want to graduate with your class?" she asked for about the tenth time. It was getting old, but he needed to understand the consequence of his actions. "No graduation, then no college."

"I don't really care," he muttered.

She didn't think that was the truth. His words were tough, but the look in his eyes was more vulnerable.

"Are your parents home tonight?" she asked.

"I have no idea," he said.

"Make sure they sign your form."

He didn't answer. Simply looked past her shoulder.

What the hell was happening with this kid? It drove her crazy. "You're excused," she said, so frustrated that she could barely speak. How could she help him if he wouldn't let her?

After Toby left, she packed her shoulder bag, stuffing inside a stack of papers to grade. She'd have plenty of time tonight, since Josh would be with Blaine.

Tilda had not mentioned the dinner to Josh. She'd been pretty upset after her conversation with Blaine last night and hadn't wanted that attitude to spill out. This morning, he'd been glued to his cell phone, barely answering any questions she passed his way. He'd seemed a little off, but then, maybe that had been her imagination, since she'd still been feeling unsettled by Blaine's visit.

You're selfish, Tilda.

Ugly, ugly words. Hurtful.

Were they true? Had she been selfish?

She'd been scared. Of Russ Colton. Of having a baby at eighteen. Of the prospect of raising Josh on her own.

But had she found solutions that benefited her and Josh without regard for Blaine? Had she, indeed, only been concerned about the two of them, without any regard for others? If she looked up the definition of *selfish* in the dictionary, would she recognize herself?

Ugh. It was no wonder her head hurt.

She drove home, carried her things into the house and collapsed onto the couch. When her stomach rumbled, she managed to pull herself to a standing position. She got an apple out of the refrigerator and cut it up. Added a few hunks of cheddar cheese and a small handful of crackers. She took the plate into the family room and returned to the couch. Then, turning the television on, caught the end of a sitcom that had been popular ten years earlier.

When everything had been simple. She'd been married to Dorian, and they'd been enjoying raising Josh.

She was so tired. Days of not sleeping were catching up with her. She closed her eyes. And woke up with a start sometime later. The evening news was on.

She looked at her watch. It was almost six. When Josh had said he'd be late, she hadn't expected this. Blaine would be here at six thirty. She checked her phone, to see if Josh had sent a text or called. But there was nothing.

She called his phone. It went to voice mail. She sent a text: Where are you?

There was no answer.

She didn't want to panic. But, truth be told, her heart was racing in her chest. She opened the app that would allow her to track the location of Josh's phone. When she saw the address, she breathed a sigh of relief. His school. He was at school.

At band practice still?

She thumbed through her contacts and found Isaac's number. His friend answered on the second ring. "Hey, Josh's mom,' he said.

"Hey, Isaac. Is Josh with you?"

"Uh...no. I haven't seen him since after school."

"You mean after band practice?" Isaac played the tuba.

"There was no band practice today."

Her heart had been racing and now might have skipped a couple beats. And she felt the burn in her chest, making it hard to breathe. "So, the two of you walked home after school together."

"Yeah."

He'd already said almost that—probably thought she was losing it. "Did he have his phone, Isaac?"

There was silence. "I don't know. Maybe not."

Josh loved his phone. He always had it. That, and Isaac's cryptic tone, sent a chill up her back. "Did something happen today, Isaac?"

"Kids are saying stuff. You know, online. About Josh being a Colton."

Oh, God. "Bad stuff?"

"I don't know. I ignored it and told him to do the same."

Her son was a sweet kid who did not have very thick skin. She wanted to know what people were saying but that wasn't the important thing. "Did Josh mention going anywhere else but home?"

"No. But he wasn't exactly talking to me," Isaac admitted.

What? They were best friends. If Josh didn't think

he could talk to Isaac, then he might not think he could talk to anyone. "If you see him or hear from him, tell him to call me right away, okay?"

"Sure," Isaac said and hung up.

His phone was at school, but she didn't think he was. She thought of all the places he might go if he needed to talk to someone. She dialed her parents.

"Hi, honey," her mother said.

"Hi, Mom. Is Josh there by any chance?"

"No. Howard," her mom yelled, her mouth almost away from the phone. "Have you heard from Josh?"

"Nope. Why?"

She did not want to worry her parents. "No big deal, Mom. I was just expecting him a while ago, and he hasn't turned up."

She kept her mouth shut about what Isaac had told her. She didn't want her parents to be scared.

"Did you call the school?"

"Maybe I'll do that," she said. "Don't worry. I'll let you know once he gets here," she promised before hanging up.

She called the main office of his school. It rang and went to voice mail. Everyone had undoubtedly left for the day. But she knew people at that school. She scrolled through her contacts, found Sarah Trent's name. She and Sarah, Josh's homeroom teacher, had bowled together on a teachers' league the prior year.

She dialed. When Sarah answered, Tilda worked very hard to keep her voice calm. "Hey, Sarah, it's Tilda Deeds. I'm having a little trouble tracking Josh down tonight. He's not answering his cell but the app on my phone says his phone is still at the school. Could he still be there?"

"I don't think so. I left the school an hour ago, and

it was pretty deserted. This time of year, the kids scatter pretty fast after school."

"You've got keys to the building, right?"

"I do."

"I know it's a lot to ask, but could you meet me there?"

"Of course. Look, I'm only ten minutes away. I'll meet you at the south door."

"Thank you, Sarah." Tilda hung up.

Where the hell was he? She tried his cell one more time. Straight to voice mail.

She ran to put on shoes and was in the garage in less than a minute. Got into her SUV, raised the garage door and backed out. The weather had changed. Earlier, it had been clear but, like it often happened in Colorado, a storm had blown in, and now precipitation was falling. It was sleet, that ugly mixture of snow and rain that would turn to ice on the roads as the evening temperature dropped.

She glanced at the clock on her dashboard. Six fifteen. She drove as quickly as she could, all the while trying to make sense of what she knew. Josh had left the building with Isaac and had gotten as far as Isaac's house. Then, between there and home, had he somehow realized that he'd left his phone at school and returned for it, only to be locked out? Was he outside the doors of the building right now, waiting for someone to exit so that he could slip in and retrieve his phone?

Not her kid. He'd have found a phone to use—either at one of the nearby stores or back at Isaac's house—and called her for assistance. She was a teacher, after all. She knew how to get things done at a school. Would know people that could get the door open.

Her kid was smart. And action-oriented. He wouldn't just stand around hoping.

There was something wrong. Maybe nobody else would believe her, but she knew. She thought about calling her parents back. For so many years, they'd been her go-to people. The third leg of her three-legged stool.

And she almost pressed the button on her phone that would have had them come running but realized suddenly that there was someone else that she should call first.

Josh's father.

And then mentally kicked herself for not calling him earlier. Was it possible that Josh was there? She didn't think Blaine would deliberately keep her son away from her, but perhaps he didn't know that Josh hadn't filled her in.

It was crazy how life worked. Earlier, she'd have been really irritated that Josh had gone to see Blaine without permission, but now, all she wanted was for him to be hanging out with his dad.

She found Blaine's contact info and pressed the number. He answered on the second ring.

"Tilda?"

"Is Josh with you?" she asked. Then sucked in a quick breath. She couldn't let him know that she was losing it.

"No. What's going on?"

"You haven't talked to Josh?"

"No," he replied. "I'm still planning on taking him to dinner tonight. I'm less than ten minutes away."

"Oh, Blaine," she sobbed. "I think something is very wrong. I can't find him. I don't know where our son is."

Chapter Ten

When Blaine had seen Tilda's number flash across his phone screen, he'd immediately gotten tense, thinking that she was calling to cancel his dinner with Josh. He'd not expected that she'd tell him that his son was missing.

He was a trained soldier, capable of rapidly sorting through complex situations. But a crying Tilda pulled at him, and he had to work to stay focused. He didn't want to waste valuable minutes because he hadn't listened well.

"What time did you expect him?" he asked.

"Five or five thirty, because he sent a text at noon, telling me that there was band practice. But when he wasn't home by six and wasn't answering his cell, I called Isaac, who is also in band. There was no practice."

Kids lied. Didn't necessarily make them bad kids, but he didn't like the idea that Josh had deliberately tried to fool his mom. "Has this happened before?"

"He doesn't lie, Blaine," she said, her voice hard. "At least never before," she added.

Before you came back. That's what he heard, even though she didn't say it. He pushed those thoughts aside. Plenty of time to be pissed off later. "Did you try his cell?"

"Yes, and I tracked its location. It's at his school. I'm on my way there."

"I'll meet you," he told her. He knew where the middle school was.

"Thank you." She sounded as if she was about to cry again.

"I'm sure it's fine, Tilda," he said softly. Didn't know why he felt the sudden urge to comfort her, especially given what she'd implied, but it clawed at him that she was upset. "This is Roaring Springs," he added before he hung up.

Small-town America. Colton Country, some in his family might even have joked. Safe.

But was anywhere really safe anymore? He immediately thought about Decker's wife, Kendall, and how she'd been injured while attending a show at his cousin Bree's art gallery. And then Bree had almost been shot, and Rylan Bennet, Blaine's good friend from the army, had taken a bullet for her.

Some people just didn't like the Coltons. And Josh was the Colton that a lot of people were talking about right now.

He continued driving with one hand but with the other dialed Josh's cell phone twice. Both times it went right to voice mail. He left a message the first time. "Josh, it's Blaine. Very important for you to call me or your mom right away."

His phone never rang. He pulled up to Roaring Springs's middle school and saw Tilda was already there. She was sitting in her car but got out when she saw him. They met on the sidewalk. Neither of them had an umbrella, and they were getting wet fast.

"I called a friend to unlock the door. She's a teacher here," Tilda said. "Sarah Trent."

He did not recognize the name. And he did not see anybody waiting for them. If she didn't get here soon, then he was going to find another way inside. "Walk me through it again."

She didn't argue. "Isaac confirmed that the two of them left school together and walked to Isaac's house. He thought Josh was headed home. He did say that Josh wasn't talking much, that he'd been upset by some things he'd seen online."

"What things?"

"I don't know. It had something to do with him being a Colton."

Christ. "Okay. We'll figure it out. Where else have you checked?"

"He's not with my parents, and they haven't talked to him. I didn't tell them that he's…missing."

"He's not missing, Tilda. He could be inside this school, at this very minute. Maybe he got caught up in some after-school activity, lost track of time. Did he know I was taking him to dinner?"

"No. I didn't have a chance to tell him."

That probably wasn't true. Maybe she'd been hoping he'd cancel. He saw a woman pull up, park quickly and get out of the car. She had an umbrella. Tilda waved to her.

"Thank you so much for coming," Tilda said. "This is Blaine Colton." She waved in his direction. "Sarah Trent," she added, for his benefit.

"You're Josh's dad," Sarah said, her tone knowing. She looked at Tilda. "Word has gotten around school," she told her, perhaps somewhat apologetically.

"I heard there might have been some stuff online," Tilda said. "Stuff that might have upset Josh."

Sarah had her keys in the door. "I didn't see it, but

it's very possible. I swear, these kids can be absolutely vicious to one another. They'll write things down for the world to see that they would never have the guts to say in person."

Tilda knew this to be true. Periodically, she monitored Josh's social media. But always with his knowledge. Always by his side. And once in a while, he'd voluntarily show her something.

But that hadn't happened tonight. Why?

The building door swung open. "You said that you tracked his phone to here?" Sarah asked.

"Yeah. I have an app. I can make his phone ring, which should help us locate it."

"It's pretty quiet in here," Blaine said. If Josh was involved in an activity, it wasn't generating any noise.

"Yeah. The cleaning crew doesn't come in until much later, and then I think they're only here for a couple hours," Sarah said.

"I want to check his locker. It's the logical place for his phone," Tilda told her.

"Do you know the number?" Sarah asked.

"Four thirty-six."

"Okay. That's on the second floor."

Sarah left her wet umbrella by the door and led them down the hallway. The doors to all the rooms were open, and Blaine suspected that was to make it easier for the cleaning crew. He quickly looked in every room as they passed. As a result, he was a little behind Sarah and Tilda when they stopped in front of a locker on the second floor. But he heard a ringing coming from within and knew that Tilda had activated the phone.

"I've got the combination somewhere," she said, tapping on her phone. "I had to get his books when he had a bad cold earlier this year."

It took her another minute, but then she dialed the combination lock and easily opened it. The phone was on the top shelf, sitting on a single sheet of paper. Blaine picked the phone and then the paper up by the edge and held it so that he and Tilda could both read it. The message was brief and clearly intended for anybody who'd come looking for him. Like his mother. *Don't worry. I'm okay. I'll be home tomorrow.*

Tilda said a four-letter word that Josh would have caught hell for.

"Yeah," he acknowledged. That did about sum it up.

He glanced at the rest of the locker, hoping that it might offer some clues. It looked like any locker he remembered. Books and notebooks stacked on the bottom shelf. A hooded sweatshirt hanging on a hook. "Josh's?" he asked, pointing to it.

Tilda nodded.

He pulled the sweatshirt off the hook. It would have Josh's scent and would make tracking easier, if it came to that. His friend Max worked with service dogs and might know where to quickly get a scent hound. "I'd like to look through the rest of the school," he said, turning to Sarah. He didn't want her locking up the building before he'd cleared it entirely.

"Fine," she agreed.

Blaine turned to Tilda and wrapped his arm around her shoulder. "We're going to find him," he reassured her. "We will. Now call Isaac. Ask him if there's any place that he knows that Josh would go to if he wanted to get away from it all. Ask him if the two of them have talked about any cool places around here lately. Get him thinking."

He waited until she nodded. Then he gave her shoulder a tight squeeze and took off. There was only one more floor for him to search. It wouldn't take him that long. His gut told him that Josh wasn't close by, though. He'd walked at least to Isaac's house. They had confirmation of that. From there, he'd gone somewhere.

They could contact the police. The note dismissed the concern of foul play, but still, missing kids were high priority. The more eyes looking for Josh the better. But if that was going to happen, he had to talk to his parents first, let them know what was happening. They would hate the publicity, once people made the connection that the kid in question was a Colton.

He could mobilize the family. The Coltons had resources. Horses that could go places that cars couldn't. Employees that could quickly be marshaled into extra boots on the ground. Access to helicopters and experienced search and rescue personnel.

But if Josh was already getting taunted because he was a Colton, any anonymity that he might have would be blown after tonight. It was a very real consequence if his kid simply wanted a couple hours of alone time.

He finished the search of the third floor pretty quickly and rejoined Sarah and Tilda, who was still on the phone. He listened to her side of the conversation.

"Thank you, Isaac. This has been very helpful." She hung up.

For the first time, she looked hopeful. He didn't demand to know what Isaac had said. Sarah was still there, and they needed to get out of the building.

"I'm all done," he said. "Thank you for meeting us here."

"Of course," Sarah replied. "Is there anything else I can do?"

"No, thank you." Tilda leaned in to give the woman a quick hug.

Blaine thought there was little doubt that she hadn't seen the note. But if Tilda had trusted her enough to have her open the school for them, perhaps she could be trusted to keep her mouth shut, and the whole episode wouldn't be flashing across social media in fifteen minutes.

The three of them walked outside, and they waited while Sarah got into her car. The second she shut the door, he turned to Tilda. "What?" he asked.

"Isaac said that when he and Josh were skiing last week, they had binoculars with them and saw a cabin to the west of the Running Deer slope. They'd joked about it being a great place to hide."

There were luxury cabins scattered around the property. They offered privacy for guests who wanted that. But he was pretty sure this cabin wasn't one of those. The cabin west of Running Deer had been there since his grandparents had homesteaded in these mountains. It wasn't used for anything, but Russ had always insisted that it be kept on the property. He was sure it was always locked. And with the temp hovering around twenty tonight, it would be damn cold up there if one was stuck outside.

He briefly explained the location to Tilda. When he finished, she ran her hands through her long hair. "There's a bus that runs from the bus depot to The Lodge."

He was aware of that. "And he might have made it before the chairlifts shut down for the day. Once he started down the mountain, he'd have had to go off-trail."

"He's pretty good on skis," she said.

He was. But it would be a very challenging run. On a good day.

Which wasn't today. The temperature was dropping,

and the sidewalks were already getting slick. Up on the mountain, it would be even colder. The slopes could have a thin layer of ice on them, making them treacherous to navigate.

"I think we need to check it," he said simply.

"I'll come with you," Tilda said.

"No." She wouldn't be safe. "I'll be able to move faster on my own."

"What if something happens to you?" she asked. "How would I know?"

"Nothing is going to happen to me. Cell-phone coverage is very spotty in those areas. I can get a satellite phone at The Lodge. Still, you may not hear from me for a while, but don't worry."

"We could be wrong," she said. "What if you go all that way and we lose hours, valuable hours, looking for him?"

It was a risk, he knew. But he'd seen Isaac and Josh together. His gut told him that Isaac had mentioned the log cabin to Tilda because he really thought Josh was probably there and he cared about his friend. "Tilda, you're going to need to trust me. To know that I'll do everything within my power to find our son, and to make sure that both of us stay safe. I'll get to that cabin. If I don't find him, we're calling in the cavalry."

"He's my everything," she said. Her voice was thick with emotion.

"I know that," he rasped. Then he leaned in and kissed her. Her lips were cold and wet. But her taste was sweet.

It was just a brief touch and over far too soon. He lifted his head. "I'll bring him home. I promise."

BLAINE DROVE BACK up the mountain, slipping and sliding on the slick road. Ten minutes into the drive, he called his mother's cell phone.

"Hi, Blaine," she said. "What's up?"

"Are you at home?"

"Unfortunately, no. Too much going on at work."

"I need to tell you something."

"Okay," she said.

Mara's tone had changed. Probably realized that this wasn't a social call. "Josh took off this afternoon."

"Took off?" she repeated.

"Yeah. Tilda and I found his phone in his locker at school, along with a note that he'd be home tomorrow."

"I see."

She'd raised a passel of kids, and he was confident that he, his brothers and his sisters had pulled some real boners. "We think he might be headed up to the cabin that sits west of Running Deer."

"I haven't been there for years," she mused.

"I'm not sure if anyone has been. But I'm going there tonight." He didn't need to explain the trip. She would understand that the road would take him as far as The Lodge, then he'd have to take a ski lift up the mountain and, from there, ski to the destination.

"Just you?" she asked.

"Yeah. I'll let Decker know what's going on if he's still at The Lodge. And I'm taking one of the satellite phones."

She said nothing for a second. Then, "Blaine, I know you survived thirteen years of very challenging situations in the military without your mother whispering in your ear to be careful. But, honey, be careful. And bring my grandson home safe."

"I will."

"Where's Tilda?"

"At home." His vehicle slid to the right, and he carefully brought it back onto the road. "I've got to go, Mom. Think about staying at The Chateau tonight. These roads are pretty bad." Blaine hung up and focused on driving. He went as fast as he could, but it still took thirty minutes to make the fifteen-minute drive. The precipitation that was falling right now was more ice than snow, and it was going to make moving on skis or foot very treacherous.

At The Lodge, he went to find Decker, who was still in his office. When he explained the situation, his brother immediately volunteered to go with him.

"Thank you but no," he said. His kid, his problem. He didn't need to drag anybody else into what could be a difficult and likely dangerous effort. "Mom also knows what's going on. Just in case." *In case I don't come back.* Those were the words he didn't need to say. They both knew. He'd be very near the area that they currently had closed because of avalanche risk.

"If you can get me up the mountain, that's the only help I need." During the week, the ski lifts stopped operating at five.

"I'll make a call," Decker said.

"Thank you."

He was at the door when his brother spoke again. "What's Tilda have to say about this?" he asked, his voice hard.

"She's scared." Blaine swallowed hard. There was no need to tell Decker that he'd kissed Tilda. He still didn't know what to think about it himself. All he'd known was that it felt right. "She's a good mom."

"You think so?" Decker said, as if he didn't believe it.

His brother was still mad on his behalf. But now, instead of it making him feel better, it just made him feel badly that he'd been so critical of Tilda. "I'm going to find Josh, and we're going to figure this out. Figure out how to be some sort of family." He stood up. "I've got to get some things together, and then I'm going to take off."

"Good luck," his brother said before he got up, came around his desk and hugged him.

It took Blaine another fifteen minutes to gather the essentials that he would need. A compass, some food, water, a couple lightweight blankets, and extra clothes because Josh had likely gotten wet on his trek to the cabin. Then, of course, matches, flashlights, a headlamp, an emergency transponder, a shovel, and a medical kit that he prayed like hell he wasn't going to need. The last thing he added was the satellite phone.

He donned his ski boots and outerwear and carried his skis. Once he was outside, he put them on. As Decker had promised, the chair-lift lights were on, and he could see a person in the control booth. He waved his hand and got on a chair. He had so much stuff on his back that he had to sit forward in the seat. He kept his face down because, even though he wore a facemask, the icy snow hurt as it hit his face.

He wasn't a praying man, but now he prayed that Josh had gotten to the cabin and found a way to get in.

He got off at the top and turned on his headlamp. The sun would officially set around eight, in a half hour, but it had been such a cloudy, dark day that it was already hard to see. The tall pine trees didn't help because they blocked any light that was available.

He was grateful for his generally good sense of direction. And the fact that he was still in tip-top shape and good on skis was certainly a plus.

A very good downhill skier could go about one thousand vertical feet in two minutes. On perfectly groomed trails. In good conditions.

He was going to have to go about two thousand vertical feet, off-trail, across rough and icy patches, in the dark, with gear on his back. If he made it in less than an hour, it would be a damn miracle. It frightened him again to think of Josh doing the same thing. Of course, it had been light then, a little less cold, and he'd probably been traveling light. Still. He was a thirteen-year-old boy. He wouldn't have the same stamina as Blaine.

So, in addition to everything else, he was going to have to keep his eyes peeled for the boy and stop every couple minutes to listen for unusual sounds.

And hopefully keep away from any wild animals who might take exception to him being on their turf.

He planted his poles, bent his knees and pushed off.

BLAINE HAD WRAPPED his arm around her. Which meant nothing, of course. Comfort. Reassurance. A promise that all would be well.

But then he'd kissed her.

Too brief to conjure up any recollection of familiarity.

Bull. The second his lips had touched hers, she'd been swamped with a memory of how he'd kissed her after their first date. Not prom. But weeks earlier. They'd gone to the movies, and he'd brought her home. And, there, on her parents' porch, he'd leaned in and gently kissed her. She'd talked about it for days to her best friend. Had recounted in great detail the shape of his lips, his taste, the fact that there had been no tongue.

It had been sweet. Just like tonight's kiss.

And now, as she parked in front of her parents' house and stared at that same front porch, she could almost see herself and Blaine, two kids really, not having a clue that their lives were about to change forever. She would have a baby and get married. He would go to war. Radically different paths.

But they'd somehow found themselves in this place some thirteen years later. They'd been given another chance to do right by the child they'd created together. She bowed her head over her steering wheel. *Please, please, dear God, bring Josh back to me. And Blaine, too. I need them, God. Both of them.*

Tilda opened her car door. She'd told her parents that she'd call back when she found Josh, knowing they'd be worried. She couldn't leave them hanging, but she also didn't want to stress them out needlessly either.

Blaine would find him. Blaine would bring him home.

She walked into her parents' house. They were in the living room, watching television. Her dad saw her first. "Where's Josh?" he asked immediately, concern in his tone.

Her mom was looking at her now. And she very deliberately reached for the television remote and turned the volume down. "What's happened?" she asked.

"I don't want you to worry," Tilda said. After all, she was doing enough of that for all of them. "We found Josh's phone, and he left a note. He said that he'd be home tomorrow." Even as she said it, it sounded unreal. Her son was only thirteen. "He told Isaac that he needed to get away for a bit."

"Get away?" her mom repeated. "That's crazy."

"Not crazy," Tilda said. "Kids are under tremendous pressure these days. As a teacher and a mom, I know that to be true. They feel stress. Maybe not in the same way as adults, but it's real."

Her mom held up a hand. "I'm sorry, Tilda. I said

that wrong. What's crazy is that he thinks he can simply be gone overnight. Without us knowing where he is."

"We have an idea. When he and Isaac were skiing this past weekend, they saw a cabin high up in the mountains. They talked about it being a good place to get away."

"Who does the cabin belong to?"

"It's on Colton property. Blaine is on his way there now, to find him. To make sure he's safe."

Nobody said anything. She understood. It was a lot to process. "Well, based on what I've heard about Blaine's military service, there's probably nobody better. He's a real hero," her dad said.

"Which makes the other thing just so ridiculous," her mom lamented.

"What other thing?" Tilda asked.

Her parents exchanged a look. "Nothing you need to worry about right now," her dad said. "You need to focus on Josh."

She wanted to argue that it might do her good to focus on something else, but she knew they would be empty words. Her head was mush right now. "Blaine was going to take a satellite phone, since cell-phone coverage is very spotty in the mountains. Still, we may not hear anything right away, but when I do, I will call you. I promise," she added, standing up.

Her mom hugged her. "Honey, is there anything we can do?"

"Maybe pray," Tilda said. Then she walked out of her parents' house, got into her car and started to cry.

How she got herself home she wasn't sure. But ten minutes later, she pulled into her driveway and raised the garage door. Then it was into the house. She made sure her phone was set to ring, and she placed it on the coffee table. She heated up water for tea and opened up a box of cookies. She had not had dinner but knew that she'd be hard-pressed to get much down.

After five cookies and two cups of tea, she reached into her shoulder bag and pulled out the papers that she'd been intending to grade. She had to do something, and this was better than staring at the walls.

An hour later, she was half done. She sat the stack aside and stretched. Checked her phone. She'd been doing that every ten minutes. Still no word from Blaine.

She could hear the wind blowing and knew that it was likely a wicked night on the mountains. *Probably nobody better.* That's what her dad had said about Blaine looking for Josh. And for the first time, she was very, very grateful that Blaine had been there.

He had not hesitated to help.

Maybe he wouldn't have hesitated thirteen years ago, either, if you'd told him the truth. She could hear the words in her head. Knew that they were true. But that was the thing about life. You didn't get to do any reruns. Decisions made and acted upon were done. Finished.

However, amends could be made.

Please, please, God. Give me the chance to make amends. To Blaine. To his family. Especially to Josh. My baby. "Be safe," she whispered. "Wherever you are. Be safe."

She closed her eyes. And must have dozed off, because a sharp knock at the door had her jumping off her couch. She grabbed her phone to see if there were missed calls or messages. None. And it was almost nine thirty. Who could be at her door?

There was another knock. "Tilda, it's Mara Colton."

Had Blaine somehow gotten news to her? Tilda

whipped open the door. Looked past Mara, hoping against hope that Josh was somehow there. But she was alone.

"Any news?" Mara asked, proving that she was in the loop.

Tilda shook her head.

"May I come in?"

Tilda stepped back, making space. "Of course," she said, feeling awkward.

Mara closed the door behind her and then took off her coat, gloves and scarf. She draped them over the back of a kitchen chair. Tilda knew she should offer to hang them, but her brain had stalled.

Mara Colton was in her living room! And it appeared that she was planning on staying.

"I wondered if you might be at your parents' house," Mara said.

"I needed to be here." In Josh's house, with his things.

"Your home is lovely," Mara murmured.

Tilda *did* love it, but she knew it was meager in comparison to what Mara was used to. She said nothing.

Mara sat in the chair across from the couch where papers were still spread. She folded her hands in her lap. "I didn't think you should be alone, dear."

And that was all it took for Tilda to lose it. All the emotions she'd kept bottled inside flooded out. Tears rolled down her cheeks, and she lowered her face into her raised hands.

She felt a pat on her back. Mara had moved from the chair to the couch.

Tilda raised her head, turned to look at the woman. "I'm sorry," she sobbed.

"Don't apologize," Mara said. "I'm sure it's been

very difficult. But know this, Tilda. Even though I've only met Josh once, I have a feeling that he's a very smart boy, capable of making really good decisions. And I raised his father. Who was the most determined and self-directed child you could meet. He set a goal, and he achieved it. And tonight, Blaine's goal is to find his son and bring him home safely. It will happen."

Mara got up and moved back to her chair. "Now, tell me. Is that tea that you're drinking?"

BLAINE HAD BEEN SKIING, walking, half crawling: whatever it took to stay upright and moving, for over an hour. He'd slipped once and caught the side of his leg on a tree, and he suspected he was going to have a hell of a bruise. Every time he'd stopped, he'd checked his compass, to make sure that he was still on course, and shined his powerful flashlight into the distance, attempting to locate the cabin.

And now, southwest, about two hundred yards out, was his destination. It was a dark little square on the horizon. He pushed himself even harder, skiing up to within feet of the door. He pointed his headlamp toward the ground, looking for footprints. If there had been any, they'd been long erased by the blowing snow. And there were no skis and boots hanging out by the door. That didn't scare him. If Josh had been thinking, he'd have taken everything inside with him, not wanting to lose anything in the storm. Blaine took off his own skis and tucked them under one arm.

Please let him be inside.

He switched off his headlamp, not wanting to blind Josh. He turned the handle of the door. It was locked.

Raising his hand, he pounded hard against the door. "Josh. It's Blaine. Open the door," he yelled.

He waited, his heart thudding in his chest. Seconds dragged. He pounded again. "Josh, come on, buddy."

Chapter Eleven

The door swung open. And there stood his son, looking small and frightened and cold. But whole. Gloriously whole.

Blaine stepped in, dropped his skis and wrapped his son tight in his arms. Realized that one or both of them were shaking. He finally pulled back. "Good to see you, Josh," he said, managing to get words past the lump in his throat.

He pushed the door shut with his foot, but that didn't cut the breeze in the cabin by that much. Then he used his powerful flashlight to scan the room. It had been twenty years since he'd been here, but it was pretty much what he remembered. One big room, maybe sixteen feet wide and twenty feet long. A bare canvas cot was bolted into one wall. Josh's open backpack was on it. Across the way, attached to the opposite wall, were old bottom cupboards covered by a scratched, weathered countertop.

There was no other furniture, nothing that could be removed, nothing to tempt thieves. There were no appliances or even a sink because the cabin had never had running water or electricity. On the rear wall was a large stone fireplace. There was a pile of sticks in it and something that looked like wadded-up notebook paper, but it had not been lit. Josh's skis were leaning up against the wall next to it, with a wet stocking cap hanging off the end of one ski.

The cabin was freezing. The broken window on the far wall wasn't helping. The wind was whistling through. It answered the question of how Josh had gotten in. His thin body would have been just narrow enough to squeeze through.

"How did you find me?" Josh asked nervously.

"Determination and a little luck," Blaine admitted. First things first, he needed to get them some heat. "Did you try to light a fire?"

"My matches got wet," Josh said, sounding embarrassed.

Rookie mistake. "I think mine are dry," Blaine replied easily. He dug them out of his pack and lit a match. It took a few seconds for the fire to take hold, but finally, there was a small flame. "Come here," he said, stepping away so that his son could stand in front of the growing heat.

He took a minute to inspect the boy. He was still wearing his coat and gloves. When he squatted down, to get his face closer to the fire, his motor movements were coordinated. "You okay? Didn't fall or anything getting here? Didn't cut yourself on any glass getting through the window?"

Josh shook his head. "It was stupid. I was stupid. I didn't realize it was going to be this cold."

"Not stupid, Josh. Inexperienced, perhaps. We need to get that wind blocked." He unzipped his pack and pulled a square of plastic that, once he unfolded it, was plenty big enough to cover the window. Then he opened the small tool kit and removed the half hammer and a handful of nails. In seconds, the plastic was secured around the edges, blocking the worst of the wind. "Not great, but it will help."

"Better than I was able to do," Josh muttered. "I thought the door would be open. Since nobody uses it," he added.

"Nobody uses it, but like any Colton property, it still gets checked routinely to make sure it's secure, free of rodents and any other intruders."

"I'll pay for the window," Josh said. "I broke it, after all."

His son was a stand-up kind of kid. He liked that. "We can discuss that later," Blaine replied easily. "I'm glad you got inside."

"I guess I was at least that smart," Josh said, sounding discouraged.

"I never doubted that you'd be smart. And now I need to call your mom and tell her the good news." He removed the satellite phone from his pack. "I need to step outside. In the meantime, I'll bet you're hungry. I've got some candy bars, some trail mix and some peanut butter crackers."

Josh smiled. "I would eat anything right now."

Blaine tossed him the food, then pulled his collar tight and opened the cabin door. He walked a short distance and turned the phone on. He held it so that the antenna was vertical and hoped for the best. Not only was the weather, with its heavy, overcast skies and ongoing precipitation, not conducive to satellite communications, the cabin was situated in a hollow. Taller mountains surrounded them, impeding a good signal.

"Come on," Blaine muttered. He tried walking around in a circle. Tilda would be so worried. He wanted to relieve that stress.

But it didn't seem as if that was going to be possible.

He considered his alternatives, all of which involved moving to a different location and meant leaving Josh. Not acceptable.

He and Josh would leave at first light. He returned to the cabin. Josh was sitting on the floor in front of the fire, eating the snacks. Blaine sat down next to him. The cot might have been more comfortable to sit on, but quite frankly, it wasn't close enough to the fire.

"What did mom say?" Josh asked.

"Phone isn't picking up a signal. I couldn't reach her."

"I guess I'm kind of glad," his son admitted. "She's going to be mad."

"Thankful," Blaine corrected. "And maybe a little mad. But mostly thankful. She tracked your phone, and we saw the note. That worried her." He wasn't trying to guilt the kid, but he wanted him to realize that there were consequences to his actions. "She loves you very much."

"I know that." He turned his face away from Blaine. "You don't like her very much, do you?"

The question surprised him. "That's not true," he said thickly.

"I heard the two of you arguing last night."

Damn. "I'm sorry that happened. I… I got stupid when you told me that your mom was out on a date. I overreacted and didn't handle myself well."

"I don't think she even likes that guy all that much."

"Doesn't matter," he said, trying to ignore the fact that those simple words made him happy. "Your mom can date. She can do whatever she wants."

"You have a girlfriend," Josh said. It was a statement but said like an accusation.

"No, that's not correct."

"You got in trouble because the two of you had sex."

Aha. Rumors of his relationship with Honor Shayne were out there. He expected no less. But to have his son be the one to repeat them was a little tough. And he wasn't exactly sure he was prepared for a discussion about sex.

But if not now, then when?

"Adults can make a decision to become close, to enjoy a physical relationship. To have sex," he said, wanting to be honest in his communication. "That's not wrong. Where Honor—that's her name—and I erred is that we had a commanding officer who felt that our relationship was inappropriate."

"So it's true. You got kicked out of the army."

Two short sentences. A sharp dagger to his heart. "Yes," he said. "I'm not happy about or proud of that. I am, however, very proud of how I served for thirteen years." He stared into the fire. "Your mom mentioned that she'd heard that there was some online chatter about you being a Colton. Was all this that we just talked about a part of that?"

"Yeah. They said that you walked away from it smelling like a rose because the Coltons walk away from everything smelling like roses, even when they leave crap behind."

"A kid said this?"

"Yeah. He's in my class."

It didn't sound like something a thirteen-year-old would come up with. No doubt the kid had heard his parent or maybe even grandparent say something. "Josh, the Coltons have been in Roaring Springs since the 1800s. They worked very hard, and they did well. And they saved their money and invested it and made more money. That doesn't make them bad people. Just the opposite." He released a breath. "That's what people are supposed to do. Work hard, save money, invest, provide for their family. But sometimes other people see the Coltons and see the things that they have, and they're not happy about it."

"Why would that tick them off?" Josh asked curiously.

"Not sure, to be honest. Maybe they're jealous, maybe they're simply tired because they've been working hard, too, but it hasn't worked out as well for them. For whatever reason, they say things that are hurtful. Behind our backs and sometimes even to our faces." He reached out and squeezed his son's shoulder. "But as a Colton, you have to learn to toughen up a little bit, to not let it get under your skin."

"A bastard Colton," Josh said.

Blaine thought of what Sarah had said, that kids could be horrible to each other. "*Bastard* is an ugly word, Josh. It's a word that people throw around to make other people feel like they are something less." He cleared his throat and looked Blaine square in the eye. "Here's what you need to remember. I'm proud as hell that you're my son. I maybe wasn't married to your mom when you were born, but that doesn't change anything. I love you." It was the first time he'd said it. Maybe it was too soon. But he didn't care. He wanted Josh to know it.

"I don't want to have to choose between the two of you."

His son's voice was thick with unshed tears. "Never going to be necessary, Josh. Your mom and I are committed to both being great parents to you."

"I heard her crying."

Blaine wondered if he could feel worse. "I'm going

to try very hard to make sure that doesn't happen ever again."

For a long time, neither of them said anything. They simply sat in the dark, in front of the fire and listened to the sap-heavy wood crackle and spit.

Finally, Josh shifted. "I'm really glad you came back."

Hope spiked in Blaine. "Me, too."

"I'm so tired," Josh admitted.

Blaine stretched out his legs. Used his arm to guide Josh down so that his head rested on Blaine's thighs. Once his son was stretched out, he used one of the two blankets to cover him and the other one to wrap around his own shoulders. "Sleep well, son. When morning comes, we're going home."

MARA COLTON SLEPT in the spare room. In a T-shirt that she borrowed from Tilda. And in the morning, she got dressed in the same clothes that she'd worn the day before, as if that was perfectly normal, and sat at Tilda's kitchen table, drinking coffee. Tilda offered her toast. She declined.

When a text arrived on Tilda's phone at 7:12 a.m., both women jumped. Tilda grabbed for it, read the short message and let out a sob. Mara leaned over her shoulder to read the phone. Then she wrapped her arms around Tilda, and both women wept.

Finally, Mara straightened up. "I'll be going now."

Tilda held up her phone. "Blaine says they'll be here by eight. You waited this long."

"Thank you," Mara said. "But now that I know they're both safe, I'm going to go home, take a shower, change clothes and go to work. Tell Josh that I'd be delighted if he could make lunch on Saturday."

"He'll be there," Tilda promised.

"And you, too, of course," Mara added. She put on her coat and gloves. "Goodbye, Tilda."

She opened the door and walked out. Tilda hesitated just a second before following her outside, paying no attention to how cold the snowy front steps were on her bare feet. "Thank you," she said. "It was…really very kind of you to stay."

Mara smiled and got into her car.

Tilda stood on her front porch, watching her drive away, until she could no longer see the car. Then she went back inside, picked up her phone and read the message again.

We are both safe. Back at The Lodge. On our way to your house. He's okay. Truly.

She danced around her kitchen, laughing. On her second pass through, she caught a glimpse of herself in the hallway mirror.

Oh, good grief. She looked like she'd been crying all night. No way did she want Josh to see that. He'd feel horrible.

She ran to her bathroom and turned on the shower. Before stepping in, she took the time to send a quick text to her parents to let them know that Josh was safe. Her mom responded immediately, with thirteen red hearts. Likely one for each of Josh's thirteen years.

Tilda took the fastest shower of her life. Then got dressed in yoga pants and a T-shirt. She managed to get her thick hair almost dry before she gave up. Halfway down the hallway, she heard a knock.

Running to the door, she wrenched it open and held her arms out to her son.

Chapter Twelve

She hugged him tight, her nose buried in his bulky coat. Josh smelled of pine and smoke, and she hoped that meant that wherever he'd spent the night he'd been warm. She looked up, over his shoulder, and saw Blaine, who looked very tired.

"Thank you," she mouthed.

He nodded. "Sat phone didn't work. I sent the message as soon as we had cell-phone service."

Her son pulled back. "I'm sorry," he choked out.

She saw a vulnerability that reminded her of a much younger Josh. "You're safe. That's what matters," she told him.

"He's probably hungry," Blaine said. He moved out of the doorway, into the house. Closing the door behind him. He evidently intended to stay.

Likely didn't want Josh out of his sight. She understood that.

"Pancakes?" she asked, looking at Josh.

"Bacon, too?" he replied hopefully.

She smiled. Her son's face was dirty, as were his hands. His thick hair was slightly matted. But he looked whole. "Maybe you should take a quick shower," she suggested.

"Am I going to school?"

"Not today. I'm staying home, too."

"You're taking the day off?" he asked.

"Yep." She'd called in to school late the night before, when it had become apparent that it would be morning before she heard anything.

"Do you have my phone?"

"I do. And you can have it back after we've had a chance to talk. Right now, I want you to go get cleaned up."

He turned and went without another word. When he was out of earshot, she looked at Blaine. "He would usually throw a fit if I withheld his phone, and it generally takes me two or three tries and at least fifteen minutes to get him to shower. I think he's glad to be home."

"I think we're both glad to be off that mountain."

"Would you like some coffee?" she asked.

"Sure." He walked over to the kitchen table and pulled out a chair. He was limping. Just the slightest bit, but she'd become so attuned to him and his movements these last few days that she noticed it immediately. "You're hurt," she said softly.

He shook his head. "Bruised. Slid into a tree on my way there. The conditions were…challenging."

They'd have been horrible. But he'd managed to keep going, to find Josh and to ski his way off the mountain this morning. Her eyes filled with tears, and she turned away hastily, not wanting him to see. She was a wreck. But he'd already dealt with plenty. He didn't need to deal with her, too.

She poured the coffee, wiped up the imaginary spills she'd left behind and straightened the towel hanging on the stove door twice before turning around. He was watching her. She set down his coffee cup in front of him.

"Thank you," he said. "He's hungry and probably a little dehydrated and very tired, but I think he's going to be fine." He stopped, maybe because he could see that she wasn't convinced. "But if it would make you feel better, have him checked out by his doctor," he added with a soft smile.

"I might do that," she admitted. "Don't want to coddle him but it was so cold and he is just thirteen."

Blaine nodded. "And like any other typical thirteen-year-old boy, he feels bad that he might have overreacted to some stuff at school and that he underestimated the difficulty of navigating a mountain storm."

She turned back toward the counter and started pulling together the ingredients for pancakes. "Did you talk about what sent him there?"

"We did. The last few days haven't been easy on him."

She waited for the accusation, the *This is how you ruined him* barb. Girded her heart, wanting to protect it from the assault.

"I blame myself for not paying closer attention to it," he said. "For not getting ahead of it."

What? He wasn't blaming her? Maybe he'd hit his head on the tree, too? She glanced over her shoulder at him. He was staring down at his coffee cup.

"Your mother came here last night."

His head jerked up. "I'm sorry," he said immediately. "I didn't ask her—"

"I know that," she interrupted. "She just left, maybe twenty minutes ago, once she knew that both you and Josh were okay."

"I'll call her. It went okay, the two of you together?" he asked cautiously.

She added eggs to the dry ingredients, then milk. "She was very kind."

There was silence behind her. "What are you guys going to do today?" Blaine asked finally, as she finished stirring.

"What I want to do is hug him all day and ask him to swear a blood oath that he'll never do anything like this again."

"Blood oath? You are tough."

He didn't say it meanly. "I can be. And I need to walk a fine line here, today. I'll see if I can get him into his doctor's office this morning. Even assuming that goes well, I don't think it's a good idea for him to go to school. He's tired and wouldn't be at his best. But it can't be a fun, stay-at-home day. That would be rewarding his behavior. What he did was wrong, and he needs to know that."

"Parenting is hard," he said.

"Very."

"So, what's the plan?"

"I want to talk to him. I need to better understand what drove him up that mountain and help him understand that there are better ways to deal with bullies, whether they're online or in person. He was lucky. Maybe he wouldn't be a second time." That thought was too horrible to contemplate. "And I'll let him catch up on some sleep. I may try to do the same because I didn't get much last night."

"I'm sorry I couldn't get word to you."

"I understand. I'm not blaming you."

The air in her kitchen seemed heavy, and she heard the pipes echo as the water poured through them in the bathroom.

"He was scared," Blaine said, his voice low. "He broke a window to get inside, which was smart, but his matches got wet, so he couldn't light a fire. He was pretty cold when I got there."

Her heart broke for her sweet boy. He'd suffered. But if he'd also learned, she reasoned, then there was something good to come from this. The mountains were beautiful, majestic even. But now he'd experienced the truth. They were also dangerous and could test even the most capable, the most prepared.

Thank goodness Blaine was exactly that. She turned around. He'd been very brave. Maybe she could be a little brave, too. "If you hadn't been here, I… I don't know how all this would have played out."

"Maybe he wouldn't have been on that mountain."

She shook her head. "If not that, then it would have been something else. I've been so confident that I was doing a good job raising Josh, that I was really everything he needed. But he needs his father, too. And I'm grateful you were here."

She heard the water shut off in the bathroom. Blaine looked in that direction for a brief moment, then, turning back toward her, stared into her eyes. "He doesn't want us to be angry with one another, to fight," he whispered. "He doesn't want to have to choose."

She'd been saying those same words, but had her actions and reactions been saying something else? Kids were perceptive. "He shouldn't have to."

"Agreed," he said. He leaned forward. "I'm willing to try, Tilda. For Josh."

She heard the bathroom door open. It would mean letting Josh embrace being a Colton, everything she'd tried so hard to avoid for so many years. It would mean that she would have to share Josh.

It would mean being with Blaine, knowing that he would never really forgive her, but putting on a brave front every day. Exhausting.

Josh would be in the kitchen any moment, hungry for his pancakes.

Blaine was willing to try. Could she do less and live with herself?

"I'll do whatever it takes," she said. "Anything for my son."

BLAINE SAT AT Tilda's kitchen table, eating pancakes and bacon. No one was talking much. He and Josh were hungry, and Tilda seemed content to just sit and watch her son eat.

He hadn't expected her to cook him breakfast, but she'd sat a plate in front of him. It was the second meal that they'd shared together as a family, the first being at his mom's house. This felt significantly different, significantly more relaxed. Almost…normal.

Not that he really had a clue what normal family life was. After all, he'd been raised by Russ and Mara Colton.

He'd been…restless. That was perhaps the best word to describe it. Restless to get away from Colorado, from a place where his destiny seemed predetermined. For those few weeks when he'd thought that Tilda was pregnant, he'd seen his chance to leave, to change everything, disappear.

So, now, to come back to this, was more than a little startling. And he hadn't handled it the best. And his son had been witness to that.

He could do better. He *would* do better. He stabbed his last bite of pancake when Tilda's phone buzzed. She picked it up, studied the text message and frowned.

"Who's that, Mom?" Josh asked.

"A parent of one of my students."

"You give your cell-phone number out to all the parents?" he asked.

She nodded. "At the beginning of the year, at parent–teacher night. We talk about all the ways that I'll communicate with them and how they can communicate with me." She paused. "It's funny, though. I don't remember this parent being there. I'm sure I've never met her, and now she wants me to come to her house."

"You do that?" Blaine asked brusquely. It didn't sound like a great idea to him. Kind of like approaching a deserted building that nobody had scouted out and cleared in advance.

"No one has ever asked before," she admitted. "But I'm grateful that she's reached out. Her son, Toby, is the one who is in danger of failing my class and not graduating. I don't want that to happen."

"That's the kid that you were meeting with after school."

"Yes."

Animosity had rolled off that kid. And an apple didn't necessarily fall far from the tree. Tilda could be walking into a very hostile situation with no one to protect her. "Are you going to do it?"

She put her phone aside. "I shouldn't. It's against school policy. A couple of years ago, a teacher went to a student's house, and there were some accusations of inappropriate behavior on the part of the teacher. He denied it, but it was a mess for the school." She sighed. "But I really do want to talk to these parents. Maybe there's another way. I'll work on that later. Because today," she said, smiling at Josh, "I'm all about this kid."

Blaine figured that was his cue to leave. He picked up his empty plate and carried it to the sink. "Thanks for breakfast. It was delicious."

"That's nothing," she said, waving a hand dismissively. "You should taste my French toast."

"Another time," he said. Tilda looked lovely this morning. She had flawless skin that required no makeup. And her long, dark hair had always been stunning. She'd truly been the prettiest girl in his senior class, and her beauty had deepened over the years.

He ruffled Josh's hair on his way past. "Get some sleep, okay?" he said.

"I will," his son said. "Thanks… Blaine."

Had he almost said *Dad*? Blaine could feel his heart race in his chest. Knew it didn't really matter what Josh called him but also knew that hearing *Dad* on his son's lips would be one hell of a sweet sound. "Happy to assist," he said. "See you later, Tilda."

"Did you want to take Josh out to dinner tonight?" she asked quickly. "I mean, it didn't work out so well last night."

She was willing to stay back, to give him time with Josh. But what message did that send to his son? "How about I take both of you out tonight?"

He could tell she was surprised. "Um…sure," she said, likely remembering her pledge that she could also try to do better.

"Great. I'll see you at six."

THE HOUSE SEEMED very quiet after he left. Then Josh pushed back his chair and carried his empty plate to the sink. Turned to look at her. "He was pretty great last night."

The quiet, heartfelt admission made her throat feel tight. He'd been pretty great this morning, too. "I'm glad he found you."

"I guess I didn't think things through very well."

"What happened, Josh?" she asked quietly. "What made it so important to get away?"

He shrugged. "Guys were saying stuff, you know."

"About Blaine?"

"Yeah. Him, other Coltons. Me, now that I'm a Colton." He paused. "Other stuff, too," he added, almost mumbling.

She'd been working with teens for many years. Knew that *other stuff* could be code for *things I can't talk to you about.* "About me?"

He nodded, looking miserable.

"What?" she asked gently. "Don't worry, honey. I can take it."

"That you were a whore, lying to the man you married about who was the father of your baby."

Ouch. It hurt...she couldn't deny that. But nor could she control wagging tongues and people with so much time on their hands that they filled it with stupid gossip. "I never lied to Dorian. He knew the truth from the very beginning. I told you that."

"I know, and I told them that, but they said there was no way to prove that now because he's dead."

So true. And maybe things would have been different if Dorian hadn't been there, hadn't been so available and so willing to offer a solution that seemed to meet both of their needs. Hell, met Josh's needs, too. He had a father who was *there.*

"So, here's the thing, Josh. I know the truth. You know the truth. Blaine knows the truth. The people that we love and care about have been told the truth, and they believe it. You can't care what anybody else thinks. I know that's easy to say and hard to live, but I'm going to need you to do that."

"I'll try."

"Did you tell Blaine what the kids said?" she asked.

"No. Not that part. I did tell what they said about him. That he'd gotten pushed out of the army."

What? And just that quick, she remembered the look that had passed between her parents last night and their odd remark about something being ridiculous. But when she'd questioned it, they clearly hadn't wanted to discuss it. She hadn't cared last night because she had much bigger things to worry about. But now, she wondered if her parents had heard something. "What did Blaine say about that?"

"He said it was true."

Wow. "Did he say why?"

"He…messed around with another soldier, a woman, and got in trouble for it. She has a weird first name. Honor."

She felt a pain in her chest. Had Blaine loved the woman? Did he still love her? Who was she? She had a thousand questions. But even if Blaine had offered up details to Josh, she should not be pumping her son for information on his father's sex life.

"Your dad's friends are not our concern. Here's what I think you need to focus on, Josh. I think your dad was a good soldier, and he's a good man."

"I just want school to be over with."

"Soon," she said. "But we can't really deal with problems by hoping that they'll go away."

"I know that. But it will be easier if I don't have to see the creeps who are saying these things every day."

Hard to argue with that.

"Can I have my phone back now?" Josh asked.

"Are you ready for that? You might see things on there that are going to be hurtful."

"I'm just going to ignore it."

"Okay. But no texting Isaac or other friends. They're in school, where you should be. No social media. You can play a few games, but what I really want is for you to catch up on your sleep and to make sure that all your homework is done. I'm also going to call your doctor's office. They may want to see you."

"Fine," he readily agreed.

She had a feeling he might agree to anything about now.

"I really am sorry, Mom."

She wrapped her son in her arms. "People screw up, Josh. Kids do. Adults, too. The important thing is to learn from the situation."

"Oh, I learned. That mountain is really cold at night. And you're a dummy if you let your matches get wet."

"Both good lessons. Now get to bed."

She sat in her quiet kitchen, staring at the wall. It had not dawned on her that Blaine might have a love interest. It was stupid that it hadn't. He was so handsome and had such a dynamic personality. Would Honor follow Blaine to Roaring Springs? Would they marry? Was Josh going to have a stepmom?

Her head was spinning. But most of all, she felt empty. At one time, she'd cared very much for Blaine Colton. Had known that he didn't feel the same and had accepted that. To the point that she'd married another man. But there'd always been a piece of her heart that she'd reserved for Blaine.

It felt a bit as if that part was breaking right now.

Chapter Thirteen

Blaine had gotten about an hour of sleep at the cabin, and like Josh, he should have been headed to bed, but he was too wired to sleep. He'd driven from Tilda's house back to The Lodge, but now, instead of getting some shut-eye, he sat in his vehicle. It was still too early and too cold for there to be much outside activity. Only a few guests were milling around the grounds. Inside, the restaurants and coffee shops were probably doing a brisk business, but he'd already had enough of that.

In the quiet warmth of his vehicle, he could admit that he still felt a little numb from the experience of searching for and finding Josh. Not in the physical sense. His bones had thawed, but mentally, he was still a little raw. He'd done search and rescue missions before. But never with more on the line.

As a parent, the need to do whatever it took to keep his child safe had been instinctual. But instinct still took effort, and as he and Josh had skied down the mountain early this morning, he'd thought about the huge responsibility that Tilda had taken on. It was some of what Sloane had been trying to tell him when she'd lectured him about being too hard on Tilda.

It was true. He hadn't been there for the ear infections and the croup. Hadn't dealt with playground falls and bad dreams. Dorian had done that for Tilda. For his son. And maybe it was time to stop being angry at a dead man and start being thankful that Tilda had not been on her own, too weighted down by worry and responsibility to be a good parent.

Because she'd done a damn good job with his kid.

And was continuing to do so. Even this morning, she'd been thinking more about what would be best for him than what her own needs might be.

He'd told her she was selfish. That gnawed at him now. He'd been angry but should have known better. As a parent, she was selfless, and to question her love of or her commitment to Josh was plain asinine. He wouldn't do it again.

Blaine saw a couple male employees exit the staff entrance. He didn't know their names, but he recognized their faces. They were carrying cardboard boxes and talking animatedly. He rolled down his window to try to hear, but the wind carried their voices the other direction.

They each went to a vehicle, tossed their box in the back seat and drove off. Blaine opened his door, walked inside and went to find Decker. Earlier he'd sent a text letting Decker know that he and Josh were both back, but his brother would want details.

When he got to his brother's office, Penny gave him a quick smile, but she wasn't her normal friendly self. She told him to wait, that his brother was meeting with a couple managers. Ten minutes later, a man and woman, both midforties, came out of Decker's office. His brother followed them out and shook hands with both. "Thank you," he said to them.

The two left without looking at Blaine. He wasn't sure why, but he got a creepy, crawling feeling up the back of his neck. "What's going on?" he asked, as he followed his brother back to his office.

"Why do you ask?" Decker said. He motioned for Blaine to have a seat and then joined him at the small table.

"Because I saw two employees leaving with boxes, like they might have cleaned out their lockers. You're holed up with two managers. And Penny is acting weird."

"Just a little turnover. We're a business. That happens. So, things went well with Josh?"

"Yeah. He was at the cabin. We're going to need to send somebody up to fix the window when it gets a little warmer. We stayed the night and then skied down this morning. Stopped here for my vehicle, and right now, he's crawling into bed with his stomach full of his mom's pancakes."

"You two have a chance to talk about what sent him running into the mountains?" Decker asked.

"We did. Some kids were giving him a hard time about me. Word has gotten out that I had a little assistance with my discharge status."

"I see," his brother replied.

"You don't seem to be surprised."

Decker stared somewhere above Blaine's head.

"What?" Blaine demanded.

"Damn fools," Decker muttered.

"Who? Me?"

"No. Not you. Couple of our best maintenance guys were going on about the same thing this morning. Their managers warned them to stop, but they just picked up speed. It was upsetting the rest of the crew. Managers told them they were suspended, to take a few days off to think about their actions. They said that they'd rather quit than work for the Coltons. *The very, very privileged Coltons.*" He did the last part in air quotes.

Damn. "I'm sorry."

Decker waved a hand. "It's just a tough time to lose a couple more men. We already have somebody on leave for back surgery, and another one needs a couple weeks off to get his mom settled in an assisted-living facility."

"I'd be happy to help," Blaine said. "Pick up the slack."

"That's not—"

"Listen, it's going to warm up finally, which means we'll be off the slopes by early next week. I'll have the time. I'm pretty handy."

"This isn't glamorous work," Decker warned. "It's everything from changing light bulbs to unclogging sinks to providing some basic supervision for subcontractors that are on-site. Our maintenance office produces work orders. You'll be expected to take what comes your way."

"I can do that."

Decker shook his head. "Fine. I'll let the managers know that you're filling in. When can you start?"

He really needed a quick nap. "Right now," he said.

Three hours later, his stack of work orders about half-done, he headed across the lobby towards the maintenance office in the lower level to pick up some glue to replace a guest's bathroom tile. He had just pressed the button on the service elevator, when he caught a glimpse of a man in the lobby that made him stop short.

Davis James.

He'd never spoken to the man, never been introduced in any way. But he'd seen pictures. And heard plenty.

Davis James was Honor Shayne's ex-husband. The marriage had been over before Blaine and Honor's relationship had begun. And they hadn't spent too much time talking about him. But from what little Honor had said, he'd thought the man might be a little unhinged.

And here he was, in Roaring Springs.

What would bring Davis James, who, last he knew, lived in Stamford, Connecticut, to Roaring Springs, Colorado?

The elevator doors opened, but Blaine ignored them. He was confident that Davis James had not seen him. The man was engaged in conversation with the concierge. He continued to watch. Five minutes later, after James had turned around and given the lobby one final expansive perusal, he left via the front door.

Blaine crossed the lobby fast and saw him get into a nondescript black sedan that screamed rental car. The man drove away.

The concierge was a young woman that he hadn't met. "Hi," he said, approaching. "I'm Blaine Colton."

"I know who you are," she said. There was no malice in her tone, simply an acknowledgment that his presence at the hotel hadn't gone unnoticed.

"And you are?" he asked, with a smile.

"Patty," she said.

"Well, Patty, I'm hoping you can help me with something. The man that you were just talking to, who was it?"

Patty looked down at her desk. There was a name scribbled across a notepad. "Jim Park."

Blaine was confident that he wasn't mistaken. Davis James had an interesting face—it was narrow and long, with a square chin and hooded eyes. The description sounded worse than it was. He was perfectly fine-looking, just memorable.

So, now there were two questions. Why was he here,

and why was he lying about his name? "What did he want?"

"Just information about Roaring Springs. Special Events passed him off to me after they finished their tour. He's thinking of booking a wedding here."

Damn long way to come for a wedding. Of course, he could be marrying someone from Colorado. But none of that explained the name thing. "Who did he talk to in Special Events?"

"Janey Maxwell."

"Got it. Thanks." Blaine flashed another smile and took off for the second floor. In five minutes, he was in Janey Maxwell's office. She was midforties and had a no-nonsense demeanor. When he asked about Jim Park, she rolled her eyes.

"I'll admit," Janey said, "I was surprised that he wasn't with his fiancée. Not that many grooms come for the initial discussion about the wedding venue. We generally don't see them until they're dragged in, once the bride has made a decision."

"When's the wedding?"

"Next fall. He said they had some flexibility and would work around our availability. I gave him dates for October and November, and he was satisfied. But I didn't think I was ever going to get rid of him. He wanted to see everything. Ballrooms. Dining options. Guest rooms. Exercise facilities. Pool. And he took notes and pictures of everything."

Blaine kept his face neutral. "Did you happen to see any identification?"

"No. That's not something we ask for."

Of course not. "No problem. Could you do something for me? If he calls or comes back, would you let me know? Before you see him?"

"Of course. Did I do something wrong?" she asked.

"Absolutely not."

"Okay," Janey said.

He was almost out the door before she spoke again. "Mr. Colton?"

"Yeah?" He turned.

"I… I heard what happened with the maintenance staff this morning, and I just want you to know that most of the employees here are very supportive of the Colton family. We're grateful for the jobs you've brought to Roaring Springs, for the investment you've made in the community. And I…" She paused. "Well, I had a son who served in the Marines. Did a couple tours in Afghanistan. Came home in one piece, thankfully. But he's got some stories. Well, I just want you to know that I'm also grateful for your service."

It was a heartfelt thank-you, and it humbled him. "I appreciate that. Truly. And please let your son know that I'm grateful for his service."

He left the office, thinking that he needed to talk to Honor, to see if she might have any idea why her ex would be in Roaring Springs lying about his name. He thumbed through his contacts on his phone and found her. He dialed, it rang four times and then flipped over to voice mail. "Honor, it's Blaine. Hope you're doing okay. Can you call me when you get this message? Thanks."

He hung up. Frustrated. But then looked at the work orders still in his hand. He had bathroom tile to glue on.

It was almost five before he got back to his desk. Honor had not called back, and he contemplated trying her again. But didn't. She would call.

He returned a few work emails that needed immediate attention and then shut his laptop down. He would come in early the following day to clear the rest. Right now, he had time to grab a quick shower before he drove down to the valley to meet Tilda and Josh for dinner.

He hoped they'd had a good day together. Shortly before noon, she'd sent a text that said the doctor's visit had gone well. He'd been busy enough that he should have been able to easily put thoughts of her aside. But it hadn't worked that way.

He could see her standing at the stove, cooking pancakes. Could see the absolute joy on her face when she'd opened the door and hugged Josh. Could see her surprised expression when he'd suggested they all have dinner together. And now he was very much looking forward to that.

Twenty-five minutes later, freshly showered, he started his car in the staff parking lot. Before he put the car in Drive, he heard his cell phone ring. He looked at the display. Honor.

"Hello," he said.

"Blaine?"

They'd parted on friendly terms, both of them accepting that what they'd had was over. It was no wonder that she might be curious about why he was calling. "Hi, Honor. How are you?"

"Good. Busy," she added. "How are you?"

"Back in Roaring Springs. Working for my brother Decker, at The Lodge."

She said nothing. Was probably surprised that he'd decided to stay in Roaring Springs. "You'll do great at whatever you try," she said finally.

"Thank you. The reason for my call is that I'm pretty sure I saw your ex-husband at The Lodge today."

"Davis?"

"You have more than one ex-husband?" he teased.

"No. But I can't imagine why he'd be there. He lives in Connecticut."

"He told our Special Events people that he was looking for a location for a wedding reception. His wedding. And he's going by the name of Jim Park."

"That makes no sense to me. I mean, I did hear that he'd been doing some online dating. Maybe he uses an alias for that. Certainly not the best way to build a relationship though." She hesitated. "And, who knows, maybe he met somebody from your neck of the woods. But that's just conjecture. It's not like we're sharing confidences these days. I haven't seen him for months."

"Do you know anybody you could ask?" Blaine asked.

"Maybe his sister. We're still on friendly terms. She always sided with me through the divorce proceedings. But she's a flight attendant. Does overseas travel. It may take me a few days to get in touch with her."

"That should be fine," he said. "I appreciate it."

"No problem." She paused. "I hope you're doing well, Blaine. I…care for you. I always will."

"Same here," he said. It had been a brief affair that had nearly had devastating consequences. It dawned on him that it wasn't all that different from his relationship with Tilda. But in that case, the consequence had been Josh.

Devastating when a person was eighteen, not married and had plans that didn't include a baby. Now, not devastating in any sense of the word. Time had a funny way of changing perspective. He thought about telling Honor about Josh but realized that wasn't the type of relationship they shared.

Who was it that he could tell his confidences?

Tilda. Her face flashed in his head.

"Thanks, Honor," he said and hung up.

He drove down the mountain. There had been no fresh snow today, so the roads were clear, especially the closer he got to town. He pulled up in front of Tilda's house and killed the engine. When he knocked on the front door, it didn't open right away. He knocked again. Harder.

It swung open. Josh. With earphones on. "Sorry," his son said. "I was listening to music."

"No problem." Blaine reached out and ruffled his son's short hair. "Did you get some sleep today?"

"I did. It felt great," Josh said.

Blaine looked around. "Where's your mom?"

"She had to run an errand." Josh looked at the clock on the kitchen wall. "I thought she'd be back before now," he added, sounding puzzled.

"Check your phone," Blaine said, seeing it on the table.

Josh picked it up. "No messages."

"Okay, let's just call her." He pulled his own phone and dialed. It rang four times before going to voice mail. "Hey, Tilda. I'm at your house, and we were just wondering when you might be home. Give me a call."

"I hope she's okay," Josh said, concern in his voice. "She's not usually late."

"I'm sure she's fine. Are you wearing that to dinner?"

Josh looked down at his sweats and T-shirt. "Mom told me to put on clean jeans and a sweater. And to brush my teeth."

"Go get that done," Blaine said. He sat on the couch, holding his phone. Minutes went by. He heard Josh in the bathroom, running water.

Ten minutes later, Josh was back in the living room. Tilda had still not called. And Blaine didn't like that.

"Do you know where her errand was?"

"I'm not sure. I think she said something about the dry cleaners."

Couldn't be more than a couple of those in Roaring Springs. He looked it up on his smartphone. There were two. "Let's go," he said. "We'll meet your mom downtown."

They were two minutes away from their first stop when his phone rang. It was her. "Hey," he answered.

"I'm sorry," she said. "I know I'm late for dinner."

"No problem. Everything okay?"

"Well, not really."

His anxiety ratcheted up. He took a sideways glance at Josh. "Are you hurt?"

"No. My car can't say the same, though."

"Were you in an accident?" he asked.

"No. I…well, I'm not sure how to say this because it sounds so awful. But I was running some errands, and I came back to my car and all four tires were flat."

Two might go flat at the same time, but all four? Not happening. "We're two minutes away, Tilda. Where are you right now?"

"In the parking lot behind Smith's Cleaners. Watching a tow truck load up my car."

"Why don't you go back inside the building?" He pressed his foot down on the accelerator, edging up another ten miles per hour.

"Why?"

"Just do it. And stay away from any windows."

"But—" she began.

"Tilda, please."

"Fine."

Chapter Fourteen

Blaine was the first one into the dry cleaners. His look took her in, from head to toe. "You're okay?"

"Of course," she said. Tilda didn't want to admit that she was a little rattled. She kept her voice down, not wanting the young woman behind the counter to hear everything.

"You and Josh stay here," he said. "I'm going to take a quick look at your tires."

"I'll save you the trouble. They were slashed."

He didn't look surprised. "You need to call the police."

"Already did. They just left."

"Smart girl," he said.

It was crazy, but just that small praise was enough to make her warm. Which was welcome because she was cold after standing outside for so long. First, talking to the police. Then, waiting for the tow truck.

"I'm sorry that I missed your call. I had my phone on vibrate and didn't realize how late it had gotten."

He waved a hand. "Just glad you're okay. Are the police canvasing the area?"

"They're going to try to see if there's any camera footage from either the city or from one of the merchants. Also, going to check to see if similar complaints come in or whether this was an isolated incident."

"Did you tell them about your student, Toby Turner?"

She shook her head. "I don't have any reason to believe that he did this."

"How can you be so sure?" Blaine asked, his tone confrontational. "After all, you're the person standing between him and graduation."

"He knows that's his fault. He hasn't done the work. I'm not picking on him."

"Tilda, he's still a kid. They react with emotion, not with logic."

Josh, who'd been quietly observing the conversation, held up a finger. "Can speak to that," he said.

It broke the tension in the room. Tilda relaxed for the first time in over an hour. "Something is definitely going on with Toby. I don't know what that is. What I do know is that if the police descend upon him because I've pointed them in his direction, I'm never going to find out. I have to have confidence that they're going to be true to their word and investigate. If evidence leads them in his direction, that's different."

"It's your decision," Blaine said, maybe still a little begrudgingly. It touched her that he was so concerned.

"As long as we're all here, maybe we could just go get something to eat," Tilda said.

"Yes," Josh said immediately. "Italian?" he asked, pointing at the restaurant across the street.

"Fine with me," Blaine said.

"Carbohydrates always make me happy," Tilda murmured. She turned to pick up the garment that she'd come for.

"That's your prom dress?" Josh asked, pointing at the garment.

"Prom dress?" Blaine repeated.

"Mom has to chaperone the senior prom on Saturday night."

"The teachers take turns," Tilda offered.

"Pretty," Blaine said, sounding a bit bemused.

She felt heat move through her body. Was he recalling that she'd gotten pregnant on their prom night? She tried to read his face but didn't have a clue what was going through his mind.

She tried to focus on the here and now. It *was* a pretty dress. Royal blue silk with a fitted bodice with lace overlay, an empire belt and a flare skirt that hit right above the knee. She'd bought it for a wedding two years ago, and this would be the second time she'd worn it. "Thanks," she said, tossing it over her arm. She reached for the door, and they walked across the street.

They were seated, and a few minutes later had placed their orders. Then Blaine leaned forward, looking at Josh. "You know, I took your mom to prom the year we were seniors."

Surely he didn't intend to tell Josh *that* story.

"No way," Josh said. "That's cool."

"Very cool." Blaine winked at him. "She wore a red dress that night. In fact," he said, reaching for his wallet, "I can show you a picture."

She almost choked on her water. He had a picture of them. And when he pulled it out, she saw that it was creased and lined, as if it had logged some miles in his wallet. "Oh my gosh," she managed.

"You were pretty," Josh said.

"Before I became old and haggard," Tilda teased, desperately needing to lighten the moment. Blaine had carried around a picture of them all these years. That, combined with all the other things that had happened, was almost too much.

For more than twenty-four hours, since waking up from her late-afternoon nap to find that Josh was missing, she'd seemed to be at a fever pitch. Even today, while at home with him, she'd felt oddly off-balance. Had tried to brush it off, telling herself that it was because she wasn't where she was supposed to be—at work. That she'd probably had less than two hours of sleep the night before. That she'd contemplated the very worst thing a parent can think of—that her child was not safe and would not return.

But it was more than that. And now, after the tires incident, she definitely wasn't up to taking on a surprisingly sentimental Blaine.

Fortunately, he didn't seem inclined to do that, either. He put away the photo without further comment and asked about Josh's summer baseball season. Then they talked about the upcoming film festival. It attracted so many people that her church even got in the act and operated a taco stand in the area that the city approved for exactly that purpose. She'd volunteered in the past and was planning on doing so again.

Blaine talked about being excited for his family. Wyatt would soon be a father. Decker was a newlywed, and Sloane had recently remarried. He mentioned picking up some more responsibilities at The Lodge and amused them by relaying an encounter with one guest, who swore that the carpet in her room was moving. When Blaine had tried to clarify if the carpet was loose and coming up from the floor, the woman had insisted that the pattern was moving, back and forth, sometimes disappearing altogether.

"I wasn't sure what I could do for her," Blaine admitted.

"Perhaps she purchased some of the state flower," Josh said.

Blaine frowned.

"Marijuana," Tilda explained.

"It's legal here," Josh said, his mouth full.

"Chew, then speak," Tilda reminded him gently.

"I didn't think of that," Blaine admitted.

"Well, not that I really know anything about it," Josh rushed to say. "But a guy hears stuff, you know."

Blaine locked eyes with Tilda. "Right answer," he said, clearly amused.

They had ice cream at the end of their meal, and it all seemed so right—that she and Blaine should be having dinner with Josh. She reminded herself that this wasn't natural, that it was a planned activity, in hopes of creating a more normal family experience for Josh.

That threatened the joy she felt, but she resolutely pushed it away. She wanted a couple hours of fun. Light after the darkness.

Blaine drove them home. "Do you mind if I come in?" he asked, as he parked in front of their house.

Josh had already showered that morning, and she didn't want to delay getting him in his room and settled down. "Tomorrow is a school day, and Josh is going to need to go early in order to talk to his teachers about what he missed today."

"I'd like to talk to you."

That sounded a bit ominous, even though he said it easily enough. She glanced at Josh, in the back seat, who didn't seem to have even heard. He was looking at his phone, laughing at something on it.

"Sure," she said.

Once inside, she immediately told Josh to head for his room. "Lights out in thirty minutes," she said. "But give me a hug first."

He rolled his eyes but wrapped his arms around her. Then he surprised her, and maybe Blaine, too, when he did the same for his father.

"Wow," Blaine said, sounding a little shocked, after Josh had left the room. "That felt good."

"I know. Hugs are the best. I don't even feel badly that I have to ask."

"I think it's good that you do. I don't remember there being a whole lots of hugs in my house. We probably all could have used more."

She didn't want to talk about Russ and Mara Colton. It seemed like a good way to end what had turned out to be a very nice night.

"Would you like some coffee?" she asked.

He shook his head. "I need to tell you something."

He sounded very serious. Tilda said, "Okay."

"I want you to hear this from me. Not some second-hand version that doesn't even resemble the truth." He leaned forward on the couch. His voice was lowered, as if he definitely didn't want Josh overhearing. "I mentioned that I was picking up some additional responsibilities at The Lodge. What I didn't say is that I need to do that because a couple employees quit unexpectedly today, after raising a commotion about Coltons getting privileged treatment. Specifically me."

She had a feeling that she was about to get the details of what Josh had mentioned earlier. She admitted that she was glad, that it had been gnawing at her most of the day. "Because?"

"Because my discharge from the military was changed, from Dishonorable to Honorable. I had an affair with a woman. Her name was Honor Shayne. Unfortunately, the commanding officer took a dim view of the situation and did a full-court press on both of us to make examples out of us. I knew he was wrong, and I was confident that I could get the situation changed. But before I could do that, my father intervened. Called my Uncle Joe."

"President Colton."

"Former president, yes," Blaine said. "Anyway, he did get involved, and what should have happened anyway came about pretty fast. Word of that has evidently gotten out, and the story has become so convoluted that some people think I committed something akin to treason and was let off the hook because of my name."

She had so many questions including *Did you love her* at the tip of her tongue. But it didn't appear that she was going to get a word in edgewise because he was picking up speed.

"I need you to know about this because I saw Honor Shayne's ex-husband at The Lodge today. He was investigating potential wedding-reception venues. He's not from this area and, oddly enough, he was using a different name. When I talked to Honor, she couldn't shed any light on it."

He'd talked to Honor. Very recently. Today, in fact. That fact was so enormous that it made it harder to concentrate on the other things he was saying. But now he'd moved on to her tires.

"...your slashed tires."

"What?" she scrambled to catch up.

"I said we can't ignore the possibility that Davis James has something to do with your slashed tires. To have something so unusual happen on the same day that he's spotted in the area warrants consideration."

"I don't even know him," she said. "He doesn't know me."

"It's Roaring Springs, Tilda. He wouldn't have had to talk to too many people before he heard that Josh was my son. That you were his mother. Important to me."

She was important to him. He'd said it almost offhandedly.

"Am I?"

He had pulled his phone from his coat pocket and was thumbing through it. "Are you what?" he asked, looking up.

"Am I important to you?" she whispered.

He put his phone down. The air in the room seemed very still. She heard the bathroom door open and then Josh's door open and close. She could hear the tick of the kitchen clock, the sound of a car very far away.

"I would never want anything bad to happen to you, Tilda."

He hadn't answered the question. Should she repeat it? Like she would for one of her students. Perhaps move closer, to make sure she had his full attention.

He'd kept their prom picture. That had to mean something.

"I need to know something," she said. "And maybe it's not my business. But I want to know if you and Honor are still…together."

Blaine shook his head. "It's been over for some time. I'm not unhappy about that."

Relief flooded her body. Maybe Blaine wasn't willing to editorialize about her importance to him but he wasn't pining for another woman. Knowing that, she could better focus on the more immediate issue.

"Let's get back to Davis James. How can you be

confident it was him if he's using a different name?" she asked.

"He's got an unusual face. I've seen photos."

"Describe him," she said.

"I can do better than that. I found this online earlier." He picked up his phone and, in just seconds, was holding it out to her.

She looked at it. He was midthirties, straight brown hair, cut short, with a narrow long face and deeply hooded eyes. "I've never seen him," she said.

"Good. Let's keep it that way."

"Are you going to tell the police that he's in Roaring Springs?"

Blaine nodded. "I'm going to contact Liam Kastor, Sloane's new husband. He's a detective. Do you remember him from high school? He was good friends with Fox."

"I do. In the last couple of years, we've seen each other at a few community events. Nice guy."

"I need to congratulate him on the marriage. I wanted to make it back for that, but I was in Washington, the whole discharge thing. Anyway, I think I'll get his advice."

"Good idea."

He stood up. "Just be aware, Tilda. That's all I'm saying. By the way, how are you getting to work in the morning?"

"I was going to call my parents."

"I'll take you."

She shook her head. "That's crazy, Blaine. You'd have to drive from The Lodge into Roaring Springs. Didn't you just say you picked up extra responsibilities, not less?"

"I'll be fine," he said dismissively.

"I need to go early." She wanted to check to see if the sub who had covered her classroom had left any notes. It was likely wishful thinking that they'd made some progress. Undoubtedly, she would have to repeat the lesson.

"Fine. What time?"

"Six thirty," she said.

"What time does Josh go?" he asked.

"He normally leaves the house about seven fifteen. But he should probably go in a little early, too, to get his assignments that he missed."

"I'll drop you both off."

"Josh walks," she protested.

Blaine shook his head. "Not tomorrow. Not until I've got a better handle on what Davis James is doing in Roaring Springs. Not until we know more about who might have slashed your tires. I can pick you both up tomorrow afternoon, too."

Oh good grief. "There's no need for that. I've made arrangements to have my car returned to the school parking lot. I'll have my own wheels back. And Josh has band practice. It's Isaac's mom's turn to pick the kids up after that."

"Okay." He walked toward the kitchen, checked to make sure the bolt lock was flipped on the back door and came back. "Is your phone charged?"

She pulled it out of her purse. "Yes."

"Okay. Keep it close. If you hear anything tonight that makes you nervous, call 9-1-1 and then call me. Do not hesitate."

"You're making me a little nervous."

"I don't mean to. But sometimes just being mentally prepared to take action gives you that one-second advantage, and that's the difference between success and failure." He opened the door, and cold air blew in. He seemed to hesitate.

Was he going to kiss her again?

Time seemed to stand still.

Finally, he gave her a quick smile. "Lock this behind me. Good night, Tilda."

"Good night," she managed, as the door closed. She immediately locked it because she suspected he was standing there, waiting to hear it. Then she pulled back the curtain and watched him walk to his car.

Broad shoulders. Straight spine. Easy stride.

Confident. Protective.

Sexy.

But evidently not interested in kissing her again.

Chapter Fifteen

Blaine called Liam on his way back to The Lodge.

"Welcome back. Sloane tells me you're working at The Lodge."

"I am. And I got a chance to congratulate her, but I wanted to reach out to you. I'm sorry to be calling you so late."

"No problem. Sloane is drying Chloe's hair, and then I'm doing bedtime stories. I've got a minute. By the way, congrats to you, too. On being a dad. I'm pretty new at it, but I got to tell you, it's pretty damn great."

"Thanks," Blaine said. "I just don't want to screw it up too badly."

"Can't screw up love. And that's what kids need."

"You're right. Anyway, besides our mutual congratulations, I wanted to talk to you about something."

"Tilda Deeds's tires?" Liam asked.

"You heard about that?"

His friend chuckled. "It's a small police department. Responding officer knew of the connection between Tilda and you, and that led him to give me an FYI."

"Well, I guess I'm grateful that word travels. It saves me some time. Anyway, here's what I need for you to know. I had a relationship with a woman while I was in the army. Her name was Honor Shayne. Her ex-husband, Davis James, incorrectly blames me for the breakup of his marriage. And today, I saw him at The Lodge, supposedly scoping out locations for a fall wedding reception."

"His own?" Liam asked.

"Again, supposedly. But he's using the name Jim Park. I touched base with Honor today, who is still connected with his family, and she's as puzzled as me."

"Do you have a recent photo of Davis James?"

"I do," Blaine confirmed. "I'll text it to you after this call."

"Okay. I'll share it around and let it be known to watch out for him. How's Tilda?"

"She and Josh are home. House is secured. She knows the importance of taking precautions."

"I can make a call," Liam told him, "and have the overnight officer take a couple drive-bys, just as an added precaution."

"Thanks. I'm taking Tilda to work tomorrow, since her car is out of commission."

"Okay. Let me know if you see Davis James again, or if he makes contact in any way."

"Will do. Thanks again, Liam. I appreciate your help."

"No problem. You're family, Blaine."

TILDA GOT UP extra early the next morning. She told herself that it had absolutely nothing to do with the fact that Blaine was taking her to work. If she took an extra ten minutes on her hair and an extra five on her makeup, and put on her nicest pink button-down and gray dress pants, it wasn't a crime to want to look nice for her job.

Right?

When she heard a knock on the door, she pulled back the curtain to make sure Blaine's vehicle was at the curb before going to open the door. She unlocked the dead-bolt, her fingers fumbling. "Morning," she breathed, as if she'd just completed a 5K.

Get a grip. She was acting as if *she* was the thirteen-year-old in the house.

"Morning," he said, his voice a little husky, as if he hadn't yet used it much. "You look nice," he added. He stared at her for an extra-long second. "I don't remember any of our teachers looking so hot."

She waved a hand, but she could feel the heat build in her body. It was going to be embarrassing if she had to step outside to cool off. "Josh isn't quite ready. Would you like a cup of coffee?"

"Sure. I didn't take time to get a cup before I left."

She poured coffee for both of them, and they sat at the table. "Hungry?" she asked.

He shook his head. "You don't need to feed me, Tilda. I'll grab something at The Lodge." He took a sip of his coffee. "I spoke to Liam last night. He'd already heard about your tires getting slashed. I let him know about Davis James and sent him a photo. He'll keep his ear to the ground."

Her toast popped up. She buttered it and took a bite. "What are you going to do if you see this man?"

Blaine shrugged. "Well, that depends. If it's possible, I'll talk to him. Try to make him understand that he should have no beef with me. If he's confrontational, well…he and I are going to have a problem."

"Don't get yourself in trouble over him. He's not worth it."

Blaine smiled. "I won't. But I'm also not going to sit back and let him wreak havoc on me or my family."

She was confident that Davis James wouldn't stand a chance against Blaine. "Doesn't seem all that bright

of him to pick a fight with you. He has to know that
you were a Green Beret. That you could, I don't know,
break him apart."

"Think I'm a tough guy?" he teased her.

No doubt about it. In excellent shape, he was six feet
of pure muscle. "If I was a betting woman, I'd put my
money on you."

"Wouldn't want you betting against me," he said,
brushing the pad of this thumb across her lower lip.
"And don't want you going to school with crumbs on
your face."

She let out a sigh. What about going to school in a
highly agitated state, because it had only taken that
light touch to manage that? "My hero," she said weakly.

He nodded. "Now back to business. I think Davis
James is smart enough. Honor said that he was an electrical engineer and super good with new technology."

She heard Josh's bedroom door open. She got up to
put bread in the toaster and pulled a box of cereal from
the cupboard.

"Hey, sport," Blaine said.

"Morning," Josh mumbled. "It's barely light outside."
He sat down, groaning as if he was ninety-three.

She ignored that. After pouring his cereal in a bowl
and buttering his toast, she brought his breakfast over
to the table. "It's warmer today, but you'll still need
your winter coat."

"Ski season over?" Josh asked, looking at Blaine.

"It's a matter of days," he confirmed. "The temperature
difference between here in the valley and on the mountain might enable us to make it through the weekend."

"Can I go Saturday?" Josh asked, switching his attention to his mother. "That's probably going to be my
last chance."

"We'll see," she said noncommittally.

Josh looked at Blaine. "Universal parent response when the parent isn't prepared to make the decision or doesn't want to fight about the decision."

Tilda tried but failed to hold back her smile. "Eat up. We need to get going."

Josh rolled his eyes but started shoveling his cereal in. Five minutes later, they were walking out the door. She sat in the front, and Josh took the back. "Your car is so clean," she said.

"I suppose. The military makes you neat."

Tilda made a mental note to pick up any trash in her own vehicle. She wasn't a slob but had been known to have a discarded coffee cup or two rolling around in her back seat from time to time.

Josh leaned forward, stuck his head over the seat. "Why is it, exactly, that you're taking Mom and me to school, Blaine?"

Blaine gave her a sideways look. "What did your mom tell you?"

"She said that you didn't want us to have to bother Grandma and Grandpa for a ride."

"That's true," he said. "Remember what I told you the other night—that there are some people who'd like to see the Coltons run into some trouble? Well, with your mom's tires getting slashed, I think it's important that we all be a little extra watchful."

"Do you think that's because she's a... I mean, she's not a Colton, but she's kind of close."

Blaine smiled. "What you need to know is that both your mom's and your safety are important to me. So, be sharp."

"Got it."

Blaine pulled up in front of her school. Before she

got out, she turned to look at Josh. This morning he'd seemed very much like the old Josh—the Josh who would never run away, never make her stay awake all night, waiting to hear.

"You're okay with going back to school, right?" she had to ask. She would not tell him that she'd come this close to calling Isaac and asking him to watch Josh, to make sure he was okay. Josh would want to strangle her if he knew that.

"I'm fine," he said. "The guys that were saying stuff are jerks. Always have been. Probably always will be. I'm just going to ignore them."

"Good plan," she said. She turned to Blaine. "Thanks for the ride."

"No problem." He reached out a hand, put it on her arm. It was light, impersonal. But she could feel the heat cutting through layers of fabric. "Same goes for you, you know. Be sharp," he added, in case she didn't get it.

"Of course." Tilda got out of the car. He cared. He definitely cared. She felt energy zipping through her and resisted the urge to skip up the steps.

But by two o'clock that afternoon, she was dragging, and the idea of even walking up steps was challenging. Her final class was filing in the door, taking seats. When the bell rang, she took attendance.

Toby Turner wasn't there. Missed class time meant more missed assignments. Tilda wished she knew what the hell was going on at the Turner home. She'd responded to the text that she'd received, saying that she was unable to come to their house but would be happy to meet in a public place of their choosing. Then she went on to say that if transportation was a problem, she was happy to pay for a ride service to pick them up. She had gotten no response.

Once she dismissed class, she sat at her desk, looking over her notes. She looked up when she heard the door open. Expecting Raeann, she was surprised to see Stacey Grand, the secretary from the office. The woman had a message slip in her hand.

"This call came in about fifteen minutes ago. The gentleman said that he didn't want to interrupt you during class time, but he needed to get a message to you." She handed Tilda the white slip.

Need to see you. Can you come to The Lodge after school? I'm working on the third floor, east wing. Blaine.

She immediately thought of Davis James. Had the man shown up again? Was that why Blaine needed to see her?

She stood up fast, noting that the secretary was still standing there. She didn't know the woman well. She was still the temporary who was filling in for their regular secretary.

"Thank you," Tilda said.

"You probably don't remember this, but the two of you were seniors when I was a freshman."

"I didn't realize that, Stacey. Is Grand your married name?"

"Yeah. I was Stacey Bender. I thought that Blaine Colton was the cutest boy in the senior class."

Tilda smiled. "I thought he was pretty cute, too," she admitted.

"I'm glad you two got back together."

Was there anywhere in this town that she and Blaine weren't a topic of conversation? "Oh, we're…" She started to say that they weren't together, to put an end to the speculation. But she remembered that Blaine had told both her and Josh to be sharp. And that included talking about her personal life with somebody who was a virtual stranger. Stacey was saying innocuous things, but perhaps she lurked in the Colton-hater camp. "Thank you," Tilda said. "Well, I should be going."

Stacey left her classroom, and Tilda quickly put on her coat and boots. The streets were sloppy with melting snow. She found her car easily enough in the almost-empty teachers' parking lot, and once inside, she looked again at the message slip. There was no callback number on it. Either Blaine hadn't left one or Stacey hadn't written it down.

No matter. She had Blaine's cell number. She started to reach for her phone but stopped. He hadn't wanted to bother her when she was working. She could do the same, given the fact that he was probably really busy covering for the employees who'd quit their jobs the day before.

She also resisted the urge to call Josh and verify that he was at band practice. That was not their usual pattern, and she needed to demonstrate trust. Instead, she sent a text.

Going to The Lodge to see Blaine about something. I'll be home by five.

She didn't get a response, but she didn't expect one. The band teacher made them put their phones away during practice.

After putting on some music, she started the car and drove up the windy mountain road. She parked in one of the main lots, closest to the east wing. Then it was in and up the elevator. When she got out, she realized that most of the floor was under construction. Walls had been removed, and she could see electrical wiring. In some areas, heavy plastic hung, maybe to block off space or perhaps to trap in dust. She didn't know for sure. The floor had been ripped out, down to the cement. It was eerily quiet. She didn't see anyone.

She took a few steps. "Blaine," she called out. The space was so empty that her words echoed back to her.

Maybe he'd finished his work and returned to his office. She would go there. Turning, she retreated the distance she'd ventured and pressed the elevator button. The minute she took her finger away from the button, the light went out. Was it just the light, or was the elevator not working?

But it had been just minutes ago.

A chill ran up her arm. She reached into her purse and fumbled for her phone. Dialed Blaine's number.

"Hey, Tilda," he answered. "What's up?"

"I'm here, on the third floor. In the east wing."

"What?"

"I got the message you left at school. I'm here on the third floor, but I don't see anyone."

"Tilda, I didn't leave you a message."

"But—"

"Stay where you're at," he said, his voice sounding calm, yet very directive. "I'm coming to you. I'll be there in five minutes. Okay?"

"Yes. Of course." She hung up before she could beg him to hurry.

There was no reason to be scared. Daylight was still coming in through the big windows. There had to be security personnel in the building and, knowing Decker Colton, they were well trained. She just needed to wait.

Five minutes wasn't very long.

And then she heard a door open at the end of the hallway.

BLAINE MOVED FAST, but his office was in the far-west area of the building, and there was a lot of real estate to navigate. When he got to the east wing, he saw a maintenance sign on the doors of the elevator that indicated it was shut down for service. That was odd. He didn't know they had anybody in, working on elevators.

Screw it. He took the stairs…two at a time. When he got to the third floor, he realized the door was locked. Not unexpected. He fumbled with the keys on the ring attached to his belt before he found a master that worked. Once open, he ran, almost skidding around the corner.

There was Tilda, her arms wrapped around herself. She looked scared.

"Hey," he said. And he pulled her in tight to his chest. "You're okay," he said, his voice close to her ear. She was shaking, and he wanted to kill whoever had played this little joke on her.

"I'm sorry that I'm such a baby," she murmured, her voice muffled by his shirt. "But right after I got done talking with you, I heard a door open, and then it sounded like something was being pushed across the floor. Every horror movie I've ever seen flashed through my head." She pulled back and looked him in the eye.

"Only family dramas on this channel," he said.

That made her smile. Like he'd hoped.

"What's going on?" she asked.

"I'm not sure. What time did I supposedly call you?"

"You left a message at the school office, about two forty-five," she told him. "The secretary walked it down to my room after school. It never dawned on me that it wasn't legitimate."

"Of course not," he said. He'd been covering for the missing maintenance workers until about one o'clock.

Then he'd gone back to his own office because he had to prepare for a three o'clock meeting that had unexpectedly gotten cancelled. "Did the sounds you heard come from that direction or that one?" he asked, pointing to opposite sides.

"That way." She gestured to her left. "But I never saw anyone. I wasn't sure what I was going to do if I did. I'd already tried the elevator, and it didn't seem to be working. Although I'd come up in it just minutes before."

"Let's go take a quick look," he said, wrapping an arm around her shoulders and leading her to the left. Near the door at the end of the hall was a work cart, loaded with tools, almost in their path. "Could that have been what you heard?"

"Maybe," she said. They walked around it, and he dropped his arm from around her shoulder. There was a push bar on the door. He put the heel of his hand against it.

It didn't budge. It was locked.

Exit doors were never locked from the inside. Basic safety. People needed to be able to leave via the stairs in the event the elevator wasn't working or not safe to use.

But the area was under construction. Maybe that made a difference. He simply wasn't familiar enough with The Lodge to know.

"Are we stuck up here?" she asked worriedly.

He shook his head. "I came up the other stairs. Let's go try that door." They backtracked but found that it also wouldn't budge. "Must have locked behind me."

She glanced at his keys. "Nothing to unlock on this side."

"Nope," he said.

She held up her phone. "I'm calling 9-1-1."

"No need. There's a freight elevator down that hallway. We can use it."

That seemed to make her feel better. "Josh is going to think this is hilarious, when we tell him that we were locked in," she said.

"Yeah. Maybe we keep this one between us." While he was happy that she seemed more relaxed, he couldn't say the same for himself. Tilda had said that she'd heard something being pushed across the floor and a door closing. Somebody had been up here. He didn't see anybody now, thank goodness, but that meant that they'd somehow gotten off the floor. Had they jammed the door behind them somehow?

He didn't think he was being melodramatic. Somebody had lured Tilda to this isolated space on a pretense of meeting him.

That somebody was up to no good.

The sooner he got Tilda off this floor and off the property the better. "Right there," he said, pointing at the freight elevator. "It's not pretty like the other elevators." He pressed the button, and the door opened.

She stepped forward. "I don't—"

She felt herself pitch forward before she suddenly was roughly pulled back and shoved aside. She landed hard on her rear end and was about to protest when she realized that she very much had gotten the better end of the deal.

"Blaine!" she gasped.

His body was stretched over the open shaft. The tips of his work boots were braced against the near edge of the elevator shaft, and his forearms were perched against the metal frame on the far side.

He'd somehow managed to save her and catch himself. But he couldn't possibly maintain that position. Still on her rear, she edged forward to get a better look. It was a dark and seemingly bottomless pit. At least three stories, she reasoned.

A sure death.

Chapter Sixteen

"What can I do?" she said, her mouth dry. She was afraid to touch him, afraid to disturb his tenuous balance.

"Well, don't tickle me."

Her heart flipped in her chest.

"Calling 9-1-1 is back on the table," he said.

She reached for her phone, so very grateful that she hadn't dropped it down the open shaft. Her fingers were shaking as she punched in the three numbers. She put it on speaker.

"This is 9-1-1. What is your emergency?"

"I'm on the third floor of the east wing of the Colton Lodge. A man is…suspended over an open elevator shaft. The freight elevator."

There was the slightest of pauses before the operator replied. "We've got a team responding. Are there any other injuries?"

Not yet. "No. Just hurry."

"Please stay on the line," the operator said.

"Put it on hold," Blaine told her. "Try Decker's office." He rattled off the number, and she dialed. How the hell could he be in such control?

The phone rang three times before it was answered. "Decker Colton's office. Penny speaking."

"I need Decker," Tilda blurted.

"Mr. Colton is in a meeting."

"Get him!" Tilda said. "It's an emergency. Third floor. East wing. Hurry." She hung up. Blaine was moving. Well, part of him was. One hand at a time, he was edging his body to the left.

He was attempting to *walk himself* around the corner. It meant that he had to pick up a hand, move it four or five inches, and repeat the process with his other hand.

The muscles in his arms, shoulders and back were taut and defined. He showed no fear. It was amazing to watch.

And terribly frightening.

"Wait," she said. "Help is coming."

"Never been one to count on somebody else," he gritted out. His voice was showing the strain of his physical effort.

He'd gotten as far as the corner. Now his feet were moving. He wasn't lifting them up. No, just twisting and turning his ankles, sliding them to the left.

Now his body was in the shape of a backward *C*.

"Tilda, with your fanny on the floor and your feet braced against the wall, take hold of the back of my belt," he said.

She did what he instructed.

"Good girl. We're doing fine here. Now, on the count of three, I want you to pull back, with everything you've got. Don't take your feet off the wall."

She wasn't strong enough. He outweighed her by at least seventy-five pounds, and she'd have little leverage. "Okay," she said. If he could be brave, then so could she.

"One. Two. Three."

She pulled. Just as he swung his body up and back, a flip of sorts.

It was awkward but good enough.

He tumbled over her legs, one shoulder hitting the floor. Momentum sent him into a somersault, and he rolled and, finally, came to a squat. He grinned at her and opened his arms wide. "Good job, darling."

With a sob of relief, she threw herself into his arms. And they just sat there, on the dirty floor a foot away from the open shaft, and held each other.

His effort had been superhuman. A lesser man would never have been able to pull it off. "Oh my God. How did you do that?"

"I didn't," he said. "*We* did. Thank you, Tilda Deeds." And then he pulled back enough to bend his head, and he kissed her. There was nothing light or comforting about this second kiss. It was hard, intense. Filled with the raw, unbridled emotion of having cheated death.

She could have kissed him forever. But when the door to their right sprang open, so hard that it almost hit the wall behind it, and Decker Colton rushed forward, Blaine lifted his head. But he didn't release his hold on her.

"*This* was the emergency?" Decker said.

Blaine smiled. "No. That was the emergency." He pointed toward the elevator shaft. "Doesn't look quite as scary now, but when I was hanging over it, face-down, seeing nothing but blackness below, it looked pretty damn bad."

Decker walked over to the still-open shaft. "What the...."

As his voice trailed off, Tilda heard the sounds of feet trampling up the same staircase that Decker had emerged from. In came firemen and paramedics. Then the police. She saw Liam Kastor and gave him a little wave.

She figured a representative from the Roaring Springs newspaper wouldn't be far behind. If there was a person in the town who had not yet heard the saga of Tilda Deeds and Blaine Colton, that would be short-lived.

Decker was already on his phone, demanding answers from his maintenance staff. An EMT had slapped a blood-pressure cuff on Blaine and was shining a light in his eyes.

Questions were flying. Blaine's explanations were concise, with absolutely no embellishment, but the emergency personnel were clearly astonished.

All she knew was that Blaine no longer had his arms around her, and his lips were long removed.

And, in a room full of people, she felt very alone.

THE MAINTENANCE SUPERVISOR had been adamant. The passenger elevator had not been scheduled for maintenance. Which meant no one was working on it. Once Decker had quietly communicated that to Blaine, the two of them had quickly agreed to keep the need-to-know circle small. It did not include EMTs, firefighters or the additional lodge employees who'd responded to the scene.

It had taken a while to clear the area. They hoped that everybody had gone away thinking that, as usual, the Coltons were a lucky bunch. That it was a workplace incident that had gone better than it probably had a right to.

Liam and Officer McDonald, who'd taken the report on her tires getting slashed, had stayed behind. The two of them, Decker, Tilda and Blaine were still on the third floor.

"Walk me through it," Liam said.

"The school received a call from somebody claiming to be Blaine, asking me to meet him here," Tilda said. She glanced around. "When I got here and the place was deserted, I called him."

"I knew I hadn't called her," Blaine jumped in. "And I have to admit, while I was walking here, I figured it might be somebody trying to mess with us. But, even when I saw the sign on the elevator that it was down for maintenance, I didn't get worried. However, when I realized the doors off the floor were all locked, I knew something was amiss. That's probably what heightened my awareness that there wasn't something quite right with the freight elevator."

"Just in time," Tilda said.

She'd been a half-step ahead of him. If he hadn't been able to grab her and pull her back, it could have gone so differently. The terrifying vision of her lying three stories below, limp and bleeding, flashed in the back of his head. She would likely not have survived the fall. If she had, the lifelong ramifications might have been significant.

He wanted to hurt whoever had done this. Badly.

"Clearly, after Tilda's arrival," Decker said, "somebody disabled the elevator and slapped a sign on it so that nobody would report it and provoke an inquiry to the maintenance staff. We have cameras almost everywhere in the public areas of The Lodge. That certainly includes the area around the elevator." Shoving a hand through his hair, he said, "My most senior security person has verified that, sure enough, there is footage of someone, dressed in a maintenance uniform with a baseball cap pulled low on his forehead, placing the sign. Unfortunately, this person doesn't appear to be on staff."

"Davis James?" Liam asked.

"Impossible to know. Camera angle didn't pick up his face," Decker said. "We don't have any cameras on the door to the mechanical room. It's controlled by badge access. Security had already verified that it was accessed by an employee at the right time. Unfortunately, said employee was nowhere near the mechanical room. He was in another area of The Lodge. That's been verified by two other employees and a camera." Decker paused, looking unhappy. "The employee had noticed that he'd misplaced his badge earlier this morning. He did not report it. Said he was confident that it would turn up. That is being dealt with separately."

"It has to be someone with some mechanical knowledge," Blaine added. "Locking some doors and putting up a sign could have been done by a monkey, but getting to the elevator controls and hitting the right buttons takes some knowledge."

"I keep wondering who the intended victim was," Tilda said, her voice soft, as if she might be afraid to say the words out loud. "Me. You. Or the both of us."

"It's a crazy thing. I can't remember anything like this ever happening before," Decker muttered, barely looking at Tilda.

Blaine knew his brother was still distrustful of Tilda. "None of this is her fault," Blaine said sharply.

"I didn't say it was," Decker retorted.

Blaine kept his mouth shut. Officer McDonald was looking too interested, and Liam was clearly uncomfortable. Tilda simply looked confused.

"Decker, we're going to need the sign that was on the elevator," Liam said. "And copies of any security footage that you have. We'll dust the maintenance door for fingerprints but will have to rule out anybody who has a legitimate reason to be in that space."

What he was nicely saying was that there was no way to conduct the investigation without people realizing that it likely hadn't been as simple as a workplace incident. It would be more bad publicity for The Lodge. He and Decker exchanged a glance.

"Do what you need to do," Decker said. "We need answers. And you should probably know something else. We've had some minor thefts and vandalism around the property. That happens from time to time, and we generally treat it as an internal matter, without police involvement. But, honestly, the illegal activity seemed to pick up in the last week. Now I'm wondering if it has something to do with this, so I want to be absolutely transparent."

"We'll get the details of that after we take a look at the maintenance room. Will you be in your office?" Liam asked, looking at Decker.

"I will. I'll have my security guy go with you."

They waited while Decker got that sorted out. Ten minutes later, it was just Decker, Blaine and Tilda on the third floor. Blaine turned to Tilda. "We'll figure out who did this. They'll pay."

"I really don't want Josh to know," Tilda admitted. "It will scare him."

The first call Tilda had made had been to Isaac's mom. Without giving her any explanation, she'd arranged for Josh to stay at Isaac's house after the boys were picked up from band practice. Blaine had been relieved to hear that. Somebody was attacking him or his family. Until he found out who, they all needed to be on high alert.

Which was why he'd made a decision. He wasn't sure

how Tilda was going to feel about it, but he didn't really feel as if he could give her a choice. And having Decker there to witness the conversation might just help him.

"We'll need to tell him enough that he's not blind-sided by the news if he hears it from somebody else," Blaine said.

"Okay. Bare bones," Tilda conceded.

"I'm glad Dad wasn't here to see this," Decker said.

Russ was traveling for business. He'd left early this morning and would be gone for a couple nights. "Agree," Blaine said simply.

"He'll need to be told," Decker said. "Not only because you're his son. This is also his business."

"Agree," Blaine repeated. "Can you take care of that?"

"Yeah. I'll get to both Mom and Dad. And I'll stop by Molly's office and make sure she knows how to respond to any guest inquiries about the incident. Probably should tell Seth Harris, too."

Blaine wasn't crazy about widening the circle of those having knowledge but knew that Decker would be discreet with the details. And Seth was a likely contact for questions, maybe even from the press.

Blaine looked at Tilda. "I don't want you and Josh alone in your house."

She looked at him blindly.

"We can get you a room here," Decker offered. "Or I'm sure Mom has space at The Chateau. Definitely at Colton Manor."

"That will be pretty disruptive for Josh," Blaine said. "I'll move into your house instead."

Tilda opened her mouth, but no words came out.

Decker looked at his brother. "You think that's a good plan?"

"I do," Blaine said.

"But…" Tilda said, her voice trailing off. She was staring in the direction of the freight elevator. "What will I tell Josh?"

"Tell him that I needed to give up my room here at The Lodge for somebody else. He's not going to know the difference," Blaine said.

"He'll be so excited he probably won't question it," she admitted.

Tilda didn't seem as excited. But he didn't care. He could keep the two of them safe. That was all that mattered.

Chapter Seventeen

Blaine was moving in. She couldn't very well admit that, years ago, when she'd been carrying Josh and even after, she'd fantasized that he'd left the army and come home to live with her. Because he loved her. And after finding out about Josh, he'd been even more committed to her, to their family.

Now it was happening because somebody had tried to kill her or him or both of them.

They'd left The Lodge just before six. She'd waited in Blaine's locked office while he'd gone back to his room to grab clothes and other essentials. Since she had her car, and he was going to need his own vehicle, he was now following her down the mountain road. She was grateful to have the twenty minutes alone to collect her thoughts.

She had a third bedroom. And he could share the second bath with Josh. There was really no reason that his presence in her home needed to affect her that much.

She gripped the steering wheel. It was better than pounding her head against it. Who was she trying to kid? Having Blaine in the house would change everything.

She pulled into Isaac's driveway and got out. Blaine stayed in his vehicle, which was now idling at the curb.

She walked up the front sidewalk and knocked. And, then, somehow, managed to make polite conversation with Isaac's mom while Josh gathered up his things.

What she had said, however, she could not remember three minutes later when she and Josh were back in her SUV. "How was your day?" she asked.

"Okay. Science was cool. Dry-ice day."

"Lucky you," she said. "And band practice?"

"Good," he replied. He was looking in his side mirror. "Is that Blaine behind us?"

Her son was observant. Much like his father. "It is," she said.

"Why is he following us?"

Josh was essentially the same as her, she realized. Ever since he'd been a little kid, he'd reacted better to things if he understood the *why* behind the request. She and Blaine needed to find a way to tell him the truth without scaring him to death. "Because we have something we want to talk to you about."

He gave her a long look. "That doesn't sound so good."

"It's not bad," she assured him. For you, she added silently. She was another story.

"Can I have a hint?"

"We're six minutes from home," she said. "Patience is a virtue."

He said nothing for a minute. Then, "Maybe you'll remember that the next time you're waiting for me to clean my room."

She laughed. Despite everything, her kid always had the ability to make her laugh. "I love you, Josh."

"Uh-huh," he said, as if he wasn't sure.

Tilda turned into her driveway, opened the garage door and pulled in. After switching off the engine, she heard a car door slam behind her and knew that Blaine was already out of his vehicle. She pasted a smile on her face. She could do this. She could invite the only man she'd ever loved into her home, into her life, only to have him leave. Again.

She'd survived it once.

But then again, at eighteen, she hadn't maybe realized all that she'd lost. This was one of those times that the wisdom gained through years of living wasn't necessarily a blessing.

She opened her door.

"Hey, sport," Blaine said to Josh.

"I saw you behind us," their son admitted. "But Mom is being pretty sketchy about why."

Blaine looked at Tilda. "You doing okay?" he asked, his voice concerned.

"Great. I'm thinking that pizza sounds good for dinner. We could get it delivered."

"Sold," said Blaine.

They walked in through the garage door. Josh dumped his backpack on the kitchen table and slung his coat over the back of a chair. Then he plopped down onto the couch. "Out with it," he said.

"Blaine is going to be staying in our guest room for a little while," Tilda told him.

Josh looked at both her and Blaine. "That's cool, I guess. But why?"

Sometimes he seemed much older than thirteen. And because of that, she wasn't exactly sure what she should tell him. But thankfully, Blaine didn't seem to have the same problem, because he jumped in.

"Your mom and I are concerned about a couple things that have recently happened. You remember that I told you about Honor Shayne?"

Josh nodded.

"Well, her ex-husband is in Roaring Springs. I saw him at The Lodge yesterday. And, today, your mom and I encountered a situation where somebody faked a call to your mom's school, pretending to be me, to get her up to The Lodge. We believe this was an attempt to cause us some problems."

Blaine was telling the truth, just not the whole truth.

"Is he the one who slashed Mom's tires?" Josh asked.

"He could be. The police have been advised to watch for him. But I just talked to them on my way down the mountain, and they don't know where he is. No activity on his credit cards nor any record of him staying at any of the local motels."

"He could be using another name," Josh said.

They'd checked everything under *Jim Park*, but that had also been a waste of time. "Actually, we believe he has been. Jim Park. So be aware of both Davis James or Jim Park. Until he's located, I'm going to be sticking close. And your mom and I need your cooperation. We may need to limit our activities for a few days, and we'd appreciate you going along with it."

"Maybe I shouldn't go to school," Josh said, his tone very serious.

Blaine smiled and shook his head. "Good try, sport, but no. You'll be fine at school. Either your mom or I will drive you and pick you up. We'll keep to our routines. The one very important thing, however, is that I don't want you telling anybody—and that includes Isaac—what's going on. Or posting anything on social media that indicates that I'm staying in the house."

He was their secret weapon. Willing to put himself at risk for them.

She stood up so fast that she almost got dizzy. "Let me show you to your room," she said.

Josh gave her a look, like she might have been rude. She did not care. It had been a harrowing day, and in truth, her nerves were hanging on by a thread. The *what ifs* were plaguing her. What if Blaine hadn't pulled her back from the open shaft? What if he'd followed her in and they'd both tumbled downward?

What if they'd both died before she'd gotten a chance to tell him that she was sorry that she'd deceived him? Sorry that she hadn't been better equipped to stand up to Russ Colton?

"You want me to call in the pizza?" Josh asked.

"Sure. Anything you want," she replied.

"That means mozzarella sticks, too," he said, picking up his cell phone.

"Fine," Tilda conceded. She couldn't worry about something as mundane as a dinner order. Motioning for Blaine to follow her down the short hallway, she opened the door of the spare bedroom. "Here you go. I… I hope the bed is comfortable. I haven't slept in it."

"It'll be fine," he said. He followed her into the room and shut the door behind him. "Hey," he murmured, his voice soft. "Are you okay with this?"

"Of course," she said. "You're the one who is being inconvenienced."

"Not an inconvenience. The two of you are the most important people to me."

Was it horrible of her that she wanted to be more than important? Being important wasn't the same as loved. "I need to set the table."

She practically ran to the kitchen. She pulled plates out of the cupboard and silverware out of the drawer. Josh was just ending his call.

"Twenty minutes," he said. "Want to start a movie?"

"Sure." She finished setting the table and sat down on the couch next to Josh. Blaine joined them in just a few minutes, but she focused on the screen, as if it was the most interesting thing she'd ever seen. When the doorbell rang, she moved, but Blaine was faster. He got the door and paid for the pizza.

They devoured most of an extra-large pie and ate every one of the six cheese sticks. Blaine had just thrown away the box and put their plates in the dishwasher when her cell phone rang. She didn't recognize the number.

"Hello," she said.

"This is Officer McDonald."

"Hello, Officer," she said.

Blaine motioned for her to come to the kitchen. "Put it on speaker," he mouthed.

She did. "What can I do for you?"

"I wanted to give you an update," he said. "We've been unsuccessful in getting any good camera footage that allows us to identify who might have slashed your tires."

She was disappointed but not surprised. If it had been Davis James, he seemed pretty good at covering his tracks. While it was frustrating that it couldn't be pinned on the stranger, she was oddly grateful that they weren't calling to tell her that it had been Toby Turner. She didn't want that to have been the case.

"We'll keep our eyes open and ears to the ground but wanted you to know where we're at with this," he said.

She appreciated that and knew that, if she lived anywhere else but Roaring Springs, she probably wouldn't have gotten this phone call. Even here, it likely had something to do with the family relationship between

Liam Kastor and Blaine and the…well…quasifamilial relationship between her and Blaine. She suspected it might also have something to do with the crazy things that had been happening in Roaring Springs over the past few months. The police were likely on high alert and attempting to be super responsive to their citizenry.

"I appreciate the update," she said. They ended the call, and she looked at Blaine. "Well, I guess that's that."

"I'm worried about you chaperoning the prom this weekend," he said. "I'd prefer that you back out."

"I can't, Blaine. A few years ago, they were having trouble getting teachers to do it, so they put it in our contract. I'd have to be dead or near death, as substantiated by a physician, to get out of it." She said the last part lightly: it was the standard joke the teachers used when they talked about the obligation. "Besides, I won't be doing it alone."

He cocked his head. "Is Chuck Pearce going with you?"

What? "No, of course not." She'd not heard from Chuck after their last date. His reaction to learning that Josh's real dad was a Colton had been telling. Plus, she'd never considered inviting him to go with her. She didn't mix her professional and her personal lives. "I meant that there would be other teachers. My best friend Rae-ann Johnson will be there."

"Oh," he said, having the grace to look a little embarrassed that he'd jumped to the conclusion that she had a date.

"I'll be fine there. I guess I don't want to assume," she said, "but you're okay being here with Josh that night? I should be home by midnight."

"Sure. No problem."

They stood awkwardly in the kitchen. "I guess I'll

finish the movie," she said finally. She wasn't sure what they were even watching.

"Great." He followed her back to the family room.

When the movie ended, she turned to Josh. "Bedtime. No video games."

He groaned and then rolled off the couch. Stood and stretched. His T-shirt pulled up, and she could see his ribs. He was too thin, but he ate like a horse. The empty pizza box was proof. "Good night," he said.

"I'm going to turn in, too," she said, in Blaine's general direction. "Tomorrow is a workday." Then she practically ran to her bedroom. Closed the door tight and immediately went into the attached bath.

She showered, dried off and got dressed for bed. But before climbing in, she opened her door just a crack. There were no lights on in the family room, and the television was off. Blaine was probably in the guest room.

She wasn't going to think about him being down the hall.

Instead, she was going to think about what she needed to accomplish in the final three weeks of the semester. Yes, that was better.

She lay in the middle of her bed. Who was she trying to kid? All she could think about was Blaine Colton. About how incredibly brave he'd been when he'd been hanging over the elevator shaft, how incredibly strong he'd been, and how incredibly wonderful it had felt to have him hold her in his arms.

Today's word of the day, class, is incredibly.

Ugh.

Silently she said a string of words that would never, ever be eligible to be the word of the day. Yup. That about summed it up.

THE BED WAS comfortable enough, and given that he'd missed sleep earlier in the week when he'd gone after Josh, his body needed rest. But his head was too full.

Tilda was upset. About something. He understood if it was the close call this afternoon. But he had a feeling that it was more.

He wanted to talk to her. And he didn't want to wait until morning because they'd both be in a hurry to get to work. He slipped out of bed, crossed the room and opened the door.

He stopped outside Josh's door, feeling a ping in his heart. How many nights had Dorian stood outside this room, listening for sounds from within? How many times had he opened the door and stood over Josh, watching the boy sleep?

But oddly enough, instead of feeling grief and anger that the man had those experiences, for the first time he felt acceptance and some measure of joy that his son had been loved, well-cared for. That Tilda had not been alone to raise their son.

Funny how a near-death experience made a person reevaluate.

He opened the door. The room was mostly dark, but a small night-light was plugged into an outlet on the far wall. It gave off enough light that he could study the face of his sleeping son.

He seemed very young. And innocent. And it was sort of shocking to Blaine to think that he'd been a mere five years older than Josh when he'd left for the army.

He hadn't handled things well with Tilda. But he'd really been just a kid, not nearly as mature as he'd thought he was.

Maybe it was time they had the conversation that they hadn't been able to have as eighteen-year-olds. He left his son's room and walked down to Tilda's, hesitating just a second before knocking softly.

"Yes," she said.

He opened the door. There was a night-light in her attached bath. That and the fact that she'd left the blinds partially open and moonlight filtered in offered up enough light. She was in her bed. "What's wrong?" she asked, sitting up fast.

"Nothing," he said, motioning for her to stay put. "May I come in?"

"Uh…sure." She scooted up in the bed until she was sitting with a pillow behind her.

Her hair was hanging down, and it looked damp. She wore no makeup, but then again, she'd never needed any. She had on a loose, white T-shirt, and he couldn't tell what else because the sheet and blanket were in the way. There was no chair in her room and, not wanting to tower over her, he sat at the far end of the bed, by her feet. "We need to talk," he said.

"About?"

"About the fact that I've been kind of a jerk."

Her pretty eyes opened wide. "I gave you a pretty good reason."

"No, I gave you a pretty good reason to hide the pregnancy from me. After all, I was almost giddy with relief when you'd said you miscarried. You painted a nice picture of me to Josh, but it wasn't the truth. I didn't want to stay in Roaring Springs. I didn't want to be forced into joining the Colton Empire and dancing to my father's tune. I didn't want to be married. And I sure as hell didn't want a baby." There it was. The bald and ugly truth.

"We were very young," she said softly.

"We were. You know, I just had that epiphany as I

stood over Josh's bed and watched him sleep. We were just five years older. How the hell did we think that we were equipped to deal with something like a pregnancy?"

"Other people have. Other people do."

"Of course. And you're one of those people, Tilda. You carried on. Alone. You had to have been so scared."

"I cried every night," she whispered. "For nine months. I've never told anybody that. And I would never want Josh to know. But every night. I was just so overwhelmed."

He could just imagine that. He moved closer to her and reached for her hand. Her skin was very soft, very warm. "I don't want you to ever feel that way again, Tilda. I'm here now. I'm not going anywhere. You're not in this alone anymore. I should have handled things better thirteen years ago. I'm sorry I didn't."

"A hundred times I started an email to you."

His lips twisted into a rueful smile. "You sent just one. A *Dear John* letter."

"I thought it would be best. You wanted to move on. I wanted you to have that chance. But after I sent that one, I drafted others."

"That you never sent," he said.

"You're an honorable man, Blaine. I knew that you'd find a way to come back. But it wouldn't have been for love. It would have been out of obligation." She sighed. "And in some crazy way, I guess I convinced myself that I was doing you a favor by letting you go. And once Josh was born and Dorian and I were married, that made me sleep easier at night."

He scratched his head. "I don't like the idea of you sleeping with Dorian. How sick does that make me? I'm jealous of a dead man."

"I…came to love Dorian. And I was very grateful to

him. And he was wonderful with Josh. But…he wasn't you, Blaine. He never could have been."

"The two of you did a good job with Josh. I may hate Dorian for some reasons, but overall, I just have to be damn grateful to him."

"I'd like to think that the two of you might even have been friends."

Blaine grimaced. "Let's not push it."

She laughed and looked so beautiful in the moonlight. And before he could think about what he was doing, he reached for her and pulled her into his arms. "I love hearing you laugh. I want you to be happy and to sleep easy every night. I…" He stopped. He'd almost said that he loved her, that he'd *always* loved her.

Her forehead was resting against his shoulder. "We did one thing right," she said, her voice soft.

"What's that?"

"Josh."

He pulled back, just far enough that she could lift her face. Her lips were very close. "He's perfect," he rasped. "Like his mother." Then he bent his head and kissed her.

THEIR THIRD KISS. Different than the other two. Seeking. Smoldering. Intense, but perhaps with a hint of question.

Yes, yes, her heart sang. Oh God, she'd missed him.

"Tilda?" he said, his voice husky, his mouth close. He was unsure, and it made him all the more perfect.

"I want…," she whispered.

"What do you want? Tell me."

There was no time to be coy. Too many years had already been wasted. "I want you. In my bed."

He evidently didn't need to be asked twice. She

drank him in as he stood and tossed off his T-shirt. He was beautifully made, his muscles honed from years of demanding physical exertion.

He reached for the waistband of his sweatpants.

But she held up a finger. Motioned for him to come close. Then swung her legs over the edge of the bed and spread them. The hem of her white T-shirt pushed up and her blue bikini panties peeked out.

Thirteen years ago, she'd been shy and awkward and wouldn't have dreamed of taking the lead. But now, it felt right. He stepped toward her, breathing fast.

With her thumbs, she slid his sweatpants and boxers down his lean hips. Let them drop to the floor. He was naked.

Thirteen years ago, she'd been afraid to look. Now she boldly reached out and stroked him.

"Aaagh," he moaned.

"Shush," she said gently. Then she bent her head forward and took him into her mouth.

"Oh," he sighed. "You're killing me." After a few minutes, he pulled back. "I'm too close."

He gently pushed her back, until she was lying on the bed. "I love those panties but they have got to go."

And he was efficient in undressing her. And then infinitely slow in kissing and caressing every part of her until she was literally shaking. "Now. Now, Blaine."

And he entered her. Smoothly. No sign of the awkwardness or tentativeness that had plagued them so many years earlier. His strokes were confident and long and she could feel her climax build.

"Blaine," she begged.

"I know, honey. I know." And with one final stroke, he took both of them over the edge.

IT WAS FOUR thirty in the morning when she felt him slide out of bed. "I'm going back to my room," he said. "I'm pretty confident Josh understands the facts of life, but I don't really want to have that discussion in relation to his mother."

She smiled. But it was true. Josh finding him in her bed might upset the fragile balance they'd achieved. "I get up in an hour anyway."

"Want me to start the coffee?"

"Are you going to sleep?" They hadn't done much of that last night.

"Maybe try to catch an hour," he admitted.

"Then don't bother with the coffee. I'll wake you up by six."

He leaned down to kiss her. "Last night was…"

She held up a finger. "It was wonderful. But let's not try to figure out what it means. Not today or tomorrow or anytime until we know that Davis James and his craziness are behind us." It was an excuse. But a reasonable one.

"Fair enough."

She relaxed. Thirteen years ago, circumstances had forced their hands. Decisions had been made. Actions executed. Paths chosen. This time they needed to take it slow.

He left her room, and she lay in bed, her body feeling deliciously tender in all the right places. She hadn't had sex in four years, but damn, she'd caught up fast tonight. Blaine had fortunately been better prepared than she was, carrying a good supply of condoms in his bag.

Her body was sated and happy. It was in sharp contrast to her head, which felt muddled and oddly discontent. She hadn't been honest with Blaine. What chance did they have if she continued on this path?

But would he believe her? She had no proof. No records.

Her word against his father's. But if she didn't tell him now, it would only be harder in the future. More might be at stake.

She swung her legs over the bed. Now wasn't the time to cower in bed. Now was the time to put it all on the table, to bare the truth for inspection.

She opened her door and walked down to the spare room. She knocked lightly. The door opened immediately.

"What's wrong?" Blaine asked, his eyes already moving, looking past her.

"We need to talk."

Chapter Eighteen

"Okay," Blaine said, stepping back.

She shook her head. "At the table. I'll start the coffee." She turned and walked back to the kitchen. Made a full pot of coffee instead of the two cups that she generally started on a weekend. When she turned, he was sitting at the table.

He was so handsome, with his five-o'clock shadow and his hair falling over his forehead. He looked relaxed, but Tilda wasn't fooled. He had to know that she'd not called this meeting for no reason.

"I haven't been completely honest," she began.

He said nothing.

"A few weeks after you left, just when I'd realized that I was still pregnant, I came home from work to find your father waiting outside my house."

"My father?" Now he looked startled.

She'd been pretty damn surprised that day, too. "His car was parked in my driveway when I got home from my job. It was the middle of the afternoon." Her parents had been at work. She'd felt small and inconsequential next to the powerful Russ Colton, even before he'd uttered a word.

Once he'd started talking, she'd realized that he hadn't come in peace. "He'd come with a warning. He said, 'My son is not going to marry you. If you've got any ideas of trying to trick him into it, then you need to understand that you'll regret it. Your whole family will regret it.'"

He stared at her. "That doesn't make any sense. He didn't even know that we were considering marriage, or about the baby. I didn't tell anybody. I..."

He stopped. Closed his eyes.

"What?" she asked.

"I told Decker. Not about the baby, but that I was going to marry you."

"He told your father," she said.

Blaine nodded. "He must have. He thought I was crazy. That I needed to go to college, take my rightful place in the Colton Empire."

"My parents both worked at the wagon factory. The economy was getting soft, and I knew they'd have a hard time finding another job in Roaring Springs."

"But why?" Blaine said contemplatively. "I'd already decided to enlist. Made my decision to not join the family business."

"I suspect he didn't think I was good enough for you."

A muscle ticked in his jaw. "You know that's not true. Right?"

She had to tell him the whole truth. "What I knew at eighteen is that your family lived in a very different world than mine. And I was scared. Scared that if it ever became known that Josh was a Colton, your family would find some way to push me aside and take him away."

He didn't immediately wash away her concern. That, in itself, made her feel valued. Finally, when he did speak, he sounded weary. "I'm sorry that happened,

Tilda. You already had enough to worry about. You didn't need my father pushing you around."

"Do you think your mom knows?" she asked.

He cocked his head. "I don't know. But I'm going to find out."

ONCE JOSH WAS up and fed, Blaine dropped them both off at their respective schools. He headed toward The Chateau. The same place that Tilda would go Saturday night to chaperone the prom. He really didn't want her doing that. But she'd given him a reasonable explanation of why she couldn't back out. And, quite frankly, after the night they'd shared, he didn't want to argue about it.

The sex had been mind-blowing. And when he'd held her in his arms afterwards, he'd simply felt happy. At rest. Not a feeling that he was all that used to. He was a hard-driving guy, always had been. Always focused on the next objective.

But for hours last night, he'd simply enjoyed the feeling of Tilda, the smell of her skin, the texture of her hair. Even the very light snore when she'd sunk into her deep sleep. But he suspected she wouldn't appreciate hearing him say that.

He pulled into The Chateau parking lot. It was still early, but his mother would be working. Especially given that the film festival was less than two months away.

He found his mother in her office. He knocked on her partially closed door, and she looked up. After waving him in, she said, "I wasn't expecting you. Decker told us what happened yesterday afternoon. I am so relieved you both weren't hurt. How's Tilda doing?"

"Okay. I think she's tougher than she looks. I guess…

I guess that's why she didn't scare away thirteen years ago when Dad threatened her."

His mother sat back in her chair. Her eyes flashed, but not with questions, more so with dismay. She had known. He was sure of it. And he felt even more betrayed. From his father, he expected such behavior. But his mom was a different story.

"What the hell were you two thinking?"

She glanced at the door, as if to ascertain that it was closed tight. Yes, she definitely didn't want people knowing about the Coltons' dirty laundry. Rage threatened to overtake him. Maybe, just maybe, if Tilda hadn't been so frightened for herself, for her family, she'd have reached out to him about Josh. Maybe he wouldn't have lost thirteen years. Tilda hadn't offered it up as an excuse, but he'd heard the very real fear in her voice as she recollected the conversation with his father. She'd believed Russ Colton would carry through with his threats.

"This is awkward," Mara said.

"Really. That's all you have to say. God forbid that I do anything that is awkward or gauche in any way."

His mother drew in a breath. "It's awkward because I want to tell you the truth. But to do that, I feel as if I'm betraying your father's trust. And that's something, quite frankly, that's rather tenuous between your father and me."

He refused to feel sorry for her. "I'm not sure I can ever trust either one of you again."

It was fact, but the minute he said it, his eyes registered the distress on his mother's face, and damn him, he did feel badly about it. "Sorry," he muttered. "I'm angry. Hurt."

"I know," she said. "So, what did Tilda tell you?"

She didn't say it as if Tilda was the bad guy. That, in itself, calmed him down some. "She said that Dad came to her parents' house and threatened that both Tilda and her parents would pay if she pursued a relationship with me."

She sighed. "I didn't realize that he'd threatened her parents. But…but I suspect that Tilda's recollection is correct. Your father would have used whatever leverage was available to him."

"I don't get it," he bit out.

"I didn't know about the conversation until several weeks after it had happened." She leaned her head back and stared at the ceiling. After a long moment of silence, she finally looked at him again. "Your father wanted what was best for you. Unfortunately, he could only see one definition of *best*, and that was to join the family business, to take your rightful place in the Colton Empire." She released a breath. "And when Decker told him that you were considering marrying Tilda Deeds, that dream was threatened. Before he could decide what to do, you had enlisted and were gone. He was furious. But he couldn't fight the United States Army. So, he lashed out at Tilda. She paid a price for your decision."

In so many ways. He was just coming to understand the full consequences of what he'd thought was a decision that had only mattered to him. "Dad bullied her."

"Yes. But he didn't know about the baby. I'm confident of that."

Maybe not, but it didn't make what he'd done right. "He was angry at me for leaving, angry at the army for taking me. But he never thought to look at himself, to understand why I wanted to leave so badly."

She stared at her hands, which were clasped together and resting on her desk. "Neither your father nor I are perfect people, and we were not perfect parents or…perfect partners. And there are…situations…that I prefer not to dwell on. I've not forgotten, but I've moved on because my marriage would not survive anything less."

She was talking in euphemisms. But he'd been confident when he was eighteen that his mother knew about his father's infidelity. The strain it had put on their lives had been palpable. But was that the kind of thing a child, even when that child was now a man, discussed with his mother?

"I hated what he did," he said, proving that he, too, was skilled at vague innuendo. "To you. To the family. I hated him."

"I know," she said, looking up. "And, if it's any consolation, I believe he knows that the choices he made had a profound impact upon his relationship with you. He won't say it, but I think he wants to fix that. I think that's why he was so quick to find a solution to your discharge situation."

"He owes Tilda an apology."

"Does she want that?"

"She didn't say that. I suspect she doesn't. And ultimately, it doesn't change anything. But I swear to God, if he does anything else to hurt her or scare her, he will regret it."

She studied him. "Things are different between the two of you."

"I…care about her." He was not about to tell his mother that he loved her before he'd had the conversation with Tilda.

"I see. I have to tell you that I'm glad to hear that, son. When we all had lunch together, both of you were trying, but there was a layer of hostility there that no one could ignore. That isn't the best environment for my grandson to be raised in. You, of all people, know that to be true."

He would not make the mistakes his parents had made. And he needed to talk to his dad about this. "When will Dad be back?"

"Early Saturday."

"I have to admit that I was grateful that he was out of town when I first heard this news. I'm not sure what I might have said or done," Blaine said.

She gave him a half smile. "You wouldn't have done anything stupid. Even as a child, you were never impulsive. That's why I knew that you hadn't made a mistake when you'd joined the army. Even though everyone else was surprised, I knew that you'd thought it through, weighed the pros and the cons, and determined that it was the best option for you."

Best option for *him*. Not necessarily for everyone else. "I'd have never gone if I'd known about Josh."

"Of course not. But now, you can only be forward-focused. And do better than your dad and I did."

The one thing he'd already learned was that parenting wasn't easy. "In the military, there's a procedure and a process for everything, and soldiers drill constantly. It's the backbone of the operation. But suddenly, I find myself in a situation where there's no manual, I've had no training for what I'm taking on, and the consequences of me screwing up are the most significant I've ever faced."

She smiled for real now. "Welcome to parenthood."

He stood, feeling drained. "I'm sorry to have barged in."

"I'm glad we talked, Blaine. This is not an easy conversation for a parent to have with her child."

"I know."

"Are we okay?" she asked softly.

He leaned across the desk and hugged her. No, she hadn't been a perfect mother. But he loved her. "Of course," he said. "I love you, Mom."

"And I love you," she said, hugging him back. "Where are you headed?"

"The Lodge. I need to talk to Decker next."

Chapter Nineteen

Penny waved Blaine in. Still, he offered up a perfunctory knock before walking in.

"Hey, didn't expect to see you so early," Decker said. "Thought you might need a few hours of R&R. Everything okay?"

"Not great."

"Davis James?" his brother asked.

"No. I need to tell you something."

"You've got another kid somewhere," Decker said dryly.

Blaine rolled his eyes. "Thirteen years ago, I told you that I was going to marry Tilda. And you told Dad."

Now Decker looked uncomfortable. "That's true," he said. "I'm sorry that I betrayed your confidence. I just knew how furious Dad was going to be, and I thought it made sense for the two of you to have that argument before the deed was already done. But I truly regret what I did, Blaine. I wouldn't make the same decision today."

Blaine knew that. Age and experience had given them both some perspective. "I'm not upset about that. You thought you were protecting me. What I'm mad about is that Dad used that info to threaten Tilda after I left. Threatened her and her parents."

Decker let out a sigh, much like their mother had

done. "I can't say that I'm all that surprised. But I am sorry."

"Nobody is responsible for Dad's actions but Dad. I wanted you to know this because you need to understand that Tilda was afraid. She was afraid to tell me about Josh, afraid for any of the Coltons to know that I had a son. She wasn't mean or vindictive. I know that you…had reservations about her, but they're unfounded. I don't want you thinking badly of her any longer."

Decker studied him. "You want to make sure that I don't think badly of your girl." He paused. "Oh, hell. You're in love with her, aren't you?"

"I am," Blaine confirmed. He wouldn't spill the beans to his mother, but Decker had always been his best friend. And it felt good to admit it out loud. "I haven't told her yet. It's too soon."

"Seems to me that you wouldn't want to waste too much time. Been enough of that."

Blaine smiled. "I'll grant you that I don't have the killer businessman instinct to propel me forward, but I don't intend to drag my heels."

It was Decker's turn to grin. "Skye doesn't think too much of my business ability. She called me this morning. News of the elevator issue had reached her, and she's panicking about the film festival and a litany of other bad things that have happened. Reservations are down. Substantially." He used finger quotes around the last word.

"What did you tell Skye?" Their cousin meant well, and she busted her butt for The Chateau, taking her role as the marketing director seriously.

"I told her to stop worrying. That everything would be fine."

"That sounds like a very relaxed response from my type-A brother."

"What can I say?" Decker shrugged. "Kendall has given me some perspective about the things that are really important in life."

"Good for her. And good for you," Blaine said.

"Never underestimate the love of a good woman."

Could Tilda love him? Maybe not yet, but this time around, he would earn that love. Blaine stood. "I'm going to get to work. I want to leave on time tonight. I'm assuming there's nothing new from yesterday's incident to report since you haven't said anything."

"Nothing. Except a lot of talk among the staff. I guess the good thing is that everybody seems to think that this was way beyond a simple prank. Somebody could have been killed."

As in him or Tilda. "I'm grateful that Liam responded to the 9-1-1 call."

"Yeah. He's a good guy. And thorough. He's combing through camera feeds. And if it's any consolation, we're installing a camera in the maintenance area, as well," Decker said. "A day late and a dollar short."

"Who could have anticipated something like this?" Blaine said.

"I don't know. But don't worry, bro. We're going to be on high alert here. Everybody is looking for Davis James."

ON FRIDAY, SHE got a chance to confide in Raeann. "Blaine is staying at my house."

"In the spare bedroom?" Raeann asked, never one to wait to get to the punch line.

"Not anymore," Tilda said. And damn her, she could feel the heat rising in her face. After Josh had gone to bed on Thursday night, Blaine had once again snuck into her room.

"OMG. You go, girl!" Raeann shrieked, giving her a high five. "I'm really happy for the two of you. What's next?"

"We're sort of living in the moment," Tilda said. "I think we're both a little afraid to look too far ahead."

"I get that. How's Josh taking it?"

"Like it's no big deal to have Blaine in our house. Kids really do roll with the punches. Of course, we haven't shared how our relationship has…progressed. Not only is that not a conversation I want to have, I guess I don't want him to get too used to it," she admitted, not able to hide the concern that hovered at the back of her brain.

"Don't borrow trouble. My mother also used to say that."

"I think I would have liked your mother," Tilda said.

"She would have loved you," Raeann answered. "Go home and have some more raucous sex. And I'll see you tomorrow night. I really hope my dress still zips."

IT WAS LATER that day, almost quitting time, when Blaine's cell phone rang. When he saw it was Liam, he snatched it up. "Hello."

"I've got good news. We picked up some activity on Davis James's credit card. He bought a bus ticket in Denver. Not sure of his final destination, but it goes through Omaha, then Chicago, and finally, a couple stops on the East Coast. We do know that a couple hours after the bus left, he charged a meal at a rest stop along the way."

Blaine let out a relieved breath. "Any visual confirmation that he left town?"

"Yeah. We've got him on camera at the bus depot in Denver. He was dragging a roller bag along behind him and carrying a hardcover book."

Something to keep him busy on a long bus ride. "I'm still confident that he could be the person who messed with the elevator at The Lodge."

"I know. And if we get any credible evidence that points in his direction, we'll make sure and have a conversation with him. But it looks as if he's going home. It will be nice to know where to find him."

Yeah. Davis James was making it easy for them. And that worried Blaine. "Can you keep an eye on that credit card? I'd like to know if he's continuing to use it."

"Of course. I'll talk to you later."

"Thanks, Liam. I appreciate it."

He could hardly wait to tell Josh and Tilda. He'd checked in earlier with Tilda by text, just to make sure that her day was going well. And had done the same with Josh, once he was out of school.

Now he signed out of his computer and grabbed his keys. Tilda was making tacos tonight.

"Good news," he said twenty minutes later, once he had his coat off.

"Tacos and good news. What a night," Josh quipped.

Tilda rolled her eyes. "Ignore him," she said.

"Davis James is on a bus, headed east," he said.

"Problem solved?" Josh asked, his tone hopeful. Then, as if the light bulb had gone on, added in a much more serious tone, "Does this mean you're leaving?"

"It's good news and…" He shifted his eyes to look at Tilda. "I was thinking I might stick around for a while. If that's okay. I mean… I really like tacos."

"Yeah, sure," Josh said, as if he had the deciding vote.

"Yeah, sure," she echoed her son, smiling at Blaine. He could feel the warmth in his body. He wanted to see that smile in his bed.

All night long.

"Does this mean I can go skiing this weekend?" Josh asked. "I could call Isaac."

Even with Davis James on a bus, he didn't feel all that comfortable letting Josh get too far out of sight. But he also knew that this weekend would be the last for skiing. "Maybe you, your mom and I could go," he said.

"Like a family?" Josh asked, likely not realizing how emotionally charged those words might be.

"Yeah. Just like that," Blaine said easily. Which was an Emmy Award–winning performance on his part. A week ago he hadn't been thinking marriage or children. Finding out about Josh had changed everything. He was a dad. And he'd be the best damn one he could be. But marriage? Was that in the cards?

Would Tilda even be interested? She'd been married once and then single for the last four years. Maybe she preferred the latter?

He told himself to relax and to breathe. There was plenty of time to sort all this out. Decisions didn't need to be made today. Other than deciding to go skiing. "We'll go on Sunday."

ON SATURDAY MORNING, Josh slept late. Blaine was working on his laptop at the kitchen table. Tilda sat next to him, drinking a cup of coffee. She was terribly relieved to hear that Davis James had headed out of town. If he'd been responsible for her slashed tires or the *horrifying elevator event*, as she now referred to it, she hated the idea of him getting away with it. But she hated that significantly less than the idea that he was unaccounted for.

If Davis James got away and stayed away, fine with her.

And since he was no longer a threat, she felt significantly better about leaving Josh tonight when she was at The Chateau. She needed to be there by five thirty, and the kids would start to arrive at six. "By the way, I've got some turkey and cheese that you and Josh can use for sandwiches tonight. And chips. Josh loves those. Cheesecake for dessert."

"Great," he said, giving her a quick smile.

He didn't seem concerned. And Josh was easygoing. They would be fine. Was she fretting because she wanted Blaine to need her more? That was crazy.

Self-sufficiency was a good thing. For everyone's sake. Especially Josh's. He needed to feel that both of his parents were equally confident in providing care. Equally at ease with the idea of hanging out with him.

Isaac came over in the afternoon and the boys hung out in Josh's room during the afternoon. Blaine sat in the living room and read a book. A couple times he picked up his smartphone and texted. He didn't offer any explanation, and she didn't ask. He had his life. Just because they were sleeping together, didn't mean that she was privy to his secrets. He'd said that his relationship with Honor was over and she knew he was telling the truth. Blaine was too honorable to lie about something like that.

At four o'clock, Isaac left, and Josh took a spot on the couch, next to Blaine. She stood up. "I'm going to go get ready." She thought she saw a look pass between Josh and Blaine. "What?" she asked.

They both shrugged and gave her a look that implied that she might be the crazy one. Whatever. She needed to get hot rollers in her hair.

An hour later, she emerged from the bedroom. Josh was the only one in the living room. He barely looked up from his phone. Made no comment about her dress. Or the makeup she'd labored over. Or the hair that had been set and sprayed to hold for hours.

It was hell living with a thirteen-year-old boy!

"Where's Blaine?" she asked.

"Had to run an errand," he said offhandedly.

Tilda glanced at her watch. She hoped he got back soon because she needed to leave in ten minutes. Josh was old enough to stay by himself, but still, given that Blaine had been so insistent that they stick together the past couple days, it seemed kind of negligent to not be around when he knew that she had another commitment.

She eased into a chair, being careful not to wrinkle her dress. Had barely gotten seated when there was a knock on the door. She'd given Blaine a key. "I'll get it," she said. Davis James was accounted for, but there was no need to be stupid.

She glanced out the window and saw Blaine's vehicle. Perhaps he'd forgotten his key. Still, she checked the peephole.

What in the world...?

She looked again. Then glanced over her shoulder at Josh, who was no longer staring at his phone but, rather, at her, his face about to split open in a grin. "New plan, sport," he said.

It took her a minute. "What's going on?"

He shrugged. "Maybe you should open the door, Mom."

She did. There was Blaine, in a black tux and white shirt, looking so wickedly handsome that her knees literally seemed weak. He held out the small box he was carrying. Inside was a wrist corsage of baby yellow roses with a dark blue ribbon that would look lovely with her dress.

"Evening, Tilda," he said, his tone even.

"Evening, Blaine," she replied, trying for the same. It was hard because her throat felt as if it might be closing up. "Kind of dressed up for turkey and cheese sandwiches."

He stepped into the house. "Nobody is eating that tonight." He looked at Josh. "Ready?"

"Oh, yeah."

She saw Josh reach for his backpack, which she had not previously noticed next to the couch.

"What's going on?" she asked.

"In case you haven't already figured it out, you and I are going to prom," Blaine said. "We're going to take Josh with us as far as The Chateau, where we're handing him off to my mom. He's going to spend the night at Colton Manor. Assuming you're okay with all of that."

It touched her that he'd done all this but was still willing to give her the chance to veto the idea if she wasn't comfortable with it. "You're good with this?" she asked Josh.

"Oh, yeah. It's a movie marathon night. And there's going to be popcorn and ice cream sundaes."

"You may never want to come home," she murmured, her heart feeling very full. How wonderful for Josh to have another grandmother.

"My dad is getting home today, so he'll be there, too," Blaine said. "I spoke with him about an hour ago. He wanted to call you, to apol—" he looked at Josh. "To make sure that you knew how much he was looking forward to meeting Josh."

She thought he'd been about to say *apologize* but had

changed his mind, given that Josh was right there. That would have elicited way too many questions that were better left unasked right now. But he was also trying very hard to make sure that she didn't get any surprises, that her decision was made with full information. And truthfully? She didn't really want any apologies from Russ Colton. Yes, he'd been wrong, but now that she was a parent, she had a little better understanding of the things a parent might do if they thought they were protecting their child. "I think it's high time that Josh meets him."

She and Russ would talk and hopefully clear the air. She wanted him to understand that she'd never be bullied again. But also that she was grateful that her son was a Colton. But that conversation didn't need to happen today.

Because right now, she had a date. With a handsome man. Who made her heart flutter.

Chapter Twenty

"You look lovely," he said. It was true. Her royal blue dress was a concoction of silk and lace. Her skin sparkled and her long, dark hair curled over her shoulders. She was the prettiest girl at the dance. Although no dancing had yet occurred. But the waiters were about to clear dessert, so it wouldn't be long now.

He could hardly wait for the opportunity to pull her close. To slide up against her. To slip his hand under…

Nope. Not going to happen. She was one of the official chaperones of the event. Therefore, they were going to have to keep it G-rated. But once the night was over, it was back to her house. Her empty house. With no thirteen-year-old boy who had the potential to overhear. Not that the sex had been bad. Just the opposite. But still, they'd had to be a little restrained.

Tonight, they might christen every room. The kitchen table seemed sturdy enough. Would certainly give him something to smile about whenever he ate his breakfast cereal there. Which, if he had his way, would be more often than not.

He'd recognized a few of the other teachers. Some had been teaching there when he and Tilda had been students. A few others had been students at the same time. The rest, like her friend Raeann Johnson, were strangers.

All seemed to have an interest in him. Not because of who he was but because they liked and cared about Tilda. That was immediately obvious. And she had a strong rapport with the students who were there.

"I feel a bit like a goldfish in a bowl," he admitted from the corner of his mouth.

"It's not me," she denied. "It's the seventeen-and eighteen-year-old girls who are staring at you, which in turn is causing their boyfriends to narrow their eyes in your direction."

He'd seen a couple of those looks, and it had reminded him of how his fellow soldiers had looked at the enemy forces. "I'm taken," he said lightly. This wasn't the time or the place to tell her what was in his heart.

She turned to look at him. "This is really very nice," she said. "And totally sneaky. I'm not sure I am comfortable with you and Josh being in cahoots. Sometimes I already feel overmatched."

"The corsage was his idea."

"I didn't think he knew anything about corsages," she mused.

"I think he looked it up on his phone."

"Aha. Finally, it becomes a tool," she said. "The flowers are lovely. I catch a whiff every time I raise my fork. And the food was delicious. We need to tell your mom."

The Chateau had hit it out of the park. The food had been excellent, the service was very attentive, and now the lights were dimming just as the DJ started the first song. "I still kind of miss the gym with the paper streamers."

"Me, too," she agreed. "But as a chaperone, I'm very grateful that The Chateau takes care of all the cleanup.

Once the last song plays and all the kids are gone, we're done."

"Can't wait," he said, winking at her. Then laughed when she blushed. "Come on, beautiful," he murmured, taking her hand. "Dance with me."

THEY WERE TWO hours into the dancing, with less than an hour remaining, when she whispered to Blaine that she needed to visit the ladies' room. She weaved her way through the crowd, smiling and greeting students who looked way too grown-up in their ball gowns and tuxedos. Everything was running smoothly. Nobody had attempted to spike the punch, and with the exception of one girl's zipper breaking, there had been no wardrobe malfunctions of any significance. The zipper had been fixed with a few strategically placed safety pins and some two-sided tape magically offered up by the manager on duty.

The restrooms were located at the end of the hallway. She went in, took care of business and was washing her hands in the sink when the door opened.

Toby Turner staggered in. She could smell the liquor on him.

"This is the women's restroom, Toby," she said, her heart starting to beat fast. He was just a kid. She shouldn't be afraid. But he was six inches taller and probably fifty pounds heavier than her.

"We're not in school. You can't tell me what to do." His tone was belligerent.

"We're at a school function. Get out," she said, her voice as firm as she could make it. There was nobody else in any of the stalls. Nobody to help her.

He took a step towards her.

She held up her hand. "You're going to get yourself into trouble here, Toby. You've been drinking, and you're not making good decisions."

He swayed. "Nobody cares. Nobody gives a damn."

"I do, Toby. I care. And I'll do what I can to help you, but you have to help yourself, too. Now, get out of here. I'll talk to you in the hallway." Where there were other people.

"No." He took another step forward.

Should she scream? Would that enrage him? Would anyone hear her over the music? How long before Blaine missed her?

She judged her chances of getting past him and didn't think they were that good. He was drunk and swaying, but there wasn't much room to maneuver by him.

"Toby, I know you're a smart kid. Be smart. Step—"

The door behind him opened. He whirled. "Get the hell out!" he screamed at a startled girl.

She stepped back, letting the door close. Tilda didn't know if she'd seen her or not. If she had, surely she'd go get someone. "She's going for help," Tilda said, with perhaps more confidence than she felt.

"Doesn't matter. Neither one of us is getting out of here."

BLAINE WAS CHECKING his watch for the second time when a young girl, her long blond hair almost flying behind her, came running up. She almost skidded to a stop in front of him. The look on her face scared him. "What?" he asked.

"Toby Turner is in the ladies' room. With Ms. Deeds."

"What?"

"He screamed at me to leave. He didn't look right."

Blaine ran. He'd always been fast, but now it seemed as if it was taking him forever to cover the hundred plus yards. He stopped outside the door, listened but could not hear anything, and pushed on the door.

It didn't budge. It had been locked from the inside. "Tilda," he yelled. "Tilda, can you hear me?"

"I'm here, Blaine."

"Okay, honey. Open the door, then."

"I…can't just yet," she said.

Now a crowd was gathering behind him. "Go back into the ballroom," he told them. "I need everybody out of this hallway. Now."

They went. Everyone but Raeann Johnson and her husband.

"Are you hurt?" Blaine asked through the door.

"No," she said.

His heart maybe slowed, but he didn't think so. He was running on pure adrenaline. "Toby, this is Blaine Colton. I need you to listen to me. You need to unlock this door and let Ms. Deeds come out. Right now."

"No." The kid's voice was shaky.

Blaine knew the layout of The Chateau. He'd been around when it had been built. Like most of the rooms in the building, there were windows to let in natural light and fresh air. For privacy's sake, the ones in the restrooms were high. And above the restroom was a guest room. With a balcony that was nice and long but not terribly deep.

He turned to Raeann. "Call the police, ask them to patch you through to Liam Kastor. Tell him to come without lights and sirens. Let the manager on duty know what's going on." Then he was off.

He ran up the stairs and pounded on door number

318. A man wearing pajama bottoms and nothing else opened it. "What?"

"We have an emergency below you." He pushed his way into the room, not sparing a glance at the woman who was in the bed. He opened the balcony door, stepped out and looked over the railing.

Yes. If he did it just right, he could hang down from the balcony and get his feet onto the ledge outside the bathroom windows. If he wasn't careful, however, he was going to fall three stories.

He'd be careful. But he also needed to be fast.

Tight to the building, he swung his left leg over the railing edge and then his right. The tips of his shoes were resting on the narrow outside edge of the wrought-iron railing. He squatted, moving his hand all the way to the very bottom. Then, holding on tight, he stepped off the edge. His body jerked, no longer supported, and he felt the pull in his right shoulder that was now bearing all his weight.

He stretched but could not reach the ledge below him. Looking down, he saw that he was still a couple inches short.

He wasn't giving up now. He let go and dropped.

When his shoes made contact with the ledge below, he tightened his core and pitched his body forward. He hit the exterior wall hard enough that the brick scratched his face, and he dug his fingers in, praying that he wasn't simply going to bounce off.

When he didn't, he stopped only long enough to take a deep breath before he moved toward the window. He edged his head around the sill, confident that he would be able to see into the lit room but they would not see him in the dark outside.

There she was. Standing. Her back to him. Her left

hand rested on the sink, and he could see the flowers on her wrist. He could see just enough of the side of her face that he knew she was talking.

Toby Turner was facing him, his back to the locked door. His hair was disheveled, and his face was red. He was staring at Tilda as if intently listening.

Blaine did not see a weapon. But Toby was big enough that he could still hurt Tilda badly. No way was he going to let that happen.

The windows were the kind that slid open to the side, with a screen covering half. If he got the glass open the whole way, it would be enough space for him to go in, feetfirst.

He grabbed the latch, praying it was unlocked. And gently pulled. Like everything else at The Chateau, it was a high-quality product that was impeccably maintained. It slid, soundlessly. The screen was still in place, but that couldn't be helped. He was going through.

He hit the ground hard, bent his knees to absorb the shock and then shot upwards. Tilda turned, he reached out and grabbed her arm and, in one swift motion, pulled her behind him. Now he was closest to Toby Turner, who was looking at him as if he was seeing a ghost.

"You okay, honey?" he asked, not taking his eyes off Toby.

"Uh…yes. How…" Her voice trailed off.

He figured she was looking up at the window and suddenly had a pretty good idea of how he'd done it. "He didn't touch you?" he rasped, needing to be sure.

"No. He's been drinking, Blaine. He's…not himself."

"Here's what we're going to do, Toby," Blaine said. "You're going to unlock that door. And we're going to walk out of here." If the kid decided to launch himself in his and Tilda's direction, Blaine would have no choice but to take him down.

"Are you calling the police?" the teen asked.

They were likely already there. Hell yes, thought Blaine. He'd locked Tilda in. Scared her.

"No," Tilda said, her voice surprisingly strong. "But we are calling your parents. And we're waiting for them to pick you up. And then we're going to have a conversation. And you're going to tell them how you feel."

Blaine turned slightly. What the hell was she talking about?

She gave him a quick smile, but she was really focusing on Toby. "And then you're going to go home and sober up, and then start working. You've got weeks of assignments that need to be turned in. You've got three days."

"Really?" Toby asked, his voice hopeful.

"Really," Tilda said. "But this is your only grace offering. You blow this and you won't get another chance from me."

"I won't blow it. I promise."

"Unlock the door, Toby," Blaine said.

He did as instructed.

Blaine wasn't confident about what lurked beyond the door. "This is Blaine Colton," Blaine yelled. "We're coming out."

"Blaine, it's Liam" was the response. "Everything okay?"

Blaine let out a breath. He hadn't wanted to get shot by some eager police officer. "Yeah. Tilda will exit first. Then Toby Turner and me."

"Step aside, Toby," he said, no longer yelling. "Let Ms. Deeds pass."

And Blaine thought Toby was going to do just that. Instead he squared his shoulders, looked straight for Tilda, and said, "No."

Chapter Twenty-One

Tilda's heart sank. "Come on, Toby. It's over," she said. She was no longer afraid for herself but for Toby. He was no match to Blaine.

"I just… I just want to apologize," Toby said.

She let out her breath. "I accept your apology," she said evenly. "Now I'm walking out of here."

Toby stepped back. When Tilda exited, she saw Liam with six more officers from the Roaring Springs Police Department behind him. Other than that, the hallway was clear. She was grateful. It was unlikely that most everyone wouldn't hear some version of the story of Toby Turner and her in the ladies' room, but at least their exit wasn't going to be on social media.

"You okay?" Liam asked.

She nodded. "He's an intoxicated and very mixed-up kid. But he didn't cross the line. He never touched me."

"We can still arrest him. On a litany of charges."

"No. Absolutely not. We're calling his parents," she said. Toby and Blaine were out of the bathroom, standing near the door. Blaine motioned for Toby to take a seat on the floor. Then he wandered over.

"Thanks for coming," he said to Liam.

"No problem. Tilda says she's not interested in pressing charges?"

"That's right," Blaine confirmed.

"Okay," Liam said, shrugging. "I hope the kid understands the break you're giving him. And you…" He gave Blaine a pointed look. "I get that you're the director of Extreme Sports for The Lodge, but you're not a superhero. No more hanging off balconies and kicking in windows."

Hanging off balconies. She'd had some idea of how he'd managed to get in, but to hear it described made her feel slightly sick.

"Just a small drop, and only a screen," Blaine said lightly, perhaps seeing that she was close to vomiting on his shoes.

"Where are all the other students?" Tilda asked, needing to focus her attention on something else.

"In the ballroom. We were just discussing the merits of moving all of them as well as all the guests when Blaine sounded the all clear."

It could have gotten a whole lot more complex and certainly more public if Blaine hadn't found a way in. She was beyond grateful. "I'm going to call Toby's parents now."

"I'll go with you," Blaine said quickly.

She almost told him it wasn't necessary, but one look at his face told her that would be futile. He wasn't letting her go anywhere with Toby, even if it was simply to sit in some comfy chairs in the main lobby.

"You might want to call your mom," Liam said to Blaine. "The manager on duty felt she needed to be in the loop."

"Will do," he said. "Thanks for your help."

"No problem. Love it when we're not really needed."

WHAT *HE* NEEDED was a stiff drink, but since the chaperones had done such a good job of keeping the fruit punch pure, he was going to have to wait.

It took twenty-five minutes for Toby Turner's mother to arrive, and another fifteen for his father. The parents had evidently stopped living together a few months earlier. There was a bitter custody battle in play for Toby and his three younger siblings.

While they were waiting, Tilda got Toby some coffee to drink. He might not have been legally sober by the time his parents arrived, but he was steady on his feet, and he wasn't slurring his words.

Blaine gave Tilda, Toby and the parents their privacy, but since the only one of the group he really trusted was Tilda, he stayed close enough that he could hear most everything. Neither parent had a clue that Toby was failing because all their contact information in the school's computer system had been changed. By Toby, who had access to his mother's password. They had not sent the text message to Tilda asking that she meet them in their home, either. Toby had done that, knowing that it was against school policy. He'd thought Tilda would give up, but instead, she'd offered up alternatives.

There was crying and a few harsh accusations, but in general, it appeared that both mom and dad were substantially impressed with the gravity of the situation and, quite frankly, greatly relieved that the episode tonight hadn't turned out significantly worse.

The credit went to Tilda, who had stayed professional and calm and offered unwavering support to her hurting student. And by the time the Turners left, Toby and mom in one car, dad in another, she looked spent.

"Let's go home, honey," he said.

She shook her head. "Chaperones stay until the end."

"You can't be serious. You're not going to go back in there and dance."

She looked at her watch. "There's fifteen minutes left. Come on. I think they're just about to play our song."

"We have a song?"

"We will."

TILDA SANK INTO the car seat and tilted her head back to rest it against the cushion. "I am so tired," she admitted.

"I wonder why," he said. "You had a hell of a night."

She hadn't wanted to talk about it inside. That's why she'd insisted they return to the dance. They'd been present for the last three songs, and then the ballroom had emptied out pretty fast. The kids were interested in doing what kids did after prom was over.

She and Blaine knew all too well what that activity was for some of them. And tonight, she'd told that story. To a young man who'd needed to hear that kids sometimes screwed up. But in doing so, she'd sacrificed not only her own privacy, but that of Blaine's. And she probably owed him an explanation and maybe an apology.

"I need to tell you something," she said.

He glanced her way, a muscle ticking in his jaw. "I swear to God, Tilda, if you lied about him hurting you in any way, I am—" he drew in a breath "—not going to be happy."

"Not that. But I told Toby about us. About how we got pregnant on prom night, and that I hid the pregnancy from you for thirteen years."

He studied her. "You must have had a good reason."

"His parents told him and his younger siblings that they were getting a divorce about three months ago, and his dad moved out right away. His mom started drinking heavily and was often drunk by the time he and his three sisters came home from school. Toby didn't care so much for himself because he's turning eighteen in a month and had plans to leave. But his sisters are much younger. They're fourteen, twelve and nine."

"I guess I can kind of relate to that," Blaine said. "Not the divorce, but I was about that age when I became aware that my parents' marriage wasn't great and that my dad was unfaithful."

"I remembered you telling me about that," she said softly. "And I remembered how helpless you felt because you couldn't really talk to anybody about it. I got the impression from Toby that he'd taken on a lot of the home responsibilities. Was buying the groceries, trying to cook dinners, washing clothes."

"No time to do homework?" Blaine guessed.

"Let's just say that he didn't have any appetite for homework. And while he didn't come right out and say it, it seems that it was some passive-aggressive behavior. If he failed, his parents would have to feel badly about it because they were the reason."

"None of that explains what he did tonight," Blaine gritted out.

"What happened tonight was the culmination of twenty-four hours of bad judgment. Last night, he had it out with his mother. Told her she was a drunk and that he was going to make sure that his sisters were taken away from her."

"She didn't appear to have been drinking tonight."

"I know. She said that she hadn't had a drink after their conversation, that she'd been very upset about how Toby had said it to her but she couldn't deny the basic truth."

"Well, something good, then," Blaine said.

"If it had ended there. After the fight, Toby left his

home and was out all night, just driving around. He slept in his car. About ten this morning, he found some guy who would buy him alcohol for a ten-buck tip, and he started drinking."

"Did it dawn on him that he was solving his problems in the same way as his mother, who he disapproved of?" Blaine asked.

"The irony was not lost on him, evidently. Which is why he got angry. At himself. At the world. And tonight, when he saw me go into the ladies' room, he was ready to pick a fight."

"But why you? You're the one who has been trying to help him. Trying to make sure he graduated."

She shrugged. "I think sometimes we want to hurt those that we care about. And Toby might not care about me, but he couldn't deny that I cared about him. And he was determined that he was going to prove to me that he was unworthy."

"But you changed his mind?" Blaine asked.

"I was well on my way," Tilda said, humor in her tone, "when someone *dropped in* from above."

"I saw him listening very intently to what you were saying. What exactly did you tell him?"

"I got the impression that he pretty much thought his life was over, and I told him that I understood what it was to feel as if you'd made such a big mistake that you couldn't see any way to come back from it. I could see that he didn't believe me, that I was going to need to give him specifics."

He lifted a brow. "Such as…"

"Well, for starters, I told him about how angry I had been with myself for being stupid enough to get pregnant on prom night. How sad I was that I was going to be such a disappointment to my parents, who had

worked so hard for me to go to college, to do something that they hadn't been able to do. I told him how
ashamed I was that I wasn't brave enough to tell you
the truth about the baby."

"But you turned it all around," protested Blaine.
"You did great."

"That all helped me to convince him that he hadn't
screwed up so badly that he also wouldn't be able to
turn it around. He's going to have a tough time making up all the work that he's missed. I know I told him
three days but if I can tell he's putting in honest effort
and still falling short, I'm going to talk to the principal and see if he'll allow him to graduate with his class
with the understanding that Toby will get the work done
over the summer."

"Once again, you're pretty amazing, Ms. Deeds. I
totally get how you received the Teacher of the Year
award a few years ago."

She blushed. "Someone told you about that, huh?"

"Yeah. Your students are lucky. Are you worried that
Toby is going to share what you told him?"

"No, I really don't think he will." She hesitated. "But
are you concerned?"

"Nah, I don't care," Blaine said. "It's our story. I'm
not ashamed of it."

"Me either," she told him. "Now, do you think you
could drive me home?" They were still sitting in The
Chateau's parking lot. "I really want to get out of this
dress."

He smiled. "I really want to get you out of that dress."

"Is that an invitation?"

"Consider it a promise."

TILDA WAS READY the next morning at eight thirty, which
was pretty damn amazing considering that she hadn't

gotten all that much sleep the night before. They'd made love three times.

She felt a little sore, somewhat emotionally vulnerable, yet extremely relaxed. "Hey," she said, as she walked to the kitchen and found Blaine at the table.

"Hey, yourself. Coffee?"

"I can get it," she said. She filled a cup and then took the pot over to the table to refill his. "I sent Josh a text and told him that we'd be there to pick him up in a half hour." She'd been grateful last night to learn that Josh knew nothing about the incident with Toby. Mara had gotten the call from her manager on duty and had wisely chosen to keep the information to herself.

"Okay," Blaine said. "I imagine he's pretty stoked about going."

"His text back was a massive smiley face." She took a sip. "Are you still worried about Davis James? Is that why you didn't want Josh to go with Isaac?"

"It seems as if he's out of our hair for the time being. I just thought it would be nice to do something together as a family. And now, after last night, I guess I'm really glad that's the way the decision went." He scrubbed a hand across his face. "I'm still a little raw from the thought that something could have happened to you. And also, maybe I'm a bit of a control freak, and I just feel better when I'm there to protect those that matter to me."

After last night and his heroic efforts to get to her, she had no doubts that he was absolutely capable of protecting them. "You were really amazing last night," she said.

Blaine said nothing. Just sipped his coffee and drummed his fingers on the kitchen table. "You know, honey, I had plans for this table."

"Plans?"

"Yeah." And then he got up and whispered in her ear,

in rather spectacular detail, exactly what those plans had been.

"Oh my," she said when he finished. "Speaking of amazing," she added weakly. "That would be." She picked up the morning paper to fan herself.

He looked at his watch. "Twenty-seven minutes and counting."

"Then, you better get a move on," she warned as she started to unbutton her shirt.

THEY WERE TEN minutes late in picking up Josh. As they pulled in the long driveway, Tilda turned to him. "Do you suppose we could just honk the horn and wait for him to come out?"

"It's an option," he said. "But I think it may be time for you and my dad to actually come face-to-face. For Josh's sake. Are you okay with that?"

"No. But I know you're right. So I'm going to ring the bell like the confident person I know I can be."

"If that fails, give me the high sign, and we'll make a break for it." Blaine parked. He was not without his own misgivings, but it was time. Tilda and Josh were a part of his life now. He didn't want it to be awkward every time his dad's name came up.

They stepped onto the porch and rang the bell. In seconds, Josh opened the door. "Hey, you're late."

"Sorry about that, sport. Couple things required my attention," Blaine said. He saw Tilda run her tongue across her teeth.

"That's okay," Josh replied. "We were playing pool."

"Who's *we*?" Tilda asked.

"Blaine's dad and me," Josh said.

At least his dad hadn't told him to call him Mr. Colton. "Were you winning?" Blaine asked.

"Absolutely not."

Blaine turned and saw his dad. He was still holding a pool cue.

"Don't let him tell you otherwise," Russ said, his
tone amused. He turned to Tilda. "Hello. Thank you
for letting him stay last night. He's quite a boy. You
must be very proud."

Now he seemed very serious. Almost tentative,
which was not a word Blaine associated often with his
father.

"I am," Tilda said. "Very proud. And I'm glad that
he was able to stay. I want him to be able to come here,
to get to know both you and your wife. You are his
family, after all."

His father cleared his throat. "Thank you."

His mother walked into the room, looking lovely as
usual. She hugged Blaine first, then Tilda. Very quietly,
so that Josh wouldn't hear, she murmured, "I'm so glad
things turned out well last night."

"Me, too," Tilda said. "Sorry that all that drama had
to occur at The Chateau."

His mother waved her hand. "Josh, do you have your
backpack?"

"It's downstairs," he said and went to get it.

"He's a delight," Mara beamed. "And very funny.
I don't think I've laughed that much for a long time."

"Reminds me a lot of Blaine when he was that age,"
his dad said.

Blaine resisted a smile. It appeared the paternity test
was off the table. Josh bounded back up the stairs.

"Thanks for letting me stay," the teen said. He did
not offer hugs or even a handshake. That would come
in time.

"Come back anytime, sweetheart," Mara said. "You,
too, Tilda."

"What about me?" Blaine asked, feigning innocence.
His mom rolled her eyes, and his dad smiled. "You're

always welcome, Blaine," he said. "I really do hope you know that."

When they got back into the car, Tilda turned to Josh. "So, you had a good time?"

"Yeah. We watched movies and there were nine different toppings for the ice cream. This morning, Blaine's dad made pancakes."

Blaine could not remember the last time he'd seen his father in front of a stove. "Pretty soon pigs are going to start flying," he said.

"What?" Josh asked.

"Nothing. Just glad you had a good time. Now I hope you're ready to ski."

"Is Wicked still closed?" Josh asked.

"Yes," Blaine said. Before he'd gotten *busy* in the kitchen, he'd checked the internal communication that was distributed to all staff. There'd been some melt with the slightly warmer temperatures, and those charged with watching for avalanche risk had deemed it necessary to continue to close the run. It would disappoint many, but The Lodge had avoided catastrophes in the past by being extra cautious.

"Oh, man," Josh said, sounding plenty disappointed. "I really wanted to ski Wicked."

"We can ski Wonderland. It's the next run over, and plenty challenging."

Tilda turned to look at her son. "Yes, remember your poor mother. I haven't been on skis all year."

Her skis, stashed in the corner of her garage, had been very dusty.

"You were always pretty good," Josh said. "It'll come back to you."

"I hope so, or I'm going to be spending the afternoon in the emergency department."

No way, thought Blaine. Not on his watch. And the

news he'd heard about an hour ago made him even more confident. The day before, Davis James had used his credit card at a diner in Ohio, which coincided with a scheduled stop for the bus headed east. The charge had just showed up. If he'd engineered the elevator attack, perhaps he'd gotten discouraged when it hadn't worked. Maybe decided that Blaine was hard to kill.

He pulled into the lot, parked in staff parking and led them through a side door. They headed for his office, where he grabbed his ski equipment. He saw his emergency pack and avalanche beacon hanging on the hook and grabbed it. He wasn't planning on going off-trail, but he'd spent too many years being prepared for anything, and he preferred that position, even if it meant he'd have a few extra things on his back.

By ten, they were outside. The slopes were already dotted with skiers, and more would arrive over the next couple hours. In comparison to their regular crowd, however, it was a lean day. Rarely did people outside of the area expect there to be skiing this late in the season, so their travel plans didn't include a skiing trip in May. So, guests would be limited to those in the more immediate area. The bad news for The Lodge was that there would likely not be enough revenue to cover their overhead. But the good news for him, Tilda and Josh was that they'd have lots of wide-open space to ski and wouldn't have to wait in any lines for a chairlift.

They made their way to the Wonderland chairlift. This particular lift carried two, so he motioned for Josh and Tilda to go first and that he'd follow. It was crazy, but when the chairlift came up behind the two, literally scooping them up and carrying them off, he wanted to grab on, even if it meant hanging on for dear life.

But good sense prevailed, and he quickly got in place

to take the next chair as it swung around. He could see the backs of their heads; Tilda's helmet was a bright royal blue and Josh's was red, matching his coat and pants. Tilda's ski jacket and pants were black, like his.

Off to his left, he watched the gondola that took both skiing and sightseeing enthusiasts from The Chateau up to The Lodge. The gondola could hold upwards of twenty people, and it was a peaceful and relaxing way to make the journey for those not inclined to drive the mountain roads. The riders were getting a great view today. There wasn't a cloud in the sky.

He saw Tilda and Josh reach the top and easily slide off the chairlift. They moved out of the way so that he could make his descent.

"Now the fun begins!" Josh exclaimed, poking his ski poles into the snow.

"Uh-huh," Tilda said, not sounding convinced.

"You're not really nervous?" Blaine asked.

"Appropriately cautious."

"I'll stick with you," he said. "You got nothing to worry about." He turned to Josh. "You can go ahead, son. But stay on this run."

"If I get to the bottom before you do, do I have to wait for you to catch up?" Josh asked.

Blaine looked at Tilda. "I'm okay…" he stopped. This co-parenting was hard. They needed to be in sync on all decisions, regardless of how big or small.

"I'm okay with him going ahead, too," Tilda said. "Only this run. And I swear to…the snow gods…that if you pass me a second time, there's going to be trouble."

"Then, get your ski on, Mama!"

The words floated back to Tilda and Blaine as Josh took off.

"My skis are on," Tilda muttered.

Blaine laughed. "I don't think that's what he meant."

"I know what he meant. Oh, it's tough to be the mother of a thirteen-year-old who has no fear." She adjusted her goggles. Appeared to be taking in a couple deep breaths. Finally, she looked at him. "Now or never."

She started off slow, skiing a zigzag across the wide run to keep her speed down. He waited, not wanting to hurry her. At the rate she was going, he wasn't going to lose her. Back and forth she went. She was doing fine, he thought. Then his stomach tightened when he saw her lean a bit too much into her turn and go down.

But his girl got right back up. She turned to look at him and waved. He waved back. Then he used the binoculars around his neck to check on Josh, who was already a third of the way down the slope.

They were skiing together as a family. Hadn't seen this one coming.

He pushed off, eager to join Tilda. "Hey, honey, you're doing fabulous," he said.

"Oh, well," she said, her cheeks pink from cold and maybe exertion, "time will tell. If I make it through today, I'm suspecting I won't be able to get out of bed tomorrow."

She'd said it innocently, but he couldn't just let it go. "If that happens, make sure you call me," he said, his tone suggestive.

She threw her head back and laughed. "Walked right into that one, didn't I?"

"You're so beautiful when you laugh," he said. "So damn beautiful." And he kissed her. And when he felt her teeter on her skis, he held her tight. Finally, he lifted his lips.

"Race you to the bottom," he said.

"What's the winner get?"

"What do you want?" he asked, as if it was a foregone conclusion that she'd win.

"Good answer," she said. "I want…a date night. Nothing crazy or over the top, but just the two of us."

That sounded really good. "We've missed a few steps along the way, haven't we?"

"Overachievers. We couldn't wait to get to the finish line."

She was trying to keep it light, but he knew. "It's been a crazy week, Tilda. But we'll get our feet back under us. We'll figure things out."

"Of course we will," she said.

Was she confident or simply putting on a good show? He wanted to tell her that he planned on sticking around, planned on being a part of Josh's life, being a part of her life. Wanted to tell her that…

Well, he damn well couldn't tell her that right now. She'd laugh it off, tell him he was crazy. That there was no way that he could have fallen in love with her so fast. Likely wouldn't believe him if he told her that perhaps he'd never been out of love.

He planted his poles. "Ready? Set?"

She moved so that her skis were pointing downhill. Nodded.

"Go," he said.

SHE BEAT HIM to the bottom, which meant that he'd probably stopped and had a burger on the way down. As Blaine came in just seconds behind her, he pretended to be breathing hard.

"You win," he said.

She was going to protest his generosity but, instead, decided to up the ante. "That's right, I did. How do you feel about spa treatments?" The Chateau was famous for them.

"In general?"

She shook her head. "No. Specifically. As in specifically for you. My perfect date involves a partner spa day. The whole works. Massage. Facials. Manicures. Pedicures. For both of us."

He swallowed. "Sounds great."

He was lying through his teeth. "And then shopping," she added.

"More fun," he said.

"Uh-huh. When's the last time you were in a mall?"

"Not a lot of malls where I've been spending the last few years."

They'd hardly even talked about his thirteen years of service. It was time to stop teasing him. "I think you were very brave," she said.

"No yanking my chain anymore?" he asked, his voice catching.

"I haven't said it, but I'm really proud of you. Proud of what you did. Proud that were brave enough to take incredible risks to help others. It's…it's a very good example for Josh."

He stared into her eyes. There were fresh snowflakes on her lashes. "That means a lot to me," he said. "Especially given the circumstances."

She shrugged. "We were young."

He leaned close. "Young and dumb," he whispered.

"Young and dumb," she echoed, lifting her lips to him.

He was still kissing her when a spray of snow flew over them. They turned their heads, and she saw Josh standing behind them. Her stomach cramped. This was the first time Josh had seen them kiss. What the heck was he going to think? She searched his face.

He looked…well, not that concerned.

"Hey," he said, "I've already been down the hill once, back up on the ski lift, and down again before the two of you made it to the bottom. I'd ask what the heck you were doing, but that seems a little obvious."

Her face flooded with warmth. "Are you okay with this, Josh?"

"Well, besides the fact that it's my parents doing the PDAs, I've got no issues."

It was the closest thing a thirteen-year-old boy could give as far as endorsements. She looked at Blaine.

He was smiling and shaking his head. "You're something, Josh. You know that?" he said, his voice full of pride.

"Yeah, I know. I'm a pretty great kid. Now, come on, let's go."

Chapter Twenty-Two

Blaine was feeling good as he started his fourth time down the run. Some fresh snow had fallen, and the temperature was cold enough to prevent too much melt. That would all change tomorrow, when the warmer air settled on the mountain. But it was a great day to end the season.

And a great day for starting a…well, he wasn't sure what to call it. A romance. A relationship. Not a fling. Not even close. Tilda mattered. Josh mattered.

He and Tilda were still skiing together. He waited at the top of the run, letting her get a couple hundred yards ahead of him. He didn't want to rush her. She'd fallen a total of three times, but other than that, she was doing really well, and he could tell that her confidence was building. She was getting more aggressive on her skis. Josh had lapped them a couple times, waving a pole as he went by.

Now Blaine put his binoculars up to his eyes to see if he could locate his son on the slope.

And what he saw almost made him drop the binoculars.

Davis James.

Blaine looked again.

The man was on skis, further down the slope, wearing a white ski jacket and matching pants. Fortunately, no helmet, which made it possible to pick out his unusual features. Still, if Blaine had not had the binoculars and exceptional eyesight, he'd have never seen him out from this distance.

The man had been on a bus headed east, presumably back home. His credit card had been used.

Blaine wanted to kick his own ass. The man had clearly wanted to dupe them into thinking that he was leaving. He'd gotten on the bus, probably had made sure that he was visible to the many cameras that were in the bus station, so that they'd believe he was leaving town. His credit card had continued to be used but, damn it, maybe all he'd had to do was give the card to somebody and tell them to use it. Could have explained it as a pay-it-forward kind of deal.

He planted his poles and headed for Tilda. Whatever reason Davis James was here at The Lodge, it could not be good.

He easily caught up with her and motioned for her to stop. It took her a second to do so, and his heart was beating fast. "Hey, no worries but I just saw Davis James. I'm going to find Josh. He passed us about ten minutes ago, so I'm going to catch up to him."

"What? Why?" She stopped and shook her head, as if she realized those question didn't matter.

"I need you to follow me, as quickly as you can, but still safely. Can you do that, Tilda?"

"Of course," she said. "Find Josh. Don't worry about me."

HE COULDN'T SKI and watch Davis James at the same time. So he chose to haul ass down the slope. Keeping his eyes on the man took second place to finding Josh and getting him and Tilda off the slopes, into a secure spot. It took him ten minutes to catch up with his son, who smiled as Blaine slid to a stop fifty feet ahead of him, throwing snow in his wake.

Blaine held up his hand, telling the boy to stop.

"Hey," Josh said, his voice happy. Then, probably taking a cue from the grim look on Blaine's face, his son turned quickly and looked uphill. "Is Mom okay? Did she fall?"

Don't scare him. He needed him to move fast and to listen well. Being scared wasn't conducive to either. "She's fine," he said, making a real effort to sound normal. "But I caught a glimpse of the guy that we thought was on the bus, the one that wants to make trouble for me. So, we're going to get off this slope. Your mom is on her way down."

He used his binoculars to look up the slope, and he saw her. Coming fast. Much faster than she'd skied at any point earlier in the day. Brave Tilda. They were going to get out of this okay.

He turned and used his binoculars to try to locate Davis James again. But he had moved. Damn. He wanted eyes on the man. "Your mom is coming. Let's wait for her."

She was less than two hundred yards away from them, when he heard a *pop* and saw a skiff of snow fly. It hadn't been that long since he'd heard gunfire, and he recognized it now.

Holy hell! Somebody was shooting at Tilda. It had to be Davis James.

He clicked through his options. To the right was tree cover that would be helpful. It was also very near the area that they'd closed due to avalanche risk.

But if Davis James was within firing range, they

were sitting ducks out here in the open. They had to go right. "Josh, that way," he said, pointing. "Go now. Go fast."

"That was a gun, wasn't it?" Josh asked.

"Yeah. We're going to get out of this, don't worry."

Josh looked up the mountain, as if to make his mom appear.

"Your mom will be okay," Blaine said, praying it was true. "Now, go."

Josh went, skiing low and fast. Blaine waved to Tilda, using both arms to signal that she should change course. He prayed that she saw him and she'd realize what he wanted her to do.

And he saw the minute that it happened. She changed course. He knew that if Davis James had binoculars, he could be watching every move they made. Would know where they were likely headed.

He used precious seconds to try to find Davis James with his binoculars but couldn't. Wearing white, which he'd likely done deliberately, he blended into the landscape.

Blaine planted his skis and followed Josh. When he caught up with his son, he motioned for him to take cover behind a tree. Then he waited several long minutes for Tilda to reach them. There were no more shots.

She stopped fast, the edges of her skis digging into the snow. "Was that…" she didn't finish her question, likely seeing that Josh was well within hearing distance.

"Yes," Blaine said. "Josh knows. Somebody definitely took a shot at you. I'm confident it came from that direction…" Blaine motioned down the hill.

"I thought this area was closed to skiers," Josh said, looking around.

Smart kid. "It is." But until he could spot Davis

James and take him out, they had little choice. He unstrapped the avalanche beacon that he wore. "Put this on," he said to Josh. *Hurry, hurry, hurry.* He didn't have to say it because Josh wasn't wasting any time.

Blaine was torn over what to do. He was worried about the shooting. Not just because bullets were deadly, but the noise, the vibration, could easily trigger an avalanche. Conventional wisdom told him to get Tilda and Josh safely secured to trees. But he wanted them to be unencumbered, able to move quickly if Davis James approached.

Decision made, Blaine slipped his backpack off, unzipped it and pulled out all the rope he had. He could handle Davis James. But what he wasn't going to be able to handle was a slab of snow coming at them at eighty miles an hour. "Skis off, both of you. Then hug the tree, Tilda. I'm going to tie you to it. If something happens, don't let go."

"Do Josh first," she said.

"Not to worry. He's next." He wrapped the rope around her and tied it. The few seconds it took him, he was thinking about the bullet, the way the snow had been disturbed, the sound. He finished, then raised his binoculars to his eyes. Scanned the area where he thought Davis James might be. Moved to the right fifty yards. Then another. Then found him.

The bastard had a gun. And if they'd have kept on course, he'd have had a clear shot at them.

He offered up a quick thanks that there were no other skiers in the area. Hopefully that wouldn't change. He didn't want anybody getting caught in the cross fire.

He was studying the man so intently that he almost dropped his binoculars, when a massive *boom* sounded, literally shaking the ground under them. What the hell had Davis James done? But, oddly enough, the look on Davis James's face was pure shock.

But there was no time to worry about that.

"What was that?" Josh asked.

"An explosion of some kind," Blaine said. The gunshot had been nothing in comparison. He used his binoculars to look up the mountain, and what he'd feared was their reality. The explosion had shaken loose a slab of snow, and it was moving down the mountain, coming straight for them. "Avalanche," he said, not having time to sugarcoat it. Damn it. He was not going to lose his family now.

He fed out another length of rope. Josh had to be tied.

Then he looked up. Damn it! It was bearing down on them. He lunged for Josh. Grabbed him.

Only to have the roaring mass of snow rip his son out of his arms.

Chapter Twenty-Three

It was over in just seconds, really. But when the snow settled, Tilda realized that everything was different. Blaine and Josh were gone, buried.

Everything, every single thing that mattered to her was gone. And she was still tied to a tree. What would her life be without Josh? Without Blaine? Not worth living.

She screamed and screamed, yelling for help, willing somebody to come. Cold air chilled her lungs but she did not stop. And within five minutes, her prayers were answered. Snowmobiles came over the hill.

It was Decker and others she didn't recognize. "Blaine," she cried, pointing towards the area where she'd seen him last. "And Josh. Blaine gave him his transponder beacon."

Decker nodded, and while he untied her, others were running down the hill. They were carrying picks and shovels, and suddenly, they merged onto a spot. "We're getting a signal," one of the men yelled.

They started to dig. Tilda floundered down to the spot and then tried to dig into the hard snow with her hands. She knew the minutes were precious. If found within the first fifteen minutes, there was a good chance of recovery. Beyond that, chances were slimmer.

There was absolutely no movement from under the snow, nothing to indicate that they were there. She understood. The snow would settle around them, as heavy as concrete, making it impossible for them to free themselves.

It seemed unbelievable that, minutes before, they'd been skiing, enjoying the day. Now the mountain seemed shrouded in a grim silence. The only sounds were the rescue crew digging and the squawking of updates from Decker's walkie-talkie.

She lifted her head. Listened more closely.

"Okay. Keep me updated," Decker said. He glanced at her. "Power is out across the property. Also, the gondola is stuck midair, a hundred and fifty feet up," he said.

"Oh, no," she said.

"Come on, guys," Decker urged on the rescue crew. "We gotta find—"

"I've got an arm!" one man yelled.

There was frantic activity. Then she could see that it was Blaine's arm, extended up. He was facedown in the snow, his other arm stretched over his head.

Was he even breathing? Tilda wasn't sure. She tried to hold back her sob but couldn't.

He lifted his head. Saw her and recognition flitted through his eyes. "Josh," he said roughly.

"Wait, wait," another man yelled. "He's got something in his hand."

It was Josh's coat. And in seconds, the men had dug out her son. Who opened his eyes, groaned a little, but managed to sit up on his own.

He had never let go. Brave, brave Blaine had grabbed

hold of his son and had never let go. Now the two of them huddled together, with her between them. And she held on to both of them, so grateful that they were both in one piece.

Blaine told Decker about Davis James. Explained where the man had been standing when he'd last been seen.

"They're already digging in that area," Decker confirmed. "We had a report that one or more people were missing. That spot was hit hard with the avalanche. Do you think he set off the explosion?"

"I don't know," Blaine admitted. "I know he shot at us but…this might sound crazy, but I was looking right at him with my binoculars when the explosion hit. He was as surprised as I was."

"Well, I hope we get a chance to ask him about it," Decker told him. "But what I'm really happy about is that all of you are safe."

"Me, too," Blaine said. "Thanks for getting here so quickly."

"We were already on our way because someone had reported hearing a gunshot."

Crazy, thought Tilda. Maybe Davis James had done them a favor. Otherwise, help would have been too far away.

Blaine was shaking his head, as if he was thinking the same thing.

"Let's get the three of you back to The Lodge and get you warmed up," Decker said.

They were helped onto snowmobiles, and in minutes, the three of them were in The Lodge, in front of a burning fireplace. A woman brought them hot chocolates. "I added whiskey to both of yours," she said to Blaine and Tilda. "Decker's orders."

They sipped in silence. When Decker found them, he had an update. "Davis James has been found. He's dead. So far, no other casualties. Unfortunately, I do have a bit of bad news. Molly Gilford is trapped in the gondola."

"Molly," she repeated. Blaine and Decker's cousin. "That's terrible," she said.

"Yeah. But the good news is that Max Hollick is with her," Decker said.

"Nobody better," Blaine said.

But still, she could hear the worry in his voice. Decker nodded and walked away.

Tilda leaned her head against Blaine's shoulder. "I can't believe Davis James is dead. Now we're never going to know if he was the one to set off the explosion." Her voice was hoarse from screaming.

"I know. But if it was him or us, I know which one I'd choose." And then he leaned close and whispered in her ear. "This maybe isn't the place or the time, but I need you to know something. I love you."

"Oh, God. I love you, too," she said. "When I thought I'd lost both you and Josh, I… I couldn't bear it. We've lost so much time, time that we can never get back. And I made a promise to myself that if we managed to get out of this, I wasn't going to waste one more minute. I need you, Blaine Colton. I need you and I want you in my life. Our lives," she added, glancing at Josh. Then she turned back to Blaine, leaned in, and kissed him hard on his hot-chocolate-flavored lips.

"PDA," Josh muttered, not looking at all embarrassed. "Hey, I've been thinking about changing my last name to Colton." He said it casually, like he might if he was thinking about buying a cool new video game.

"Really?" Blaine asked, his voice thick with emotion.

"Any concerns?" Josh asked, looking at her.

"None. Absolutely none," she said.

* * * * *

COMING SOON!

We really hope you enjoyed reading this book. If you're looking for more romance, be sure to head to the shops when new books are available on

Thursday 16th May

To see which titles are coming soon, please visit
millsandboon.co.uk/nextmonth

LET'S TALK
Romance

For exclusive extracts, competitions
and special offers, find us online:

- facebook.com/millsandboon
- @MillsandBoon
- @MillsandBoonUK

Get in touch on 01413 063232

For all the latest titles coming soon, visit
millsandboon.co.uk/nextmonth